ONE
step
CLOSER

KAHLEN AYMES

Cover designed by R. A Mizer; Shoutlines Design
Book Formatting by Cassy Roop of Pink Ink Designs

Cover photography: © AdobeStock #88664278
Published by Kahlen Aymes Books, Inc.

Visit the author's website: http://www.KahlenAymes.com

ISBN ebook: 9781370532056
ISBN Paperback: 9780996734462

Version: Sample: 2016.10.25

ONE
step
CLOSER

prologue

THE NIGHT THAT RUINED EVERYTHING

H E WAS GOING TO KILL HIS best friend. He was literally going to *fucking kill him.*

The party was buzzing and so was Caleb's brain. He didn't know the time, but it had to be somewhere around 3 AM, and anger was simmering just below the surface.

He was thankful it was winding down and most of the guests had already left because he was agitated and pensive. The few who lingered were all part of his best friend, Dex's, crowd. He knew Jake and Bret because they were part of the same group he used to hang with when he was younger, but there were several new faces.

Caleb had been hell-bent on making his father's life a living hell. Dex and his friends were rough, tough, and tattooed. They walked a fine line between right and wrong; more unruly and wild than the preppy crowd that went to the private high school his father demanded he attend. However, that was sort of the point. The three other guys and two women that remained he'd never met prior to this evening when they'd shown up with his old friend.

Hard to believe how much could change in four years. Look at *Wren*.

His eyes had been unwillingly glued to her all night, stalking her every move.

The beer in his hand was probably the sixth he'd had in less than two hours, but he wasn't drunk. The time at home had been a combination of heaven and hell. He'd been dying to see Wren and they'd had some great times together in the week he'd been back in Denver, but the familiar aches in his heart and groin hadn't magically abated during their time apart. He silently chastised himself for being foolish enough to think that it would ease as she grew into a woman. His breath left his chest in a loud sigh.

Sure, the alcohol was giving him a buzz, but it wasn't enough to kill the burn in his gut or the pressure in his chest as he watched Dex put the moves on Wren. Caleb had asked him to watch out for her in his absence; but Dex was supposed to protect her, not want her. No one fucking wanted her as much as Caleb had wanted her, or for as long. He'd been tortured with wanting her. He'd been tormented for years with it, but everyone thought of them as siblings. The very thought made Caleb's stomach turn.

Someone was speaking to him, but he barely registered the sound of the female voice. His eyes were trained on Dex's arms snaking around Wren's back and waist, under the luxurious curtain of loose blonde curls that rained to just above her hips.

Caleb lifted the beer to his mouth and took a long pull. "Hmm?" he asked of the woman standing close to him as he sat, half-assed, on the back of a sofa. The music was blaring over the state-of-the-art stereo system, and he strained to hear her, but his eyes never left Wren.

"So this is your last year at MIT? Dex said you two were gonna start some sort of motorcycle company together. That's so cool. My dad is part of an MC."

Dex's dad, Darren, had a shop and he had learned a shit load from the two of them; and more importantly, they'd become like family in the years after Caleb lost his mother. Darren was a stand-up guy who'd never abandon his kid, and Caleb envied the close relationship Dex shared with his father. Sure, he was a laborer and Edison Luxon had a successful corporation, but in Caleb's eyes, Darren was the better man. He had ten times the respect for him.

Caleb met Dex at a high school wrestling meet when Caleb was thirteen and Dex was fifteen, and the two of them had become friends. Caleb spent as much time as possible at Darren's shop and with Dex's family. Dex was sort of a wild child, and his parents were less strict than Edison was, but there was a strong sense of mutual respect in their family.

Caleb and Dex hadn't been angels growing up, but at least, Dex could count on his parents to have his back. It was completely unlike the abandonment that Caleb felt from Edison. Most of the time, Caleb acted out just to get his father's attention. It hardly ever worked. Edison would deliver a cold lecture, calmly deal with the situation by paying someone off, and then forget about his son until the next time he got into trouble. Caleb had come to the conclusion that the only thing he could do was get the hell away from his father as soon as he was eighteen. Somehow even that got fucked up.

"Yeah. We've talked about it for a long time, that's why I'm studying mechanical engineering. It's not that easy; we're both dead broke, and his Dad's shop can't spare him right now. A lot has to happen first," Caleb answered.

"But..." the young woman began, waving her hand around at the expensive surroundings. "It looks like your family is rich—"

Caleb cut her off. "Don't get excited, honey. These are my old man's digs, not mine." He huffed. The only reason he even came home, ever, was because of Wren. The music changed to a slow, deep rhythm.

"But this place..."

"Yeah. My dad is swimming in it, but hell will freeze over before I'd ask him for a damn thing. He'd just hold it over my head for the rest of my life, or at least, the rest of his." He could elaborate that his father was a control freak, or explain the reason he hated Edison so much, but he'd most likely never see her again. So, what was the point? Besides, he was preoccupied with what was happening across the room.

Caleb glanced down at the woman for the first time since their conversation began. She had hair so dark it looked black in the dim light. Her makeup was overdone making her skin tone a deep tan, and her clothing was tight and cheap. She was a sharp contrast to Wren's natural, blonde beauty. Caleb tried to remember the name Dex had mentioned when he'd introduced her earlier.

Was it Marie? He wracked his brain. *Maryann? Michelle?* He knew it was an "M" name, but not sure exactly what. *Fuck!*

Movement in his peripheral vision made his eyes return to Dex and Wren. Aside from the girl at his side, everyone else was playing pool on the other half of the big room, except for the one couple dancing. Caleb's chest was tight as he tried to breathe; it physically fucking hurt to watch.

Dex was pulling Wren close, pressing her against him and they were swaying softly to the song. Wren seemed to be enjoying herself. Her head was tilted up to look at Dex; she was smiling alluringly. She was so beautiful when she was happy. How could she keep getting more fucking beautiful every time he saw her?

Wren laid her head on Dex's shoulder, her hands slipping up around his neck, clearly losing herself. She had just turned eighteen a month earlier, but Caleb was sure she'd had a drink or two; which was enough to make her less inhibited.

Caleb swallowed. He was mesmerized, unable to look away from the two of them. It was nothing short of torture knowing it was impossible for him to touch her the same way Dex was able to. Not only was she the daughter of his father's second wife, she was younger by close to three years. Sure, he could protect her from that abusive bitch. He could spend time with her. He could even fantasize about her, but that's where it stopped. Even though Wren had developed a kind of crush on him at first, he'd never considered they could be more. He loved her. He'd always loved her, but he'd always considered her off limits.

He tried to keep making small talk with the girl whose name he couldn't remember. He nursed what was left of his beer, until he caught sight of Dex's hand sliding down over Wren's ass to the hem of her dress and then creep up slightly; underneath.

Caleb's eyes narrowed and adrenaline started to flood his veins abruptly clearing the alcohol haze. Suddenly the music was deafening. The beat was pounding in his head like a hammer; the dim light flickering with the beat. It was getting brighter with each hit of the base drum.

"It looks like Dex likes your little sister."

Caleb's nostrils flared, and the skin of his face felt as if it was lit on fire. He ran a quick hand over the scruff on his jaw trying to alleviate it. The girl reached out to touch his muscled bicep.

Caleb clenched his teeth. "Wren *isn't* my sister."

The girl rolled her eyes. "Whatever. Stepsister then. Same diff."

No. It wasn't the same thing, not even close. If the "M" girl sensed Caleb's irritation, she didn't show it.

His instincts made his muscles coil, and it was all he could do not to fly across the room and pummel his best friend down to the floor. He still fought in the occasional underground fight club, but he was in even better shape now. The boxing club at MIT was official, and kept him lean and honed. He could still beat the shit out of anyone who challenged him. He could probably do it even easier than before, and right now; he wanted to pound Dex into the fucking ground.

Didn't he know how Caleb felt about Wren?

When Dex's hand rose higher under Wren's dress, his intent to grab her ass full on, Caleb couldn't stand still any longer. He dropped his beer and the glass bottle broke with a loud crash on the hardwood floor; making the girl beside him jump.

"Party's over," Caleb growled deeply.

The girl looked dumbstruck as Caleb left her standing there and moved quickly across the room to shut down the music.

"Party's over!" he said, louder this time; shouting so he would be heard over the music.

Dex and Wren split apart when the music stopped abruptly and everyone in the room was staring in Caleb's direction with blank looks on their faces. However, they sat down their drinks, and began putting on their coats.

Dex's hand slid down Wren's arm and his fingers closed around her hand, as he took a couple of steps toward his friend. "What's up, man? Why? The house is empty."

Caleb met his eyes unflinchingly. "I'm tired. Everyone out." Caleb's tone was low but the only sound in the silent room. "Now."

Dex looked incredulous, and shook his head. "Why Caleb?"

Caleb continued to stare him down, his eyes menacing. "I said; I'm tired." He was livid and he didn't even understand why he was so fucking pissed off. Shit, if he'd been dancing with a beautiful girl he was into, he'd probably have copped a feel too.

Wren pulled her hand from Dex's grip and walked to Caleb, looking up into his face. She looked so damn innocent, her brilliant blue eyes wide. "Cale, what's going on? We were only dancing."

Caleb looked down into her face, his eyes softening at the confused look in her blue eyes, and his thumb lifting her chin briefly. "Stay here."

The others, sensing the palpable tension between Dex and Caleb had already started to file up the stairs to the outside door. Caleb nodded in the direction of Bret, who was waiting for the two girls to precede him up the stairs, then followed.

"I don't get it, Caleb. I mean, what the hell?" He took two steps in Wren's direction.

"You don't have to get it," Caleb commanded, nodding at the stairwell. "You just have to get the fuck out of here."

Dex looked pissed, then glanced down at Wren. "You wanna come with?" he asked Wren.

Caleb shook his head once and in one second had moved in front of Wren, to separate her from Dex. "She stays." His tone insisted compliance.

"Caleb, this makes no sense, man. We were having a good time dancing."

"Yeah, I saw," Caleb hissed. The fingers on his right hand began curling into a fist at his side, and he had to mentally insist it didn't fly and punch Dex right there. "I want to talk to you. Outside."

Dex's eyes widened. Suddenly he understood. Defiantly, he made a move in Wren's direction, intending to kiss her full on the mouth just to piss Caleb off, but Wren, sensing it wouldn't help the situation between the two men, backed up even further behind Caleb.

She'd danced with Dex and purposefully let him get a little too familiar with her because she felt hurt that Caleb was letting Michelle monopolize him on his last night in town. However, she didn't intend for the two of them to out and out brawl, and she didn't see it coming. She would have preferred spending the evening alone with Caleb; talking, driving around, or watching a movie together; but it hadn't been her choice.

"Unless you want to die, I suggest you get the fuck out! Now!" Caleb seethed.

Anger flooded through Dex, as well. His friend was overstepping. He didn't do anything wrong, and he'd be damned if he'd cower to Caleb's jealousy.

"Just go, Dex. Go on," Wren implored, peering at him from behind Caleb's solid form. Caleb was poised to strike, and Wren could feel his anger vibrate in the air around them like electricity.

Dex was built; lean and strong, but Caleb was a competitive boxer and formidable; he easily had thirty pounds of muscle on Dex. Wren didn't want Dex getting pummeled or Caleb regretting his actions afterward, which she was certain he would. They'd been friends for as long as she'd known them both and the last thing she wanted was to see their friendship ruined.

She mentally kicked herself for leading Dex on. She was confused by Caleb's sudden anger, but it made her heart trip around in her chest at the same time. She felt excitement at the prospect he might be jealous; making her own adrenalin flow.

Wren liked Dex and he'd taken great pains to fill Caleb's shoes after he left, but no one could ever take Caleb's place. Wren had been in love with Caleb for years, but he was older and not once had she imagined he'd reciprocate her feelings. Even now, habit made her push down that daydream.

He was just acting like the protective older brother, as he had since the day he found out about her mother's treatment of her. He'd changed her life, and that was the beginning of her hero worship. Before she knew it, her schoolgirl crush had eventually matured and grown into full-blown love.

Dex turned and pulled on his leather jacket. He started to climb the stairs with Caleb following closely behind, leaving Wren standing in the middle of the big room, alone. "I'll be back in a minute," Caleb said over his shoulder as he left.

Dex's motorcycle was the only one left in the wide driveway at the back of the house in front of the five-stall garage, signaling that everyone else had already gone.

Before Dex could say a word, Caleb used both of his hands to give Dex's shoulders a forceful shove that sent him stumbling and falling backward into his bike. The machine fell over with the loud clang of metal bashing against the pavement, and leaving Dex sprawled face-up over it.

"What the fuck were you doing touching her like that? Wren is off-limits! You were supposed to protect her, not try to get in her pants! Have you touched her before this?"

"Son of a bitch!" Dex shouted. "You just wrecked my bike! You're gonna pay for that!"

"Answer me!" Caleb's chest was heaving. "What's going on between you two?"

Dex scrambled to sit up, pushed his weight up off the fallen motorcycle with his hands, and lunged at Caleb without answering; hitting him hard in the middle with his shoulder. Caleb grunted as the breath was forced from his lungs. He stumbled backward but didn't fall. He pushed Dex back and soon the two were going at each other with fists swinging. Caleb took a hit on the jaw, pain exploding in his face, before he managed to land a hard right hook to Dex's temple. He followed it with a solid left upper cut to his jaw.

Dex fell backward, hard onto the pavement, and landed with a guttural grunt.

"What the hell is your problem? For Christ's sake, Caleb, we're friends!"

Caleb looked down at Dex, his breathing heavy from the exertion of the fight, the conflict of his emotions getting the better of him. "Yeah, but friend or not, touch her again and I swear I'll mother fucking kill you!"

"Wren isn't fifteen anymore, Caleb!" Dex returned, out of breath and moving to get to his feet. "She's an adult and she doesn't need big brother's permission to dance with me."

If anyone was painfully aware of Wren's age and how she'd blossomed into a gorgeous and graceful young woman, it was Caleb.

"I saw what you were doing, and dancing was the last thing on your goddamned mind! I could deal with a random guy; but not you. Anyone but you, Dex!"

Their eyes met and Dex could see the pain on his friend's face. He'd watched Caleb come to Wren's defense at school, with her mother, or anyone who made fun of her or hurt her for years. He should have seen that Wren was more to Caleb than he'd ever admitted. It was clear that brotherly was not how his friend felt about Wren, and that it wouldn't matter who was trying to get with her; Caleb wouldn't take it well.

Dex nodded and put up his hand to keep Caleb from hitting him again, while he was down. "Okay, man. You should've said something."

"You should've known." Caleb's brow was furrowed with a scowl firmly planted on his face. He turned his back and reentered the house, running his hand through his over-long hair, anger still pumping through his veins as he went down the backstairs to the lower level. He probably didn't need another drink, but he wanted one. His body was still on fire, and his mind was raging at him. He took a deep breath, not sure what the confrontation with Wren was going to be like. She was sitting on one of the big recliners that were lined up in front of the big projection TV on one end of the room.

Caleb walked past her, between the theater set-up and the pool table to the wet bar along one side. Foregoing the beer waiting in the full-sized refrigerator, he reached for a glass and the crystal decanter of amber liquid. It was his father's expensive single malt scotch. He'd never liked that shit. He was feeling in need of something stronger, so he poured half the glass full and downed it in one big swallow. It burned all the way down; Caleb could feel it run down his esophagus and into his stomach, the heat leaving a trail that didn't lessen the tightness in his chest.

He refilled the glass and turned, his gaze intense as it settled on Wren. The music was still off and Wren hadn't said anything. Caleb had fought his desire for Wren for years. Ever since he'd seen her as she really was without that hideous disguise she always wore when she and her mother first moved in with the Luxon men. The scotch, along with the beer, might be impairing his judgment just a little, but damn, if she wanted to grow up; he'd help her.

His eyes seared over her body, taking in the short dress that left her legs bare and gave Dex easy access to her ass. Anger flared inside him again.

"I don't understand you, Caleb—" Wren began, but he held up his hand to stop her. He took another swallow of the scotch then sat the glass down on the mahogany bar and walked purposely toward her.

She was amazingly beautiful, and he'd had enough fantasies about her to last a lifetime. He couldn't resist the blonde curls that tumbled down her back to her waist. Her dancer's body was slight and firm, her skin flawless and smooth. Caleb's cock was already hard, but blood surged again, making it throb even more painfully inside his jeans.

Their eyes met and locked. Wren could sense a danger behind his eyes, a look that had never been directed at her. Her body quickened and heat pooled inside her at the intensity in his eyes as he slowly unbuttoned his white shirt. When he got to her he reached out and took both of her upper arms in his hands, forcefully pulling her up to stand in front of him, close enough to feel the heat radiating between them. She smelled amazing. Like spring flowers with a hint of vanilla. He leaned down and ran the tip of his nose from her shoulder, up the cord of her neck until his mouth was next to her ear.

He spoke in a guttural whisper. "You wanna play with the big boys? Then, play with me."

Wren's breath sucked in with an audible gasp. She was shocked and excited at the same time. Caleb's right hand lifted and his fingers traced over the top of her shoulder, up her neck and under the curtain of her hair to tangle it as he cupped her head. His left arm began snaking around her waist to pull her hard against his body, his fingers curling to fist in the soft cotton material of her dress.

She could feel his erection pressing and pulsating into her hip. This was something she'd wanted, but never thought would happen. Her hands landed softly on his bare chest as he tilted her head up. His skin was warm under her fingers, like hot silk and the beat of his heart hammered against her fingertips.

"Caleb," she murmured, just before his mouth swooped down to engulf hers.

His mouth was not tentative, but rather hinted at the long denied hunger he felt. Instinctively, Wren opened to allow his tongue access and almost swooned at the combination of her emotions, her body's response, and Caleb's obvious possessiveness. It didn't take more than a couple of seconds before Wren's arms were snaking up to wind around his neck and she was kissing him back, kiss for kiss.

"Oh, God, Wren," Caleb moaned against her mouth then bent slightly to lift her legs up and around his waist. He took her weight easily and began walking into his room that was off the far side of the entertainment room, separated only by a bathroom and the short hallway. Wren's hands found their way into Caleb's hair, her hands desperate to bring his mouth closer. The feeling of her body opening was unfamiliar, but welcome. Her heart was beating so hard; it had her blood pounding in her veins.

He kicked open the door to his room and it banged against the opposite wall before he lowered Wren down to his bed. He followed her down, his knee parting her thighs. The feel of him pressing his hard erection into her softness was delicious and she welcomed Caleb into the cradle of her body. It was just as amazing as she'd imagined, Caleb was hungry and ardent, wanting her with an abandon that made her heart race. He had his elbows resting on the bed, his arms holding his weight to keep himself from crushing her. His lower body ground into hers.

He couldn't help it; he closed his eyes, taking her luscious lips and tongue in a series of deep and demanding kisses that invaded her mouth like he wanted to invade her body. They made out for endless minutes. Each kiss was deeper and longer than the last. His body pressing and moving, drawing a response from Wren that she wasn't prepared for. A delicious ache began deep inside her, causing her hips to surge and rise to meet his.

Caleb could feel the heat from her body through her panties and his jeans and he needed to be closer. He reached between them with one hand and pulled open the button of his jeans before sliding the zipper down, and pushing up her dress. His dick was so hard it was pushing out of the waistband of his boxer briefs. He allowed himself the luxury of a couple of thrusts; dry humping against her, the head of his cock pushing into the moist material of her panties. It left them both panting, and urgent; their hands frantically pulling at the other's clothes.

Wren was inexperienced and wasn't sure what her body was craving, except that it was in need of something to ease the delicious ache. What she was sure of; was that Caleb could give it to her. His hand moved up and cupped her breast, her erect pink nipple straining against the lace of her bra. He pulled the cup down, and rubbed his cheek on the top swell, letting the scruff of the day's growth of beard tease the stiff peak before his mouth closed around it.

Caleb had his share of experience and his hands and tongue knew how to draw sighs and moans of pleasure from a woman, but this was Wren and she meant the world to him. He was hungry, his desire boiling over, almost beyond his control. Despite the alcohol he'd consumed, he was aware of her innocence and tempered his movements. He teased her breasts with his tongue, his hand dipping into her panties to begin a slow rub that had her moaning his name. The soft sounds she made drove him to insanity.

"Uhhhh, Cale... Uh... mmmmm...."

She was slick and hot, and he was dying with wanting her, but he took his time and brought her body to slow climax. He continued running sucking kisses from her breasts up her neck, until his mouth claimed hers, swallowing her cries as she came. His dick was throbbing to the point of pain. After wanting her for years but telling himself she was off limits, he was finally lost to his long-suppressed desire for her. His resistance was gone.

Her body jerked against his hand multiple times, her back arching and his name tumbling from her open mouth. Caleb moved back so he could look into her face, anxious to gauge her reaction. Her lips were parted in desire, her eyes languid; her sighs contented.

"You are so beautiful," he said softly. "So fucking beautiful. I've wanted you, Wren."

"For how long?" she asked in wonder.

"Forever," he said simply. His voice was thick with desire as his eyes burned down into hers. The darkness kept them both in outline and shadow, but he could see her eyes sparkling, reflecting the small amount of light coming from the dimly lit entertainment room.

Her hand reached up and her fingers traced his jaw. "Oh, Caleb. Me, too."

His hips thrust forward, and the head of his dick pressed against her most private and untouched flesh.

"Mmmm," she sighed then whispered, "That feels nice."

"Oh, God. I don't know if I can stop. I want you so much."

One arm was cradling her head as Caleb let his hand run down Wren's body, over the luscious, but not overly large curve of her breast. His hands explored over her rib cage and down to lay on the flat of her stomach beneath her belly button. Wren's dress was bunched up, but Caleb still had on his open jeans. His shirt had somehow disappeared with the assistance of Wren's urgent hands.

"I want to feel you, Wren. Skin on skin."

She tasted the remnants of scotch on his tongue while they were kissing, though he didn't seem the least bit intoxicated.

His eyes were clear and his words were not slurred. He continued his gentle exploration of her body with his hand and mouth at the same time as his lower body delivered slow and deliberate, teasing, thrusts designed to renew her arousal.

"Caleb." Wren's hips surged against his and she reached up to pull the dress over her head in silent agreement. When Caleb lowered his chest to hers, it was like a slice of heaven. "Don't stop."

"Wren—" he began. It felt amazing, but he didn't mean for things to go this far, and though he wanted to push his body into hers, he hesitated.

"Don't stop," she insisted, reaching down to touch him. She'd never touched a man before and the size of him should have scared her, but it didn't. "I trust you, Caleb. I know you won't hurt me. I want this," she whispered. "I want to know what it feels like to be with you."

Caleb's mouth crushed hers, while her body communicated that her need was as intense and incredible as his was. He loved how she tasted and smelled. He loved how perfectly they fit together. Most of all, he loved that she wanted him as much as he wanted her. When Wren's hands started to push down his jeans, he lifted his hips and let her, and she managed to get them down far enough for his cock to spring free. He pushed against her slick heat with a groan. Her panties were slippery; damp with her arousal, and Caleb's movements caused his erection to slide into the folds of her flesh. She was hot and he ached to push all the way into her.

After rolling to his side and pushing his jeans further down and kicking free of them and his boxers, he could look down upon Wren. He was in awe of the exquisite outline of her body in the low light, clothed only in a black lace thong. She was the sexiest thing he'd ever seen. He reached out and hooked his fingers around the lace at her hips and slowly peeled them down and off of her legs.

Wren was mesmerized, her eyes drawn to Caleb's erection, proud and full. It bobbed away from his body until he settled back down into her, his mouth finding hers, and the passion between them stealing his reason. He played with her body, kissing what he could reach, but Wren's legs wrapped around his hips refusing to let him move away.

Caleb withheld himself as long as he could stand, careful to bring her close to climax again so it would be less painful for her. He knew in his soul she'd never been with anyone else before, and God help him, he didn't have the strength to deny what they both wanted.

The kisses grew in urgency as their fevered touches and thrusts grew more intense, until finally Caleb guided his cock to her opening. She was so hot and tight... all of his muscles coiled; he couldn't stop himself.

"Wren, God... I can't help it." He eased into her slightly, feeling her muscles tense, and she gasped. Caleb pushed in all of the way, feeling the resistance that confirmed her virginity, until he was completely sheathed inside her. Caleb teased her mouth with gentle, yet passionate kisses, his mouth playing with hers, as his body moved within hers.

After a few seconds, Wren's hands were raking down his back and she was moving in unison with Caleb's thrusts. Caleb was as gentle as he could manage, slowly wringing a response from her body. This was something he'd been waiting for, something he thought could never happen. It was better than he could have imagined and he wanted their lovemaking to last.

She felt amazing, and Caleb let himself get lost in her. The morning might bring regrets or awkwardness, but for now it was beautiful, amazing, and his heart was full of her. They kissed and clung together, their bodies working together to bring the other pleasure, perspiration forming a thin, salty veil on smooth skin, Caleb's hands wandered; delivering gentle caresses that made everything more perfect than Wren could have dreamed.

"Wren, I shouldn't come inside you."

The alcohol had caused him to forget a condom, but he wasn't drunk enough to disregard the possible repercussions of being so reckless.

"It's okay, don't stop, now. Don't stop, Cale."

Wren was the only person to shorten his name. Ever. Love for her rushed through him. He desired her with an urgency that ate at him, yes, but he loved her more than anything. He'd dreamed of his name coming from that luscious mouth in breathy passion, and now it was happening. Finally.

Her movements urged him on, despite her inexperience, and the pressure continued to build as she started to squeeze and milk his cock with each and every thrust. It pushed both of them over the edge.

Only when he felt her body spasm around his, did Caleb let himself thrust faster to end his self-inflicted torment. The beautiful torment that ended in an explosion of sensation, and light. Caleb closed his eyes, and breathed out Wren's name as he came hard.

They were both breathing hard, but Caleb bent down to claim her mouth with his, lightly licking the center of her top lip; sucking it into his mouth. She responded by pulling his lower one into her mouth. Fuck, it was amazing. He nuzzled against her cheek with his nose, and then placed a kiss on her temple, pulling out of her body, rolling over and pulling her into his embrace in one movement. He didn't want to move and Wren seemed content to stay where she was, snuggling into Caleb's shoulder, her arm across his waist, and her leg hooking his.

His eyes were tired, and he was physically sated; he should be falling asleep in his big bed; with Wren. Instead, he was staring at the ceiling in the dark, wondering what in the hell he'd just done and what repercussions it would have on their relationship.

What would Wren think of him in the light of day? Would she think that he took advantage of her? Would she hate him for taking her virginity, or think he had no respect for her? Would she feel embarrassed or even, humiliated? Wasn't he the one who always protected her? If only he'd protected her from himself and his fucking moment of weakness and jealousy. He was beating himself up for sleeping with her and not using a condom. The last thing he wanted to do was fuck up either of their lives by getting her pregnant. He'd always protected her, except tonight.

Ugh! He inwardly groaned. As amazing as the night had been, he wished he had a time machine to rewind the evening.

Suddenly he felt claustrophobic and fidgety, and he needed to get out of bed.

He slid from beneath Wren, who was sleeping so soundly she hardly noticed, remaining on her stomach and moving into the pillows.

Caleb knew he had to figure this shit out, and he was feeling he needed separation from Wren to do it. He wasn't thinking straight and he needed to clear his head. Obviously, he couldn't think straight as long as he was touching Wren. Distance was what he needed and he was thanking God he had three more months of school.

He quietly packed his bag, using the flashlight on his iPhone so he could see what he was doing, and called a cab to come pick him up. On the way to the airport, and the five extra hours he sat there waiting for his flight, he tried to convince himself that he was doing it for Wren. He tried to make himself believe that if she woke up full of regret, she could pretend it didn't happen and she wouldn't feel any shame or embarrassment. If she didn't mention it, he wouldn't either. Maybe she'd think he was drunk and didn't remember, and that would be her out.

But really, it was *his* out: he wasn't ready for this one night to fuck up his relationship with Wren. He couldn't bear it if she looked at him as less than he'd always been to her. Either way he'd failed her, and he couldn't live with that.

chapter
ONE

CALEB LUXON COULDN'T CRY FOR the loss of a man he barely knew. He didn't hate his father as much now as he did when he was younger. The bitterness was not as pungent now, but so much of what his father had done was unforgivable. The most grievous hit, was forcing Caleb to leave the one person he loved most in the world; the only person he'd *ever* loved, beyond his mother.

Wren.

Now *there* was a loss he could mourn; a loss that was still so acute it would slice him wide open if he let it.

Over the years, he'd become an expert at shutting down his emotions, but whenever he thought about Wren a deep ache took root inside his chest and regret flooded every cell of his body. The abyss between them ate at him every day from the moment he opened his eyes until he fell asleep at night. It didn't matter that he hadn't had a real conversation with her in what seemed like forever. It didn't matter that both of them had moved on. It didn't matter that she didn't seem to need him anymore. Wren was always his first and last thought.

When they'd first met, Caleb wanted nothing to do with her; she was introverted and strange, and at the time, and he had more than enough of his own problems. By the age of sixteen, he already hated his father and was consumed with doing everything he possibly could to make the man's life a living hell. Wren and her witch-mother had been just two more knives in his back.

He still cringed when he thought of the day that ice queen, Veronica, moved into his house; her very presence was his father's misguided attempt to erase the memory of his mother, Celine. Caleb knew from the moment he'd laid eyes on her that she was a narcissistic money-grubber who had no interest in his father other than his success, wealth and the influence bought by both.

The sick part was that Edison Luxon knew Veronica was a plastic bitch from the moment she'd come to work for his company, Lux Pharmaceuticals, but it didn't seem to matter in the least. Sure, she was beautiful, in a fake, calculated, surgically enhanced sort of way.

Caleb's father would never pick anyone less glamorous given the cosmetic empire built on his brains and Celine's amazing face. Caleb remembered his mother as kind and graceful; elegant even, and not just beautiful. She was a high-fashion model, and Edison met her at a company event for the launch of a new line that he helped develop, and Celine represented. As a boy, his father had told him to believe in love at first sight, because he and Celine were living proof.

Caleb huffed at the irony. His mother had been ten times the woman Veronica would ever be. A modeling career was the only thing they had in common. She was hired to represent the Lux brand when his mother had been unable to continue. Caleb often wondered if his father was banging her even before his mother lost her battle with cancer. Edison was never around those last, hard months, and his absence had festered into a deep resentment and disdain within his son. It didn't help that Edison basically abandoned Caleb in the process, leaving him to be the one to watch his mother wither and die, to be the strong one she leaned on. It was a lot to expect of a twelve-year-old boy. Caleb's throat constricted as emotion tightened his chest and made his eyes burn.

He remembered his disgust at the way his father pandered and gave Veronica everything she ever wanted. To Caleb, she was constantly screeching in that intolerable shrill, fucking voice, prancing around the house in those obnoxious hooker heels that clicked on the hardwood and marble floors. He couldn't stand that bitch, but at least she was momentarily placated when his father threw money in her direction, which took her attention off of Caleb and Wren. *Especially, Wren,* Caleb thought. Money was something that Edison had plenty of, and if it bought a bit of peace for Wren, all the better.

Life was still hell for them, but at least, it helped. He shook his head at his sad contemplation. It was good that money didn't mean shit to Caleb since his father squandered so much of it on someone so obviously conniving.

Caleb sighed heavily, regretting the hatred he wasted on both of them. As much as he despised Veronica, and at the time, his father for marrying her, he realized that if it weren't for that turn of events, he would never have known Wren. That would be a tragedy; maybe the biggest tragedy of his life.

The day he first laid eyes on Wren was still crystal clear in his mind. The day was traumatizing considering he'd felt like an orphan for the past four years. His father had just dropped the bomb that he'd married the woman whose face had replaced Celine's in the company advertising campaigns; and done so without warning his son it was coming. Caleb had been hurt and furious; completely taken by surprise. He barely knew the woman, and was in shock.

"You married that plastic bitch?" Caleb had rushed up and shouted in his father's face. He'd just come home from high school and Edison was waiting with Veronica in the drawing room of the huge house, and Caleb had been hit with it square in the face.

"What the fuck, Dad? Why did you have to marry her? Just throw cash at her if you want to fuck her! How long has this been going on?"

Veronica, dressed in a bright red dress, at least had the grace to flush at his outburst, the shade of her face, almost matching her dress. She had nearly white, bleached blonde hair, done up as if she were Cinderella going to a ball, and her body, overly thin, even for a model, sat with perfect posture on the sofa across from the large marble fireplace in the elegant room. Caleb had balked, thinking she looked more like a doll than a person. She was boney and it was clear her face could be harsh underneath the thin veil of beauty. She'd been staring at the big oil portrait of his mother hanging over the fireplace, her eyes hard and calculating as they roamed over it. Caleb remembered hating that she had even laid eyes on it.

Veronica had been startled by Caleb's booming voice, but quickly regained her composure and spoke in a sickly, sweet tone. He had glared at her quickly, and then looked away to lock eyes with his father. He could see through her ploy like a freshly washed window.

"Now, Caleb, I'm sure—" she began.

Caleb's head snapped around in her direction again. His overly long hair, getting in his eyes, as he impatiently pushed it off his forehead. "Was I talking to you, bitch?" he yelled, his face was red; the skin on his face felt as if it were on fire, his heart beating so fast it felt like it would fly from his chest.

"You can be sure of nothing; other than I hate your skinny ass! This is my mother's house! Get the fuck out!"

"Caleb!" Edison shouted back. "Veronica is my wife! You will treat her with respect! She and—"

It was bad enough that his father hadn't been present in his son's life for the two years since Celine had died, but to bring in this... whore. Caleb couldn't take it. He felt as if his mother was dying all over again, and his father, cold as stone; didn't give a damn. The pressure inside his chest was debilitating.

His throat had tightened and his eyes welled with angry tears.

"The hell I will!" Caleb's voice cracked with emotion.

"Your wife is in Lakeland Cemetery! You're dishonoring Mom, Dad! You reduce yourself to this—? This piece of sh—!" He indicated the woman sitting on the sofa, but his father interrupted.

"Enough!" His father bellowed, but after a beat, his demeanor had returned to the cold, dead-like lack of emotion that Caleb was used to. "I understand you're upset, Caleb. I should have prepared you. But it is what it is, and you have to accept it. It's good for the business and in everyone's best interest. I'm your father, and you'll conduct yourself in the way your family name demands. I don't have to ask your permission and your mother would want—"

One frustrated tear slipped from Caleb's eye and he'd quickly wiped it away. Unwilling to show any weakness, he turned his back on his father and Veronica, the helplessness he felt nearly crushing. "Fuck you, both."

He'd seen Wren for the first time, then, and he'd stopped short, embarrassed to be seen crying. The small, timid girl cowering near the doorway between the drawing room and the foyer, had been dressed all in black, her unnaturally black hair cropped in a short, but shiny bob, and her eyes almost completely hidden by black eyeliner. He'd sniffed and used the back of his hand to wipe at his nose, squared his shoulders and calmed his voice.

"You don't give a shit about my best interest, just like you didn't give a shit about what my mother needed! You are not my father!" he shouted and walked from the room, past the gothic-looking girl hovering uncertainly in the doorway.

"Caleb!" His father's voice boomed behind him, but he'd

only lifted both of his hands to flip the double bird from behind.

Not his finest moment, in retrospect. Especially considering Wren was watching everything.

It was a few weeks later, right after he'd gotten his driver's license with the help of the housekeeper and his father's friend, that he'd pulled a few grand from the bank account his mother had set up for him before she died and bought a used motorcycle against Edison's wishes. He spent hours and hours fixing it up. When it was running, he stayed out until all hours, resentful that he had to go home to that God-forsaken house at all.

He blew off all his preppy friends and started hanging out with a different crowd, picking anyone his father would consider the most undesirable, or morally repugnant. He skipped school, stole a few cars, and got arrested twice. If it annoyed Edison Luxon, cost him money, or otherwise disrupted his carefully controlled life, the better Caleb liked it. Payback was a bitch.

Caleb met his best friend at a wrestling match and the rest was history. Caleb was into motorcycles and Dex's dad owned a local motorcycle shop and they spent a ton of time hanging out there after school. Dex was everything Caleb wasn't; tattooed, tough, and loyal to his dad. He was a couple years older and had taken Caleb under his wing. He helped him fix up an old beater bike, and introduced him into a regional fight club, which quickly consumed him. Soon Caleb was muscular and strong, and Dex was like the older brother Caleb never had. The fighting helped Caleb deal with all of his personal issues. Somehow beating the shit out of someone helped ease his internal turmoil and gave him an outlet for the hatred and anger that had overtaken his reason.

The money he made when he won was a bonus, but even better, his father abhorred his fighting. Edison's disapproval spurred Caleb on and he smugly displayed every black eye, cut lip, or set of bruised knuckles just to taunt his father. He never lost a fight and sometimes he imagined the person he was pummeling was Edison. It helped, if only for a few minutes.

When Edison married Veronica, Caleb was well entrenched in his new life and wasn't home much. He learned in the months following, that Veronica's thirteen-year-old daughter Wren was a dramatically stark contrast to her mother. Veronica was loud and intrusive, beautiful and aloof, and the girl was quiet, wore dark, shapeless clothing, and always had her eyes completely camouflaged by the overabundance of black eye makeup. She kept entirely to herself, and Caleb thought her name didn't suit her at all. She looked like a witch, not a beautiful bird.

Wren barely spoke, and hardly ate. He barely knew she was in the house unless Veronica was shrieking at her. His mind had written her off as a freak, and he decided to stay as far away from both of the women as he possibly could. He couldn't bear his father, he couldn't bear his new stepmother making changes to the house as if trying to erase his mother's memory, and he had no tolerance for the quiet girl who haunted the house like a dark ghost.

The girl had been enrolled into the private school Caleb attended, but didn't fit in at all. The uniform was at odds with her emo style and she didn't make any friends. The preppy bastards there had a hay day making fun of her, but even the crowd of misfits and delinquents Caleb hung with after school, thought she was weird. But then, everything changed.

Caleb let out a deep sigh at the sudden pain the memory caused.

"Ugghhhh!" he muttered under his breath. "What the hell am I doing here?" Though his father had unexpectedly tried to make amends years later, their relationship was never close. Now, since the old man was dead, what the hell was the point? That house was already haunted and this new ghost was far less significant to Caleb than that of his mother, or his memories of Wren.

Still, Caleb put one foot in front of the other and plodded forward. Everything was a blur as he made his way through Denver International Airport. The noise of planes, announcements, and the massive crowds of people rushing to get to and from their gates, all melded together in an annoying, white noise haze.

He was tired. Exhausted. His mind flashed with memories, and his heart seized with apprehension. Would Wren come home? Would he see her? He was both anxious and terrified. Everything was so screwed up. It had been for the past five years, since the spring break before he graduated college. He'd fucked it up, huge, and then, impossibly, made it even worse. What his father started, he'd managed to finish.

His head throbbed and his eyes burned from lack of sleep as he walked toward the exits, pulling his one small roller bag behind him. He was tall like his father, his shoulders broad and his body ripped and strong, but his eyes were like his mother's; such a deep blue they sometimes hinted of violet. Caleb squinted in the morning sun as he left the building. The bright June weather was beautiful, the sun's warmth kissed by a light northern breeze, and the lapis sky loaded with cottony white clouds. The Colorado climate was moderate, even in the dead of winter or the height of summer; the low humidity made the temperature feel more comfortable than the thermometer belied.

Caleb pulled his sunglasses off the back of his head and shoved them on. He knew he looked like a slob and he didn't care. After all, his father wouldn't be able to ridicule his appearance this time. As morbid as that might be, it was something.

Coming back to Colorado didn't leave Caleb riddled with memories of his father, or even his mother, but instead, thoughts of a crying young girl, begging him not to leave her just before his nineteenth birthday. His thoughts continued to flood with images of another time when her tears ripped him to shreds when he'd said "no" to the only thing she'd ever asked of him. That girl, and the beautiful woman she'd become, was all he could think about.

Caleb swallowed at the tightness in his throat. He'd gone from avoiding her at all costs, to having her clinging and crying when he tried to say goodbye without losing it himself... and then she was the one to leave him, once and for all. The memory still cut like a knife.

Raising his right arm to hail one of the passing taxies, Caleb climbed inside when it stopped in front of him and let his bag land on the seat next to him. The cab reeked of cigarette smoke, but once he was securely inside he closed his eyes and leaned his head back onto the seat, forgetting to give the driver directions.

"Where to?" The cab driver asked in a raspy voice that, along with the odor, confirmed he smoked about two packs a day. Caleb cracked the window to hopefully alleviate the stench, and looked out at the Rocky Mountains in the background. They were majestic as they rose from the western horizon, creating layers upon layers in different shades of green and brown, fading into a haze the further away they were, with the snowcapped peaks of higher elevations; like their crowning glory.

Caleb raised his head and his eyelids fluttered open. "Um..." He wasn't sure if he was supposed to go to the estate in Downtown Denver or the one in Evergreen. He pulled out his phone and found the text from the secretary of his father's lawyer. *Downtown*, it said. "530 South University."

The cabby whistled. "The Polo Club area?"

It was an affluent collection of old and new money; the houses all valued at several million dollars with substantial grounds, especially for the center of the city. It was minutes to his father's office, which had amazing views of downtown and the Front Range. The stone house was magnificent, though it didn't matter that it was a beautiful property. It was nothing more than a huge museum or mausoleum to Caleb; just a cold and empty shell.

"Yes." Caleb didn't feel like elaborating. He was staring at the phone in his hand, his thumb automatically sifting through his contacts until Wren's name appeared on the list. He sucked in his breath. Should he call her? The last time he'd spoken to her had been Christmas Day for ten minutes, and the conversation had been painfully stilted.

The taxi pulled away from the curb and merged into traffic. The estate was a good thirty minutes or more from the airport, depending on traffic.

He sighed and put his phone back on the clip on his belt.

"Are you just visiting, or is Denver your home?" the driver asked.

Caleb considered this. He hadn't considered this house his home since his mother died. "Just visiting. I grew up here, though. My father died yesterday." His response was devoid of emotion and short.

"Oh," the cabby paused, feeling awkward that his questions brought up such a subject. "I'm sorry to hear that."

"Thank you," Caleb's voice showed no sorrow or regret. He was so tired, he should try to sleep on the drive but he had little trust that the driver would take the most efficient route, and though his father was dripping in money, he wasn't. He had plans to start a business of his own, and he had to save every cent he could because he didn't want to rely on his father's last name, money or connections.

It wasn't that his father hadn't tried; he sent him a check every week for five years, but Caleb never opened a single one of them. Instead, he shoved them all in the biggest drawer in the kitchen of his apartment, always meaning to burn them, but not quite getting around to it. They sat in the drawer, as if leaving them untouched would allow him to forget things he didn't want to think about. It was just easier. But some things were harder to forget, even when he pushed them down.

He glanced out the window, watching the industrial areas of east Denver pass as they made their way toward the city center. Denver was beautiful to the west, north, and south, but between the airport and the city, it was less appealing.

"Where did you come in from?"

"San Francisco."

"I've never been there."

"It's really beautiful. I love the bay, but this..." Caleb watched the Rocky Mountains get closer and realized how much he missed them. When he was very young, his mom and dad would take him on camping and fishing trips in the national forest, and skiing at Breckenridge, Aspen, and Keystone. Before his mother got sick, his father had been a different person, and those were happy memories.

"The Rockies are so magnificent. Too bad about all this industrial shit out here." The backdrop was breathtaking, but what populated along the highway, between the airport and further into the city was dirty and unkempt; a succession of junk yards, dilapidated buildings, and litter. "Sad."

"Yes. I've lived here my entire life. I'll never leave Colorado."

Caleb didn't answer, wondering if the new law that legalized weed had anything to do with the driver's love of the state. Coming home stirred a lot of memories and he preferred to let his thoughts drift rather than engage in superficial conversation.

The first time Caleb spoke to Wren, he'd he'd padded

into the kitchen in a pair of grey sweats sitting low on his hips. He'd just worked out in the fully equipped gym his father installed in the basement of the house and needed to get something to drink. The gym was outfitted with the best fitness equipment, a bag, and a complete set of free weights. He'd been lifting for thirty minutes followed by running five miles on the treadmill, and was dripping in sweat and dying of thirst.

The kitchen was massive and set up with all the best appliances; the industrial stuff you might find in a restaurant kitchen. He pulled open one side of the stainless steel double door refrigerator to examine the variety of beverages lined up neatly inside, along with yogurt, fresh fruit, cooked chicken breast, vegetables, and other healthy foods, stocked at his request by the housekeeper. Everything in that house was the finest, biggest, and newest. Caleb sometimes wondered if it was his father's way of trying to make up for not being a real part of his life. He saw his father's lawyer and the household staff more than he saw his own dad.

The house had always been amazing, but since his mother's death, it was more sterile, somehow. It was missing the laughter, the warmth, the music Celine always had playing, the smell of his favorite cookies baking, and the expensive perfume she always wore were conspicuously absent.

The "stuff" aspect seemed to be more pronounced since she'd died as if his father was trying to compensate for her absence with material things. Practically every room had been remodeled, other than his mother's suite, which he'd begged his father to leave as she had left it. On this, at least, they were in agreement, and Caleb had secretly rejoiced at the nasty argument that ensued when Edison had refused Veronica's attempts to convert it into a giant closet and changing room. She was so fucking vain; Caleb couldn't stand it. It may have been the moment that Edison had begun to regret his decision to marry her.

The light from the inside of the refrigerator flooded over his sweat-drenched torso as he leaned in to grab a bottle of water when a noise from about ten feet away caused him to pause and glance toward the table in one corner. Natural stone tiles covered the floors; and the walls were lined with mahogany cupboards and topped lighter granite counters, with darker backsplashes.

Nothing looked out of the ordinary to Caleb as he stood, casually propping open the door with an elbow while he unscrewed the cap of the water bottle and took a long pull. A chair leg grated against the stone tile as Wren shifted in her hiding place, causing him to stop drinking abruptly; water spilling and dripping down his chest.

"Shit!" It had been ice cold on his hot skin. He leaned down to look more closely in the direction of the noise; but the kitchen was huge and it was dark, other than a small light above one side of the counters by the sink, and that from the open refrigerator door. Everything was engulfed in shadows. The large, granite and mahogany island was lined with stools on one side and the oversized gas stovetop on the other; opposite the double ovens on one wall. He let the door of the refrigerator close and moved stealthily toward the table, crouching slightly to look under it.

Surely, there wouldn't be vermin skittering around the Luxon house. The staff was on autopilot to care for the home and the grounds, and his father would tolerate nothing less than perfection.

There was a small, dark form cowering in the corner, on the floor. Caleb's adrenaline began to flow, but he was smart enough not to make any sudden moves.

He glanced at the security panel by the door leading from the kitchen out into the giant garage. Nothing was amiss; the system was on and working, but there was definitely someone there.

He quietly moved to the island and set down his water, and opened a long drawer where the knives were kept. His hand folded around the handle of a particularly large chef's knife, and he pulled it out silently, sliding the drawer shut simultaneously.

"Who's there?" he demanded, his voice harder than normal, taking three stealthy steps in the direction of the shadowy figure, his movements controlled. He'd put down bigger opponents than this with just his fists, but if this was an attempted robbery, there might be weapons to contend with. "I said who's there?"

"Caleb, it's just me. Wren." Her voice was soft and she sounded frightened. Wren. Her name seemed to suit her tone, even if her general style was more in line with Satan.

He visibly relaxed, the hand holding the knife falling to his side, irritated that his stepsister would be sneaking around the house. "What are you doing hiding in corners, for fuck's sake? I could have cut you."

He hadn't made any effort to talk to her or learn anything about her in the two months since she'd moved in with her horrible mother, and he didn't intend to start then.

"I was—" she stopped. "I'm sorry. I was..."

"Spit it out, girl, and get up off of the floor, already." Caleb walked back and put the knife away with a clang and slammed the drawer too hard. He was irritated that she was even living in his house, let alone lurking around like a scared rabbit.

She scrambled to her feet, and though Caleb hadn't turned on the main light in the room, he could see she was dressed in some ungodly black tent of a shirt over baggy pajama pants. He frowned when he looked at her face, as he closed the drawer after replacing the knife. Why was she wearing that awful makeup at this time of night?

Wren was stunned just looking at Caleb. He stood there in the low light and she stared at him, unable to move. "I—I'm sorry," she stammered. "I was just—"

Caleb's face twisted as he went back and picked up his water to untwist the cap again. "You were just, what?"

She was holding something in her hand and she was trying to hide it; and then looked down toward the floor. "I was looking for something to eat."

Yeah, he thought. She could use some meat on her bones.

"Have at it," he said casually, his hand waving at the refrigerator. "And the pantry is through there. Jonesy keeps the place loaded. You don't need to sneak around like that."

Wren looked up at Caleb as he went to the pantry, threw

open the doors loudly and went inside. It was a walk-in and he went in to rummage. After his workout, his stomach was rumbling, too.

He found some crackers, bananas, and cereal bars, then went to the refrigerator to get some sliced cheddar cheese, the chicken, and another bottle of water. Wren was still standing in the same place he'd left her and Caleb's eyebrow shot up as he brought the food to the table. He pulled out one of the chairs, not caring about the noise he was making. "Well? Sit down, why don't ya?" he asked, annoyed. He wasn't used to someone acting so scared. "I'm not gonna bite you."

He wondered if she was bulimic or had other issues considering her oversized clothes that hung on what, judging by her face, he could tell was a waif-like body.

"Shhhh!" Wren said softly.

"Why?" He asked wryly?

"Aren't you afraid of waking everyone up?"

He shook his shaggy head with a wry grin and sat down. The sweat was drying, and sticking a few wayward tendrils of his dark hair to his forehead and side of his face.

"Um... no?" He shrugged, his tone laced with incredulous sarcasm. "I'd rather it bother the shit out of them, but it's not likely. This house is way too big to hear what's going on in here from way up in the bedrooms."

"Oh," Wren said quietly, and seemed to visibly relax. "Okay."

He nodded at the food in front of him on the table. "Sit."

She'd done as she was told and then reached for the plate he'd handed her helping herself to a few crackers and a piece of cheese, and placed them on it. "Thank you. Aren't you having any?"

He hadn't planned to eat, since he'd just worked out, but thought if he went back to his room, she might not eat anything, and she looked like she'd blow away. Besides, he'd already decided he was starving.

"I don't usually eat after a workout." By then she'd taken a small bite, and he sat down. Her eyes glanced up, guiltily, as if she'd done something wrong by eating.

"Oh," she said, using a hand to cover her mouth, full of food.

Caleb watched her as she shoved her mouth full. "But, I'll make an exception." He reached for a cereal bar and started to open the wrapper. "You look like you're starving to death," Caleb observed. "Why?" He'd heard about girls who starved themselves, or ate and then forced themselves to throw up. He'd never seen her eat much either time he'd had to suffer through dinner with the family since Wren and her mom moved in.

"Um... I don't like to eat in front of my mother."

Unexpected anger rushed over Caleb and it showed on his handsome face. "Why not? My dad's rich enough to feed her, too."

Wren shook her head, picking up another cracker. "She doesn't want me to be fat."

"Fat?" Caleb was incredulous. "She's got more meat on her than you do, though, I guess not much."

The girl shrugged. "She was a model by the time she was my age, and so I think she's just trying to help me."

"Are you into it? My mother was a model, too. She was always watching everything she ate. I think never being able to eat has to be depressing as hell."

Even in the low light, Caleb could see the hollows in her cheeks, the dark circles under her eyes, and the frailty of the delicate bones of her hands and wrists she had exposed. She was painfully thin.

She stopped mid-chew and then continued, emptying her mouth before she answered. "I don't know." A slender shoulder rose in a shrug and the oversized neck of the shirt fell off down her arm. "I'd like to be a dancer."

Caleb was taken aback. "What, like a stripper?"

Wren laughed softly, the sound strangely pleasing to Caleb.

"Why do guys always think all dancers are strippers? No. Like a ballerina or on Broadway. I had classes until I was eleven, but then I had to stop. I don't think we had the money for me to keep going."

"Wow. Were you any good?"

Wren nodded. "Yeah. I was in the Nutcracker with the Colorado Ballet for two years. Only one other girl from my ballet school was asked to perform with them. We were part of the studio competition team, too."

Caleb's eyes widened. He didn't know much about dance teams and such, but it sounded impressive. "Holy shit! You must be really good."

Wren nodded sadly. "Pretty good. I wish..." She let her regretful words trail off.

"I can speak to the asshole and ask him to cough up the

dough," Caleb offered.

Wren quickly shook her head. "Oh, no. Please don't. I couldn't."

"Sure you could."

"No, please. I'd be punished for even speaking about it."

Caleb downed the last of his cereal bar, and then asked, "Where's your dad?"

"I don't remember him. I've had a couple of stepdads. Off and on."

Caleb's lips thinned as he pressed them together. "Rich stepdads?" he asked knowingly. If that were the case, though, Wren should have been able to remain in dance. Her mother had no issues spending his father's money, so he decided Veronica was a worse bitch than he thought.

"Part of the time, I... I guess?" Wren made it sound like a question. "Where's your mom?"

"She died when I was twelve. Cancer."

She gasped. "Oh, I'm sorry. I didn't mean to—I thought they were divorced."

He waved a hand to silence her. He didn't talk about his mom with anyone. He didn't share how his father had become a coldhearted bastard. The conversation was about to turn down a path he didn't want it to. "Don't worry about it. I'm gonna go to bed." He pushed back from the table, picking up his bottle of water. "Can you put shit away? I may want to piss off my dad, but Jonesy's another story."

"Jonesy? You mean Mrs. Jones?"

Caleb hadn't called the housekeeper Mrs. Jones since forever, and no one did. "Yeah. She's a cool old lady. Unless *you call her Mrs. Jones, that is."*

"Caleb, can you wait for me to go? I mean, sure, I can put stuff away, but, um..."

"What?" He was getting impatient. This was more interaction than he'd wanted to have with her, but she looked so frail and scared, the protective instinct in him made him hesitate.

"I don't want my mom to come down here and see me with this food. If you're here, you can say you're the one eating."

In that conversation Caleb got the first glimpse of Wren's true relationship with Veronica, and it would soon become even clearer.

When the cab pulled up to the gate of his family home, Caleb had to lean out of the window to talk to the security guards to get them to open the gate. The house was enormous, the grounds still perfectly manicured, and just as he remembered, like a fortress. As the cab drove up the lane to the front, the sun was dipping to hide behind the low clouds over the mountains, making the late afternoon seem like twilight.

"Here you go," the cabby said, and then informed Caleb of the fare total.

Caleb took a roll of cash out of his front jean pocket and peeled off two bills. "Thanks, man. Keep the rest."

"Thank you, son. Again, sorry about your dad."

"Yeah," Caleb answered as he pulled on the door handle. "So am I."

The cabby was unaware of the double meaning behind Caleb's words.

chapter
TWO

THE HUGE HOUSE FELT LIKE A TOMB.

How fitting, Caleb thought. He wasn't sure what to expect out of the day or week in front of him. The house was empty when he arrived late yesterday afternoon, and he'd spent the evening in his mother's old room, laying on her bed and watching TV. Surprisingly, it was still untouched; though he wondered how his father managed that all these years... he thought for sure the hag would have won out eventually. It still held the faint scent of Celine's favorite perfume, which was one of his father's first formulas for Lux. Caleb lived in that house until he left for college, but his mother's rooms were the only places he felt at ease.

His mother's death had been one of those moments that change you. 60 little seconds and *boom;* your life will never ever be the same. He could think of a few others that occurred since, and again, images of Wren raced through his thoughts, but he tried to push them down and focus on the task at hand.

As Caleb sat on the large, expensive leather sofa in his father's study, he was faced with another of those horrible, unforgettable situations.

These were the kind of events that are burned on your mind forever and you remember exactly where you were, what scent surrounded you, how you felt, or what music was playing... because they were that powerful.

Some of these times left an indelible stamp that Caleb resented, rebelled against, and wanted to forget. Most of them were agonizing, but a slight few had been like the most amazing dreams. Yet, still... even those could still cause incredible, irreversible regret.

He glanced up; his dark blue eyes meeting older, sadder ones. Finally, though he'd fought it, the question had to be asked.

"Is she coming?"

His father's friend, and long-time lawyer, Jonathan Westwood, was as distinguished, polished, and stoic as his father had been. He'd been a prominent figure around the Luxon household since Caleb's adolescence, shortly after Caleb's mother got sick and Edison virtually disappeared. Nothing seemed to rattle Jonathan; his demeanor was always steady, calm and kind.

Caleb huffed softly. Everything in the house reminded him of why he never returned; hard, and cold; silent, and lifeless... and the conspicuous lack of Wren's presence. He supposed that on the surface, the structure was elegant and posh, the kind of home most only dreamed of having, but he hated every fucking brick in this place! There may have been moments of happiness, bought at years of misery, and Caleb didn't need to be reminded.

Jonathan cleared his throat and scooted forward on the second leather couch opposite Caleb, then opened the expensive Gucci briefcase sitting on the stone coffee table between them.

The old man contemplated the younger one in front of him. He could see the same proud arrogance in Caleb that his friend, Edison, had been known for. Though Caleb's hair was thicker and he was much tougher than Edison had been, there were definitely some similarities. The circumstances of his youth had made him harder, and knowing what Jonathan knew, it was completely understandable.

"I placed a call to Wren's ballet company right after I spoke with you yesterday. Your stepsister was in Bali on vacation, but I was able to get in touch with her office," Jonathan said, carefully monitoring Caleb's response. "She should have the message by now."

Stepsister. Jesus Christ!

Caleb ran an agitated hand through his dark hair, broke eye contact, and then physically balked at Jonathan's words. Wren was a prima ballerina with the New York City Ballet.

Stepsister, his mind screamed again.

He'd come to despise that word more than any other in the English language. He'd fought the implications of that goddamned word for years, and it still made bile rise in his throat.

"Wren doesn't need to be here," Caleb said tiredly, rubbing a weary hand down over his face to his jaw.

"Yes, she does, Caleb," Jonathan responded. "She's part of this. If you choose, that is."

Caleb's eyes snapped to the other man's face.

What the fuck? he thought. What did his control-hungry father have in store for him this time? After everything, what else could he do to him? He'd already ripped he and Wren apart years before this.

"If I choose? What does that mean?" His voice took on an angry timber. "I *don't* choose for Wren, Jonathan!"

"You do this time, Caleb. Maybe you should consider that for a while."

Caleb's brow furrowed and he wanted to growl at the other man. "You said you called her already, so how in the hell was that my choice?"

Jonathan sighed heavily. Caleb's emotions had always simmered right beneath the surface; especially when it came to Wren. "You've got a lot to deal with. I thought you'd want to see her."

Caleb's scowl lessened and his brows lifted slightly, his eyes widening. Wren was a sore subject and he was pissed that his father's lawyer seemed to think he was an expert on how he felt. He didn't lean on anyone. He didn't allow himself to wallow in self-pity and he'd been strong out of necessity. Wren was his Achilles' heel, but no one knew it, not even Wren.

"I survive. That's what I do."

Jonathan sighed again. "I know, Caleb. I guess, I thought—"

"You thought what?" Caleb almost growled, his impatience,

mixed with emotions he didn't want to deal with made him harsher than he should have been.

"Nothing. Wren may not believe she's needed. When was the last time you two spoke?" Jonathan continued, always so formal in his speech that Caleb sometimes wondered what his upbringing was like.

"I don't know." But, he did know. It was Christmas, and then a brief conversation after that, on her birthday. What a cluster fuck that was. "Months, I guess."

It had been apparent after his one night of weakness that the two of them were better with minimal contact, but Caleb wasn't ready to take that demon on just yet.

"What choice are you speaking of, Jonathan? How has my father screwed me over this time?"

"Caleb, consider that your father really did love you and had your best interest at heart. I know the two of you struggled after your mother died, and I understand your resentment. However, I ask you to understand that your father was watching the woman he loved lose her vibrancy and life. That type of pain makes a man do things he might not do in other circumstances. That had to be unbearable."

Sure, Caleb had considered that before; but when you've just lost your mother, and then your father disappears around the same time, any understanding you might have flies out the window; especially when you're twelve and puberty is messing with your emotions.

"You mean he took the pussy route when he abandoned my mother, leaving her to die alone? Is that the struggle you're referring to?" Caleb returned sarcastically, his face and chest began to burn, his heart starting to pound as he relived the pain of the past. "How he married that gold-digging bitch soon after? That resentment?" Caleb snarled.

"It was four years later, Caleb. Remember?"

"Yeah, whatever. Time flies when you're having fun," he said bitterly. He got up to pace around the room, sucking in his breath. He couldn't help but notice Jonathan's calmness in the face of his rage. He ran a hand through his thick dark hair, again. "I'm sorry. I have no right to rant at you like this. It's not your fault my father was the way he was."

"I understand, son."

Son. When it came right down to it, Jonathan had been there for Caleb far more than his father ever had, and suddenly he felt guilty for his temper.

After the call from Jonathan delivering the news of Edison's death the previous day, Caleb had numbly packed a bag and gotten on a plane without much thought. He had no idea what difference his presence would make either way; when you're dead, you're dead. Does it really matter who shows up to plant you?

"What's the supposed choice I have to make, Jonathan?" Caleb asked wearily. "What suit or tie to send to the coffin slinger?"

"No." Jonathan's face twisted in consternation at Caleb's bitterness, before reaching into his briefcase and lifting up two envelopes. "Mrs. Jones is handling that. It's in here." He tapped the edge of the envelopes on his hand and Caleb watched him, perplexed. "Your father left two versions of his will. He wanted you to decide which version to have read.

Whichever you choose will go on record and the other is to be destroyed without anyone but the two of us knowing about it."

"What? Why?" Caleb's brow furrowed in confusion and his lips pressed together in anger. He'd spoken to his father maybe ten times in as many years, and only seen him once or twice.

Jonathan contemplated Caleb for a moment. The young man was still so full of fury and pain. He could tell that Edison's death hit him harder than he wanted to let on, and that regret and grief would probably hit like a tidal wave in a few days.

"One version all of it comes to you—"

Caleb's face mottled as if he wanted to explode, but he kept a tight reign on his emotions. "I don't want his fucking money."

He didn't want the cosmetic business that bore the Luxon name either. That company was his mother's vision, and Caleb felt his father had tainted that, too; when he brought that money-hungry bitch, Veronica, into it. It sickened Caleb and at the time, he'd vowed to wash his hands of his father and Lux Pharmaceuticals, as well. "I don't want anything from him. Give it all to charity."

Jonathan's watery light blue eyes were sad as he looked at Caleb. He knew he had to be full of sorrow, if not for the loss of the actual man, then the loss of the father he should have had, and didn't. No matter how strained their relationship, Edison was the only parent Caleb had for more than half of his life, and his unexpected death was bound to leave behind some damage.

"Unfortunately, that's not one of the choices. He asked me

to have you read this letter and the two wills, and then you're to tell me which version I should read after the funeral. He knew you felt this way, but he has considered Wren, as well."

Caleb sucked in a deep breath. *Of course*, he thought. The few times he'd seen any softness in his father it was something to do with Wren. He shrugged. "Okay. Give everything to her, then."

"Caleb," Jonathan began, "that isn't one of the options, either. If you want her to have anything at all... you have to split the estate equally."

Both of Caleb's hands rose to tangle in both sides of his thick head of hair and his chest expanded to bursting as he sucked in a deep breath. The company was publically traded, but his father retained controlling interest with sixty-five percent of the shares.

"I'll take it all, then sign it over to her."

"There are huge tax ramifications of doing that. Your dad made sure that couldn't happen. It isn't an option."

Caleb sighed. "Of course, not. Why would he make it easy on me? He fucked up my relationship with Wren years ago, and now he wants to throw us together?" When Jonathan didn't answer, Caleb made his way back to the sofa and sat down again. "Have you read it?"

"Yes. Just calm down and listen, Caleb."

"Can I just sell her my half for five dollars?"

Jonathan cleared his throat and smiled. He admired Caleb's protectiveness of Wren. "Not right away. You each have the option to buy each other out, if you both agree, but not for five years from the time of Edison's death. After that time has passed you can sell it to her, but not below the current market value. It's publically traded and doing so would devalue the stock for the rest of the shareholders. You can gift it to her at that time, though, she'll have to pay huge capital gains tax."

"What the hell?" Anger rose up inside him and made Caleb's chest feel like it was going to explode as heat rushed under the skin of his face like liquid fire. He tried to suck in a breath big enough to fill his lungs but they resisted. "Goddamn him!"

"If you want her to have anything going forward, you'll have to assume control of Lux and operate it together, at a profit. Even if you both agree, you can't give it to charity, outright, either. At least for the time being."

"Five years, being that time?"

"Yes."

"Then just let the board of directors run everything, until I can figure it out."

"They'll be involved, of course. They have a responsibility to the shareholders, but the shares you control puts you at the helm."

"Fine. I'll do a shitty job and they'll have me removed. The end."

"Then Wren gets nothing, Caleb. The shares will be stripped from both of you. Your mother would roll over in her grave if the company she and Edison built didn't benefit you in some way. And your history with Wren is telling, Caleb. Edison knew you'd do this, solely to take care of her."

The air left Caleb's lungs and he shook his head in absent denial. Wren had a successful career and maybe she wouldn't want to be straddled with the company and her estranged *stepbrother* for the next five years. Also, what about his own life? He had plans of his own.

"That bastard really hates me." His heart started beating so fast he felt it would fly from his chest and Caleb rose to pace the room. He flushed, realizing he should have said it in the past tense. He hadn't felt like that since his mother died, or since Wren left him the last time.

"No, he loved you, Caleb. Edison realized his mistakes and had many regrets; which he voiced to me on multiple occasions. Not the least of which was his decision to send you so far away for college. He knew he should have supported your desire to go to Colorado School of Mines so you could stay close to Wren. This is his attempt to give you a chance at the life you should have had with her. To make things right."

He shook his head. "How? It's too late , Jonathan! Even if it was all wrapped up in a nice little bow, she has a life of her own, and so do I. Don't you get it? He's still trying to control everything I do. He took my decisions about Wren away when he made me go to Boston and he can't fix it all by dropping dead."

When he was younger, Caleb had done just enough to make his father miserable, but not enough to fuck up his own life. He knew his father would always get him out of petty larceny charges or bail his ass out when he boosted cars. Even if Edison had to pay out the ass to do it, he did it; and that had suited Caleb's agenda just fine. He'd made an art out of causing trouble with the confidence his father's intervention would mean he wouldn't be convicted or even have a record.

Maybe it was arrogant, sure, but it was just the way it was. *Amazing what, and who, money could buy,* Caleb thought; disgusted.

"You're not a delinquent with a ruined future. Your dad did that, Caleb. Yes you lost your mother, yes your father was not the parent you deserved, but you did your part to make things worse. For God's sake, take some responsibility for something! The man is dead." Jonathan's voice became thicker, and he cleared his throat.

Caleb's face burned. It wasn't like Jonathan to throw around criticisms or use that kind of tone when speaking to him, and maybe he was right, to a degree; but he'd be damned if he'd give credit for his success to his father's manipulation.

"I did. I studied and graduated with honors. That was me taking responsibility so that bastard wouldn't be able to control me for the rest of my life!" Caleb's own voice rose and broke on a bitter laugh. "But look? He's still yanking my chain."

Caleb had always been interested in how things worked, and from the time he met Dex; and learned how to take shit apart and put it back together again; he'd wanted to be a mechanical engineer. He was fascinated by how things worked and he had dreams of designing custom motorcycles or cars.

Despite his teenage desire to make his father squirm, he'd been smart enough to realize that he'd never be free of Edison without a high school diploma, good grades, and decent test scores. College was his ticket out and away. He'd signed up for the SAT prep-classes, and applied to colleges with Jonesy's help. It was working out great until his father intercepted an acceptance letter to one of the schools he'd applied to. A school that would let him follow his dreams, and stay close to Wren so he could continue to take care of her.

Caleb's mind flashed to a long ago conversation when his father had insisted he attend MIT in Boston. It didn't matter what Caleb had wanted or that he'd taken any initiative on his own, Edison thought he knew what was in his son's best interest, but at the time he resented the hell out of it because he knew how his leaving would affect Wren.

Caleb could admit that his father may have had pure intentions now, but when he was eighteen his emotions ruled his thinking. He hated Edison for sending him away when Wren was so vulnerable and at that bitch, Veronica's mercy. It felt like blackmail, and Wren didn't understand, and he couldn't tell her. She was only sixteen when he left and all she knew was that Caleb was the only person in the world who gave a damn about her.

Edison was planning to divorce Veronica, and Caleb couldn't let that happen… he was terrified for her. At the time, he was smart enough to know Edison's reasons for sending him away, but it hurt so damn bad; rationalizing everything offered little comfort. Caleb had only cried a couple of times in his life; when his mother had died, and then when he had to tell Wren he was leaving her behind. He couldn't tell her he was doing it to protect her and ensure her safety; he couldn't let her know that he was being blackmailed because of her.

His mind flashed to the conversation with his father. He remembered it all so clearly.

"You can't divorce Veronica, Dad! What about Wren?

You know what will happen to her!"

Edison was sitting on the front edge of his heavy mahogany desk, contemplating his son. He knew Caleb and Wren had gotten close, but he hadn't expected this bombastic reaction from his son.

"You hate Veronica. I thought you'd be overjoyed at the prospect of my divorcing her."

Caleb began pacing back and forth in front of his father; feeling like his world was about to implode again. Wren was the only person he cared about, and Veronica would hurt her. "I do. But Wren will be at her mercy. You know what happened before!"

Edison had remained calm, his eyes calculating. "Wren's older now. She can take care of herself."

But Caleb knew that wasn't true, and he couldn't bear the thought of Wren turning back into that introverted, frightened shell of a girl she was when they met.

Caleb stopped and turned to his father, his tone pleading. "Dad. Please. Not until she's eighteen. Please, I'm begging you." It was a bitter pill to swallow after Edison's apparent disinterest in his life.

Edison was annoyed. "That's almost three years from now, Caleb. I can't put up with Veronica's schemes for three more years. I can't afford it. Not if you expect to inherit anything." His tone was sarcastically amused, but lost on his son.

Caleb wasn't worried about the money, but he knew his father's company was sound. "Dad! Please."

"Well," Edison said slowly. "I might be persuaded; if you

go to college. I don't need a fuck-up for a son. Though, God knows, you've tried hard enough to earn that title."

Caleb felt like he'd been kicked in the gut, even though he'd heard the same thing numerous times. It didn't matter. He'd gotten accepted to Colorado School of Mines a few days earlier. His last name alone would have ensured acceptance, his father's Denver-based company was well known worldwide, but his grades were solid, too. "Yeah, I'm such a fuck-up, I got into CSOM," he shot back.

"I know."

Caleb was stunned at his father's easy answer. How in the hell did he know? He hadn't said anything. "You do? How?"

"Come on, Caleb. I know everyone in Denver. My golfing buddy's brother is the president of the school."

"Fuuuuck," Caleb huffed under his breath, pissed he hadn't thought of that. Couldn't he do anything without his father's influence hovering over him? "In that case, I'm not going."

Edison folded his arms over his chest arrogantly eyeing his son. "Don't be stupid, Caleb. Of course, you're going to college. You're always insisting you don't want my help, so make something of yourself on your own."

"I'm trying, but you keep fucking it up! Why can't you stay out of my goddamned life?" Venom dripped from Caleb's words.

Edison's demeanor was stone cold. "I'll stay out of it after you graduate, but you're going to MIT, not the School of Mines."

"You can't force me to go to Boston! I didn't even apply

there!" He'd felt smug, thinking the conversation was over.

His father had simply huffed and turned away, going to the bar in his study to pour a stiff drink. "Oh, yes, I think I can, son. You obviously have initiative, and I admit, I'm pleasantly surprised, but if you want me to suffer that bitch for three more years, you'll do as I ask. It'll be MIT because it's more widely known and will offer you more opportunities, later."

"I don't need your permission. I have a scholarship for part of it, and I've saved up some of my own money."

"Stop it, Caleb. It's MIT, or nothing. I can get that scholarship at CSOM yanked. You'll do what I tell you and you'll be happy about it. You're lucky I'll let you study engineering. I'd hoped you'd pursue a biochem degree. It would be more beneficial to Lux."

Caleb had been furious, his blood rushing in his ears. "You are such an unbelievable bastard. Do you think I planned this to make you look good or help you out? I have plans of my own!"

"Caleb!" Edison shouted, finally losing control. Dressed in a black designer suit, he calmed himself then walked back to his desk. "It's settled. All I have to do is make a call or two."

"I hate you," Caleb had seethed. "What about Wren? What happens to her while I'm gone?"

"She graduates. She continues dance classes." At Caleb's surprise, Edison continued. "Oh yes, I know you've been taking her and paying for them with your blood money."

Anger exploded inside Caleb and he saw red and his fists clenched. It was all he could do not to beat the shit out of his own father. His teeth ground together. "You're such a controlling prick. Can't you let me have anything without invading it? Do you have me followed, or what? I fucking hate you!"

Edison was cool and collected; calmly smoothing his tie down the front of his shirt. "Clearly, but it's beside the point. I'll help Wren get into Juilliard, if that's what she wants; and I'll pay for it. I'll rein Veronica in, as well."

His father had played his trump card. Juilliard was Wren's dream and she was an amazing dancer. Caleb was always stunned watching her. They'd kept dancing a secret from Veronica so she couldn't sabotage it, and had to turn down more than one opportunity to dance in productions around Denver. Caleb paid for her lessons out of his fight earnings. They'd both worked so hard to make it happen without telling either of their parents, so how did Edison know?

His heart had sunk to his stomach at the prospect of leaving Wren behind, but she was all that mattered. He'd sobered and said the only thing he could say. "Okay."

It was in this very room and Caleb remembered it like it was yesterday. He made it a point to stop his thoughts; he didn't want to deal with those demons right now, because depending on which choice he made, he could be re-living that day for the rest of his life. No doubt, the next few days would be the test.

"I don't know if Wren will even want to see me, so I'm sure she won't want to be tied to me for five years. We've been through a lot." He understood why things had been strained between them, but that didn't make it easier on either of them.

"Honestly, Caleb, you should read both versions and then make a decision. It's really about what *you* want at this point," Jonathan said. "I was as surprised by the contents of Edison's letter, also, and depending on your decision, and what you've said, Wren may not believe she is needed here."

"Then why didn't you wait to call her until you knew what I'd decide?"

"Because your father knew what you'd choose," Jonathan said simply. "I was instructed to call her first."

The lawyer's words, and the fact his absentee father thought he had him pegged, pissed Caleb off. After all this time, everything that had happened, and the lives he and Wren built separately, was it still so fucking obvious?

Wren. For years she'd been the reason he did everything. The reason he stayed in high school, the reason he didn't run away from home; the reason he left... but she was blissfully unaware of any of it. *Fuck!*

The silence boomed around Caleb like a thunderclap, broken only by the painful thudding of his own heart and the rasping of the breaths being dragged in, and painfully pushed out, of his lungs.

When he'd heard the news a day earlier, he'd been like a zombie, simply going through the motions. Since then, his eyes had remained as dry as a desert. He was in shock, no question, though a sick ache had begun to take hold deep down in his gut. It was too soon to tell if his reaction was due to his father's death, his manipulative bullshit, the undisclosed details of the wills, or trepidation of a possible confrontation with Wren that had him tied up in knots.

Obviously, Wren was the main component in whatever decision he made. But, Caleb didn't understand why, if Jonathan knew what choice he'd inevitably make, why didn't he just destroy the version that gave Caleb everything? Why put Caleb through the hell of deciding, for Christ's sake? His face twisted sardonically as he sighed heavily, attempting to ease his tension. At the same time, his hand pulled at the front of the expensive linen button down he wore.

Caleb felt as if an elephant was sitting on his chest; the tightness making him feel claustrophobic and he wanted to claw at his lungs. Claustrophobic. That was the only way to describe how he felt. He didn't want to be here, he didn't want to make this decision; maybe he didn't even want to see Wren, because it always ripped him open.

My father would be so proud of himself. He has me squirming like a fish on a hook, one final time. The diabolical prick, he thought.

Caleb tried to remain passive and adopt the mask he'd become so good at plastering on his face whenever he didn't want anyone to know how he felt. A skill he'd mastered to keep his inner turmoil secret all those years ago, though it didn't mean that he wasn't ripped to shreds on the inside.

Why did love and pain have to be so fucking indistinguishable? Like living things, yin and yang, one completely impossible without the other.

Like me and Wren.

Jonathan sat on the couch watching Caleb's silent struggle as the young man's hands visibly shook while sifting through the contacts on his smart phone.

Caleb tightened his grip to steady them. When Wren's name landed on the screen, he stopped at it automatically, his eyes locked on the word as his thumb traced over the individual letters. How many times had he done this? Practice stopped him from dialing her number. It must have been at least a hundred times. So often, he needed to hear her voice, but only allowed himself to call on her birthdays or holidays, and for an occasional family event.

Caleb spent years rebelling against everything his father wanted or expected of him, He'd tried to make Edison's life as miserable as possible but in the end, Wren was the sacrifice.

Payback was hell, but it had backfired, and Edison still had Caleb under his thumb; shoving one last lesson down his throat. There was always another lesson to learn, and the harder it was, the better. Even from the grave.

Caleb almost laughed at the irony of it. He had to admit, most of the time, he hadn't appreciated his father's methods, but dying was rather extreme. Caleb had spent years telling Edison to go straight to hell, and maybe he was, but he was sure as shit having the last laugh. *That bastard.*

Caleb knew the other shoe was about to drop, the repercussions would be massive, and it would ruin everything he was about to accomplish professionally; and probably screw up his personal life.

The only thing he knew for sure were that he didn't want to make the choice. And if Wren was a factor, no doubt, she would be his first consideration; old habits were hard to break. No doubt, it would complicate things with his current girlfriend, Macy as well.

Obviously, he wasn't as good at hiding his feelings as he'd prided himself, but was he so transparent? Obviously, or Jonathan wouldn't have summoned Wren home to Denver on his father's command. He could only pray that Veronica wasn't hauling her skinny ass within a hundred miles.

The two envelopes now lay heavily in Caleb's hand, and after taking them he sat back down, this time on one of the large, matching chairs.

Since Jonathan had already read Edison's letter, Caleb hoped he could skim through it. To read it would make his father's death real, and the rest of this impossible situation more tangible. He was used to being gone from the house... but the last time, he thought he was gone for good.

"There's a method to his madness, I'm sure. He never does—" Caleb stopped and swallowed, correcting himself, "—he never *did* anything without a very calculated reason." Though Caleb wondered if it was truly noble motivation or just another thing to make his son miserable.

This shit was going to rip open so many fucking wounds.

Edison was dead, but the son-of-a-bitch was still laughing his ass off.

If only this were just about me, the answer would be easy, Caleb thought. *But, it's about Wren. It's always been about Wren.*

chapter
THREE

CALEB WAS ANXIOUS AT THE PROSPECT of seeing Wren. Would she want the security that Lux Pharm could give her, or would she just rather live her life?

He struggled with his choice. Should he tie his life to Wren's for the next five years? Her life was full now. She had a successful career, maybe a relationship for all he knew, and probably no amount of money in the world would be worth screwing it up. He sighed deeply, the sound filling the silence around him. His life was also rolling in a steady direction and whether he split the estate with Wren or kept it all himself, it would send him in a different direction; if not forever, certainly for the time being. His father had effectively plugged any loopholes that would allow him to avoid this decision, so really it didn't matter what he wanted.

But, what *did* he, want? Realistically, he and Wren had

lived on opposite ends of the country, which would complicate everything if he chose to share it with her. Though money was the last thing he wanted from his father, it would help him start his automotive design firm. But... it would mean putting everything on hold for five years, first. His thoughts raced, and Caleb ran an agitated hand down his face. He could walk away and lose everything, but then, Wren would, too. *Fuck.*

The decision weighed heavily, like his need to love Wren had always wrestled with his conscience. Apart from twice in the past, he'd always put her first. The regret he had over hurting her on both of those occasions haunted him and fought with his selfish heart. Twice, he'd made a decision about Wren, to benefit himself, and neither had turned out well. Could he make this decision without talking to her about it? Would including her only put something on her plate she didn't deserve to shoulder, and would she be selfish enough to be honest about what she wanted? Caleb had his doubts.

New anger and hatred surged for Edison Luxon. *Damn him to hell!*

Caleb's chest felt tight as he carried his one bag down to his old bedroom in the basement of the huge house; the three envelopes Jonathan had given him felt like fire in his left hand. Shit, by most people's standards, the place could be considered a mansion, but without his mom and now, without Wren, it was just an elaborate prison; a silent reminder of things he'd rather forget. Well, most of it, anyway.

He did have some good memories within these walls, on the grounds, and in the garage or pool house, but every one of them was tied to one of the two women. Though he cherished so much, he associated more with pain or guilt, rather than pleasure.

After his talk with Jonathan, it was clear to Caleb he'd have to confront all of them in the next few days or he was at risk of screwing everything up.

The basement was full of remembrances of Wren. Good or bad, happy or sad, it was full of her. It had everything they'd needed, save a kitchen, and they'd spent a lot of time there because it turned into a sort of escape.

After his mother died, he'd taken up residence in one of the spare rooms off the entertainment room down here because he'd wanted to put as much physical distance between himself and his father as possible. There was a second set of stairs leading down from the kitchen; which made coming and going undetected easier, even with the cameras and security system. With the garage entrance a few feet away from the top of the stairs, he was able to keep to himself without much notice from his dad or his stepmother. After the hag showed up on the scene, his father had been even more distracted and it was harder for Caleb to garner any attention, even when he was trying to piss him off.

God, he hated that woman. He'd wanted to kill that cold, jealous bitch on more than one occasion. She was selfish, for sure, and at times, Caleb doubted she even had a conscience at all.

At the bottom of the stairs, he turned the dimmer switch on full and the massive room was flooded with light. His room was at the far end, separated from the massive and elaborate theater room setup, by a full glass-enclosed gym on one side, and the Italian marble bathroom on the other. First-class all the way, for all it mattered to Caleb. His father's money and all of this extravagant shit designed to keep his young son placated while he blew him off, had done nothing but made Caleb more resentful. He'd needed a father, not all this material crap. His friends liked it though and his fists had earned him all the status he needed within that group, he didn't hate the admiration the money garnered. It was the only good thing to come out of having Edison Luxon for his father.

The rooms hadn't changed much that he noticed, though he wasn't paying close attention. From what he could see from the light streaming down the hallway out of the big room, his bedroom was kept clean and tidy by the ever-efficient housekeeping staff.

He hadn't been back since the spring break of his senior year in college, but all of his things, save the dirty clothes he'd left strewn around, seemed in place, just as he remembered. Caleb's eyes roamed over the bed, as the memories flooded his mind. He had mixed feelings about that visit. His relationship with Wren was changed forever. It had been a dream, and a nightmare at the same time.

He'd been such a fucking coward. Maybe if he'd been more of a man, things would be different now. Because of that one night, their relationship had changed forever. He'd been so blind with the jealousy that had eaten him alive and clouded his judgment. He was pissed at her, at himself, and Dex. His best friend moving on Wren had made him snap. He'd wanted her for as long as he could remember and seeing Dex go for her... well, Caleb didn't handle it well.

Afterward, it was too hard to lie to Wren's face, and just easier to let her think he was drunk and didn't remember any of it, though every precious second was burned on his soul like a brand. Denial of the whole thing was the easiest way to keep it from happening again. Only doing so hurt her badly, and his idiotic thinking that they could go back to the way they were before it happened, was ludicrous. It had been the best, and worst, night of his entire life.

Only physical distance and the span of years had given Caleb any type of perspective... but that flew out the window each and every time he'd seen Wren since. He was terrified of the rush of excitement he felt whenever fate would throw them back together; so damn anxious to see her, his eyes drinking in every line of her face and body, memorizing the most minute changes, yet knowing the fight he'd have to fight to keep his hands off of her would kill him. It was like some sort of sick addiction; he couldn't be in the same room with her without pain, but when she was close, he couldn't stay away from her, either.

As she grew up she became more beautiful and sexy, and every time he saw her it was harder, putting Caleb at critical risk of all of his carefully constructed control being annihilated, so when it finally happened; Wren paid the price for his weakness. It took everything he had to push her away because each time he got closer and closer to losing it. Somehow, he managed because he couldn't figure out any other way not to touch her, though seeing the hurt look on her face each time, put him in hell.

He'd crushed her. He knew it, but justified it by the age

difference and because keeping Wren at arm's length was critical for his control.

The last time he'd been in this bed, he'd cracked, and the next day he'd made the worst mistake of his life. It had destroyed her. The only time he'd felt worse than the night they'd slept together, was that time she'd flown out to San Francisco last year to introduce him to Sam. Hatred welled up inside his heart. Who in the fuck was this guy, anyway? Oh right, some fancy French ballet prick that wanted to marry her.

Caleb knew he didn't have any fucking excuse for acting the way he had; on either one of those pivotal moments. He knew he was just being a selfish prick; protecting his own sorry ass and his own selfish pride, instead of doing what was best for Wren. He'd promised to take care of her forever, and he'd failed to protect her from himself. Twice.

Despite the cooling off between them, Caleb still kept up with Wren's career, and in general, watched over her as well as he could without her knowing. He'd kept his distance, but last March he went to New York to see her perform. He'd wanted to see her on her birthday and hopefully repair some of the damage he had done to their relationship. Caleb had been stunned by how amazing she was, completely mesmerized as he watched her dance, anxious to talk to her and tell her how proud he was of her. He wanted to surprise her, however, Caleb had been the one surprised, seeing her come out of the theater clinging to a man he didn't recognize. It wasn't Sam, but it was enough to make him stop dead in his tracks.

Reconsidering his decision to show up and interrupt her

life, he'd waited a few hours and then placed a call to her instead of letting her know he was in the city. He'd already screwed one of her relationships up, and she didn't deserve it again. The memory still stung.

He dropped his bag unceremoniously on the floor, then laid the envelopes on his dresser and flopped down on his back in the middle of the big king-sized bed. Caleb's hand came up to wipe down over his face from forehead to jaw then he glanced at his watch. It was close to 6 PM and way too early to sleep despite his exhaustion.

Maybe he should read his father's letter before Macy, and especially Wren, arrived. He had to figure shit out. Macy didn't know much about Wren, other than she was the daughter of Caleb's father's second wife, and the two of them kept in touch once in awhile. He kept his memories of Wren private. Dex knew some of it, but he was the only one.

"Ugh." Caleb groaned at the memories, wishing he'd never had to come back to Denver.

The gravity of the current situation was also weighing on him. He hadn't thought about the repercussions his past with Wren would have on his relationship with Macy. Macy and he were casual, and he figured that she and Wren would never meet. Leave it to his dad to fuck that up by dying.

If it were possible, he'd have preferred to keep them eternally separate. Not because of Macy, but because of Wren. Their history was long and involved, and despite Macy, Sam, and the nameless guy he'd seen her with in New York, Caleb was in the dark about her feelings. Maybe she'd gotten over her hero worship, maybe she hated him; maybe she'd never forgive him... or, maybe she had residual feelings, as he did. Too bad she had no clue how he felt. His gut tightened. What a fucked up mess.

He'd deliberately kept his relationship with Macy on the back burner, and because he told her next to nothing, she wouldn't understand the complexity of his situation with Wren.

At least, from Caleb's point of view they were casually dating, though he realized Macy might not agree.

"Fuck." Caleb groaned and pulled out his phone. Maybe he could cut Macy off at the pass, though he knew a call would give her too many opportunities to ask questions that he didn't want to answer. Instead, his thumbs began typing out a text.

Hey. I've gotta stay a few days to sort things out.

No need for you to fly in.

Even in his mind, the words were cold and emotionless. Last week, he was all over this woman; hot as hell for her body, but now her presence would bring about a whole shit storm of implications. He didn't have the energy to answer an inquisition about his childhood, or Wren. And maybe, he didn't want Wren asking questions about Macy, either.

He shook his head at himself. He was emotionally closer to Wren, but given the state of his relationship with her, she had no right to question him about Macy. He also knew that he needed to keep Macy out of his decision about his father's estate. He was fairly sure doing so would scream he didn't have serious intentions about her, but the fact was, he hadn't spent more than a couple of minutes ever contemplating more than "fun-for-the-moment" with Macy. Maybe he could be ready for more in the future, but this thing with Wren had to be dealt with first.

"Ugh!" he groaned, wishing his head would shut the fuck up. "What a cluster fuck!"

He glanced down at the screen of his phone again and after another second's pause; Caleb sent the text, praying to God Macy would get it in time to stop her from getting on a plane.

Afterward, he got up to start stripping off his clothes. He needed a shower, and maybe he'd try to take a nap. God knew; he was tired. His eyes were burning and he was in desperate need of a reprieve from his overactive brain.

The white envelope containing his father's letter glared at him from atop the two other larger, manila ones; conspicuously sitting there, sucking at him like a black hole he had no hope of escaping.

Caleb pushed it from his thoughts. He got up off the bed and crossed his strong arms, curling his fingers around the hem of his T-shirt, he started to pull it over his head with both hands. His belt was barely unbuckled, and he was kicking off his shoes when his phone started ringing. He knew without looking that it was Macy. Reluctantly, he reached for the phone, which was still on the bed where he left it.

"Yeah?"

"Babe, you don't want me to come?" Her voice held a slight whine.

Caleb winced slightly at the endearment. He'd never thought about it before, but now it seemed awkward and uncomfortable. He closed his eyes at the same time he began to rub them both with his thumb and index finger of the hand not holding the phone.

"Well," Caleb began; searching for the words that would accomplish the two things he wanted; to keep her from showing up and keep from hurting her feelings. "There's just a lot of mundane paperwork to deal with that will take longer than I expected, and I see no point in you wasting a week of your time, too."

"Caleb," she sounded bored and annoyed, now. "We knew you'd have the will and properties to deal with, besides the funeral. So, why are you changing your mind now? I want to be there for you."

He finished pushing his jeans down with one hand, and then kicked out of them, awkwardly, while still keeping hold on the phone. "I'm not changing my mind. I told you that you didn't need to come in the first place, remember?"

"But you shouldn't be there alone."

Caleb's instincts told him to tell her he wasn't going to be alone, but he clamped his mouth shut, not ready to get into a "Wren" discussion. He felt irritated that Macy didn't listen to what he needed from her. She was just another thing weighing him down at a time when he had too much other shit to handle.

Macy continued when he didn't speak. "I can help you, and besides, I'm already on my way to the airport. I'll get in late tonight."

Well, that's that, he thought cynically. *Great.*

He'd met Macy in a bar not long after his failed trip to New York for Wren's birthday, and you could say she'd been a useful diversion for a while. They went out a few times, and he genuinely liked her; she was smart, sexy, and in San Francisco.

Macy worked for a venture capitalist, so it wasn't long before Caleb had spilled all of his dreams of starting the automotive firm, and then, Macy was plotting how she could help him. But, Caleb didn't just want to design cars, he wanted to build and sell them; that would take a lot of green, as in millions or billions of dollars, and he would need some major investors to partner with him. It seemed like fate that he'd met her.

That changed after Macy found out that Caleb was sole heir to Lux Cosmetics. She wanted to stop working on the business plan they were putting together for the pitch to her firm, thinking it would be a piece of cake for Caleb to simply ask dear-old dad for the cash.

She hadn't liked his answer. Caleb wouldn't consider crawling back and asking Edison for that kind of money. He'd rather saw off his right arm.

Caleb never planned on asking his father for one red cent, preferring to work his ass off, and Macy was a little late to the party to change his trajectory. He put in long hours at a private design firm that outsourced for several global OEM automotive manufacturers, and also offered luxury interior conversions for individuals, the healthcare industry, or various government agencies. His work ethic and creativity had gotten him promoted quickly. He made a good living and he'd acquired a lot of valuable experience, but his dream was still to start his own company. Caleb acknowledged that his drive probably came from his dad, but he did so, begrudgingly.

Caleb sighed, putting the phone on speaker and walking into the bathroom. It was huge, with a separate, glass enclosed shower, a big, jetted tub, and Italian marble from floor to ceiling. "Alright."

"Don't sound so enthused. I'm just trying to offer support."

Caleb reached in and turned on the shower. "I know. I appreciate it. What are friends for?" He interjected, knowing it would probably make her mad. The fact was, he'd rather she not come and if pissing her off worked to that end, so be it. He could mend that fence later.

Normally, he would welcome Macy's input, but he was aware she'd see his father's untimely death as a way to finance the company. And, if Wren wasn't a factor, he'd probably be on board, but Wren *was* involved, and Caleb didn't need, or want, any input from Macy on this decision. She couldn't be objective, even if she tried, and the stakes were too high. "Listen, I'm gonna hop in the shower, eat, and try to crash for a few hours. We can talk more when you get here."

"Okay. Bye, *friend.*" Macy sarcastically emphasized the word then abruptly ended the call.

Caleb proceeded with his shower, letting the hot water beat away the stress from the back of his neck and shoulders, then quickly soaped down his body and shampooed his hair. The fresh scent and heat relaxed him slightly; the soapy water running down the hard muscles of his torso and strong legs.

He decided to forgo shaving until the following morning, and wrapped a large white towel around his waist, taking another, and attempting to rub as much water out of his hair as possible. Leaving the towel hanging over his shoulder, he turned on the lamp on the nightstand near his bed then went to his dresser and picked up his father's letter.

The bed was big and took the weight of Caleb's muscled

frame easily as he flopped down on it. It was plush and expensive, like everything in his father's house, and his exhaustion made him thankful for its comfort.

He ripped open the envelope and pulled out the letter, staring at it with a sense of dread. The folded sheet of paper was wrapped around another smaller, sealed envelope that fell out onto Caleb's lap.

He scooted up higher on the bed and piled one luxurious pillow on top of another before leaning back, and setting the second envelope aside, unfolding the main piece of paper. The words were handwritten in his father's measured hand, upon the fine linen stationery of Lux Cosmetics that matched the envelope. Caleb ran a hand over his face, before beginning to read.

> Dear Caleb,
> I know you and I haven't had the best relationship since your mother died, and for that I am deeply sorry. I realized that I forced you into situations and to do things you didn't particularly want, and it is my wish to make amends; even at this late date.
> It's too late for you and I, Caleb, but it's not too late for you and Wren. Obviously, I knew how you felt about Wren, or I wouldn't have been able to leverage her so succinctly. Again, I'm sorry, but at the time, I thought I was doing what was in your best interest and what your mother would have wanted; ensuring you received the best education money could buy.
> As you know, Lux is publically traded, however,

I own the majority share. It's important to keep the majority so that the board can't oust the family in a hostile takeover, so keep that in mind. Jonathan will be able to offer valuable guidance should you need it.

There are two versions of the will; one gives all of my shares in Lux, and the three properties to you in full. The other splits everything equally with Wren. This puts the fate of the company, as well as your future with Wren, completely in your hands, son.

I'm hoping giving you this last, admittedly major and albeit late, choice, will somehow let you define your own future. Choose wisely.

The other envelope is an overdue explanation. You deserve one, though you may not want it. That's another choice only you can make. I'll understand if you'd rather burn it than read it.

I am proud to call you my son.
   With Love,
   Dad

Caleb let the letter drift to the top of the rich silk of the burgundy comforter, huffing out his breath in angry retort, his throat thickening in protest to the emotions welling up inside his chest. He'd be damned if he'd shed tears for a man who would wait until it was impossible to make amends, to even fucking try. Was this some sort of sick joke?

Way to be a prick till the end, Pop, Caleb thought wryly. *Thanks.*

He was somewhat relieved that whatever was in the other

envelope wasn't glaring off this same page; but the letter he'd just read was wholly unnecessary since Jonathan had already laid it all out in their earlier conversation. Caleb had a brilliant mind and it didn't take a brain surgeon to realize that the crux of it all was in the other envelope. It would hold the hammer to the proverbial nail.

At least, he didn't have to read it if he didn't want to.

His phone began to ring and he reached for it, glancing down: it was a number he didn't recognize.

"Hello?" he answered.

"Caleb, darling, I'm so sorry to hear about your father."

Caleb visibly cringed. He was shocked by the voice on the other end of the phone, though he shouldn't have been. Veronica didn't come off any less bitchy or annoying despite the pseudo attempt at a sympathetic tone.

"Ah! Step-monster! I wondered how long it would take you to start sniffing around like the vulture you are. You certainly don't disappoint," he retorted sarcastically. He could almost hear her claws come out through the open phone line.

Veronica laughed nervously, ignoring his sarcasm. "Now is that any way to be, given the circumstances? I just wanted to offer my condolences to you and to—," she stumbled a bit before she continued. "Um, Wren. I know she and Edison were close over the past few years."

Obviously the bitch was fishing and Caleb realized that his stepmother had absolutely no idea whether Wren was in Denver or not. He almost laughed out loud. His disdain for the woman was barely contained when he spoke; his tone harsh. "Fishing is for seagulls, not vultures, Veronica. You get nothing about Wren from me, and no, you don't get any of the money, either. Buh-bye, now." He hung up on her without filling in the blanks then glanced down at his smart phone. "No Caller ID" was the only identifier, making it impossible to block the number. "Bitch."

He threw on some old flannel pajama pants and a T-shirt he found in one of the drawers and meandered upstairs in search of the delicious aroma coming from the main level of the house. His stomach was rumbling and he realized he hadn't eaten since that morning.

When he found the kitchen, Mrs. Jones was at the stove frying something, and the counter was lined with pies and breads.

"Hey, Jonesy," Caleb murmured and the old woman turned, a sad smile flashing across her face.

"Oh, Caleb!" She put down what she was doing and rushed around to hug him. His arms wound around the plump older woman to return her embrace. "Are you hungry?" Jonesy pushed back to look up into Caleb's face.

"Starving." Caleb nodded, letting her go and then went to the refrigerator and pulled it open. The shelves were lined with trays of salads, fruit and vegetable trays and more desserts.

"Wow. Look at this spread. Are you expecting everyone within the Denver city limits to come to the wake? I didn't think dear-old dad was that popular." Caleb knew he sounded scornful, but he felt little need to put on a façade for the housekeeper, a woman who'd seen him grow up and knew every nuance of what went on in this house.

Jonesy turned, pulling up the front of the apron that was

tied around her waist and used it as a towel to wipe off her hands. "You know me, dear. I like to be busy. And your father was very respected, Caleb. There will be a lot of people coming to his funeral. We have to—"

Caleb interrupted her. "Put on a show?" His face twisted and he shook his head, leaning into the refrigerator in search of a beer or something else to drink. "No beer," he huffed. "How could I forget beer was beneath *Edison Luxon*?" He lowered his voice mockingly. "Single malt scotch and Dom Perignon all the way."

Jonesy pulled the skillet off of the hot burner and shut off the heat angrily. "Caleb." Her tone was stern. "Your father may have been less than he should have been to you, and no one can make you respect him, but the man is dead. He built an empire for you."

Mrs. Jones wasn't just an employee of his father's estate; she'd been a fixture in the house for Caleb's entire life, and so she wasn't overstepping her place in her tone. She and Jonathan were the closest thing to family he had left.

Caleb found a bottle of water and let the door of the refrigerator shut. He shrugged, looking at the woman. "I don't want it. Do you think money and mansions can justify everything he did?" His brow dropped into a frown as he began to unscrew the lid off the plastic bottle, and shook his head. "It wasn't for me. All it did was assuage his guilt, and he deserved to keep every last shred of it for how he turned his back on Mom, Jonesy."

The old woman sighed and started to pile food from one of the containers on the counter onto a plate. She turned and put it in the microwave, and pushed the button to make it start. As it whirred into operation, Caleb lifted the lid on one of the other containers and fished out a thick piece of buttered French bread, taking a giant bite.

When Jonesy sat the plate piled with steaming lasagna and a smaller one with a fresh Caesar salad on the table, Caleb, still munching on the bread, took a seat behind it, set his water bottle down and picked up the fork she provided. It looked and smelled delicious. Macy never cooked, and it had been years since he had home-cooked meals.

Jonesy looked hard at Caleb for a few seconds; as if she were having a mental conversation with herself then pulled out the chair across from him and sat down. "He made sure you were educated; that should mean something. He was good to Wren after you left. He's responsible for her career."

Jonesy knew the pain that Edison suffered after the loss of his wife, and though it was no excuse for abandoning his young son, she understood that kind of pain. Her own husband and baby girl had died in a car crash when she was a young bride, and no pain had ever compared to it. Caleb had suffered too, but he would surely suffer more if he couldn't find forgiveness in his heart.

The food was good, but something inside Caleb didn't want to hear anything good about his father. Especially, when it came to Wren. He stopped eating and put his fork down on the plate with a clang.

"*She* was responsible for her career, not him. He kept me away from—" Caleb stopped at the shocked look on Jonesy's weathered face. She had to be in her mid-seventies by now, and he felt regret at his tone. "I'm sorry."

The old woman reached wrinkled hands across the table, both of them taking one of Caleb's. He felt claustrophobic and wanted to pull his hand away but resisted out of respect.

"I know you don't want to see any good in your father, dear, but it was there. He was a man filled with pain, Caleb. When he lost your mother, it broke him."

Caleb's throat tightened against his will and it was all he could do not to scream at Jonesy not to plead Edison's case, and that it was a lost cause, though if he were honest, as a grown man, he could understand that. His piercing blue eyes met older ones. "I lost her, too. I was twelve years old, and I lost my father, even before she died. We both lost him, and she didn't deserve that, Jonesy." Caleb's throat tightened and tears blurred his vision. He didn't like showing weakness. He blinked twice and cleared his throat. "Even if I could forgive him for abandoning me, I can't when it comes to Mom."

Jonesy patted Caleb's hand, and he pulled it away as gently as he could manage.

"I know, honey. It was wrong of Edison to do things the way he did, and I don't agree with most of it. He did realize after a time, Caleb, and he tried to make amends but by then, you were on a rampage. You didn't make it easy on your father. I know he had regrets and he tried to make up for it in the only way he knew how."

"How was that? By making a shit ton of money and forgetting I existed? By bringing that plastic whore into my mother's house?" Caleb's anger returned and he resented anyone trying to make his father look like a white knight;

about anything.

Jonesy sighed and shook her head sadly, sitting back in her chair. "No. By making sure you got a damn good education and by building up the company for you like your mother would have wanted. Caleb, you're so bitter. Edison married Veronica because he thought it would be best for you to have a mother, not because he loved her. He couldn't love anyone after Celine."

"I thought you knew everything, Jonesy! I never wanted to leave Denver; Dad blackmailed me to go to MIT. He made me leave Wren in the clutches of that psychotic, evil witch, and I couldn't even tell her why. Do you know how hard that was?"

"Caleb, Wren was taken care of. Your father made sure she had everything she needed and she was safe. He even got her into Juilliard."

Caleb stood and picked up the plate with the lasagna, shoved the water bottle under his arm and reached for the salad plate.

Anger festered in Caleb's chest and heat began to race like fire under his skin. "I love you, Jonesy. I owe you a lot for always taking care of me after mom died, but he *did not* get her into Juilliard. Wren earned her place among those students. He made a couple of calls and arranged her audition, and then paid her tuition. He used his money, because that's all he knew how to do. He wasn't some saving grace, Jonesy. He ruined everything I wanted." *With Wren*, his mind screamed.

Maybe, Caleb didn't know about the suite of rooms that Edison had remodeled for Wren, or how Edison sent Veronica off on duties for the company over half the time to keep her away from Wren, Jonesy thought. *But given how close Caleb and Wren had been... how was that possible?*

Jonesy could see the resentment seething inside Caleb and because he'd just lost his father, she decided not to press. She could only hope that eventually Caleb would be able to understand his father's motivation, and to forgive him for his misguided methods.

Caleb began to walk from the room, intent on taking the plates with him downstairs to watch a movie and maybe get his mind off the memories. He felt like his chest was ready to explode, and he didn't want to talk about his father or Wren any further.

"Thanks for the food," he muttered over his shoulder.

"Caleb, about the service..." Jonesy stopped him. "There is a place for your father inside the mausoleum, and the service has been arranged for Monday. The funeral home will take care of notifying the media with the obituary Jonathan wrote. Unless, of course, you'd like to write one?"

Caleb turned, still laden with plates. "No. No, I don't. I'm sure what Jonathan wrote is fine."

"Alright," Jonesy nodded her silver head. "Jonathan mentioned the will is being read early Monday evening. Is there anyone I need to notify to be in attendance? What about Wren?"

"She's on her way already."

The old woman's eyes lit up. "Oh!" She smiled softly. "It will be so nice to see her and to have the two of you back together under one roof."

"Yes. I've arranged for a car to pick her up," Caleb rambled, unsure why admitting he'd taken care of Wren's ride felt like a bigger confession. "Tomorrow."

With that he left, using the stairs off the kitchen to retreat back downstairs, then choosing one of the black leather recliners directly in the middle of the surround sound setup, and in front of the big projection television. There were trays hidden inside some of the arms of the chairs, and Caleb juggled the plates into one hand, so his other was free to pull one out. He found the remote, flipped on the Direct TV and wolfed down his meal, setting the empty plates on the seat of the recliner sitting next to his. Caleb made a mental note to take them up to the kitchen later.

He was uneasy, feeling physically sick inside. It wasn't the nauseous; puke your guts out kind of sick, but the empty, desolate, hole-in-your-chest kind of feeling. Caleb didn't want to think about his father's death, the gravity of the decision hanging over his head, or dealing with the pressure he'd undoubtedly get from Macy. And Wren; all he could do was hope he could figure out a way to make things easier between them.

He realized it would be almost impossible to rest, and despite the distraction and white noise drone of the television, he wasn't able to fall asleep. The chairs were the finest leather, and luxurious. More comfortable than most beds he'd ever slept in. He got up and pulled a blanket out of one of the closets in the hallway leading by the bathroom. He recognized it as one Wren used to use regularly. He hesitated briefly, before taking it with him back to his place in front of the television.

Caleb settled back in and tried to concentrate on the

movie playing on Cinemax but all he could think about were his father and Wren. His eyes were unseeing, though trained on the screen as his mind ran rampant.

When he was seventeen, he and his father had gotten into a particularly nasty argument about a long vacation the two adults were taking. Normally, Caleb would have rejoiced at having the house to himself for a couple of weeks, but his stepsister was younger and being left in Denver with him. He still wasn't acclimated to Wren, and even though he'd started watching out for her at school, he didn't want to be responsible for her because his father decided he wanted to bang his new wife to the French Riviera. But, that was when he'd discovered who Wren really was, and looking back, he wouldn't have changed anything about it.

Caleb closed his eyes, and took a deep breath. Remembering more shit about Wren wasn't going to help him sleep, but there was no helping it. She was everywhere in this house. After the first few months of knowing her, they spent a lot of time in this room, watching TV and basically hiding out from their parents. Wren hated Veronica as much as Caleb hated Edison, and that built a strong bond between them.

He could see it in his mind as if it were happening all over again.

After the blow out with his dad, Caleb snuck out through the back stairs, so upset he considered never coming back. His adrenaline was on overload and he needed to get rid of his aggression. He called his best friend; gunning to find a fight club event, but it was a Sunday night and the two boys weren't able to find any openings on short notice.

They'd ended up in a more dangerous part of town, looking in a circuit that they weren't regulars in, and Caleb's smart mouth had landed them both in a brawl. Dex and Caleb were tougher and stronger than most boys their age, but they were outnumbered four-to-one by one of the more ruthless gangs and they got their asses handed to them. In all honestly, they'd been lucky they came out of it alive.

There was no denying that Caleb had gotten into some trouble, most of it on purpose to piss off his father; he'd gotten arrested twice, but he wasn't stupid enough to dabble in gang warfare.

Caleb and Dex had no choice but to leave the destroyed car and run away like hell was on their heels. It wasn't easy because of the injuries; Caleb's face was turned into hamburger, and he'd taken a few kicks to his ribs, his knuckles battered and bruised. Though he'd had some awful pain in his chest and side, Dex was the one who needed medical attention since his shoulder had obviously been dislocated, his arm hanging painfully loose at his side.

Even worse for Dex; his prize 66 Mustang that he'd rebuilt with his Dad and brother had been trashed with a tire iron, and then torched. Dex's dad, Darren, was livid at their recklessness, but he still came to get them; delivering Caleb home after spending two hours in the ER getting Dex's shoulder reset. Caleb was badly beaten, but contended he didn't need any medical attention; and had insisted on waiting in the backseat of the car during the hospital visit.

Caleb had been lucky. His own father was out of town with the plastic bitch to some cosmetic convention and he'd had a few days to heal up. Except, he really had the shit beat out of him, and he was worse off than he, Dex, or Darren, originally thought.

chapter
FOUR

SHE WAS NERVOUS.

Wren Brashill hadn't been back to Denver in two years, and she hadn't spoken to Caleb since her birthday. She'd been sad that day, even though she had a date with Victor that evening; Caleb didn't call until late that night, and she'd suffered waiting for it all day. Though they didn't keep in touch as much anymore, she still missed him everyday.

Everything had been so messed up since they'd slept together when she was eighteen, and Caleb pretended he didn't remember it the next day. It had hurt her deeply because she'd loved him in secret long before that. To date, she still hadn't confronted him about it; still hadn't told him she knew that he was fully aware of what happened between them. Before that night, he'd been the one person she leaned on: the only person she trusted. God knew her life before knowing him had been hell. She lived inside herself, finding it a safer place than the world where her mean and vindictive mother hated her. Wren had only known solitary confinement inside her own soul, hating herself as much as she hated her mother.

Her fingers traced over the faint scars that remained on her wrists from the times she sought to ease her mental pain, with self-inflicted physical pain. Her dark garb and reclusive behavior had hidden those scars from her mother, but never Caleb.

Wren closed her eyes; her right hand closing over her left wrist where a white ink tattoo now resided over those scars. She remembered the pain she'd gone through and the solace that Caleb had become to her; he protected her and she'd grown to trust him implicitly. Caleb had adamantly insisted she be herself and stop hiding behind her disguise once he'd confronted Veronica and warned her to stop her cruel ways or face his wrath. Wren still worried about the faint red lines on her wrist would be seen by counselors or teachers, and had been ashamed of the scars; ashamed of the weakness they represented, though Caleb insisted they should be worn like medals of battles fought. He'd been tough as nails, though he had this innate vulnerability that she'd seen on rare occasions when he'd let his guard down.

She sucked in her breath as the memory washed over her, her heart swelling with benevolence that only Caleb could inspire. She recalled that night like it was yesterday; the two of them snuck out of the house after their parents had gone to bed and he'd taken her to a late night tattoo parlor on the back of his motorcycle. It had been the first time she'd been that close to him, the first time her body had been plastered up against his back, and then, he'd held her hand the whole time. She'd only been fifteen, but already, she'd been in complete awe of him.

Her fingers lovingly traced the lines of a white stallion on the inside of her wrist. Caleb thought she chose white ink because it would hide the scars but still be subtle. He thought Wren chose that horse at random. Neither was true.

To Wren, Caleb had always been impervious and strong, but now, worry over how his father's death was affecting him, consumed her. Caleb and Edison's relationship had never been easy, but this was as final as it ever would be; no more time for second chances. A regretful shudder ran through her slight form.

Her own relationship with Edison had grown closer in the years after Caleb left for college, and she was thankful. With Caleb gone, he was the only thing keeping her awful mother at bay. It was strange that he'd become more of a father to her than she'd ever known and sadly more, than he'd ever been to his own son. The thought filled her with sorrow. Caleb was so good and giving; he deserved much better than he'd gotten from his dad. He deserved everything.

A plethora of emotions flooded over her whenever she thought of the dark-haired boy who had at first intimidated her, but later became the one person she could rely on the most. Caleb did everything he could for Wren, and she worshiped him like a hero; because that's what he was to her. It was more than a crush; she was closer to Caleb, even when they were fighting like cats and dogs, than she was to anyone else in her life. As time wore on, she was losing hope that anyone would ever touch her heart the way he had.

Caleb had been her tough, gentle savior; and Wren wondered if it would be possible for her to help him, now. She wanted to, and maybe even needed to. More than anything, she regretted the distance that had grown between them over the years. She longed to offer comfort and melt away the abyss that the past had created.

Wren and two of her best friends had flown to Bali during a break in their performance schedule and she'd been lounging on the beach with a book she'd been trying to find time to read for the past three months, when the bellman's shadow fell over her. He gave her a message informing her to phone Edison Luxon's lawyer, Jonathan Westwood.

Trepidation had filled her and she quickly rose, at the same time pulling her cell phone from the beach bag that was resting beside the lounge chair she'd just vacated. She gathered her things and began walking briskly into the hotel; Ainsley and Michelle had both called after her.

"Wren! Where are you going?"

"What is it?"

"I have to make a call! Something's wrong!" She'd shouted back at them.

It had to be bad. She talked to her stepfather more regularly than she did her own mother, and so the lawyer's name and title on the message filled her with dread. Her hands shook violently when she dialed the number, already guessing the reason for his call. Her worst fears were confirmed moments later when she got to her room and Jonathan confirmed that

Edison had died.

"What happened?" she'd asked, her face crumpling, and the thickness of tears cracking her voice. "When?"

"Last night. Mrs. Jones found him in his bed. Looks like a heart attack. I'm so sorry, Wren. I know the two of you were close."

Wren wiped away a tear with a quick hand, holding the phone to her ear with her shoulder, already pulling out her suitcase and rushing to the dresser in her hotel room to begin throwing her things haphazardly inside.

"When is the funeral? Is Caleb coming in?" she asked, still crying softly, her snuffles permeating through the phone. Given the state of their relationship and knowing how Caleb felt about him, it wasn't a given. Someone should be there, though. How sad to die and have no one but business associates to mourn you?

"The funeral arrangements will be made tomorrow. Mrs. Jones is handling most of it, I think. Caleb came in earlier today, but too late to do that. He's at the Denver house." It was 1:00 in the afternoon in Bali, which made it 9 PM Denver time.

"Oh God." Her voice was anguished. "Is he okay?" Her throat felt tight and swollen as tears tumbled down her cheeks. Thoughts of Caleb engulfed her. She felt a sudden urgency to get to him. He said he hated his father, but Edison had been the only parent he had for the past sixteen years; they were each other's only blood relative. Edison had an older sister, but she had died years earlier, and they weren't close. They were so estranged, from what she'd learned from Caleb, that his aunt hadn't even put in an appearance for Celine's funeral. Wren worried the implications would be devastating when it finally resonated with Caleb that he was the last in the Luxon line.

She had to go to Denver. And, she had to go now. For a split second, Wren worried that things would still be awkward and strained between Caleb and her considering the last time they'd seen each other, but she hoped they would fall into the easy closeness they'd always shared before...? Well... *before.* So much time had gone by; maybe things between them would be healed.

"You know Caleb, Wren. He's always been strong, but I'm not sure this has hit him yet. He's been pretty stoic," Jonathan replied.

"That's what I'm afraid of. I'll get there as soon as I can," she said.

Wren was worried about Caleb. Even in those times when she was spitting mad at him, completely hated him, never wanted to see him again, or he'd crushed her heart... she worried about him. And, she loved him. There was no denying it, and she'd stopped fighting it years before. She'd tried to build a life without him, but even so, she still loved him more than anything. She could convince Caleb to the contrary, but she couldn't lie to herself. He'd saved her life; and she'd saved his. He was the one man she measured all others against, and they'd all fallen short. Even Sam.

"Thank you, Jonathan."

As she hung up the cell phone and tossed it on the bed near her purse, her breath caught on a sob. Unspeakable sadness for the man who had died, and for Caleb, engulfed her as she bent at the waist, catching herself by one hand pushing into the mattress. Wren cried hard for both of those losses, sobs wracking her small frame for a good ten minutes.

Finally, she gathered her composure, took a quick shower to rid her skin of sunscreen, dressed quickly, and finished packing. She called her friends to tell them she was leaving, and within an hour was at the United Airline ticket counter forking over her passport and a credit card.

Wren spent the next twelve hours traveling and thinking. A young girl, traveling with her parents from Los Angeles to New York, sharing Wren's final leg to Denver where they were making a connection and recognized Wren from her lead role in the U.S. tour of Cinderella a year before. The girl's chatting and obvious excitement helped to take Wren's mind off of the sadness.

She wore no make-up and looked far younger than her twenty-four years, her luxurious blonde curls pulled up in a loose, messy bun. Her blue eyes were tired, and her iPod was shoved into the lightweight hoodie she'd taken to wear on the plane. Once her plane landed and she made her way into the main terminal and past the security checkpoint, Wren saw a large man dressed in his black chauffeur uniform, holding a cardboard sign with her name on it. He'd told her his name and picked up her bags without added small talk and soon she was falling asleep in the backseat of the limousine, she assumed Jonathan had hired to pick her up.

Without going home to New York, she only had what she'd taken on her vacation, and it hit her that she didn't have anything appropriate to wear.

She'd cried for the first twelve hours after she'd learned of Edison's death, hiding behind her sunglasses and plastering her face against the inside of the airplane. Thank God for her window seat.

When the limo pulled into the neighborhood of the magnificent Luxon home, Wren sat up and tried to do some damage control to her appearance, using her phone's reverse camera mode to look at her face. She looked like hell, and after a minute put the phone away in acceptance. It wouldn't matter to Caleb, anyway. He'd seen her at her worst, and this was hardly the time to worry about it. It was just before noon, Denver time, and she'd have jet lag for a day or two, at least. Her eyes were tired and she couldn't stop a yawn.

As the limo drove around the circle drive in front of the big house, Wren's hand rose to touch the gate locket that was always nestled under her clothes, except when she was on stage. It was a small pendant consisting of three layers that were connected by one hinge at the top. The top one was filigree made from 18 karat gold and embedded with a scattering of diamonds in the ornate design that swung over the two others behind it. Each one held a picture of Caleb, one when he was a baby and another, a candid of him from high school she'd placed there. The three gates hung on a long fine gold box chain; the diamond cut making it glisten in any type of light.

Wren's fingers traced the outline of it, subconsciously making sure it was still safe, as she so often did. It was precious; so precious. Only one other person knew it was there, nestling against her skin, and he meant even more than the locket.

She took note of a white Toyota Camry with Colorado plates. She assumed it was Caleb's rental because Edison usually drove a Mercedes and housed them in the big garage at the back of the house. Though she hadn't been back for two years, she doubted her stepfather would ever leave a vehicle in front of the house, despite the gated property.

The air smelled fresh, even though Denver was nestled on the eastern edge of the mountains and at times pollution settled over the city in a brown haze. Today was not like that.

For the past couple of years, Wren's life was busy and full, and she didn't spend much time thinking about the time she spent under her mother's vicious control. Looking at it, she had to admit there were several fond memories of this house, of Edison, and of course, Cale.

It was in this house there were a lot of firsts between her and Caleb.

She stopped her thoughts, and began to pull her suitcase up to the door. The fine cobblestone in the driveway was beautiful, but it made it hard to pull the heavy bag because the wheels got stuck in the crevices between the stone more than once.

The limo driver had gotten out, but Wren was anxious and he didn't have the time to make it around the car to open the car door for her. He quickly stepped around to pick up the bag, and carry it up the three steps onto the huge covered porch. The house was grand; modern with rustic touches that made it fit in perfectly with the backdrop of the mountains in the near distance. It was built with native Colorado stones and lumber and would have fit just as perfectly in Vail or Evergreen.

There was a huge lamp-like chandelier hanging high above the door, the ceiling towering up to the second story. Wren remembered the large curved staircase in the foyer held another, more ornate, light fixture sparkling with crystals that shone through a brilliant round window feature above the outside door.

"Thank you for coming to get me," Wren murmured, glancing up into the man's face. He looked sad, his dark eyes understanding. "Um, I'm sorry, what was your name?" she asked in a quiet voice.

"Jared."

Wren nodded. "It's nice to meet you, Jared."

"Thank you. I'm sorry for your loss, ma'am. I've been instructed to be on call for you during your stay; to take you anywhere you need to go." He reached into the breast pocket of his dark suit and produced a white business card with his name, phone number and the limo company on it.

Wren stopped looking for the key in her purse, wondering if it would still work in the lock. "Well, that was nice of Jonathan, but it was unnecessary."

"Jonathan?" The man looked confused for a second then shook his head. "No ma'am. Mr. Luxon sent me."

For a moment Wren's heart stopped, thinking he was referring to Edison, but realized he was speaking of Caleb. The driver leaned in, reaching past Wren to ring the doorbell.

"Oh, there's no need—" Wren began, as she pulled out her key fob and fumbled for the key to the front door.

The heavy door opened and a stout, grey-haired woman

stood there, her kind brown eyes widening in surprise.

"Oh, my goodness! Wren!" The old lady's voice filled with emotion as she reached out to wrap chubby arms around the younger girl. "It's so good to see you, but I wish it were under better circumstances. You look so wonderful, but so thin!"

Wren wrapped her arms around Mrs. Jones, and inhaled the light scent of floral perfume and something she must have baked earlier in the day. She knew she looked horrible from lack of sleep and traveling, as she lost herself in the comfort of the arms of the woman who was the closest thing to a grandmother she'd ever known.

"Jonesy!" Wren's eyes filled with tears. "I've missed you."

"You, too, child. Come in. Come in." Jonesy moved back into the house and took Wren's hand in hers when the young woman entered the foyer. "You're not expecting that awful mother of yours, are you?" She huffed with a frown.

Wren couldn't help a small smile. No one liked Veronica, and Wren downright hated her.

"No." She shook her head. "We don't keep in touch all that much anymore."

"Thank God for that. Caleb would go crazy if she dared show her face."

Wren's heart raced at the mention of Caleb's name, her eyes couldn't help searching past Jonesy into the house; looking to see if he was there.

The driver stood behind Wren, holding her suitcase and waiting for instructions. He cleared his throat. "If that will be all, Miss Wren?" he asked.

"Bring the bag in, young man," Mrs. Jones said and waved

him in. "Her rooms are at the top of the stairs, third door on the left. There are two doors, but the first is open. Up you go," she commanded. "Just set it inside."

Jonesy was just as abrupt and bossy as always, though she had a heart of gold and a sweet demeanor that softened her gruffness.

"Are you hungry? You look like you haven't eaten in years!"

"It's dancing so many hours a day." Wren shrugged and smiled. "All that exercise."

"Pish!" Jonesy scolded. "You young girls are always trying to be so skinny! I will cook something for you."

Jonesy made the best food Wren had ever eaten, but she wasn't hungry. "I'd rather unpack, take a shower, and get a nap, if I can. I have jet lag, I'm afraid. It's the middle of the night where I just came from, and I'm beat." The truth was, she was exhausted, but more, she wanted the opportunity to clean up before she saw Caleb.

"Oh, for sure! How silly of me. Come on, honey." She started up the stairs, gently pulling Wren to follow behind her.

Wren looked around, trying to glance into Edison's study that was to the right of the foyer, and then back toward the kitchen and left to the great room. She wanted to see if she could find any evidence of Caleb's presence. Finally, she had to ask. "Where is Cale?"

"He went for a run, I think. That one! He always did push himself to the limit. I'm worried about him. I don't think Edison dying has completely sunk in yet."

As they climbed the long, winding staircase, that was open to the second floor, Wren contemplated Jonesy's words and thought she was probably right. Caleb was strong, and he didn't like to show his emotions, but his father's death had to have hit him hard. When the two women reached the second floor, the limo driver was just closing the door to her room.

Soon Wren was sitting on the big king-sized bed in the suite that Edison had remodeled for her right after Caleb left for college. Her mother had a fit, and though it surprised Wren at the time, it was the beginning of her new relationship with Edison. He'd had the walls between two of the adjoining rooms removed to combine them into one large dance studio, complete with a floating hardwood dance floor, a wall of mirrors, state-of-the-art sound system, and ballet bars. It was separated from her bedroom with just a door, and had become her sanctuary.

The bedroom was lush, decorated in her favorite colors of cream and wine, accented with dark charcoal, which spilled over into the luxurious bathroom. Her affinity for the dark burgundy was one of the things she had in common with Caleb.

The bed was a dark metal four-poster with cream chiffon scarves twisted and draped around, and the desk and dressers were all painted wood. The jewelry box that Caleb sent from Boston the first year after he left, still sat on the dresser, and there was a stack of her favorite books still piled up in the window seat to the left of the bed. She spent a lot of time sitting there, reading, talking on the phone or daydreaming of Caleb.

Jonesy was already unpacking the suitcase before Wren noticed what she was doing. "Oh, Jonesy. You don't need to do that. I can't wear much of those clothes here, anyway. I'll have to go shopping for a dress for the funeral. When is it?"

"A few days. Edison's body was taken to the mortuary the morning I found him, and I've already taken over his best black suit, one of his favorite white Egyptian cotton shirts, and that red silk tie."

Wren smiled sadly. "The one I sent him from Paris last year?" She'd been on a European tour with her dance company, and Father's Day was close so she'd popped it in the mail.

"Yes, it's hard to believe, isn't it?" Jonesy asked, her face sad. She had sifted through Wren's clothes and picked out the personal things she'd be able to wear, and a pair of jeans, putting some aside with intentions of washing them and neatly folding the rest to replace in her suitcase. "You're right, honey. This stuff is much too light for our spring weather."

Wren was distracted. "How is Cale handling it?"

Jonesy smiled. "Cale. No one calls him that but you, dear. Brings back memories of happier times."

Wren could almost see the questions racing around inside the older woman's mind; she was wondering what happened to create the distance between Wren and Caleb.

Wren was sad and melancholy about it, too. There were many times she missed him and longed to talk to him. But, so much had happened to change things. Still, there was a piece of her that would always belong to Caleb.

"Yes. So, how is he? He tries to be indifferent, but I know the unresolved stuff with his dad has to hurt him more than he lets on. This might..." Wren's words fell off, and she shrugged, unwilling to share the true tenor of her current relationship with Caleb.

Jonesy sighed and sat down on the bed, the mattress giving beneath her weight as she took one of Wren's hands. "He's calm and keeping to himself, but almost seems annoyed. He's been wandering around the house a bit, but mostly holed up in the basement. I made breakfast this morning, but he didn't want much." Jonesy wondered how much Wren and Caleb kept in touch or how much they really knew about each other anymore. "That boy could always eat..."

Wren nodded. "Don't worry, Jonesy. Cale's always been a loner when something's troubling him. He isn't one to show vulnerability, so he does something physical to get rid of the tension." Wren's fingers ran over the tattoo on the inside of her left wrist. The scars beneath it were faint, but she could still feel the ridges. "We all have different ways of dealing with things."

"I know, child. I just hate seeing him like this. He suffered so much when he was younger, always silent and resentful. But, thankfully, that changed when you came to us."

Wren's face took on a far away look and the corner of her mouth lifted in the start of a sad smile. "He hated me, at first, though."

"He hated everyone, and everything, for a time. You changed that. You gave him purpose." The old woman patted Wren's hand. "A reason to open his heart again."

Wren's heart swelled as precious memories flooded her thoughts. Caleb had become her everything. She developed a major crush on him from the time she was fourteen. He was sort of like a Greek God, strong and beautiful who swooped in to save her every time her mother hurt her, or the kids at school were cruel. And later, when she let him closer, he was the only one who really knew who she really was.

"It was sort of mutual, Jonesy," Wren said softly, her eyes languid. "He helped me more than I can ever tell you."

"I know, honey. You both needed someone."

"I'm glad we had you, too." Wren watched Jonesy get up and move the suitcase off the bed. Though she was still sturdy, she wasn't as young as she used to be and Wren jumped up to help her. "I'll do that. It's heavy."

"Pish!" Jonesy dismissed, waving Wren away. "I'm not decrepit yet, dear. It's almost empty now." She set it up and then wheeled it into the large walk-in closet that still held many of the clothes Wren had left when she went off to Julliard. She closed the closet door and then moved to the end of the bed where the stack of dirty clothes were piled and waiting. "I'll just put these things in the wash. You get a shower and a nap, now. I expect Caleb will be home for dinner, and that *woman* is here." Jonesy's voice took on a sour tone and Wren's eye's widened.

"Woman? Does the white car on the front driveway belong to her?"

"Yes. She arrived about an hour before you, after Caleb had already gone. Her name is Macy. I'm not sure if she is a friend or something to do with his work. But what I do know is she is nosy and bossy. She's been snooping around this house and asking all sorts of inappropriate questions, like she owns the place. She asked where Caleb's room was, but I put her in one of the spare bedrooms at the back of the house." Jonesy's disapproval was evident.

Wren's eyebrows rose and she inhaled a short breath. "I'd guess they're more than friends if she expected to stay in his room." Wren swallowed. She couldn't help the stab of pain that shot through her at the thought of anyone else sleeping with him in that bed, after the night they'd spent together. Wren's heart did an involuntary plummet, but she tried to hide it. Her hope of private time to speak with Caleb alone, dashed.

"Mighty presumptuous, if you ask me." The old woman sniffed. "You'll meet her soon enough, but for now leave her to me. You just relax for a while and get situated."

"Okay. Thank you, Jonesy." Wren leaned forward and gave the old housekeeper a big hug. "I'm so glad to see you."

"I love you, doll." Jonesy wrapped her plump arms around Wren's thin body in a tight hug. "I'm gonna make you a big dinner and a cake. You're way too thin," she said again. "I thought those days were over." As she pulled away, Jonesy's face twisted in a wry expression.

"Of course. I do have to stay trim, but dancing as much as I do, I can eat more than you might think. But no cake." She smiled and then yawned, her eyes closing and her hand coming up to cover her mouth. "Oh, excuse me. I'm so tired."

"Nonsense. I'll bring you up a snack and some water while you're in the shower, and then you can have a nice long rest. I'll plan dinner for eight, and I *am* making cake, and you'll have a nice big piece, young lady! That's that!" With a wink and a bright smile, she exited the room, her arms full of clothes, leaving Wren to her thoughts.

Her room was much the way she left it and she'd find some

clothes to kick around the house in, though she'd have to go shopping before the funeral for a suitable dress. Her first pair of ballet slippers hung, tattered and worn, over the mirror on her dressing table, which was lined with tickets to various ballets and concerts that she'd attended with Caleb. After he'd left for MIT, Edison had attended some with her and through it was awkward and stiff in the beginning, it was one of those occasions without her mother's shrewish presence, when Wren got to know the older man and discovered some of the secrets that he should have shared with Caleb.

Wren was filled with regret for them both. Full of sorrow at the loss of the only father-figure she had ever known, for the regret Caleb must surely be suffering now that Edison had died, and for the loss of Caleb in her own life. No matter what had gone on between them, he was still the most important person she'd ever known, and something had to be done to fix things between them.

Maybe Edison's death, though a great loss and tragedy, would give them another chance. They were both older, and she hoped they'd be able to forgive each other enough to know each other again, at least. Though, now, with this woman, Macy here, it might not be as she'd wished. She closed her eyes at the thought. Caleb had been the center of her world for so long, and she missed him more than she wanted to admit.

Wren sighed. She was glad to be back home in Colorado, though she was nervous about seeing Caleb after so long. Rising from the bed to walk to the window she looked out over the back yard with the pool house and large multi-layered deck, with the Rocky Mountains majestic in the background.

That pool house was where her world changed forever, when she realized how much Caleb really meant to her. That was a night she'd never forget, and a memory she'd cling to for life.

chapter
FIVE

IT WAS STILL LIGHT OUT, THOUGH THE sun was low on the western horizon, as Caleb finished his run, enjoying the crisp air and scenery. The neighborhood hadn't changed that much since he left, but still it felt different.

He pounded out the path he was familiar with; subconsciously unaware of even where he was going, but then added a few more miles in the opposite direction because the responsibility of the coming days weighed on him heavily. The decision to continue running longer than he normally would, briefly registered in Caleb's mind; his thoughts were consumed with his father's death, and the uncertain future in front of him.

Macy's connection had been grounded due to a large line of thunderstorms and she was stuck in Phoenix, and rather than spend the night sitting at the airport waiting in case the weather cleared, he'd encouraged her to stay at the Hilton at the airport and try to catch another flight when the weather cleared this morning.

He rationalized that he was being considerate, but really, he was hoping he'd get a chance to speak to Wren in private before Macy arrived. Though, he conceded, if weather was a problem in Phoenix, the chances of Wren's flight being delayed out of LAX would be likely, as well. That worry was dismissed when the driver from the limo company had called to let him know he'd safely delivered her to his father's estate. That might have been the reason for his extra-long run. He wanted to see her, but it had been two years, and they hadn't parted on the best of terms. Over that time, their phone calls had moments of closeness and regret, but most of the time, the distance between them boomed, making communication awkward. Caleb fucking hated it.

He was breathing heavy as he jogged the final mile back to the house, not even sure what time it was, but the white Toyota on the circular drive signaled Macy's arrival. Awesome timing.

Shit!

He stopped briefly and let his head fall back in silent frustration, inhaling a deep sigh and preparing himself for what was next. He wished he'd thought about the cluster Macy being here would cause and insisted she stay in California.

"Oh, well. Might as well get it over with," he muttered.

Caleb squared his shoulders and resumed a slow jog the final few hundred feet up to the house, to the front door, and then grabbed the knob and pushed it open without hesitation.

He was sweaty, his T-shirt stuck to his muscled torso and his hair plastered to the skin of his forehead and the back of his neck. If nothing else, it would allow him a brief escape to clean up.

The house smelled good; like something sweet had been baking earlier in the day, overpowered now with a savory scent of meat roasting and fresh bread. Caleb glanced around the entry and noticed two red roller bags sitting just inside the foyer, beside the wrought iron and marble table that sat beneath a large ornate mirror. His blue eyes darted quickly around, glancing into the empty great room and then at the closed door to his father's study on the other side.

He could hear faint sounds coming from the kitchen, wondering who he'd find in there with Jonesy. He didn't recognize the bags, but most likely they belonged to Macy. Caleb sighed again as he walked casually through the house, unsure if he was anxious or uneasy. As he got closer, he picked up Macy's voice asking Jonesy questions. Her tone was strained and it appeared the old woman was reluctant to provide the answers.

"You'll have to ask Caleb. It's not my place to discuss family matters."

Macy was perched on one of the stools watching Jonesy pile fluffy white icing onto one cake layer, but her back was stiff and the look on her face showed her annoyance. Always polished perfection, her long brunette hair was slicked back into a tight chignon, and her red business suit and high heels impeccable, despite her layover. Caleb walked up behind her and reached out a hand to place on her back.

"I see you made it safely," he said calmly, careful not to startle either one of the women.

Macy turned, the expression on her face lighting up in a bright, red-lipstick lined smile. She was a beautiful woman; her voluptuous curves always showcased to their best advantage by her wardrobe. "Caleb!"

Her arms slid up his shoulders in an attempt to hug him, but Caleb stalled her, instead leaning in to place a short kiss on her full mouth.

"I'm a sweaty mess. You'll ruin your suit if you get close right now."

Caleb's demeanor was decidedly different than the easy-going and jovial man Macy knew, but then, his father had just died and it was to be expected. She made no further attempt to embrace him, though her hand reached up to lay against his cheek; her dark brown eyes searching his face for a clue to what he was thinking. "Are you okay?"

Caleb moved away, effectively breaking the contact of her hand as he reached in to pick up one of the fresh rolls cooling on the counter and pulling a piece of it off before popping it into his mouth. "Yeah," he said, walking away to open the refrigerator. "Fine."

Jonesy took notice of Caleb's coolness to his supposed "girlfriend" and wondered if it was because he'd overheard her meddling questions as he'd entered the room. She seemed overly concerned with things that were none of her business.

Caleb grabbed a bottle of water and opened it, leaning his hip against the counter behind Jonesy, who was facing Macy across the island where she was working, and took a long swig of the cool liquid. He used the back of the hand holding the bottle to push the hair back off of his forehead, his eyes searching for any sign of Wren.

"Smells good, Jonesy. What's for dinner?"

"Roast beef, garlic mashed potatoes, and strawberry cream cake."

The cake was Wren's favorite and Jonesy's silent signal to Caleb that she was in the house somewhere.

"Sounds delicious," Macy put in. "I've been watching her make that cake and it is positively spectacular. If it tastes as good as it looks, we're in for a treat!"

Jonesy offered a small smile, but it didn't go all the way to her eyes as she arranged sliced strawberries over the top of the icing, then placed the second cake layer over it. "It is," she said matter-of-factly, reaching for the bowl containing the remaining frosting and repeating the process.

Caleb walked around the room so he could see Jonesy's face. She looked perturbed, her eyes downcast as she worked. "That's for sure." Caleb's tone was designed to make the housekeeper smile. "Jonesy is the best cook in the known universe. I don't know how I've lived without her all this time."

"Pfft!" Jonesy snorted. It had the desired effect as Jonesy looked up and offered Caleb a genuine smile. "Flattery would sway me if you weren't so stinky! Off to the shower with you! Dinner is in an hour."

Caleb walked around and leaned in to kiss Jonesy's plump cheek, grateful for her steady presence. He realized now how much he relied on her when he was younger and how thankful he was that she was still part of the Luxon household. It was another thing to consider in his decision. Jonesy was family. "I love you, Jonesy."

"Of course, you do. What's not to love?" The old woman grinned at Caleb. He returned her smile, but his eyes were questioning and Jonesy recognized it right away. "She's upstairs sleeping." She answered Caleb's unanswered question.

Macy's head snapped around to look for Caleb's reaction. He seemed to physically relax, and nodded slightly.

"Good." When he started to leave the room, Macy stopped him.

"Caleb, please take my bags. I'd like to freshen up myself."

Caleb stopped, mid-stride, and turned around at the same time Jonesy huffed.

"Nothing wrong with the room you have, in my opinion," Jonesy put in promptly, continuing her task of finishing the cake.

"But—" Macy began, a scowl beginning to form on her features.

Caleb's hand went up to waist level, to stop her, noting her perturbed expression. The last thing he needed was a throw-down between Macy and Jonesy. Macy was used to getting her own way, but even though Jonesy was paid a wage for her work, she was more like the matriarch of the family and used to taking charge. His eyes implored Macy to can her response. "I'm sure that it's fine. I'll be glad to deliver the bags, though."

Macy was clearly angry, but Caleb nodded his head, indicating that she should follow him out of the room. "See you in an hour, Jonesy."

As he walked into the foyer to pick up her bags, and Macy followed.

"Caleb!"

He bent to pick up one of the bags in each hand, foregoing pulling out the handles so he could wheel them. He wasn't sure what room Jonesy had given Macy and there might be carpet or rugs on the way. When he straightened with the bags, the muscles on his biceps bulged slightly, though he bore the weight easily. "Jesus. Did you bring your entire closet? Lead the way."

Macy didn't tell him where her room was, nor did she start walking in that direction. "Why can't I stay in the same room with you? It's not like we're kids, and you're her boss!"

"Macy, come on." Caleb was unmoving in his resolve but he kept his tone low. They were still within earshot of the kitchen and who knew if Wren would show up at the top of the stairs any minute. "I don't want to argue and I'm not up for getting into it with Jonesy either. Please, show me the way to your room and we can talk about it."

Macy waited a beat, and then preceded Caleb down the hall behind the staircase to the back of the house. "She stashed me in the farthest part of the house. She hates me and I didn't even do anything to her!"

Caleb remained silent until he deposited the cases on floor of her room. It was lavishly furnished with polished hardwood floors and a thick area rug in the center of a seating area situated at the end of the bed, where a big screen TV was mounted on the wall above a fireplace. It could be watched from there or from the bed. The room was done in soft yellows, gold, and light jade green.

"This is like the Ritz. She probably put you back here because it's private. You have everything you need."

Macy huffed, throwing her purse on the middle of the king size bed. The linens were the finest money could buy; plush and comfortable. "I *need* to be with you. How am I supposed to help you if I'm exiled to the outer limits?" Her lips took on a petulant pout, though the woman Caleb knew her to be was always controlled and mature. It was out of character.

Caleb contemplated his words; knowing in soothing her, he'd have to say things he didn't really mean. "I'm glad you're here, though I have a ton of meetings and we won't be able to spend much time together. It's a funeral, not party-time."

Macy's expression got hard, angry at his choice of words. "I know it's not a party." She unbuttoned her jacket and kicked off her high heels. "Obviously."

Caleb's hands landed on his hips as his stance changed. "Look, I told you there is a lot of shit to deal with this week."

"I know." Her expression softened. "I know there are a ton of things that need dealing with, but do you need to do it all yourself? After the funeral, we can just hire people to do it all. Real estate agents, lawyers, brokers... I don't like to see you so stressed over things."

Caleb was uncomfortably aware of his state of bodily odor and sweat. His shirt was sticking to him and his hair was plastered onto his forehead and was starting to itch. He reached up to scratch his temple in irritation.

"My father is dead."

"Yes, but you hated him, so I don't really understand all of this pent up anxiety. And why is your stepsister here? Aren't your parents divorced?"

Her blasé attitude as she stripped out of her blouse and skirt just pissed him off, and it made worse by her reference to Wren. To be fair, she had no clue what he was and would be dealing with and he could tell her just to shut down the conversation, but he wasn't sure he wanted to.

"There's more to it. Wren is here because she and my father were close and he wanted her here."

Macy hesitated briefly before going into the bathroom, wearing only a lacy white bra and thong. She was always so perfectly coiffed. Even down to her lingerie, and usually, that would turn him on, but as it was, he barely noticed. "Is she in the will?" Macy's tone was casual, but Caleb knew she was bristling.

"For Christ's sake! It's a *will*! No one knows what's in it until it's read." This new side of Macy wasn't sitting well with him. He knew she had his best interest at heart, but he didn't want to see any ill will toward Wren. She was innocent in the entire thing. No, the decision was his and his alone. And really; it was none of Macy's goddamned business. He didn't even have to tell her he'd been given a choice. If he decided to split it with Wren, he could let Macy believe that was how the will was written. For that matter, he didn't have to tell Wren, either, though it would affect her and she deserved to be part of the decision. But would she be honest about what she really wanted?

"I suppose."

The water started to run in the bathroom, and Caleb

decided to make his exit.

"I'm gonna go shower. We'll talk more later."

Macy popped her head around the corner of the bathroom doorway. "Or," she said silkily, "We can shower together. Come on, baby."

Normally, he'd never pass up such an invitation, but his mind was racing and he wanted to check in with Wren. If he didn't see her alone before dinner, it was doubtful he'd have luck in getting her alone.

Caleb glanced over his shoulder to see Macy's beguiling expression as she stood in the doorway, and then shook his head. "Now is the wrong time. "

"Babe—" she started to protest.

"Not now," he said forcefully and left the room. He inhaled in agitation as his feet quickly took him to the other side of the house and the curved staircase that went to the second level. Knowing Wren was this close; he couldn't stay away. He wanted to see her as quickly as possible.

It took him less than three seconds and he was standing in front of the mahogany door that led to Wren's bedroom. His father had allocated at least a third of this level to her when he did the remodel shortly after Caleb had gone off to MIT, and for that, at least, and he was thankful. Finally, Wren had been able to be open about her dancing, and not have to hide it from her jealous shrew of a mother.

Once he was there, though, he hesitated. There was absolute silence and he wondered if she wasn't still sleeping. His hand lifted to lightly brush the wood surface before he flattened it and laid his palm on the door. Her presence in the room beyond it convinced Caleb's mind that the wood was warm and he could almost feel the vibration of live electricity running through it.

She was here; just feet away. The closest he'd been to her in two years.

It seemed like he and Wren were defined by a series of two-year periods. She was in the house two years before he had to leave, two years later he'd made love to her after that damned party, two years after that she'd brought that producer home with her to San Francisco and they'd had that blow up at Fisherman's Wharf. It had been just over two years since that had happened.

He laid his forehead on the door, his hand still splayed out next to it, as he thought about it all. His heart was thudding hard in his chest, like he'd been running a marathon, drowning, or *dying*. The air being forced in and out of his lungs actually hurt as they protested.

She was here. Right here. Now what the hell was he going to do?

He strained to hear inside her room, but there was no sound. Yearning to see her, his hand found its way down to the doorknob and wrapped itself around it. He even began to turn it, but then he stopped, his broad and usually solid shoulders, sagging in defeat.

Fuuuucccckkkk! His mind screamed.

He was stronger than anyone he knew. He could take on his father, win every fight inside the ring, but he was completely wasted by a tiny girl. Fucking helpless.

Caleb swallowed and straightened, reluctant to leave, but

used the excuse of her possibly being asleep to turn and hurry back down the hallway to the stairs and then to his suite in the basement. He was shaking. Literally shaking.

Damn it all. He needed to talk to her without Macy, Jonesy, or Jonathan listening in. He'd have to find a way to take Wren aside after dinner, to see if they could even communicate, if she still held any ill will toward him, and if he could gauge what, or rather if she'd even want anything to do with him or Luxon Pharmaceuticals.

It would be easy to separate from Jonesy after the meal concluded, but Macy was another story. Clearly, he'd made a mistake in allowing her to be here given their casual status. He could kick himself, but he didn't think it through in his haste to leave, pack and get here. He hadn't even considered Wren would be in residence. "I should have known," he murmured; chastising himself. To be fair, his father hadn't known anything about Macy, and he wouldn't have cared, even if he did. Wren would still have been summoned to Colorado either way. How else could Edison make his son squirm to the greatest extent possible?

Old habits are hard to break, and it was extremely difficult for Caleb to recognize Edison Luxon did anything for him, despite what the letter had said.

Deciding the outcome of his own life was bad enough; everything would change. But deciding Wren's fate, too, was the part that ate at him. Why couldn't he make sure she had half of the fortune, without the need to completely uproot her career and her life? How was making someone, whether himself or Wren, give up their career goals, acceptable? Was

Caleb's dream of designing and building cars and cycles, or Wren's dream of dancing any less important than Edison's precious company?

Caleb felt like a butterfly in one of those shadow boxes with his wings pinned down, and his father's supposed posthumous gesture of "good will" was the pins.

chapter
SIX

Dear Caleb,

I know there is no way to make amends for all of the sins I've committed against you. Though I've tried in the past, and am trying again now, a dying old man's last chance to do the right thing may be futile. If you're reading this, then it gives me a bit of hope that one day you may at least understand.

I have no excuse for my behavior. My lack of a relationship with you is my greatest regret. I can only hope that in telling you the truth, you'll at least have some peace and an explanation. God knows you deserve one.

Nothing can justify a father turning his back on his twelve-year-old son; there is no excuse for disappearing from your life, and abandoning you and your mother those last months before she died. I know I have no right to ask for your forgiveness, but I do, nevertheless.

When I first learned Celine was sick, my whole world came crashing down around me. We had an amazing life, a successful company, an incredible son; life was idyllic, so how could it end? The pain was horrific. I couldn't accept that I would lose her, and it was unbearable to watch her change from the beautiful, vibrant woman she'd been, into a shell of her former self. I exhausted myself searching for a doctor who would have a different diagnosis or miracle cure. I spent an astronomical amount of money and traveled the world over talking to doctors, but there was nothing to be done for her type of brain tumor.

Every doctor had the same answer: it was inoperable, her pain would get worse, she'd begin to forget things or lose use of her motor skills, and medication would have horrible side effects. The feeling of hopelessness, failure, and despair was like nothing I'd ever felt.

I neglected my company and my son, and I couldn't face your mother, I couldn't face you. I'd failed both of you because I couldn't save her.

I have no other explanation except I simply couldn't handle the pain. I went to work to rebuild Lux. It was her legacy, and in that at least, I wouldn't fail her. I used it as an excuse to block out her illness until she died and I closed down. I felt like I'd died myself.

My grief was unbearable and you were a reminder of her: every time I looked at you, I saw her in your eyes. It was unfair to you, and the worst thing I could have done.

You were already so angry by then; I thought it was easier on both of us if I just kept working. Your resentment was justified, and it only solidified the distance that I needed to function.

It was the worst mistake of my life. The worst thing I've ever done.

Over the years, I tried to make amends in ways you are not even aware of, and others you didn't agree with. I can only hope someday you will come to see that most of what I've done, even marrying Veronica, I did, because I thought you needed a family. I thought she would be kind, and her presence, along with Wren's, would bring some happiness back to your life. Looking back, I know at least one thing good came out of it. Wren.

I know I was wrong to force my will on you to go to Boston, but at the time, you were reckless and spiraling out of control. I wanted you to have a good life, and guide you along a better and more stable path. I feared that the crowd you ran with would influence you in a destructive direction. Right or wrong, I wanted to separate you from that possibility.

You are a far better man than me, and it's obvious you love more selflessly than I am capable of. I should have let you live the life you wanted, and trusted you to take the right path. I had no right to stand in your way.

I understand that you may be angry to hold the responsibility I am placing in your hands, but I hope you can see that this is my way of proving my faith and trust in you. Finally.

No matter what you decide to do, I want you to be happy. I am proud to call you my son.
Love,
Dad

Caleb's whole body was shaking as he finished reading his father's last words to him. His eyes burned with unshed tears, his throat ached, and he felt like two steel bands wrapped around his chest, preventing him from breathing normally.

What the fuck? He waits until it's too late to say this?

Wren had been so tired she slept through dinner, and afterward, Caleb managed some time alone when Macy had to take a call from her firm. He retreated to his father's library, grateful for her distraction so he could read Edison's second letter.

He was in shock at its content, but still he was overwhelmed with emotion. Caleb wasn't sure if the explanation inspired forgiveness, or only made him more pissed off at his dad.

How dare he do what he did, then act like a whiny bitch instead of a man? A man, who should have been strong for his dying wife, and for his son.

Did he think Caleb could just forgive him so easily? Did he think a few words on a page would change the years of hatred and resentment? Was Caleb supposed to thank his lucky stars for this huge fucking "gift"?

Rather than make his life easier, it shifted the weight of the world onto his shoulders. Was he supposed to be grateful? And, what about Wren? Did Edison Luxon even give one fucking thought to what this could do her life? What if she didn't want any of it?

Caleb tried to take a deep breath, but was only partially successful. His lungs felt rigid and resisted his effort as the words on the page blurred. *Goddamn him!*

"What is that, Caleb?"

Macy's voice sounded from somewhere behind where Caleb sat on one of the leather sofas and she startled him. He jumped slightly, and then quickly began to fold the letter back up, not wanting her to see it.

"Nothing." His voice thickened with emotion.

"Is it from your dad?"

Nothing annoyed Caleb more than redundant questions. Who else would it be from? When he didn't answer, Macy pressed him.

"Are you okay?"

"I'm fine." He cleared his throat, still holding the folded piece of paper in his right hand.

"Caleb, why won't you talk to me?"

"Why? What good would it do? It won't change anything."

"True, it won't bring your father back, but it might help you work through your feelings."

Caleb huffed. "I don't know what I'm feeling. It's personal. Why do you want to know, anyway?"

He was agitated with the conversation as he refolded the letter, and folded it again; small enough to shove into the back pocket of his jeans.

Jonesy's worry about Wren had dominated the conversation over dinner and echoed his own. He'd been preoccupied all evening, while Macy's displeasure had been written all over her face on the couple of occasions that he'd voiced his concern. He should be grateful for her softer tone now, but he only wanted to be alone. If Wren wasn't here, then alone was the next best thing.

He wished the few minutes he managed to himself would have lasted longer and Macy hadn't tracked him down to start pelting him with a barrage of questions.

"You're so distant. I don't like it," Macy continued, using one hand to pull through her long dark hair, now loose from the bun she'd worn it in earlier. Caleb wondered if she really gave a shit or she was bored out of her mind and just going through the motions.

The letter left him raw, and conjured up feelings toward his father he didn't even realize still existed. Regret at the lost time and relationship they could have had, sure, but he was royally pissed at the same time. Turmoil had him all screwed up on the inside, and Macy's nagging was the last thing he needed.

There were a few seconds hesitation before Caleb retorted, anger lacing his voice. "That's unfortunate, but not really a consideration."

Macy was stunned for a beat, but then huffed in frustration. "Wow. That was a dick thing to say. I'm trying to help you, Caleb. I just want to make you feel better."

Caleb had regret that his words may have hurt her, but then realized coming here was her own choice. He didn't ask her to join him. "There's nothing you can do, and I said; I'm fine. I have a lot to deal with, and I'm just preoccupied with everything that needs to be done. I told you not to come out here. There are some things that I have to do on my own."

"Caleb," Macy forced her voice to grow softer and more sympathetic even though his words pissed her off. She had no intention of doing anything to alienate this man. He was strong and beautiful, intelligent, and now to find he was heir to a huge cosmetic brand she'd used for years; made him close to surreal. She should have put two and two together. His last name, *Lux* Cosmetics; his hometown of Denver, the company being headquartered there; she couldn't believe she didn't figure it out before this.

Maybe she could convince him to give up his silly automotive venture and travel the world with her. Now that he was loaded, why would he want to work his ass off starting a brand new company from the ground up? "I thought we were close enough that you'd lean on me. You don't have to be strong all the time."

Caleb grimaced and huffed in agitation. "That's who I am."

He felt like his insides were about to explode. He didn't like Macy pressuring him to talk about things he was still trying to reconcile in his own mind. And, if he were honest, she didn't seem sincere. She was just digging for information he had no intention of sharing.

What was upsetting him? he wondered. Was it Macy's prying, his father's death, or the major decision hanging over his head? Was it Wren being in such close proximity, or the fucking letter? Maybe, it was all of it.

He felt something, but he couldn't really categorize it. He was pensive, anxious, his chest felt tight, but he was still trying to get his head around everything, and up to this point had been pretty much numb. He shook his head. Nothing had changed from ten minutes earlier, so why was he struggling? Sure, Edison Luxon had sired him; so what? He hadn't been anything like a father for many years. Why should the small act of dying change anything? Why should a few paragraphs scrawled on a page make a difference?

"I know, but—" Macy began, but Caleb cut her off.

"You don't know anything about how I feel, Macy." He didn't say it to hurt her, but it was the truth, and he wasn't in the mood to sugar coat anything. "You're clueless about my father and my life growing up."

Anger reared inside Macy. Caleb was being an asshole and she wanted to tell him so. The problem with that was that it might drive a bigger wedge between them and that didn't suit her agenda. She tried to calm herself.

"Why don't you tell me, then? I know you have to be sad. Even if you hated him, he was still your dad."

"An unfortunate fact I had to come to terms with long ago. DNA doesn't make someone a father. He's dead; there's no use crying over someone who stood in the background of my life except when he was trying to make me miserable. Dying might be the biggest favor he's ever done for me." It was a sad reality, and Caleb's defensive anger at the letter he'd just read was fresh. "So no. I don't *have* to be anything; least of all sad."

"Oh, Caleb. That sounds sort of pitiful." Now Macy's voice sounded sad, but Caleb just shrugged and leaned forward to lean his elbows on his knees.

Pitiful. The word made his blood boil. *What the hell did she know about it?* He needed a drink, but he didn't' want to start drinking with Macy. He could use alcohol to relax, and then follow with a leisurely fuck with a willing woman, except he found he had zero desire to be close to Macy tonight.

Caleb shrugged, hoping she'd drop it and leave him alone. "It is what it is. Go to bed. I need some time alone."

***

UPSTAIRS, IT WAS DARK when Wren awoke; well past 10 PM. She bolted up in bed, frantic that she'd missed dinner, and quickly leaned over to snatch her phone off the bedside table so she could check the time. The last thing she wanted was to be disrespectful to Jonesy after she'd cooked the meal, or Caleb, by seeming like she was unfeeling or insensitive to his pain over Edison's death.

"Oh my God! Really?" she said to herself, dropping her phone and then scrambling from the bed to throw on a pair of jeans and the one long sleeved T-shirt she had packed. She rushed into the ensuite bathroom to look at her appearance. She was rumpled, her face was red on one cheek where she'd slept on it, and her blonde hair was a snarled mess.

She wasn't sure if she'd find anyone still around, or if she'd even be able to apologize for missing dinner. It was hours beyond when Jonesy said the food would be ready. The skin of her cheek felt hot as she touched it, and then dropped a tube of moisturizer on the vanity in her haste; it knocking a powder compact, three eye shadows, and an assortment of other make-up to the tile floor in a loud clatter.

"Ugh!" she moaned.

The blush compact fell open and shattered on the tile, sending chunks of the now broken pink powder all over the floor, and puffs of it into the air. Wren began to cough at the same time as frustrated tears welled in her eyes and batted at the offending particles that were trying to make their way into her lungs. When she bent to clean up the mess, the wad of toilet paper she'd grabbed to do the job only smeared it around more.

She felt like bursting into tears. The last thing she wanted was to let Caleb down. Considering the time change, Jonesy would understand her missing the meal, but there was no excuse for not being awake to offer her support to Caleb. Whether he'd want it or not, she wasn't sure, but even if he rebuffed her, she had to at least try.

Wren threw the paper into the toilet, and stood to stare at her reflection in the mirror again as the cloud of dust cleared. She sniffed, grabbed a toothbrush and quickly brushed her teeth, then ran a quick brush through her hair. Makeup would have to wait; she'd already wasted enough time.

Slipping out of her room, she quickly rushed down the hall. On her way down the stairs, she could hear voices coming from Edison's study. One she didn't recognize and one she dreamed about on many lonely nights. One she loved more than anything.

"Caleb."

A woman's voice made Wren's foot pause; her downward descent on the stairs halted.

Surely this was the woman Jonesy had referenced that afternoon; Macy. She sounded very sophisticated with a level of polish Wren never dreamed of attaining. Without even laying eyes on her, it was obvious Macy was expensive with a haughty air. It came through in her tone.

Wren had traveled the world and met some amazing people, but she knew she didn't possess that type of sophistication. She was a prima ballerina with one of the premier ballet companies in the world, yet in her own heart she was still just a girl who danced.

"I said; I need to be alone. Why can't you respect that?"

Wren's breath left her body at the subtle hint of anguish in Caleb's tone. He hid it well, and anyone who knew him less wouldn't catch it.

She hadn't heard his voice in person for a couple of years, and now it was a combination of resignation and defeat. Her heart squeezed painfully inside her chest. It was almost like he was physically touching her, pouring his pain into her. Wren found herself sinking down to sit on the stairs, mid-flight. Her hands came up to slowly wind around the spindles of the ornate railing, unable to stop from listening. However, nothing followed but an uncomfortable, dead silence.

Powerless to do anything else, Wren stood up and continued toward the study entrance, moving slowly; her bare feet making no sound on the polished marble floor. Peeking in through the open door, she could see Caleb sitting on one of the sofas; his back to her. Wren felt as if a lightning bolt jolted through her at the sight of him. She'd missed him more than she could deny.

He was leaning forward as he sat; unmoving. A sleek brunette was perched next to him, rubbing back and forth on his back.

His demeanor was stiff, unwilling to accept any comfort from the woman Wren barely noticed. Her eyes were trained on Caleb's back and bent head, the material of his white dress shirt stretched tight across his arms, shoulders and back.

Macy scooted closer to him as Wren appeared in the doorway to the room hesitating to interrupt, but unable to move or rip her eyes away. Her heart was beating so hard she could feel the pulse throbbing in her neck and wrists, her chest was ready to burst, and her breath caught in her throat.

"I want to comfort you, babe," Macy said suggestively. "Make you forget about everything for a while. Come to bed with me."

Macy's arm slid around Caleb's shoulders and Wren almost turned to return to her rooms. This was a private scene, and one that hurt to watch.

She stopped and stifled a gasp when Caleb visibility stiffened, and abruptly stood up. Running an impatient hand through his thick dark hair, he shrugged the woman off. Wren's heart leapt at the site, and she longed for him to turn so she could see his handsome face. She was drawn to him, hungry for the sight of him, yet her feet were frozen; unable to move as she watched him from across the room.

"Please, don't! I feel claustrophobic when you do that, Macy! I don't want to be touched! Having your arms around me right now makes me feel like I'm in a fucking cage!" He took a few steps forward and then turned, wanting to shout that he didn't know her well enough to dump his entire life of bottled up emotions on the floor, but within the course of one split second his eyes landed on the slight form of the woman in the doorway. His heart and mind recognized her right away and he stopped dead.

His stomach dropped as his brain connected the image of the long blonde hair, beautiful face, and sad expression; Wren's eyes were wide as she stared at him.

"Wren." The word fell from his lips softly, and as if against his will. Caleb started moving toward her.

Macy's head snapped around instantly to search for the source of Caleb's attention.

The moment Caleb said her name, tears started to flow and Wren's feet were flying as she ran to meet him halfway. Caleb caught her up in a tight embrace, and her arms wound around his shoulders as he pulled her close against him.

There was no stopping his reaction, and no thought that Macy was watching; she may as well have disappeared.

Caleb held Wren in a crushing embrace. His strong arms held her tightly to his chest and her arms locked around him. He smelled amazing; just like she remembered, and he felt like home.

"Oh, my God, Wren." Caleb's voice caught as he felt her start to shake against him, his body absorbing her racking sobs.

Wren buried her face in his neck as he lifted her off the ground further into his embrace, unable to keep the torrent of emotions at bay. "Oh, Cale. I'm so sorry! I'm so sorry, Cale."

Wren wasn't sure if she was expressing sympathy because of Edison's death, or pouring out all of the apologies needed to make everything okay between them.

Caleb's arms tightened again, his heart soaring at the sound of her voice; saying his name as only she said it. He wanted to get closer as if contact between them would be the balm he needed. Wren was the one person who knew him better than anyone ever could, a source of comfort like no one else, and he didn't want to let her go.

His heart swelled and fell at the same time, his pain intensifying and easing simultaneously, and his tears began to fall like rain, the dam of his pain finally bursting. He cried hard, and Wren's heart shattered like glass.

"Cale," she said brokenly.

He was overwhelmed with emotions as he held her, unable to quell his violent reaction. "Oh, Wren. I'm so glad you're here." Caleb's voice was tight, his throat felt swollen and his heart thumped heavily inside his chest. God she was tiny and it felt so good to touch her. "I didn't know how much I needed you here." Seeing her after so long, and the reality of his father's death; the finality of it, and the too late declaration of fatherly love; finally hit him. His emotions over the letter he'd just read, and finally seeing Wren after so long collided, and the result was cataclysmic.

"My dad..." He cried into her shoulder, sinking to his knees on the fine Persian rug and bringing her with him. They literally melted together, both seeking and taking comfort from the other. "I never thought I'd feel this way."

Wren's voice broke on a sob as the two of them clung together in the center of the big, masculine room; both of them overcome with grief. "I know. I'm suh-sorry. Suh-sorry I fell asleep. I should have been with you."

Caleb's big hand moved from her back to cup the back of her head, his fingers tangling in her long blonde hair. "Hush. You're here now."

She was, and he was so grateful. He hadn't realized how much he needed her near to somehow make sense of any of this. As his tears ebbed, Caleb turned his face to kiss her temple as he inhaled deeply to gain some control over his rampant emotions, his chest tight with love for Wren and the loss of his father. Nothing could be done about their relationship now, and though he'd been hurt and hated Edison for years, the chance to know his father was lost forever. But his chance with Wren was *now*. The realization hit him like a ton of bricks.

She pulled back just enough to look into his deep blue eyes, now glassed over with tears, his eyelashes wet and spiky, longing to comfort him. He was still beautiful, but his hair was shorter. She lifted her hand to touch the side of his face. "Oh, Cale." Tears still fell onto her cheeks, and he wiped at them with his thumb. "He loved you. I know he did."

Caleb's eyes closed, his expression twisting as he fought to regain control. Why couldn't his father have said that before it was too late? For years he'd hardened his heart and convinced himself it didn't matter; but it mattered more than anyone knew. Even Wren.

All Caleb could do was pull Wren close again and bury his face into her shoulder. He was still shaking and all she could do was hold him close, cry with him, stroke his hair, and whisper words designed to comfort him. He was helpless to his feelings and helpless to his reaction.

Caleb succumbed for only a short time, but then reason

took hold of his mind, strength took over and he got it together.

He'd lost control of his emotions only a couple of times in his life, and it wasn't something he was proud of. He was a master at hiding his feelings and he was embarrassed when anyone saw any type of weakness in him. And Wren... He'd always taken care of her, and she was the last person he wanted to witness him falling apart.

"Uhuhum..." Macy cleared her throat. She watched the two of them fall apart right in front of her and her heart seized. Caleb hadn't told her much about Wren, but she'd always assumed they weren't close and that they had a typical stepsibling relationship when the parents married later in life when their children are older. Given Caleb's abhorrence for his stepmother, Macy had expected casual indifference for Wren, certainly not this explosive reaction to the girl.

At first impression, Wren looked about eighteen years old and though beautiful, was very frail. Jealousy welled inside Macy. He didn't want comfort from her, which said a lot about his inner strength. Obviously, that wasn't the case with Wren. She sucked in a slow breath to quell her rising agitation.

Caleb glanced up to where Macy was standing and his eyes locked with hers, noting the pained expression left undisguised on her face. A wave of guilt rushed through him. He swallowed and began to disengage with Wren, though Macy had already started a brisk walk from the room.

Wren saw a blur in her peripheral vision and pulled completely out of Caleb's embrace; suddenly aware of what had just happened in front of the other woman. She felt horrible about it. This was Caleb's girlfriend and she had to be hurt after what she had just witnessed.

"Caleb, stop her." Wren stood up and brushed at her wet cheeks with both hands, then quickly wiped them on the hem of her shirt. She turned toward the retreating figure and called out her name.

"Macy, right? I'm so sorry. It was rude of me to hover and barge in like that. It's just that I knew I missed dinner and felt I should apologize to everyone. "

Macy stopped and turned back into the room, trying to hide her displeasure at Caleb's behavior. She reminded herself of the reason for this little reunion and that the circumstance might warrant a little levity. His reaction was testimony to the pain he really felt, though she wished she'd been the one allowed to comfort him. It made her wary of Wren and she questioned the truth of Caleb's feelings for the young woman.

Macy sized Wren up again. Her face had a delicate beauty; her features fine with vibrant blue eyes, her body so small, she looked as if she might blow away in a strong breeze. If Caleb was protective of her, it was easy to see why.

Wren held out her right hand, taking a step forward, toward Macy. Caleb, now on his feet, was unsure of what to say, and stood watching. "I'm Wren. It's nice to meet you."

Macy's expression lost a bit of its strain as she slowly took Wren's hand and shook it. "The stepsister." She nodded and smiled stiffly. "I'm Macy. Caleb's—"

The hair on the back of Caleb's neck stood up. The label grated on him like fingernails running down a chalkboard, but worse, he wasn't ready for Wren to believe his relationship to Macy was more serious than it really was. He was acutely aware he'd look like an asshole either way.

"Um, Macy and I are working... uh, she's helping me find financial backing for a business idea." The words rushed out of Caleb's mouth, and he ran a hand through his hair nervously, his eyes flashing to Wren's face. He wanted to gauge her reaction; unsure why he felt guilty, and prayed the conversation would move away from the topic.

Wren paused as the handshake ended, and both of them looked at him. Wren's features held a faint curiosity and Macy's hardened as her mouth pressed into an angry line. Awkward was an understatement. *Fuck.*

"Oh," Wren said. Her voice was soft and she smiled gently at Macy. It was evident the other woman was hurt and angry. "I thought you two were together."

"So did I," Macy retorted, shooting Caleb an angry look.

Wren felt the tension between them, and she wanted to make Macy feel better. "You know guys; most of them are commitment phobic."

"Yes." Macy smiled and seemed to relax. "He's just shy about sharing."

Caleb bristled, wondering what or who Wren was basing her comment on.

"Cale, is there anything to drink?" Wren asked hopefully, raising her eyebrows and glancing suggestively at the bar. She needed a distraction and a way to move the conversation away from its current course. "Wine, maybe?"

He nodded and went to the bar without saying a word. He wasn't sure how he felt about this apparent kinship between Wren and Macy. Wren still held a beguiling innocence in stark contrast to Macy's razor sharp edginess, and the protectiveness inside him reared. What would Macy say to Wren? He'd already decided he wanted to keep distance between them, and that looked like it was shot to hell. He found some red wine, opened it and poured three glasses.

It wasn't long before Wren and Macy were engaged in conversation about Macy's firm, how she and Caleb had met, and Wren's production schedule for the upcoming season. Macy was a talker and had a lot of questions, which Wren answered graciously.

As Caleb sat on the opposite sofa, enthralled watching the animated way Wren talked about the torture of many long hours of practice, the grueling touring schedule, and her love of traveling the world. The joy that radiated from her made his heart constrict a little, and he wished he'd shared some of it with her.

He should probably just take the fucking estate and not bog her down with the responsibility of helping him run the company. It was clear she loved her life as it was. His mind railed as his conflict filled him. He already knew most of what she was saying, and even though they didn't keep in close contact anymore, she was a still a priority. Despite their differences, Caleb made it a point to know where she was at all times.

He was listening, but the words morphed into the background as the conversation between the girls continued. He simply could not take his eyes off of Wren's face. She was so beautiful; still so beautiful.

He remembered the first time he saw her without that

horrible black wig and awful dark eye makeup she habitually wore after coming to live with the Luxon men. He thought she was an utter freak before the night he and his friend had gotten the shit beat out of them. The night Dex's Mustang was destroyed; when Dex's dad had dropped him off at home after taking Dex to the hospital. He wondered if Wren remembered that night with as much clarity as he did. It had changed the way he thought of her, looked at her, and made him want to get to know who she really was.

chapter
SEVEN

CALEB REMEMBERED IT AS IF IT were yesterday. Even though he was observing the two women interact; his mind was filled with that night.

The first time he'd seen her as she truly was; he'd been stunned. Despite his injuries and haze of pain, he'd barely been able to believe his eyes as she tended to his wounds. He was in as bad of shape as Dex had been and should have been seen by a doctor, too. He hadn't wanted to burden Darren more than they already had, and he'd put on a tough front, hiding how badly he was hurt. It turned out he'd had at least three broken ribs and the pain had made it impossible for him to get downstairs by himself. He'd collapsed at the top of the stairs, and lay there in a helpless, moaning heap.

Like an angel, Wren had appeared; her long blonde curls flowing loose, her eyes not masked by the black makeup she usually wore, and the blush on her skin not hidden beneath a whitewash of foundation.

At first, he thought he was having a hallucination brought on by a pain-induced hazed.

"Caleb!" When she spoke, and he recognized her voice. He remembered how stunned he was; how absolutely speechless he'd been as he stared into her beautiful face, framed by all of that glorious hair.

"Wren?" he'd asked as she knelt beside him on the marble tiles of the kitchen floor, his hand reaching toward her face. He grunted in pain and fell back on the cold floor, cradling his mid-section. "Is that you?"

"Oh, Cale. What have you done?" His face was bruised and swollen, his knuckles broken and bleeding, so she'd done as he asked and not called his dad, or a doctor. Instead, she taped up his ribs, cleaned his hands and the cut above his left eyebrow, and bandaged him up as best she could. All without judgment.

In those few hours their relationship slowly began to change. She'd pulled his arm around her neck, put another around his waist to take some of his weight as she helped him carefully down the stairs and into his bed. He was exhausted and out of breath, pain wracking his body; his ribs throbbed, his knuckles burned and his head pounded, and still; he couldn't take his eyes off of her in the low-lit room.

"You can't tell my dad, okay?" He groaned in pain as she let him down as gently as possible. "I mean, ever?"

"What will he do?"

"Lecture me to death. I'll be better by the time they get

back, and he'll just be an asshole."

"Okay." She nodded and turned to leave the room. "I'll let you get some rest and check on you in the morning."

Caleb was panting slightly, out of breath from the exertion and his injuries, embarrassed to be so broken in front of her. He was seeing her as she really was, with new eyes... and he'd never look at her in the same way again.

"Wren, wait." He put up a hand and she turned back around. "Why?" His brow knitted and he shook his head in confusion? "I don't get it. You're so—"

She stopped and turned toward him again, a small shrug lifting her slight shoulders. "It's just... easier. My mom doesn't like me when I look like this."

Despite his weakened condition, rage welled up inside Caleb's chest and real hate for his stepmother began to fester. From what he'd seen Veronica didn't like Wren when she looked gothic, either. "What? She wants you to hide what you really look like? Is she that vain? She can't handle that you're more beautiful than her?"

When Wren looked down and shrugged again, embarrassed to be called beautiful after so many years of being told she was ugly and worthless. She was frightened at the very thought of being more beautiful than her mother. She had tasted the consequences of that, too many times.

Caleb exploded. "That is so fucked up, Wren!" Pain had sliced through him as his muscles coiled with rage; his first instinct to act. "If I could, I'd beat the shit out of her. What kind of twisted bitch is she, to do that to her own kid?"

"Caleb, it's okay. I'm used to it."

He shook his head. "No. No, it's not okay, Wren! It's so fucked up."

"She forgets about me when I disappear. She doesn't hurt me as much when I wear that stuff."

Caleb had never been so livid in his life. Not even his own father's lack of caring about him could compare to how heinous this was. It was one thing to forget about your kid and another to physically and emotionally abuse them. "You will never put that stuff on again, Wren. Never, do you hear me?"

"She'll—"

"I never want to see that fucking shit covering up your face or that wig hiding your hair again!" Wren started to protest and Caleb held up his hand to stop her words. "I'll deal with Veronica. She won't hurt you, I promise."

He fell back on the pillows exhausted, the exertion making him cough and the spasms sending pain rocketing through his midsection. "Aw, fuck."

Wren had hovered for a couple of seconds then reached into her back pocket for her phone. "You should go to the hospital, Cale."

He shook his head and put a hand to stop her from calling an ambulance. "No. I'll be okay. I've had worse beatings than this." He huffed softly, lying back again. "You did a good job taping me up. Can you get me some water, please?"

Wren had gone to the master suite and rummaged through the medicine cabinet to find a vile of Vicodin and brought it, along with a glass of water to him.

"Take one of these. It says on the label it's for pain."

Caleb didn't question where she got the pills, he just downed the one she handed him and closed his eyes. She spent the night, and the next, on the couch in the entertainment room in the basement, so she could check on Caleb and hear him if he needed anything. She'd nursed him, brought him food, and helped him back and forth to the bathroom; until a few days later when he was able to move around by himself. She'd even skipped school to take care of him. When his dad and Veronica came back from their trip two weeks later, Caleb could move without grimacing, his bruised face and knuckles were healed, and Wren... was Wren.

The shock on Veronica's face when she'd returned to see her daughter without the disguise had been priceless. Edison had been quietly astonished for a split second, but then nodded his silent approval, and went about his business like nothing had changed.

The morning after their return, his dad had gone to Lux and Caleb stayed by Wren for the inevitable confrontation that would come from his step-hag. Wren had been pensive but Caleb had reassured her he'd be by her side through it all. They'd been having breakfast in the kitchen when Veronica marched into the kitchen for coffee at a time when Jonesy had been cleaning in the other room.

"Caleb, I'd like to speak to Wren."

"Isn't she gorgeous?" he'd asked casually, and set down his spoon, locking eyes with Veronica, and silently throwing down the gauntlet. "Who knew? Oh, right. You did."

Wren sat as still as stone next to Caleb, unable to meet her mother's eyes, fear keeping her quiet. It made Caleb physically sick that Wren would be so intimidated and afraid of this vapid woman.

He stood up and moved to stand in the space between where Wren was sitting at the table and Veronica stood in front of the refrigerator, his voice deadly calm. "You won't touch her again. You won't tell her what to eat or not eat. You won't tell her how to dress or make her ashamed of how beautiful she is. You won't raise your hand or your voice to her, ever again."

Veronica had cackled in her shrill, waspish laugh; casually brushing off his threat. "Shut up, Caleb. You're just a kid no one cares about. Your father will—"

Something inside Caleb snapped at her harsh words. He bolted into action, grabbing Veronica, turning quickly and roughly pushing her up against the wall. The entire thing took less than a second. He used his forearm to press against her chest, using his weight in to hold her still. Wren gasped loudly at Caleb's show of force, but remained unmoving. His ribs weren't one hundred percent and his movements caused him a great deal of pain, but it was masked with his anger.

Caleb's face was inches from Veronica's; so close he could feel her breath on his face as she gasped and exhaled in her surprise at his abrupt actions.

"Look, you don't know me, but I can make you disappear. Literally." He leaned in even closer so he could lower his voice; looking down as he towered over her. "So don't. Fuck. With. Me." He punctuated each word for emphasis. "I know everything, you vain, wicked bitch. Touch Wren again and I promise you'll be very, very sorry."

He had lied because he didn't really know everything Veronica had subjected Wren to, but he could guess. It was only after she felt safe that she'd shared the details of how Veronica beat her, starved her, berated her and made her hide inside herself, behind that horrible black wig, and harsh makeup. She told him that she dealt with the emotional abuse, by starting to self-mutilate.

"Do you understand me?"

Veronica had met his eyes and sneered, her bright red lips contorting in a hateful expression. "Your father won't stand—"

Caleb's lips lifted in a devious smile as he simultaneously gave his stepmother another sharp shove. "My father is a lot of things, but he's my father. Haven't you paid attention? I can do any damn thing I want and he'll bail me out. That's the beauty of it. Your pussy isn't so amazing that he'd forsake me or sully his precious company and the Lux name. Trust me."

Veronica stilled, shocked from the bluntness of his words and the realness of his threat. She no longer struggled to free herself from Caleb's grasp, her eyes meeting the blue steel of his, but her features belied an untouchable and conceited smugness that told Caleb she wasn't backing down. Hate welled up inside his chest and he wanted to pound his fist into her smug expression.

After half a minute, Caleb released her and turned back to Wren. She wasn't finished with breakfast, but he needed to put space between himself and Veronica. He held out his hand to Wren, who took it readily. "You're with me. Let's go."

You're with me. Those words resonated like no others.

From that moment, Caleb made Wren his responsibility in every way, and he still felt as strongly about it now as he had then. He blinked to regain focus on the two women as they talked, the memory causing pain, pleasure, and pride.

"Are all ballerina's as tiny as you are, Wren? I've been to a ballet or two and I don't remember the girls being so small. From a distance you must look like a child."

Macy seemed like a nice woman and their conversation up to that point, had been good. Wren had regret at the possibility that the earlier scene had hurt her, but these last words felt like a thinly veiled jab. Even though Wren could understand how Macy might resent her presence, it still hurt. But, what was worse; her presence was an obstacle to being alone with Caleb and she desperately wanted to talk to him. She was worried about him, and she longed for some time to reconnect. As long as Macy was here, she couldn't get close to Caleb.

"Do you mean that I'm short?" Wren began hesitantly. "I'm a little shorter than average, I guess... but then, I'm always en pointe, so that adds a few inches."

"Oh. That makes sense. It must destroy your feet, though. I always imagine really nasty feet under those beautiful shoes."

"Macy." Caleb was annoyed with Macy's obvious slam of Wren, and pissed she felt the need to say something like that. "Really?"

Macy had the grace to flush but looked incredulous. "What? I didn't mean anything by it."

"It's okay," Wren reassured Caleb, then turned her

attention back to Macy. "I have had my share of blisters, and bloody tears in the skin, broken toenails, that's for sure."

"You had that stress fracture, too. Right?" Caleb interjected almost absently, and Wren's eyes narrowed on him. She couldn't ever remember telling Caleb about that: it had happened not long after the debacle with Sam, when she was refusing Caleb's every attempt to contact her. She'd been pushing herself harder in practice in attempt to forget her misery at another thing standing between them. It didn't matter that her relationship with Sam had been destroyed over it. She decided she needed to ask Caleb how he knew about it when they were alone.

"Don't things like that make you want to stop dancing?" Macy asked, demanding Wren's attention again. "I mean; surely there's something else you could do?"

Wren smiled and shook her head, choosing to ignore that particular comment. Apparently Macy never had a dream or something she loved as much as Wren loved to dance.

Her lips lifted in a wry smile and she shook her head slightly, causing her curls to move gently around her face. Caleb noticed and then looked down, hoping neither of the women noticed his rapt fascination with Wren.

"Not so far. That reminds me of something." She looked at Caleb who now was staring into his wine glass. "Cale?"

He didn't answer and looked deep in thought. The conversation must be boring him silly.

"Caleb, did you hear me?" Wren's voice registered for the second time and this time he looked up at her.

"Hmm? What?" He lifted his glass and took a swallow of

the rich Cabernet.

"I asked; when is the service?"

"Oh. Monday."

Despite the driver saying he was at her beck and call, she'd rather drive herself. "Is that white Toyota outside yours? Can I borrow it tomorrow? I'll need to get a dress and shoes. I was in Bali and I have nothing appropriate to wear to a funeral."

"Bali!" Macy said. "I've always wanted to go there. How marvelous. Maybe someday we can go, Caleb. I'm sure Wren would be happy to give us tips on where to stay or what to see there."

A small huff escaped Caleb, and his mouth flattened in disgust. He was silently cataloguing every time Macy tried to stake her unjustified ownership on him, and every time she came off callous in light of the reason they were in Denver. His eyes landed back on Wren to gauge her response.

"It was pretty, but I was only there two days when Jonathan called with the news of Edison, so I barely have anything to offer." Her eyes darted across to lock with Caleb's. "In any case, all I have with me are shorts, swimsuits and a couple of sundresses, so I definitely need to go shopping."

"It's Macy's rental," Caleb returned. He'd hired the driver to be on call for Wren, but Caleb capitalized on the opportunity. "But, I'll be glad to take you. We can use one of Dad's cars."

Wren offered a wide smile for Caleb. It would be nice to spend some time with him like they used to. She'd rather they take Caleb's old motorcycle like they often had when they were younger, but with Macy along, that wouldn't be possible.

"I'd love to explore the shops with you!" Macy said

enthusiastically, quickly deciding there was no way Caleb was going off alone with Wren while she was anywhere in the vicinity. *No. Way.* She could see the intense way Caleb studied Wren and the she was anything but stupid. She needed to find out the true nature of their so-called relationship, so she planned to ask him the first chance she got. "Is there any area of Denver notorious for the best shops?"

"If I remember correctly, I think Cherry Creek has a couple of big stores. Honestly, I just need a simple black dress. I'm not really in the mood to spend hours at it."

"I adore shopping." Macy yawned, putting an elegant hand to her mouth, her vibrant red nails perfectly manicured. "And what else are we going to do, anyway? As Caleb said, the funeral isn't until Monday, and Jonesy has everything arranged."

Caleb glanced at his watch then stood up, holding his hand out to Macy. The conversation was giving him a headache. Macy's lack of sensitivity was grating on him, and he could tell it made Wren uncomfortable, too.

"It's getting late, Macy. Why don't you head on off to bed?"

"Aren't you coming?" she asked innocently as she placed her hand in his and he pulled her up.

Caleb's mouth pressed into a firm line. He hated games and this was definitely a game. Given she had her own room and he'd already told her he wouldn't be joining her. The comment was solely to stake her claim on him for Wren's benefit.

Wren stood and smoothed down the denim covering her thighs, preparing to say goodnight and go to upstairs to her room.

Caleb shook his head, then leaned in and placed a short kiss on the outside of Macy's mouth. "No. I'm taking Wren to the kitchen to get her something to eat. She missed dinner, remember?"

Macy opened her mouth to speak, but Caleb directed his words to Wren before Macy could respond.

"Jonesy made a plate for you. You have to be starving."

Wren was hungry, but more that that, she wanted a moment or two alone with Caleb.

"Yes. I didn't want to impose by asking."

Caleb frowned, shaking his head incredulously. "This is your house, too, goof. Come on."

When they left the room that was off the foyer and staircase he nodded in the direction of the kitchen and said goodnight to Macy a final time. Macy didn't look pleased, but if she didn't want to make a scene, she had no choice but to turn and walk down the long hall to the other end of the big house. No doubt an unpleasant confrontation was in front of him, but Caleb wanted to spend some time with Wren. Alone.

"Ready?" Caleb nodded in the direction of the kitchen, and they walked side-by-side in silence. Caleb set his almost empty wine glass on the marble countertop of the freestanding island and then opened the refrigerator.

There was a covered plate containing juicy roast beef and perfectly mashed potatoes. The smell made Caleb hungry all over again. The large plate was accompanied by two smaller ones, which he knew would contain salad, and a slice of the delicious strawberry cake. When the roast beef and potatoes were warming in the microwave, he returned to set the smaller two in front of Wren.

She was studying him as he removed the coverings from the plates.

He felt her eyes watch every movement he made, as if her long, slender fingers were touching his skin. He could literally feel her. Not much had changed, in that regard. He was overtly aware of her at all times.

When the steaming roast beef was sitting in front of her, she spoke. "This looks amazing, and it smells delicious."

Caleb nodded. "Good old Jonesy. There's strawberry cake. Your favorite."

"Yes. She's amazing. I've missed her."

"Me, too." *Have you missed me, too?* He wanted to ask.

Now that they were alone, words were harder to find. Even though there was much to say, the years and distance, combined with their last painful argument hung between them.

Caleb opened a drawer and handed Wren a fork, then grabbed the unopened bottle of red wine sitting on the counter. He took the corkscrew that had been sitting next to it and made short work of opening it.

Wren had forgotten her wine glass in the library, so he pulled another down from the cupboard and filled it, and then added some of the rich red liquid to his own. He glanced up at Wren who was just beginning to slowly fork up some of the mashed potatoes.

"Caleb—" Wren began hesitantly. "I'm sorry about earlier."

He sat down across from her, his brow knitting as he contemplated her words. "What for?"

"Well, interrupting you and Macy, sleeping through dinner. And, about your dad."

Their eyes met and locked. "Nothing to be sorry for."

"Nothing?" she asked softly, needing the reassurance only Caleb could give.

He knew she didn't mean for what happened tonight. She was talking about surprising him with Sam to San Francisco. "No. What happened was my fault. I should have done as you asked."

Wren's throat tightened involuntarily. There was so much to clear up between them and she wanted all of their misunderstandings and missteps to magically disappear, but she knew it wouldn't be that easy. She opened her mouth to ask him to elaborate, but didn't get the words out in time.

"Why aren't you eating?" Caleb took a drink from his wine, leaning back in his chair. "Aren't you hungry anymore?"

"Yes, I guess; but I hate eating alone. Do you want some?" The corner of her mouth lifted in the start of a smile. They needed to talk it all out, but she just wanted things to fall back into the easy way they used to be, first.

"Remember the first time I found you hiding under this table?" He huffed out a small laugh. "God, you were so different, then."

"We both were, I think."

Caleb stood and went to get another fork, then sat in the chair next to Wren's. He dug his fork into her food when she shoved the plate a little closer to him. "That's true. I was a punk."

He was sitting so close she could feel the heat radiating

between them, emanating a small healing that Wren soaked up like parched earth in the rain.

She laughed softly. He was right, he was, but his toughness was part of what she loved about him. "You had a little chip on your shoulder, maybe. Macy seems nice. Have you known each other long?" She finally took a bite of the delicious food at the same time as Caleb did.

"A few months." Caleb shrugged off the question, but Wren had to acknowledge that if Macy was here, in Denver, with him, then it had to be more serious than he was letting on. "Sorry she was so nosy. I haven't told her that much about you, so naturally, she's curious."

Wren hated the way she had to search for things to say. They hadn't spoken since the phone call on her birthday, and Wren found herself struggling. She wanted to blurt out that she was sorry for bringing Sam to San Francisco, that she knew he remembered their night together, and so much more.

"I understand."

They fell silent for a minute or two, both of them eating from the same plates, leaning toward each other, eyes meeting for a brief second once or twice. It was nice, and some of the strain between them melted away.

When she pulled the cake toward her and took one bite, her eyes sparkled at him. "Go on. Help me. You know I can't eat all of this."

Caleb chuckled softly. "If you insist." He dug in with her.

When she'd had enough, Wren reached out to touch him, her fingers wrapping around his left wrist, causing him to pause.

"Are you okay, Cale?" Her blue eyes searched his. "I mean, really?"

"Yeah, sure." One shoulder lifted in a half-assed shrug. "Sorry about before."

Wren shook her head. "You don't have to be sorry with me." *Hasn't our history taught you that?* Her mind screamed with all they'd been through and all he meant to her. "You're obviously hurting. Hatred is as fragile as love... isn't it?" Her soft words, though soft, held the hit of a hammer.

Caleb set down his fork, and turned his hand so his fingers could close around hers, and nodded. "How'd you get so smart?" His eyes glassed over and he swallowed hard. "I just wish I'd known the whole story, before."

"I don't think you were ready to listen." Their faces close as they both leaned on the tabletop, the situation intimate, and their voices low.

"Probably not."

Wren knew him better than he knew himself. So much, it sliced right through him.

"What about now? Do you know how he felt?" Her eyes were soft and imploring, her voice sweet and searching.

"Do you?" Caleb asked, his brows elevating a bit. How much had his father told her when he'd refused to listen?

She nodded slightly, leaning on her arm, her eyes never leaving his handsome face. It was easy to see how exhausted he was. His hair was shorter, but he was still the same beautiful, golden Caleb. His arms, shoulders, and chest were bigger; his legs stronger; his presence even more intimidating, if that were possible. Her heart stopped in her chest at his strength and good looks.

"A little, I suppose. Don't be angry with him. He told me about your mother, and how much he loved her. I know he loved you, too, Cale. He wasn't great at expressing his feelings, that's for sure; but he only married my mom so you wouldn't be alone. He knew he wasn't present in your life and... well, I'm really thankful he did, Caleb." Wren's voice caught and a tear tumbled down her dewy cheek. "I only wish he could have told you some of this when he was alive."

"How long have you known?" He backed up a little, angry that she would keep something like this from him.

"Last year. His health was failing, and I think he knew he wasn't going to be around for long."

"Why didn't you tell me?"

Wren could feel him emotionally pulling away and she reached out again, this time holding his hand. "I should have. I know that, but I was afraid of hurting you, and we had issues of our own to clear up, first. We still do."

"I know we do."

"I was hoping we could talk while I'm here."

"Me, too." His fingers closed around hers and squeezed slightly.

"But, with Macy here—"

Caleb huffed impatiently. "We'll have time," he promised. "I'll *make* time, Wren."

He wanted to get this thing with his dad and the estate out of the way first, unwilling to let it influence any personal conversations that were in front of them.

He pulled the letter from his back pocket, pain welling up

inside his chest. In another life, he would have gotten angry and disputed anything good anyone would have said about Edison Luxon, but not tonight. Not after... the letter and his time with Wren.

"All this time, I've blamed him for everything, but now—" He stopped and leaned back, breaking their connection, and used that hand to rub the back of his neck, then reached back and pulled out the letter. "I'm not so certain." He held it out to her. "Read it."

Wren hesitated to take it from him. "Are you sure?"

"Yeah." He set it down in front of her and pushed his chair away from the table and scrubbed his face with both hands. "I want you to read it."

Given the lateness of the hour, Caleb hadn't turned on the recessed fixtures and the only light was from a small one over the sink and the moonlight streaming in from outside. It cast a low blue glow through the multi-paned windows: each with an ornamental arched pane at the top. They framed a curved alcove that bowed out and created the quaint nook where the kitchen table sat and added elegance to the space.

The house was quiet and Wren could sense Caleb's apprehension as she reached for the paper and unfolded it, unsure if she should read it to herself or so he could hear her.

"Do you want me to read it out loud?" she began, glancing up to gauge Caleb's reaction.

Caleb shook his head. "I've already read it," he said shortly, with a shake of his head. He was feeling uncharacteristically emotional, and he didn't need, or want, to get sappy in front of Wren. "I don't need to hear it again."

"Okay."

Caleb moved away from her to pace slowly around the kitchen, finally stopping to lean his hip against the granite countertop on the opposite side. He studied her features as she read his father's words. Her face took on a pained expression and a tear tumbled from one eye, then the one from the other. She used one hand to wipe them from her cheeks. She closed her eyes and small cry broke from her. "I'm so sorry, Cale."

"How much did you know?"

Wren shook her head, and looked up into Caleb's face, her eyes sad. "Only that he had major regret about his lack of relationship with you and he missed you. I think he struggled for a long time, but was unsure how to reach out to you in a way that you would respond to. He should have tried harder."

Caleb's mind flashed to the drawer full of letters sitting in his apartment in San Francisco. "He did. He tried for years." Caleb stopped to look out the window, his face hard, and a muscle working overtime in his jaw. "I was a prick. He sent a bunch of letters, but I never read them," he bit out. "Never opened any of them. I figured it was just money and I wasn't going to help him assuage his conscience by taking cash."

Wren felt her heart break, his sadness palpable; as if it were her own. She knew he couldn't change anything and beating himself up wouldn't help.

"He wouldn't want you to blame yourself, Cale. He wasn't an easy man to read. He was the adult, and you were a young boy who lost his mother. He knew how much she meant to you, and how much you must have suffered."

Caleb's muscled frame was rigid and as Wren looked at

him, she studied his profile, and could feel his coiled tension. The fingers in his right hand curled into a fist. "I was so mad. So many times, I wished he'd been the one to die." His voice was full of pain, as the words tore from him. "I fucking hated him with every breath I took. You saw how much."

Wren nodded, though he didn't see her acquiescence. She knew what he went through growing up when they had formed an affable alliance against their parents. She hated her mother at least as much as Caleb hated his father and she understood his anger and pain; then the apathy that became a welcome alternative. They'd been unlikely allies against a common enemy.

"Maybe I deserved his indifference."

Wren got up and went to Caleb, standing behind him as he stood still as stone, and staring out the window. Her heart ached with love and grief for Caleb. She wanted to touch him; to offer reassurance, to take away the ache in his voice and heart. Without considering her actions, her arms slipped around his waist and she pressed up against his strong back and leaned her head against him, between his shoulder blades.

Caleb was massive in comparison to her, and she was like a flower curling around him. Her hands fanned out against his hard stomach, her fingers finding the definition of his abs beneath his shirt. "Stop, Cale. I won't let you do this to yourself. Your dad wouldn't want that. None of it was your fault." Her arms slid fully around him and held him tight against her body. "I can't bear it. You've had enough pain. Enough."

Caleb sucked in a deep breath, the action bringing her even closer. He could feel every curve of her body pressed so closely against his back. He could feel her breathing, could feel how she shared his pain. His hand came up and he ran the flat of his hand from her elbow down to her hand, and then wrapped his fingers around hers.

"When did you turn into the strong one?"

Wren's arms tightened around him. "When I met you. "

"Oh, Wren." Should he just spill his guts? Would it fix everything? "I've got so much to say to you. How long can you stay?"

She nodded against him, unwilling to end the contact between their bodies; needing the closeness as much as he did.

He wanted to apologize for how he acted the last time he'd seen her, he wanted to say a hundred things... he needed her forgiveness.

"How long do you need me?"

In that moment a miracle happened; a sort of beautiful irony that taunted Caleb with its fragileness. It was as if he'd never screwed everything up between them. But would it stay this way?

How long do I need you? Caleb thought. His heart raced to the point of exploding, and he wondered if Wren could feel it.

Forever.

chapter
EIGHT

Aᴛᴇʀ sᴀʏɪɴɢ ɢᴏᴏᴅɴɪɢʜᴛ ᴛᴏ Wʀᴇɴ forty minutes earlier, Caleb discarded his shirt, and unbuttoned his jeans, leaving them on and throwing himself on his big bed. Lying back, he stared at the ceiling with one arm bent so his hand rested between underneath his head. His mind was working overtime, bombarded with thoughts of Wren. He thought talking to her would help come to a decision regarding the will, but the conversation hadn't moved deep enough.

Part of him didn't want to know much about her life, and part of him wanted to know every damn thing. How could he make this decision without her? "Uhhhhhgggg!" He groaned into the empty room, his fist clenching into the comforter.

Obviously, she loved touring with her ballet company, but sharing Lux with her would mean she would want for nothing throughout her whole life. As much as Caleb hated thinking about it, he had to consider that money could bring out money-grubbers. Given her experience with Veronica, surely, Wren would recognize men with ulterior motives, but Caleb wondered if being wealthy would ruin her chances at real love.

He felt sick inside at the thought. Regardless of how it would grate on him, he wanted her to have a happy life. No matter what that was or who she ended up with. Wren deserved someone to worship and adore her. Caleb sighed heavily, the sound filling the silence of the room.

He needed to clarify a few things with Jonathan before he could make the decision. Would splitting the estate mean Wren would have to stop dancing completely or could they let the board of directors run the company and go about their respective lives? Was that what Caleb wanted?

His father's entire orchestration of this was to create a situation where he and Wren would be in constant contact. Caleb knew it, but he didn't want to be selfish and just follow his heart. He had to do what was best for her. But what was that?

"Fuck!" He spat, and then ran his hand over his face in agitated impatience. He still wasn't sure what to do. Seeing Wren had stirred something deep inside of him, though he knew he had no right to feel that way. He'd let her down twice over the years, and her reaction earlier in his father's study was more than he'd deserved or expected. He should have known she'd be loving and supportive despite everything; that's who she was: who she'd always been. Too bad he went and fucked it all up. And, then made it worse.

The room was pitch black, and so quiet. He could hear the

soft whir of the heat blowing in through the vents, and feel his own heart beating in his chest. Suddenly, Caleb heard a loud noise from the other room that made him sit straight up.

"Wren?" he called out softly.

A few seconds later a shadowing figure appeared in the doorway and the room was suddenly flooded with light as Macy threw the switch, and Caleb was momentarily blinded.

"Wren? What the hell, Caleb? What exactly is she to you and why are you expecting her to creep into your room?"

Even as he blinked at the sudden and unwelcome brightness, Caleb could feel heat rushing up his neck and into his face. Macy had effectively caught him thinking about Wren, and she knew it. He scowled at the woman standing over his bed.

Macy's face wore an angry expression, her dark hair swinging around her shoulders as she walked around to the other side of the bed. She glared at him as she stood there in a slinky chemise.

Caleb scooted to the edge of the bed, stood up and brushed past her. "My relationship with Wren is none of your business." When Macy opened her mouth to protest but he continued. "You and I are dating, Macy. That's all. You have no right to make demands of me. Jesus Christ! My father just died! Wren was close to him and she's hurting, too."

"Yeah, I saw that earlier," Macy retorted sarcastically. "Didn't look like Edison was who she was close to."

He walked into the other room, his intent to get a stiff drink from the bar in the entertainment room. He reached into the refrigerator situated behind the bar for a beer, when he heard her footsteps behind him. Macy followed him and stood there in awkward silence, watching his every move.

"I thought I made it clear that we weren't going to share a room here." He had serious doubts he'd ever share a room with her again, given his current state of antagonistic indifference toward her. What the hell did she think?

"I know, Caleb. I'm sorry." Realizing her mistake, Macy's voice turned low and pleading. Caleb could hear the slightest tremble in her words. "I just wanted to comfort you."

Awesome, his mind reeled as he lifted the long neck bottle to his lips and took a long pull. That was just what he needed; to feel guilty on top of everything else. He turned to face her, but remained behind the bar. "I don't need comfort, and I don't want sex."

"You certainly looked like you needed comfort from Wren earlier."

Caleb's head made an almost imperceptible shake, anger welling up inside him.

"We have a history. She's the only person who understa—" He stopped and changed his words. There was no way he was going to spill such personal memories. "Look, I'll deal with the estate and then see where we are."

The light from his room filtered down through the hallway, and those from the deck and backyard shone in through the windows. His head hurt and he didn't want to turn on more lights, but he didn't want Macy to think he had any type of romantic intentions, either.

"Where are we, Caleb?" She shook her head and folded her arms across her chest. She wasn't crying, but she wasn't happy. Her face said it all, even in the dimness of the room.

"No clue," he said without hesitation. "I might have to stay in Denver for a while. The start-up may have to take a backseat until I get my head around everything." He took another drink, draining half the bottle.

"But, this inheritance is the answer, Caleb. You'll sell everything then have more than enough money to start your firm. It solves everything. Right?"

Caleb was shirtless as he stood there, tall, cut, and unmoving until he set his empty bottle down and bent to get another beer from the fridge. Her words should have been expected, but he was still surprised. "Don't you want to do your job, now?" he asked, unable to keep the slight tinge of sarcasm from his tone.

Macy walked toward him and leaned on the bar, her eyes dark and imploring. "That's not what I meant. The design firm is your dream. Now you can have it without owing anyone. That's all."

He ran a hand through his mop of hair. It was short on the sides and the back, but the top was longer. "No, that's not all. Not even close."

Caleb backed up to lean on counter by the sink of the wet bar. He wanted to keep the Italian marble bar top, that Macy was almost sprawled across, between them. She shook her head and shrugged slightly. "Then, what?" she asked, until it dawned on her, incredulity showing on her pretty face. "You have to take care of your little sister? Is that it?"

Caleb huffed angrily. "Wren is not my *sister*. How many times do I have to fucking say it?"

"But, it has to do with her, doesn't it." Macy stated. It had to be some sort of misguided loyalty Caleb felt for the young woman. "Like how?"

Caleb struggled with how much he was willing to share with Macy. He'd already settled that it was none of her business, but maybe he could tell her just enough so she'd stop pressing him about Wren and back off long enough so he could get her out of town while he dealt with things. "Like, she gets part of it, and there's a clause that states we can't sell for five years." He silently hoped the five years would be the dealbreaker he needed.

Macy let out her breath, her eyes wide. "Wow, that sucks. Your dad really was a prick."

Caleb considered his next words carefully. They were only partially true, but Macy was smart and she wouldn't just take a placating answer designed to shut her up so he could move to the next subject. "I worry that my step-hag will show up. I know her and she'll descend and lay in wait like a vulture after a kill. I've always protected Wren from—well, let's just say, I've always protected her."

"Always protected her, why? Living here? In the lap of luxury, what could she possibly need protection from?"

"That's not my story to tell."

Macy moved slowly around the end of the bar, intent on getting closer to Caleb. When she was a couple of feet away, her arm snaked out and she ran the fingers of her right hand down the hard contours of his stomach. He was so effing delicious: his shoulders and arms were strong and defined, his stomach flat, but ripped, the six pack and V made her fingers itch to touch him. She'd want him even if he wasn't gorgeous, but it was a bonus.

Caleb's hand closed around her wrist to stop her descent to the open waistband of his jeans, and at the same time spoke softly. "I'd appreciate it if you'd keep this quiet. I don't want Wren to know that I already know what's in the will." He moved around her without touching her, leaving her to stand there blankly watching him move away.

She could sense a new distance between them and she damn sure knew the reason why. It wouldn't do. It wouldn't do at all. Something had to give. She had to figure out how to get rid of that little ballerina bitch, and fast.

"I'm exhausted. I'll see you in the morning," Caleb said flatly.

With that, he disappeared into the hall, the light to his room went out, and she heard the door to his room close with a click. It was like a thunderclap in the silence.

"Uh uh," she said softly to herself as she walked up the stairs and deciding to take a little exploratory trip through the house in search of Wren's room. If she didn't get a chance to talk to her alone on their little shopping trip tomorrow, she'd just have to figure out a way to get her alone at some point. She needed to know Wren's intentions and feelings for Caleb before she could figure out how to deal with her.

"No little dancing orphan is going to ruin the future I have planned for us, Caleb Luxon. Especially, not now. No way in hell."

***

IT WAS NO WONDER THAT Wren couldn't sleep.

It could have been her long nap and the jet lag, but it was also because she was haunted by the events of the evening. She dug out some of her old dance clothes from one of the drawers in her mahogany dresser: a leotard, tights, and a short chiffon wrap skirt that tied around her waist. She slipped on a pair of pale pink ballet slippers; thinking a good workout was just what her body needed. Ballet could help ease tension and clear her mind.

Given the lateness of the hour, she kept the music and the lights low. She'd decided on contemporary, rather than classical music, as she often did when she was dancing just for herself. The stereo speakers were excellent, and on her way to turn on the music, she passed by the vanity that matched the rest of the furniture in the room.

The only pointe shoes she had here were the first ones she'd ever owned, and they were very well used. Caleb had bought them for her years ago and they were beat up so bad they offered little support anymore; the fabric was peeling away from the tips to expose the hard structure beneath. Despite their condition, Wren couldn't bear to throw them out; they might was well have been made of gold. Untouched for years, they hung by their ribbons over the corner of the mirror in a position of honor and memory. She made a mental note to take them with her when she traveled back to New York.

With Edison gone, it wasn't likely she'd be visiting very often. Depending on what Caleb's plans were, she had no idea if he'd even keep this house. Sadness flooded through her at the thought of never being in this house again. There were some hard times within these walls, but it held so many great memories, too. Her heart skipped a beat as she ran a hand lovingly over the ripped and frayed satin of the shoes she treasured as if they were the Hope Diamond.

She remembered when Caleb had surprised her by taking her to a dance studio in one of the northern suburbs the day after her fifteenth birthday. She could see it play out in her mind as if it were happening right then and there.

His face had been bruised and his lower lip split from the fight he'd fought the night before. It had been a few months since she'd stopped dressing in her disguise, and he had made sure he was with her whenever Veronica was around.

With Jonesy's help, the two of them had been able to keep pretty good track of the modeling shoots, promotional trips or vacations that Veronica went on with Edison, and Caleb kept a handwritten note in his front right jean pocket. They began to look forward to the freedom they gained when their parents were gone. Caleb made Wren a priority whether they were in town or not.

Wren's eyes started to burn, and her throat ached.

He'd been so diligent in his efforts to keep her safe at home and at school. Her mother had been less cruel once Caleb warned her off, however she still kept Wren from dancing, which was the only thing she wanted in the world. Forbidding her daughter from taking classes was her one last avenue of torture.

When they pulled up to the outside, she was excited to see where there were.

"Cale, what are we doing here?"

"You like to dance, don't ya?" he asked with a lopsided grin.

It was a cold March day and he'd stolen the keys to Veronica's Mercedes. When he'd shown up after school in it, she wasn't even afraid of her mother's wrath because she was with Caleb; hesitating a mere three seconds before sliding into the luxurious leather seats.

"Yes!" Wren was giddy with happiness. "But—"

"But nothing! Come on." Caleb had been almost as excited as she was.

He took her hand and pulled her with him across the parking lot; toward the studio, then in through the door. The smell of the sweat, rosin, and wood assaulted her nostrils and brought back many happy memories of when she was very young. Her face almost hurt from the big smile she couldn't quell.

"May I help you?" A young woman, with her dark hair scraped back in a tight bun and dressed in a leotard, had asked from behind the front counter.

"Yeah. I'm Caleb Luxon. I called last week. About the lessons?"

Joy filled every cell of Wren's body at the words, though she was uncertain they'd be able to carry it off or how she'd afford it. She was certain she wouldn't be allowed to continue, though she would be satisfied with just an afternoon on the wood.

The woman's face twisted wryly and she smiled. "For you?" Her eyes skated over Caleb's face, handsome, even though he was injured.

He laughed. "No. I spoke to Emily Mason about lessons for Wren Brashill."

The girl's expression changed, as recognition dawned on her. "Oh, yes. Emily told me you'd be coming by today. She's teaching a class until 4:30, but instructed me to help Wren get the paperwork filled out."

The woman handed Wren a clipboard with a form on it and a pen attached, but she hesitated to take it. "Cale, I can't." She shook her head adamantly.

He put one arm around Wren, took the clipboard from the receptionist with the other, and turned her toward the waiting room in one motion, speaking in low tones right by her ear. "Yeah, you can. I'll handle the hag-a-saurus."

"But—"

Caleb nodded toward a chair, indicating that she should sit down, and then handed her the clipboard when she did. She looked up at him, towering over her. Even in a heavy leather jacket with his hair flopping boyishly over his forehead, he looked tough as hell, his vibrant blue eyes piercing. "Come on. You're doing this." His expression was adamant and she started to hope it was possible.

"How will I get here?"

Caleb's mouth thinned in frustration and he rolled his eyes. "Wren, will you have a little faith? I got this." Their eyes locked and his lips lifted in a sly smile. "Fill that thing out, but put down my cell number, not your mom's. You just hafta trust me."

And she did. She trusted Caleb more than anyone in the world. She put the pen to the paper.

"You'll be required to pay for the first month and the registration fee, up front," the counter girl mentioned.

Caleb turned back toward the counter, pulling a wad of cash out of his coat pocket. "Like I said when I called, she's more like a professional. She needs the real good lessons. Advanced stuff."

"Caleb," Wren called and shook her head. His pride showed and while it made her heart soar, she was embarrassed at the look the other girl threw at her.

"We have a package for nine to twelve hours a week; then she can take whatever classes she wants. However, to get that deal she'll need to sign up for the year. Perhaps all day on Saturday, then a couple of nights a week?"

Caleb started peeling off bills one-by-one. "Cool. How much?"

Wren's eyes widened when the girl told him the tuition and without flinching he simply handed over the cash. How would he afford nearly five hundred dollars a month? His father was rich, but Caleb was barely seventeen and his dad didn't give him that kind of pocket change.

When Wren was finished filling out the paperwork, the girl handed her a sheet of required attire and shoes she'd need. "You can get the things you need in our shop. For advanced classes, you'll need a good pair of pointe shoes, as well as slippers, lyrical, toeless lyrical, and jazz. Plus, a good selection of leotards, tights and skirts."

Wren's cheeks filled with heat. She couldn't afford all of that and anything she had from her previous years dancing didn't fit her anymore.

"Sure. Thanks," Caleb said to the girl. "What about shows?"

"Shows? Oh, you mean recitals?"

"Yeah. Recitals." He nodded.

"Twice a year in June and November, and costumes will need to be purchased in advance for each of her numbers."

"Awesome. I can't wait to see them." He smiled at the girl, then down at Wren. He grabbed her hand and proceeded to pull her into the shop.

It was loaded with beautiful costumes, as well as many styles of dance apparel. Some were less adorned and relied on the cut for the style. Her eyes searched for the most basic, and she picked up a price tag.

"Cale, this is sweet of you, but it's too expensive."

"Shhh," he ordered, taking the list out of Wren's hand and giving it over to the clerk. She was a very thin older lady with steel grey hair, who looked exactly what Wren imagined a prima ballerina to look when her career was over and she was getting on in years. Still graceful, hair still wound in the tight bun, still beautiful and elegant. "We need everything on this list. The good stuff," Caleb told her.

"Caleb you don't realize how much that will cost. Just a couple of the basics will be fine."

She wandered forward, unable to help herself. She looked through the pretty things with longing; not because of the price of the allure of the expense or quality of the items, but because of what they represented. It has been so long since she'd been able to dance. She was drawn to the round table circled with various ballet shoes and slippers, she reached *out to ghost her fingers longingly over the soft pink satin of a pair Russian pointe shoes.*

"Yeah. Let's see." Caleb pulled out the cash he had left and preceded to count it, and then took the few steps needed to reach the shop clerk and stopped in front of her. "I have eight hundred on me. So whatever we can get with that, today."

Wren turned abruptly. "Cale! Oh, my gosh! That's too much."

Caleb ignored her. "Start with those pink things she was just looking at."

"What size?" the woman asked with a smile.

Caleb walked up behind Wren and took the shoe from her, turned it over, and looked at the sole, and then inside, examining it thoroughly. "I always wondered how these things worked." He tapped one toe on the table and it made hollow sound. His eyes widened. "You actually wear these things? They must be torture. I'd rather take a fist in the face," he teased, then nudged her shoulder with his. "What size, Bird?"

Wren laughed softly, though her heart was full to bursting that he'd want to do this for her and pay for it with his fight club money. "It's still too much, Caleb."

"Size?" he persisted.

"Six."

Caleb turned to the woman with a brilliant grin and repeated it. "Six it is!"

When the lady disappeared into the back room to gather the shoes in the appropriate size, Caleb spoke; a laugh lacing his voice. "You deserve it. I'll just have to beat the shit out of a couple more guys every week. Not a big deal."

A huge smile broke out on her face and she hugged him tight, reveling the feel of the strong arms he wound around her. He lifted her off the ground as if she weighed nothing.

"Thank you, Cale. You take such good care of me. No one has ever made me feel this special." She turned her face, kissed his cheek and buried her face in his neck.

"You are special."

When the woman brought out the shoes and some toe pads, Caleb knelt in front of her to help her try them on. She felt like Cinderella at the ball. It didn't matter that he fumbled with the ribbons and got confused because there was nothing to distinguish one shoe from the other.

He looked up at her wryly. "What the hell?" he asked perplexed. "Which is the right?"

Wren giggled and took over. "They're both the same. Until you wear them awhile and they form to your feet."

His lips lifted in a soft smile. "Oh, no wonder." He lifted her right foot and fumbled to slide one on. His fingers were gentle as they grazed her skin when he wound the ribbons around and around her ankle. His awkwardness and lack of ability to tie them properly were utterly endearing to Wren. He represented such juxtaposition: tough guy trying to tie pointe shoes with his big bandaged hands. He was so cute she couldn't stand it.

It was the very moment when she fell madly in love with him.

What more could a girl want? Prince Charming buying her shoes with money he'd taken a beating for.

Amazing.

That's the word her mind always chose when she thought of Caleb.

Her eyes welled with tears as she went to the ballet barre in front of the mirrored wall on the east side of the studio room, and lifted her leg to put her right heel over the barre. Her left foot fell into turnout as one arm rose gracefully above her head and her posture lengthened. Wren's hands and body naturally assumed ballet pull up and heart forward position from her years of practice. With her neck long, fingers and arms poised, she bent at her waist, her left arm reaching toward her right foot as she stretched.

She'd been with her company less than a week prior and her body was still nimble, and she moved through the standard warm-up moves their Ballet Master put them through before every practice or performance.

Finished with her stretching and warm-up, Wren began to dance in the middle of the hardwood floor, letting the soft and gentle music overtake her. The lyrics about love and loss caused emotion to well up inside and overtake her in such a way that the rises and falls in the music dictated her steps. With practiced precision and flawless technique, she performed a series of Arabesques, Chasse's, extensions, Jete's and Fouette' turns, not even aware of her movements.

When the song ended, Wren was startled by the sound of clapping coming from the doorway of her studio. Her heart lurched and her head snapped around to find Macy lurking there. The woman would have had to walk through her bedroom uninvited to watch her dance.

Wren's breath left her body and her hand went to her cover her heart. "You scared me, Macy."

The dark-haired woman straightened from where she was leaning on the door jam to walk into the studio. "Sorry," she said casually. "This is some set-up."

Wren walked quickly to the other side of the room to turn off the music, and Macy took note of the way she walked. The way her knees and toes turned out from her hips screamed ballerina and Macy wondered if she always walked like that.

Wren was nervous about being intruded upon during such a private moment. She used shutting off the music as an excuse to turn her back and brush the tears from her cheeks.

"Yes, I've always loved it. Edison had it done for me after Caleb went off to college. He was very generous."

"I can see that." Macy looked around and peered through the adjacent door that led into Wren's bedroom. "A little dancing suite, all your own. How convenient."

Wren grabbed a small towel and made the pretense of wiping the back of her neck and face. It was strange having Macy sneaking around the house and watching her dance in silence. It felt creepy and awkward.

"I couldn't sleep. The jet lag and the long nap before must have done a number on me."

Macy went into Wren's bedroom to continue snooping, and Wren could do nothing else but follow her through the doorway to watch her casually inspect the room and pick up odds and ends; examining everything.

Macy was a good 5 inches taller than Wren, but she wasn't intimidated.

"Macy, can I help you with something?" Wren asked hesitantly, lifting first one foot, then the other, to peel off the ballet slippers.

Macy turned to look at Wren. "I couldn't sleep either. Caleb seems to think we can't do the nasty in this house, and I'm not used to sleeping without him."

"Oh." Wren's cheeks and neck began to flush uncomfortably. That was a little more information than she wanted. "Well, it was his father's house. And, I'm sure he's not himself, considering his reason for being here." She went to a drawer and took out an oversized sweatshirt that Caleb had sent her from MIT. She pulled it over her head, and shoved her arms into the sleeves. She'd often worn it over her leotard after a workout because it made her feel closer to him while he was in Massachusetts.

"MIT, huh? Caleb's?" Macy sat on the end of the queen size bed and watched Wren untie the skirt and lay it over the back of the chair at her vanity.

Wren flushed at Macy's correct assumption, but she was starting to get angry. The line of uncomfortable questions coupled with the intrusion, were starting to wear on her. "He sent it to me while he was away at school. It was new."

"I see." Macy's eyes narrowed. "I think we should have a little chat." She patted the bed, as if it were her right to invite Wren to sit down in her own room. "I'll tell you all about me and Caleb, and you tell me all about your relationship with him."

"Um..." Wren's delicate fingers flitted over the top sheer chiffon on the back of the chair. She struggled with whether she should tell her to get the hell out, or be casual and get this out of the way. It was inevitable, given the way Caleb had melted into her in front of Macy, earlier. "I'm not sure what you want to know."

Wren didn't think she wanted to know anything at all about Caleb and Macy, nor could she tell her very much about her own relationship with him. He wouldn't want it either, in any case. "Caleb doesn't really like people talking about his business."

"Aw, come on; it's me and you. We're the two women in his life. Surely the rules don't apply to us."

Wren's well manicured brows shot up, but she went to the head of her bed, pulled down the covers and crawled under them, situating herself against the pillows and pulling another onto her lap. It was silly, but it was a barrier between Macy and herself and she needed it, no matter how frivolous.

When Wren didn't volunteer anything, Macy launched into a set of questions. "How long have you lived in this house?"

"I was thirteen when Caleb's father married my mom."

"Where is she? Your mother?"

"She lives in California now. They were divorced just after I turned eighteen."

Macy turned more toward Wren, pulling one leg underneath her. She was wearing a pair of satin shorts and a matching cropped chemise and showed a lot of cleavage between her large breasts.

"Hmmm. I gather you and Caleb are close, or you wouldn't be here. Close for step-siblings, I mean."

Wren still wasn't sleepy, even though it was getting close

to 2 AM. "Caleb represents many things to me; the least of which is my stepbrother. My life before I came to live here wasn't good. My mother was really mean and after a while, Caleb became my friend. He wasn't afraid of her like I was, and he kept her away from me. He's very protective."

Macy nodded. "I can see that. Caleb's toughness is what attracted me to him, too. He's got this bad boy thing going on underneath all that yumminess, even when he wears a suit. But it's not just his body."

"Right. It's his attitude. He's always 'in charge'. He's always been that way." Wren stopped short. How much had Caleb shared about his relationship with his dad? She didn't want to say anything he wanted kept private. "I feel bad for him. The company and the estate will be a lot to manage."

"Yes. It's too bad his father was such a bastard to him," Macy said flatly. "But, at least Caleb has money now. When you were having dinner, did he tell you about the design firm he wants to start? It's his dream. At least, it was before this."

"No, we didn't talk about that yet. There will be plenty of time."

Macy's eyes widened and she blinked once. "Maybe not. I think he'll just put everything on the market and get back to life in San Francisco. At least I hope so. I couldn't stand living this far from the ocean."

"I love New York, but Colorado is so beautiful, especially in winter. I miss it."

"Yuck!" Macy spat in disgust. "I hate snow and slush. Nope, I'm hoping we'll be catching a flight Monday night, right after the will is read."

Wren bit her lower lip. "Do you know that for sure?"

"I know Caleb, and he hates this house and the memories it represents."

Wren's heart fell but she hid it well, though her hand shook a little as she pulled her comforter closer. The memories here with Caleb meant everything to her and it hurt to hear he detested them.

"I've used Lux cosmetics my entire life. Ironic, isn't it? Small world, I guess." Macy smiled but it seemed like more of a sneer to Wren. She certainly lacked any real warmth and didn't seem concerned for Caleb at all. That was the root of Wren's dislike of this woman. She tried to push it down, but Macy's arrogance was on the verge of obnoxious.

Wren turned onto her side and snuggled down into the covers, hoping Macy would get the hint and leave. Macy pointed to Wren's locket, which had fallen out of the neck of the sweatshirt when Wren moved to her side. "Isn't that the Lux logo? It looks familiar."

Wren's hand went to cover the precious gold and diamonds protectively, and she quickly shoved it back inside the shirt, not wanting Macy to see the photos of Caleb hidden beneath the swinging gate. The locket was the template for the Lux logo; the filigree rectangle nestled up to the "L".

She could lie about it, and maybe she should. If she told the truth, she'd have to tell the whole story attached to it, and she wasn't up for it, and selfishly, she didn't want Macy to know. Ever.

"I'm really tired, Macy. Can we continue this talk tomorrow while we shop? Visitation is tomorrow afternoon, so I'll want to go right when the stores open."

Macy smiled and to Wren's eyes, it seemed to be genuine. "Of course. Listen, I don't have any sisters, so I'd really like us to be close. I'll need a maid of honor very soon, I think!"

Wren was caught off guard and she stifled a small gasp, but tried to hide her surprise and the deep pain that sliced right through her heart. Caleb was that serious about Macy? "Uh..." she stammered and forced a smile, trying to cover. "Sure. That's very sweet of you."

Macy stood and walked toward the door of Wren's bedroom. "Nighty night."

When the door closed, Wren reached over and shut off the lamp. Maybe the darkness would be better at hiding her misery. She squeezed her eyes shut, as tears squeezed out from behind her lids. Her chest began to seize in pain. When Caleb had issues with her dating Sam, it led to a small thread of hope that maybe he had hidden feelings for her, as she had for him. But now, with Macy's declaration, it was lost.

Wren turned her face into her pillow and held it close, praying as she started sobbing, that no one would hear. The best thing she could do was to get through the funeral and get back to her life in New York as quickly as she could.

Her entire world was about to change. Edison was gone, and so was Caleb.

chapter
NINE

WREN WOKE TO A LOUD KNOCK ON her door followed by Caleb's voice.

"Hey, Bird. Are you up?"

Wren sat up and put her hand into her hair, blinking at the sunlight streaming in below the half-closed window shade. She was still dressed in her leotard after her "chat" with Macy the night before. She'd fallen asleep after she'd cried herself out.

"Wren? Are you okay?"

Wren inhaled and scooted toward the edge of the bed. "Coming!" She didn't think about what she looked like; she just hurried to open the door.

Caleb was standing in front of her, a look of concern flashing across his face. He was dressed casually in dark jeans and a dark blue button down; his hair was combed but still slightly damp from his shower, and his face was freshly shaved. The musky clean scent of his cologne enveloped her. Her heart stopped in her chest at how handsome he looked.

"Oh, crap," she muttered and turned back into her room, motioning with her hand for him to follow. It didn't occur to her that it might seem inappropriate for Caleb to be in her room. It was Caleb. "I couldn't sleep."

Caleb watched her retreating back, his eyes roaming down her slender body, still clad in the pink leotard. "You didn't sleep?" He moved hesitantly into the room, taking stock of the way the covers were pulled from one side of the bed onto the other, exposing the sheets. It was as if she had slept on top of her comforter, and the open doorway between her bedroom and the studio.

She went into the bathroom, intent on brushing her teeth and inwardly cringed at her reflection in the mirror. Her hair was a mess and there were dark smudges of mascara beneath her eyes. She picked up her toothbrush and squeezed toothpaste onto it, before turning on the water and shoving it underneath the stream. "I meant, the outfit. I couldn't sleep so I danced for a while." She pushed the brush into her mouth and began to clean her teeth.

"Oh, I can wait downstairs. I just thought we'd go to breakfast. I know you want to shop later, and then we have the visitation..." he hesitated briefly. "I wanted to talk to you."

Wren bent over the sink and spit into it, wondering how Macy figured into the equation. "So talk."

"Not here."

"Okay. Just give me a few minutes."

"When do you need to be back in New York?"

She rinsed her toothbrush and then used a glass to take a quick gulp of water and swished it around her mouth. She spit again, and then continued. "Not for two weeks, why?" Wren turned back toward Caleb and glanced around the edge of the bathroom door jam. "Do you need help with something? I can stay until the tour starts again, if you need me."

If I need you, Caleb thought incredulously.

If only he could be completely honest with her about what he wanted and needed from her.

"Just get dressed and we'll talk over breakfast."

"Is Macy coming? I know she wanted to shop." She said the words, but dreaded the answer.

"No. Just us." He was wishing she'd been awake and ready to go. The last thing he wanted was Macy intruding on this time with Wren. He needed this conversation to get clarity on the best course of action.

"Okay. Let me just hop in the shower and throw on some clothes."

"Sure. I'll wait for you downstairs." He turned to leave.

"Cale?"

Caleb stopped and turned back to her. She had turned on the water in the shower. He could hear it running, but she'd moved further into the bathroom. He could see her reflection in the mirror as she untied her skirt and let it fall. He froze, as she started to push the leotard off her shoulders, giving him a glimpse of the creamy skin of her back. His memory was filled with flashbacks of their one night together. How she felt, how she smelled and tasted. His dick twitched inside his jeans and his heart seized painfully. His hand rose to rub the back of his neck as he quickly turned away to give her some privacy, and to get a grip on his feelings.

"Yeah?"

"I don't feel like spending hours shopping. Macy seems like she loves it, but I just need a couple of dresses. I mean; this is a funeral. This isn't for fun."

"Yeah, I get it. I'll handle Macy."

"Thank you."

"I'll see you downstairs." Caleb shut the door behind him and walked down stairs.

God. He still had it so bad for her. He knew he'd never feel for anyone, like he felt about Wren, but all of the time, distance, and lack of contact hadn't changed one damn ache. Despite everything, and the conversation he knew he'd have to have with her about the two of them, after the decision was made. He wanted the will issue to be resolved and the funeral over and then he'd come clean on all of it. He'd have to if he ever expected to be in her life, and he wanted to. It was a burden his heart was tired of carrying. He owed her a lot of things; the least of all was the whole truth.

Heading to the kitchen to the smell of fresh brewed coffee, he knew he'd find Jonesy already at work. The old woman had her back to him, unloading the stainless steel dishwasher, and he didn't want to startle her. She was softly humming to herself; a tune that Caleb didn't recognize, and probably one she was making up as she went. He could see she was deep in thought.

"Good morning, Jonesy."

She looked up, her hands full of drinking glasses that she was in the process of putting away. "Oh, morning, honey. Do you want breakfast? What can I make you?"

Caleb shook his head and went to get a coffee cup from the cupboard on the other side of the big kitchen. "Nothing. I'm taking Wren out for breakfast."

Jonesy stopped for a split second and then continued in her task. "What about the other one?"

"She's in bed."

Jonesy's eyebrows shot up. "Not invited, eh?"

He picked up the coffee pot and filled his cup with the steaming liquid. "No," he answered simply.

"If you don't mind my asking; I mean it's none of my business, but why is that woman even here? It doesn't seem to me like she has your heart."

Caleb sighed and sat down at the table in the windowed alcove. "Never could fool you, Jonesy."

She huffed and bent to retrieve more dishes to put away. "No. It's about time you stopped fooling yourself, too," she said matter-of-factly.

"I'm of the same conclusion; but it really depends on Wren."

Jonesy nodded in agreement and continued her task.

"What do you think, Jonesy?"

The old woman stopped and looked at him, before getting a cup down and pouring herself some coffee. "I think Wren has always loved you. You're her sun and moon, Caleb. I think it's always been you and Wren. I'm not sure what happened a few years back to change that, but you can fix it." She took a sip of the steaming liquid. "If that's what you want."

Caleb pressed his lips together, a new determination coming over him. Taking in her words, he hoped she was right. He could always count on Jonesy to be in his corner and to give it to him straight, even though she didn't know all of the details. Fundamentally, Wren was still the same person, and so was he. One thing he was sure of, Wren knew him like no one else did, and he hoped that would be enough to mend the fences.

"Jonesy," he began quietly; looking over his shoulder to make sure Wren wasn't already coming to find him. "Has she said anything about what her life is like? Is she seeing anyone?" His heart tightened slightly as he waited for her answer; the feeling a reminder of his utter devastation when Wren had brought Sam to San Francisco and the consequences of that visit. Maybe she'd married Sam and just didn't tell him. Surely his father had known the status of their relationship before he made the will. Hope bloomed inside of him. "Sam?"

Jonesy huffed, dismissively, looking at him over the rim of her coffee cup as she was about to take another swallow. Her eyes locked with his. "Now there's a name I haven't I haven't heard for a while. Though I'm an old woman. I can't remember everything." She winked mischievously, setting her cup down to resume putting away the dishes. "Talk to her, honey. That's all you can do. And, send that other one on her way."

He inhaled deeply, wishing it were as simple as Jonesy made it sound. Macy had been supportive and they'd had some good times, and he didn't want to be a complete dick. He couldn't just send her packing. She'd want to get back to

San Francisco soon after the funeral, and he fully expected her to leave Tuesday morning.

He turned in his chair as he heard a light flap of rubber soles crossed the marble floor behind him. The sound was soft; not the loud clacking of the high heels that Macy always wore, so he knew it had to be Wren. The house was big and sprawling, and the sound echoed through the main atrium at the foot of the stairs.

"Hey, Jonesy." Wren's voice was soft and musical, washing over Caleb and making him tingle as if she touched him. Her cheeks were rosy, her face freshly washed but devoid of makeup other than mascara. Her blue eyes sparkled, the color brought out by the V-neck shirt she wore atop a pair of faded jeans. Caleb glanced down to find her feet in a pair of black Vans with the laces shoved inside so she could just slip them on. Her hair was pulled back in a loose ponytail, but several loose curling tendrils were loose, framing her face. She looked unpretentious. "I hurried. "

Caleb stood up and started to pick up his cup to put it in the sink, but Jonesy quickly took it from him, nodding toward the back door that led directly off the kitchen and into the garage. "Get out of here, you two."

Caleb smiled gently, knowing Jonesy was helping them make a speedy exit before Macy made an appearance.

"Thanks Jonesy. Let Macy know we'll be back in a bit."

Caleb grabbed Wren's hand and started toward the door. The warmth of his hand in hers sent a thrill running through her and Wren had to remind herself of Macy's words the night before. He was taken and it was time she tamped down any ridiculous fantasies of Caleb. It was time she face the reality that he might only see her as a little sister. Everything in her screamed in defiance at the thought, but maybe he pretended their night together never happened because he was ashamed and couldn't deal with it any other way. She sighed softly, telling herself that having him in her life, in any way, was better than not. The past two years had been hard, and a few stilted phone conversations were not how she wanted their future to be.

The garage was as pristine as the house. The floors all painted back and glossed with rosin; it seemed more like a showroom than a garage. There wasn't one speck of grease or dirt on the floor, and the walls were covered in sheetrock and light grey paint. "I forgot how much this place was like a museum," Caleb muttered, glancing from one expensive car to another. "Shit, there must be a million dollars worth of metal in here."

Wren's hand brushed the shiny red surface of a vintage Corvette. "It's more like a collection. Can we even drive them?"

"Sure, we can, but I'm not really feeling it."

The words welled up inside her before she could stop them. "Too bad you still don't have your old Harley. That would be like old times."

Caleb had an old beater that he and Dex had found beat up in a junkyard. It had been trashed in a wreck and needed a ton of work, including a new manifold. They worked on it for months and finally got it running. Caleb had saved up the money to replace all of the chrome and buy a new seat, and together with his best friend, it had been restored to almost perfect condition at Dex's father's shop.

"We can," Caleb said with a smile. Happiness rushed through him at the thought of stepping back in time with Wren. He began walking to the far corner of the large garage, still holding her hand and pulling her with him toward it. His objective was parked along the wall covered in a painter's tarp that he had bought to protect it. "I'm surprised Dad didn't sell it or give it away." He used his free left hand to pull the tarp off and let it drift to the ground. "It's been a while, so it might not start." Two helmets sat on the seat, as if waiting for Caleb's return and he opened a long cabinet that was one of the built-ins that he used to keep his jackets and gloves in.

Wren gasped softly, surprised the cycle was even still in Denver, and even more surprised was that the cabinet still held one of Caleb's old leather jackets.Knowing how much it meant to him, she'd assumed he'd taken the motorcycle with him to San Francisco. The vintage black cycle was just as she remembered it, the many times he'd taken her riding rushed through her mind.

Was it wrong to be this happy when someone you cared about just died? A small twinge of guilt nagged at Wren's heart because she was just happy to have this time with Caleb. She pushed Macy's words from the night before to the back of her mind as she reached out and took the helmet he handed her, watching as he removed the beat up jacket from the hook inside the cabinet. He looked at it for a split second then held it out for Wren. It was one he'd outgrown even before he left for MIT and one he'd let her use on several of their rides in the past.

"I don't think anyone's worn this, since you." He laughed softly, joy all over his features as he pulled his old helmet onto his head and swung his leg to straddle it in one motion. He finished securing the strap under his chin and then turned the key. It was a good sign when the lights in the odometer panel lit up, and Caleb pulled the bike off of it's kickstand and then kicked it back before flipping on the fuel pump. "Here goes nothin'," he said as his left hand squeezed in the clutch and his right hand flipped the start switch.

The motorcycle came to life with a deafening roar in the enclosed garage. The bright white of his smile was almost dazzling and Wren was overjoyed to see happiness on his handsome face.

Wren secured the helmet on her head and quickly slid her arms into the sleeves of the jacket before she climbed on behind Caleb, sliding her hands around his waist. Her insides were a mass of excitement as the smell of his cologne assaulted her nostrils at the same time as the exhaust rose up in a stinky blue cloud from the bike's tail pipe as he revved the engine three times.

"Hold on!" he instructed loudly.

The garage was massive and one of the doors opened as they approached. Wren knew from experience that once free of the massive garage, Caleb would gun the engine and they'd fly down the lane and out of the gated property. She couldn't help but let out a small squeal as they started to speed away from the house, the wind rushing over her face, and causing the hair hanging from the bottom of her helmet to beat around her face madly. Her arms sneaked further around Caleb's lean waist and she wrapped one hand around the other wrist. His body was solid and she longed to rest her cheek on his strong back. This was paradise. She laughed out loud, and held on tighter when he turned south and into the city.

Caleb hadn't planned on the bike, but he was enjoying every second of having Wren wrapped around his body. He'd always loved the protectiveness that came over him whenever she was around, and he loved the physical contact between them. For years, he'd wanted her and couldn't touch her, and the times they were on the bike were the only taste of if he'd had.

It was a beautiful morning and the air was a bit brisk. He wished he also had a jacket on, but to go back into the house would have meant taking a chance of Macy being awake. The warmth began to seep into him from where Wren was plastered up against his back, and he leaned into her a bit more.

The city was left behind as Caleb headed west and up into the front range of the Rocky Mountains on US-6. He didn't care if Macy would be mad that he'd disappeared with Wren, he didn't care that the wake was later in the day, he just felt free and as if the load of his pending responsibilities had been lifted for a brief time. On the back of his bike, riding up into the mountains and surrounded by the amazing scenery with Wren, it was like old times. The sky was a bright blue and the sun a vibrant yellow as it rose behind them, her slender body up against his, and her arms tight around his middle... nothing could be better.

Wren didn't need to ask him where they were headed

because she didn't care, and she trusted him completely. One or two minor, okay major, betrayals couldn't change the facts, though she did have some questions, but she refused to ruin the momentary perfection of the morning.

The wind on her face as they climbed into the mountains wasn't something you got in New York City. The fresh scent of the Blue Spruce and pine trees that rose into the sky above the rocky walls that had been blasted out of the mountains to accommodate the highway, and sun that filtered through them and flittered across her face was amazing. And Caleb. None of this could be found in New York City.

After they'd been driving for about half an hour, Caleb's stomach reminded him of their need for breakfast, so he pulled off into the small town of Golden. There was a small restaurant near The Colorado School of Mines that he liked. He'd explored the area plenty of times once he and Dex rebuilt his bike since he'd wanted to attend and get his engineering degree there.

It would have been just thirty minutes from Wren, not thousands of miles, he thought sadly. His chest expanded in a sigh of regret as he parked the bike in front of Café 13, a small, but busy restaurant known for their amazing breakfast menu, and a place that he'd been once or twice before.

He hadn't intended to go so far from town, but he'd enjoyed the drive and the company and before he knew it, they were in Golden. The shopping schedule might be a bit thrown off, but it was the last thing he cared about. This talk with Wren was imperative to making a clear decision.

The natural rock covered building was on the corner of

Main Street with a simple blue sign that looked like it was hand-painted. There were a few people sitting at outside tables that were covered by red umbrellas that they passed on their way inside the restaurant. Wren pulled at the hair by her temples and forehead as they approached the door. "Helmet head. Literally." She laughed.

Caleb smiled. "You look great." He held open the door and ushered in front of him. The warm smell of bacon, maple syrup and coffee brewing permeated the air. The furnishings were simple, round wooden tables with painted black chairs.

A waitress, dressed in jeans and a red t-Shirt greeted them. "Good morning! Just seat yourselves anywhere you like!"

"Thanks."

Caleb looked around the room. It was crowded and he found an empty table near the back by the kitchen that was a bit off from the others, pointing at it. "Is that table okay?" he asked.

Wren nodded. "Sure." She preceded Caleb in the direction of the table in the corner.

Before they were even seated, the waitress was hovering behind them with menus. "Can I get you any coffee or orange juice?" She put the menus down on the table.

"I'll just have some water," Wren said with a slight smile. The woman was in her mid-twenties and it was obvious she thought Caleb was attractive by the way she was staring into his face. She huffed to herself. *Typical,* She thought. *Some things never change.*

"Coffee for me. Black," he said before the waitress could ask. He pulled out Wren's chair and waited until she was seated before taking the one across from her. He glanced down at the menu quickly, and then up at Wren.

"What are you hungry for?" She was starving, but her eyes searched the menu items for something healthy.

Caleb knew what she was doing. "Sticky buns, bacon, eggs, and a mountain of pancakes." Wren loved pancakes, but they were loaded with calories. "Don't order bird food, Bird."

The corner of her pink lips lifted in a slight smile. Her lips were bowed and perfect, her blue eyes bright and sparkling beneath her somewhat matted down curls. Wren glanced up from the menu to meet his eyes and self-consciously started pulling and pushing at her hair. "Don't look at me. I must look a mess."

Caleb laughed and threw down the menu at the same time as the waitress set the drinks on the table. "Yeah, but who cares?"

Wren's face twisted wryly. "Gee, thanks."

"My name is Suzy and I'll be taking care of you today," the waitress said. "Are you ready to order?"

With a wave of his hand Caleb indicated she should take Wren's order first.

"I'll have an egg white omelet with spinach and mushrooms, and an English muffin with the butter on the side."

"Any bacon?"

Wren looked up and shook her head. "Nope."

"She's always on a damn diet. I'll have three scrambled eggs, four strips of bacon, a stack of pancakes, and two sticky buns."

Suzy smiled as she scribbled down Caleb's order. "Wow.

You must be a growing boy."

Wren's eyes widened and she rolled them. Caleb saw her reaction, even if the waitress didn't. He was still grinning at Wren across the table when the waitress left.

"Wow, you must be a growing boy!" Wren mocked in a sing-song voice. "Bleh!" She tried not to smile, but couldn't help it and they both laughed out loud.

"Stop it, or I'll think you're jealous," he goaded with a grin. Hoping he was right, he waited for her reaction.

Their eyes locked. He knew she was thinking of their night together and wondering what the fuck happened afterward; why he left without a word, and why he pretended like it never happened. A public restaurant wasn't the place to get into it, but it would definitely need to be addressed.

"How's Sam doing?" he asked. Inwardly he braced himself for the answer. The guy he'd seen her with on her birthday wasn't Sam, but maybe they were just having a spat. Sam was the only guy Caleb was totally sure she'd ever been serious about.

Wren's eyes widened in surprise, and she cocked her head to one side. "You wanna talk about Sam? I thought you wanted to talk about your dad and stuff."

What Caleb needed was to find out what her life was like, if she was happy with it the way it was, and wanted to stay in New York indefinitely, or if she missed Colorado and might want to come back someday. He needed details, and Sam was a significant detail.

"I do, but I want to know if you're happy. Are you?" he asked seriously, his finger and thumb of his right hand fiddling with the handle of his coffee cup. He hadn't taken a drink of it yet.

Wren studied him. He was so freaking beautiful. His dark hair had been matted down by his helmet too, but with one swipe of his hand through it, he'd managed to make it look like messy perfection, and the soft shadow of beard on his strong jaw practically made her mouth water.

Wren sat back in her chair before she spoke. "Yes. You know how much I love dancing."

This wasn't going to be as easy as he'd hoped. He felt sick inside at his next words, but the questions had to be asked. He had to know, and not just because of how it would affect his decision about the will.

"Sure, I do. But are you with Sam? Did you get married?"

Caleb already knew the answer. It didn't take a genius to do a public records search, and she wasn't wearing a ring, but that didn't mean he wasn't still in her life. He told himself he needed to know if she was seeing anyone else because that could have an direct effect on whether she'd want to be tied to Lux, and whether he'd want another man owning half of it through possible divorce. Really, he just wanted to know. Period.

Wren's mouth opened in surprise, but then she closed it. How could she tell him that the San Francisco trip had ruined her relationship with Sam? Her heart hammered underneath her ribs until she thought it would fly from her chest. She clasped her hands together in her lap to quell their shaking. She never told Caleb she'd broken up with Sam. She'd never told him anything about her personal life in the past two years, so how could he know she wasn't with Sam anymore?

San Francisco had been heartbreaking, but it also hammered home some hard revelations.

Wren swallowed. "Sam and I aren't together. We haven't been..." she stopped, not wanting Caleb to realize that the trip to see him and the events that followed had made Sam leave her. "For a while, now."

Caleb breathed a silent sigh of relief. So, what about the guy he'd seen her with on her birthday? He had to know.

"Oh, I'm sorry it didn't work out," he said softly. A piece of him was rejoicing, but another part felt bad for her. She deserved to be loved. More than anyone he'd ever known, and he'd been a complete dick to Sam. He knew it when he was doing it, but at the time his heart was on fire and there wasn't one fucking thing he could do to stop it. The poor schmuck had been lucky he hadn't pounded him into the ground.

One slight shoulder lifted in a shrug. "It's okay. I guess it wasn't meant to be."

She remembered it so clearly.

Two years earlier Sam had proposed and she'd taken him to San Francisco to meet Caleb, hoping her new relationship would ease the awkwardness between Caleb and herself after their division after he'd slunk off and never acknowledged their night together.

That weekend had served to open her eyes and made her face the truth. She'd liked Sam, but she didn't love him. He was hot and talented, and he made her feel beautiful, but he wasn't Caleb and putting the two of them side-by-side had been a mistake. Her entire life; no one could compare to

Caleb and she was kidding herself and being dishonest with Sam by attempting to hide her feelings. After the night she'd introduced them, it had been clear to Sam that her heart was someplace else.

She'd had a blow up with Caleb after their dinner and was pensive and quiet when she met Sam back at the hotel. She was heartbroken. Caleb had let her down when she needed him to help her move on with her life; to help her move on from him.

It had been an awkward introduction between the two men and an uncomfortable meal at a local steak house filled with stilted small talk, long uncomfortable silences, and a lot of wine. Caleb's dark brooding and intense stare as he sat back regarding the way Sam interacted with Wren had made his presence at the table a mostly silent, potent force. Sam had tried to make small talk, but Caleb's short answers made the evening unbearable.

"So, Wren tells me that you're an engineer?" Sam had asked after the first round of drinks.

"What else did she tell you?"

Sam's brow creased and his head cocked to one side, perplexed at Caleb's rude tone. "Just that you two grew up together."

Caleb leaned forward to grab his Dos Equis, drained it and lifted his hand to signal the waiter to return so he could order another one. "I think she left a whole lot of shit out, then."

Sam cleared his throat and shot a look at Wren, who was seated between the two men. "Um... Well, I'm sure she didn't *tell me every detail."*

"No, I'm positive of that." Caleb grunted; his eyes flashing up to lock with Wren's as she silently questioned what he was doing.

"Can we order, please?" Wren asked, trying to lighten the mood. The air between them was so thick she could hardly breathe. Caleb had always been protective and so she justified his behavior. This was the first time she'd been with a man in front of him since the night she spent dancing with Dex. She's flushed as the memory pushed heat through her body. "I'm starving."

After the compulsory return questions of what Sam's job entailed and the response about being one of the directors with Wren's ballet company, and some dumb, meaningless conversations about the San Francisco Giants and the New York Mets, the evening thankfully came to a close with Wren sending Sam back to the hotel in a cab, so she could speak to Caleb in private.

As they walked along the streets off of Fisherman's Wharf, Wren struggled with what to say. She was angry that Caleb had behaved so badly after she'd extolled his virtues to Sam the way she had. She felt disappointed and angry.

It was a damp night and Caleb had his collar turned up and his hands shoved into the pockets of his wool jacket, and Wren struggled on the cobblestone in her black stiletto heels, resigned to the fact her hair was getting spoiled by the misty air, her arms curled around her middle, holding her own long coat closer around her body. They walked slowly because of her shoes; the second time she stumbled and Caleb had to catch her to keep her from falling flat on her face.

"What the hell did you ask to go for a walk for when you have those damn things on?" he growled angrily. "It's ridiculous."

"Why are you so mad? I haven't seen you in forever and you've been a prick all night!"

He was taken aback by her question and he straightened and turned back forward to keep walking. "I'm not mad. I just don't want you to hurt yourself."

Silence followed for three or four minutes while Wren tried to muster the courage necessary for what was coming.

Her contact with Caleb had been sparse for much of the almost two years that had passed since she'd seen him. She'd been so hurt because he refused to acknowledge the one night she spent in his arms which had been heaven to her, and what she thought would be the beginning she'd been waiting for... that he was just waiting for her to grow up. It turned out nothing was further from the truth and she'd had to face it. It probably didn't help that the first time she'd been face-to-face with Caleb since that fateful night, she had another guy in tow.

"I hoped you'd like Sam."

Caleb clenched his teeth and the muscle in his jaw started to twitch, but he didn't respond. Wren reached out and touched his arm to get him to pause in his steps. She was almost running to keep up with him.

"Cale, will you please stop for a minute? Look at me?" Her voice was pleading and filled with enough emotion to make it quiver. She looked up into his face. That face that haunted her dreams, along with strong arms, the sound of her name on his lips as he came inside her.

"What? Why? Who is this guy? Are you in love with him?"

She liked Sam. Liked him a lot, but she couldn't say she loved him. Especially, not to Caleb. "I want you two to be friends."

Caleb visibly stiffened, stepping back so her hand dropped from his sleeve. "You and I never see each other. What does it matter if I like the guy?"

"Because he's asked me to marry him, Caleb. You're the only other person in the world who means anything to me, and I need you in my life or I won't be happy."

He kept walking, throwing an irritated glance over his shoulder, his voice taking on a harsher tone. "You can't marry him. He's a pussy. I can see it from a mile away. He can't take care of you; he can barely lift his fucking drink."

"Cale, stop." When he didn't she did and yelled after him. "Cale!"

He stopped and threw his arms out then let them drop to his sides heavily before turning to face her. "What?" he spat out.

"It would mean a lot to me if you'd be the one to give me away."

Caleb's surprise was plain on his face as he huffed loudly in disgust. His eyes widened for a split second, then his face changed to a rigid mask, cold and devoid of emotion. After a couple of seconds, he laughed harshly. "No." He said, with a lift of both eyebrows and a hard shake of his head. "No way."

Wren felt as if the air had been knocked from her lungs,

as if she'd just been kicked in the gut. Did he just say no? Her throat got tight and her eyes began to well with tears, Caleb's form starting to blur in the dark night and the dim light of from the street lamps. She could see his arm lift like he was rubbing his mouth with the back of his hand. Wren blinked at the tears forming in her eyes.

It was almost 11 PM on Saturday night, but there were still people milling about, despite the inclement weather and the start of a light rain. "No?" Wren asked, the words torn from her. "Really, Caleb?

He visibly flinched. She hadn't called him Caleb for years and it was like a slap in the face.

"Did I stutter, Wren? No. Fucking. Way," he punctuated the words, his eyes pained as he looked at her.

She sucked in her breath on the start of a sob. "I've never asked you for anything. Despite all you've given me, I never asked for any of it. I'm asking for this. I nee—eed you to do this for me."

"I can't, Wren!" The words ripped from him as he stormed closer until he was looming down on her, his hot breath showing white in the cold air. "I'll give you anything! Ask me any goddamned thing you want, but I can't do that. Not fucking that!"

"I need you, Cale! You're all the family I have." Her voice broke as tears started to run down her face. She had faced the fact that she had to put her schoolgirl crush of Caleb in the past and she was trying her best to move beyond it, but her heart was breaking. There was no denying the one she loved the most was standing in front of her, and it killed her

to ask this of him. "I need you to stand beside me when I do this. Please don't let me down."

"I said, no, Wren." He turned and started walking away again. When she didn't follow, he stopped and turned back. Coming closer and taking her cold hand in his and starting to pull her along with him down the sidewalk.

Wren yanked her hand free of his abruptly, and stopped, causing Caleb to turn to her again. She held out her wrist, pulling up the sleeve of her coat to expose her tattoo. "Remember this? Remember when you took me to get it? You wanted to know why I wanted it." She was crying full out now, her voice breaking. "I can't believe you didn't know. A white fucking horse?" A bitter laugh burst from her as she stood shaking in front of him. "It's you, Caleb. YOU. You are the white horse, the savior, the knight in shining armor of my life!"

Caleb's head dropped and his shoulders slumped as she railed at him. He couldn't meet her eyes. "I know that." It was a simple statement that held the weight of Thor's hammer.

Tears poured from her eyes and sobs broke from her chest. She wished she could fall to her knees into a broken mess on the wet pavement, the rain falling around her. Her heart was breaking, as much as the morning after their night together, when she gave herself so fully to him. She wanted his arms around her. She wanted her Caleb to save her once again; to save her from the misery of not being everything to him. "Then live up to it, like you always have. I need you in my life, Cale." Her voice was so soft he barely heard her words. "Please."

Wren waited for him to speak for what seemed like forever. She used her cold fingers to push the wet hair out of her eyes and blinked; unsure if the drops on her eyelashes were tears or raindrops.

When Caleb finally lifted his head, the expression on his face and the tone in his voice said it all. He was hurting as much as she was. "But you're asking me for something, I can't do. I don't know him. I can't give my blessing to someone I'm not absolutely certain can take care of you."

"That's not it, Caleb. Just... tell me the truth!" She felt like she was begging for her very last breath.

"Come on, let's go. I'll take you back to your hotel. Sam's waiting."

Pain exploded inside Wren. Every cell in her body protested and felt like it would implode and she gasped for breath. "He's a great guy if you'd give him a chance. You two are a lot a like."

"He's nothing like me," he railed. "How can he take care of you? He's a pussy who prances around in tights; my wrists are bigger than his biceps! He can't protect you!"

"Caleb, I've been protecting myself just fine! I've been in New York for more than two years without you. I'm okay." She pulled her hand from his and put her palms out at her side. "See?"

He shook his head as he lifted his hand and quickly wiped at one eye with his thumb, starting to walk away from her toward the curb. "The hell you are."

Traffic was moderate, a mixture of cars, SUVs and cabs. Caleb whistled and held up his hand, hailing one of them.

"Who else do I have to walk me down the aisle?" She took a step closer to him, reaching out her hand.

"My dad." His answer was harsh and abrupt.

A cry broke from her chest. Edison had become dear to her, but no one meant more than Caleb. She'd hoped her getting married would have taken the pressure of the sexual tension that always existed between them away and they could be close again. Caleb opened the door of the yellow cab and waited for Wren to get in. She stopped in front of him. "I miss you, Cale. Please do this for me. I want you back in my life."

He ushered her inside and she fully expected him to follow her but he only leaned in and gave the name of her hotel to the driver. "Then, don't get married."

He shut the door, hammered on the roof of the car, and then turned away as the sky opened up and rain started pouring down. She was sobbing in the backseat of the cab, and once again, Caleb was walking away from her.

When she got back to the hotel it was easy for Sam to see how upset she was, despite her attempt to convince him she looked so ruined due to the rain pouring down outside. She was in so much pain she finally broke down and told him everything. She couldn't help it, and it was the honest thing to do.

"You're in love with your brother, Wren? That's so fucking sick!"

Sam stormed around her hotel room gathering his things and throwing it all in his suitcase in angry outburst. He was hurt and Wren couldn't blame him, but there was nothing she *could do or say to change reality. She did love Caleb. She'd always love Caleb and she had to face it. She wasn't strong enough to pretend that she didn't or that she was okay.*

She'd sat on the edge of the bed, still crying softly. "Cale isn't my brother."

"Whatever," he huffed, tears in his eyes. "Do me a favor; don't fuck some other poor schmuck over and make him think you want a relationship."

"Sam! I didn't know that I felt this way. I thought I was over it."

"Save it, Wren. I'm not a fool." With that, he left her in the hotel room and she never saw him again.

The next day she took a cab to the airport alone, but the empty seat next to hers on the return flight was a blatant reminder of how alone in the world she really was.

She'd tried to build a life with Sam to get over Caleb, but he still haunted her life and owned her heart. She was wrong to think she'd see him, introduce he and Sam, and everyone would live happily ever after.

After that, she'd cried for weeks. She felt bad about hurting Sam, and sad because the ache she felt inside didn't subside. She had no hope that she and Caleb would ever reconcile. She'd get over Sam... she'd never get over Caleb.

"Is there anyone else?" The deep tenor of Caleb's voice brought her out of her thoughts and back to the present.

"What?" She looked up into his eyes, doing her best to hide how the memory affected her. "Um, nothing serious, no."

She didn't need to ask about his relationship with Macy or their future plans because Macy had made it clear the night before.

"Why not?"

Caleb took a deep breath, just as Suzy appeared with their breakfast. She set the plates down and asked, "Is there anything else you need?"

"We're all good. Thank you."

The waitress flounced off and looked over her shoulder at Caleb. He smiled, despite himself.

"Will Macy be angry that we left without her?" Wren wasn't sure why she was annoyed he'd flirt with the silly waitress, considering the woman waiting for him back at the house.

Caleb shrugged and began to put blackberry jam on one of the pancakes, then proceeded to lift them up one by one to coat them all. He took the syrup and drizzled it over the whole mess. "Nah. We'll see her later."

"Caleb, I can understand if you're upset with me." Caleb looked up from his plate, his brow creasing.

"For what?"

"Well, because your dad was good to me." Wren had a certain amount of guilt because of it. "After you left for MIT he was so much better to me than he had been to you. I feel so badly about it, and I'm sorry. I'd understand if you resent me for it."

Caleb set his fork down and met her eyes without wavering. "I don't! I don't, Wren. I'm thankful that someone stepped in to keep that bitch Veronica from hurting you. I'm sure if he hadn't taken care of you, I'd probably have killed them both."

"Caleb, no. Don't say that."

He shook his head. "I would have." Caleb wondered if

she knew why he went to MIT instead of CSOM. "You know I hated leaving you unprotected. At least he held up that end of the bargain." Caleb stopped before going any further, pissed at his slip.

"Bargain?"

"Nevermind. It all worked out."

Wren frowned and shook her head slightly. She wanted to know. "Tell me what you mean," she demanded.

"I will." Caleb wanted to wait to spill the beans about Edison using Wren as leverage to manipulate him to leaving Denver for college. She obviously cared for and respected his dad and the occasion of his death wasn't the time to disillusion her. "But, now isn't the time. Trust me."

Wren paused to consider for a moment. Things had happened to cause distance between the two of them, but the years of Caleb being the one person she could trust were deeply seated. It would take more than the denial of lovemaking or his refusal to give her away at her wedding to break that bond. Those things had hurt; devastatingly so, but Wren could be honest with herself: she still trusted him more than anyone else, and despite the pain he caused, she wanted him to be part of her life. In whatever way was possible.

"Edison was wrong to withhold love from you, Cale. You deserve love more than anyone I know."

Caleb's heart stopped dead. He had already forgotten about eating, but this gave him hope. Maybe she wouldn't resent him if he gave her half of the estate. That's what his heart and gut wanted to do. It was the only way he could ensure she'd be taken care of, and the only way he'd know she was okay.

And if he were honest; the only way it would guarantee he'd see her. For the next five years at least, until the option to sell became available. It would at least buy him some time to put their relationship back together.

In that moment, his decision was made. He didn't need to tell her there were two wills and he decided then and there to call Jonathan and let him know when they returned to the house to pick up Macy.

"We both had shitty lives for a while. Just the way it was," Caleb tried to sound casual. "Wren, are you going to eat?" he questioned.

"Oh." She picked up a knife and started to butter half of her English muffin. "What did you want to talk about?"

"Huh?" He picked up his fork and resumed eating.

"You said you wanted to talk. That's why we came here, right?"

"I just," Caleb began, "I just wanted to make sure you're okay. We haven't talked much. I came to see you for your birthday, though."

Wren's eyes snapped up and she halted her task. "Wait. What?"

"Keep eating, Bird." Caleb picked up one of the sticky buns and took an oversized bite, hoping to lighten the mood. "Wow, these are good." He shoved the plate containing the second one toward her. "This one is yours. Eat up! They're awesome."

"Cale, really?" She couldn't believe her ears. The night of her birthday he'd waited so late to call, and she'd been upset all day, waiting. "You came to New York?"

He sighed at the hurt look on her beautiful face. He still

didn't know if he should tell her the whole truth, but if he wanted to rebuild things with her, he had to be honest. "Yeah."

"But, I didn't see—"

He put up a hand to stop her words. He had to get it out. "No, I didn't let you know. I went to your matinee and watched you. You were amazing. I could barely believe my eyes."

Emotions exploded inside her. She wasn't sure if she was hurt, touched, or just angry. Her throat began to ache and her eyes filled with tears. She was still in the process of buttering her bread, and she sat still as stone, the knife still in her right hand as her wrist rested on the table's edge. "You couldn't let me know? Why?"

The pain in Wren's voice tore at Caleb's gut; deep down in places that only she affected. "I waited outside the theater. It was raining pretty hard, and you came out with a guy. I didn't want to intrude. You looked really—" He searched for the right word. He knew he had no right to sound jealous and he didn't want it to come off that way. "*Cozy.* I didn't want to ruin your plans."

Wren sat back in her chair and blinked at the tears in her eyes, trying to remember who was with her at the time. He hand lifted and she pressed her two middle fingers to her forehead, right between her perfectly arched brows. She closed her eyes and swallowed, trying to dispel the tightness. "Victor?"

Caleb felt like hell. Obviously, he'd hurt her again. "I don't know. I didn't recognize him. We hadn't talked much, and not about anything that really mattered; for all I knew he could have been a new boyfriend."

Wren opened her eyes and looked at him. If only he wasn't so fucking beautiful. She felt robbed of the time with him on her birthday and robbed of having in her life for the past few years. "He was just another dancer on the production and a friend. He's gay, Cale. How could he be a boyfriend if you didn't know I wasn't married?"

He was busted so his words rushed out. "Okay, I knew about Sam, but how was I to know about this new guy? His arm was around you, and you were laughing."

"Yeah. Because it was pouring down rain, and we were sharing my umbrella." Her voice cracked and the tears she'd been fighting won out as first one, then another tumbled in fat drops down her cheeks. She quickly reached up and brushed them away. The restaurant was crowded and she didn't want to make a complete fool of herself. "I waited to hear from you all day, and you didn't call until almost midnight. I'm so mad at you right now."

Caleb felt heat begin to rise under his skin, slowly crawling up his chest, into his neck and face. He ran a hand over his unshaven jaw. Shit! It seemed like all he did was make mistake after mistake with her.

He leaned forward to take her hand, but the table was full of plates and half eaten food. He was fucked. "I know. I'm an asshole."

She looked away, her chin quivering. "All I wanted for my birthday was to see you."

"Wren, I was feeling like a prick because I refused to be at your wedding, and knew I'd ruined it for you. When I saw that guy, I figured you had someone new, but either way— Oh, fuck it," he spat out in frustration.

The waitress was coming toward them with a coffeepot in her hand, but Caleb shook his head to indicate that they didn't need any more. Suzy abruptly turned away with a disappointed look plastered across her face.

Wren's eyes snapped around to focus back on Caleb. His expression was as pained as she felt. "I just didn't want to cause any problems. I'd already fucked things up with you. You didn't deserve to have your birthday ruined, too. I came to New York to make sure you were okay. I saw you, and you looked happy."

"I wish you would have told me. I missed you so much."

His breath rushed from his chest. He loved this woman. Loved her so much he couldn't even breathe. "Me, too. And I'm sorry. I should have manned up and did what you needed me to do."

Wren sniffed; not ready to explain what happened with Sam. "Yes, you should have. I was mad for a while, but then I was just sad. Ever since that party when you fought with Dex, it hasn't been the same between us."

She watched him carefully, looking for any indication that he would acknowledge their night together. She knew in her heart, he remembered. He'd said her name in the middle of it, so he wasn't that drunk.

"I know." Caleb looked down and started to dig some cash out of the front pocket of his jeans. "I was dealing with some personal stuff. I was still pissed off at my dad for shipping me off to Boston, and then he wasn't around at all when I came home. And then, you didn't need me because you had Dex."

"Dex? He was my friend after you left. That's all."

"Didn't look like it to me."

"That dance was the first time he'd ever touched me." She shook her head, frowning. "You are so confusing, Cale."

There didn't seem to be an easy way to end this conversation and it was going in a direction he never intended to take it. He'd spill his guts, but not in the middle of a public place, and not while Macy was in Denver. He had to be in a place to touch her, hold her and let her know how he felt; how he'd always felt, so he could make sure she understood it the way he meant it.

He threw two bills on the table without waiting for the check and then pushed his fingers through his hair uncomfortably. "Are you ready to go? Do you want to take anything with?" He noted how she'd barely touched her food as they both stood up. Caleb waited for Wren to precede him out, and Suzy called behind them. "Come back and see me again, soon!"

Caleb lifted his hand without turning around, his eyes on the long blonde curls of Wren as she walked out in front of him. She was so small and the protectiveness inside him roared. He'd hurt her again.

Why the hell was he always hurting her? He silently chastised himself; regret surging through him. He hated hurting her. He'd rather never see Wren again than hurt her. He leaned around her to push open the door to the outside, the fresh air and sunshine greeting them.

He could sense Wren's sadness and the hint of anger simmering underneath the surface, though she didn't say anything as they both put on their sunglasses. Walking beside her the few feet to the Harley, he took a chance and reached out to grab her hand in his, hoping the silent plea would hit its mark.

It must have because her fingers squeezed around his. When they were back on the bike and he started the engine, the arms around him seemed a bit tighter than on the trip up the mountain; an unspoken forgiveness. He knew he didn't deserve her forgiveness or to have her in his life, but he was so thankful for her comforting presence behind him on the ride back to Denver.

Every inch where their bodies connected was on fire. Her thighs hugged the side of his hips and legs, her head rested against his shoulder, and her fingers curled into the fabric of his shirt as she held on; her arms wrapped tight around his middle.

It was a slice of heaven.

chapter
TEN

MACY WAS PISSED. When Caleb and Wren finally showed up at the house it was after noon and Mrs. Jones had played ignorant and refused to tell her what the hell was going on. Add to it that Caleb hadn't answered any of the five text messages she'd sent during his time out with Wren.

She'd wandered through the house to look around and ended up in a large bedroom on the second floor across the hall from Wren's suite. It was very luxurious with a huge four-poster bed and sitting area by the window. The faint smell of a woman's perfume lingered in the air and a large portrait of a woman Macy could only assume was Caleb's mother. She was beautiful, her hair a lighter shade than Caleb's, but the deep blue eyes were identical. She had a softer, more feminine version of Caleb's face, but the resemblance was unmistakable.

The frame of the picture was understated so it wouldn't take away from the woman who was the focus. Celine was thin and glamorous; and Macy recognized the image as one from the Lux campaign for their signature scent; Lumineux. Celine Luxon's eyes were soft and serene, connected with the camera, the fingers of her right hand hovering by the pendant hanging on a long chain; just above the scooped neckline of her dress.

The jewelry resonated in Macy's thoughts. Her eyes widened in recognition. It was the pendant the Lux logo was based on; the very same one Wren wore. So... little miss Wren had the cherished locket. Did Caleb's dad give it to her since he didn't have a biological daughter? Her mind churned. What if Caleb were the one to give it to her?

Macy's lips pressed together, as anger and resentment resonated through her. She huffed and both fists clenched at her sides. That would never do.

She rushed downstairs to wait for Caleb in the great room, anxious to confront him. Wren had the necklace, and he disappeared with her for hours? Two and two certainly added up to four, and Macy was anything but stupid. Something had to be done. It was suddenly imperative that Caleb be kept away from Wren as much as possible and for Macy to get him back to San Francisco immediately after the funeral. She had just started impatiently pacing in front of the main window when Caleb walked in, his head down while he fiddled with his phone. It was clear he was checking his messages; finally.

"Nice of you to let me know what you were doing! Was I supposed to just twiddle my thumbs all damn day?" she said, her tone short and waspish.

Caleb's head snapped up and he glared at her.

What the fuck? he thought.

"It's only noon. Chill out," he said in annoyance. He didn't feel like he owed her any type of explanation, but wanted it cleared up before they were out with Wren. "We took my old bike for a ride and headed west. It was such a nice morning that we lost track of time."

Macy plopped down on the oversized sofa. The furniture was plush with dark green suede cushions designed for comfort as well as style. "A ride with little sis for old times sake? I can't imagine you'll see much of each other after the funeral. Not being blood and all."

Caleb's muscles tensed. She was being a complete bitch. "Some ties are stronger than blood."

"Like what? A little humping and bumping in the backseat of Daddy's Mercedes? Ooohhh." Her voice dripped with sarcasm as she fanned her fingers in front of her. Macy's suspicions were gaining strength the more she saw how Caleb acted around Wren. He was serious and more intense, and she didn't like it.

"No," he said harshly. He casually sat down in the chair at the end of the sofa, keeping his distance. "Like two parents who fucked us both up horribly. Any more questions?"

"Yes." Macy's eyes narrowed.

"Too bad. I'm not in the mood to be interrogated. No more answers." Caleb cut her off.

Macy flushed uncomfortably. Clearly Wren, and Caleb's relationship with her, was a sore subject for him. She didn't want to piss him off further; it was too much of a risk in his present state.

She got up and sauntered toward the big chair and crawled onto his lap. Caleb sat up and scooted back in the chair at her unexpected intrusion into his personal space. Her hand reached up to cup the side of his face and she bent to press a kiss to his unwilling mouth. "Come on, Cale. Let's not fight."

Cale. He bristled at Macy's use of the nickname. No one called him that. No one had ever called him that, except Wren.

"I'm not fighting... and, please don't call me that." He didn't want her on his lap so he stood up and placed her on her feet in one easy move, as his phone rang. It was Jonathan returning the call from a few minutes before "Hello?"

"Good afternoon, Caleb. So you've made your decision?"

He nodded and turned his back to Macy. "I have," he said into the phone. "Split it."

"Are you sure?"

"Yeah. I'll deal with any repercussions later."

"Right. Okay. How are you holding up?"

"I'm fine."

"If you're sure, I'm going to burn the other copy right. "

"Sounds good. I'll see you at the visitation later." Caleb used a hand to rub the back of his neck. The thought of seeing his father in a casket was disconcerting and uncomfortable. Seeing his father inside it was something he'd prefer to skip. "Is it an open casket?"

"Mrs. Jones made the arrangements, but I assume so."

Chills ran down his back and arms. *Ugh*, he thought. It would be so much less personal if it were closed. It would just be a box and less personal. He inhaled hard, his chin raising as he looked at the ceiling and then closed his eyes.

The thought of seeing his father in a casket only brought back memories of his mother's funeral. His father had been like a stone cold statue; oblivious to his twelve-year-old son crying his eyes out while Jonesy and Jonathan tried to comfort him. He'd never felt so alone as he had that day. "God. I wish it weren't."

"Your father had a lot of friends and business associates. Funerals are more closure for the living, son. Do you want to come to my office to discuss the reading this afternoon? The only people required to be in attendance tomorrow are you, Wren and Jonesy. Your father left her a bit of money for her retirement."

The resentment he was feeling because of the memory faded slightly; maybe there was some good left in his dad after all. He sighed heavily, wishing for a replay of the past few hours with Wren when he wasn't thinking about this morbid shit.

"Is it restricted beyond that?" Caleb had a feeling in his gut that the step monster would show up uninvited. "Is the will unbreakable? I fully expect that bitch, Veronica, to try something."

"It's not specified, but do you want it to be? What about Macy? Do you want her there?"

"I'm not sure, to be honest. Veronica will never leave Wren alone if—" He stopped; glancing at Macy, suddenly aware she was listening intently to his side of the conversation. "Uh, yes, I'll come over there and we can discuss it."

"I have a conference call for the next hour, but then I'll be free for the rest of the day," Jonathan replied.

"Okay, I'll call you back in an hour."

When he ended the call and turned around, he found Macy studying him, her expression softer; the snarkiness of a few minutes before completely gone from her face. She walked to him and laid a hand on his chest.

"I'm sorry, baby. Can't the driver you hired take Wren out? We can let your sister shop and we'll sneak off, alone," she suggested silkily. "It's my turn to spend time with you."

Caleb's teeth clenched. How many times did he have to tell her that Wren wasn't his fucking sister? He covered her hand with his when it started to wander up toward his neck. After his morning with Wren and the shit he learned Macy had said to her the night before, he had no desire for any type of intimacy with her.

"No, I promised her I'd take her. You aren't obligated to come if you'd rather skip it. Wren said she isn't in the mood to spend all day in the shops, and I have to meet with Jonathan before the wake."

"But, this is my first trip to Denver. I want to explore and maybe go to that old mining town after the malls. I Googled 'things to do' earlier. I was bored stiff while you were off on your little jaunt." The whine Macy's voice had acquired since she'd hit the Colorado line was back and it grated on Caleb's nerves.

He moved away from her with a huff. "I'm sorry if my father dying is interrupting your sight-seeing plans. That's not why we're here."

Macy reeled on him with narrowed eyes. "Not here for

sight-seeing?" she asked, sarcasm lacing every word. "Isn't that what you were doing this morning?"

"No."

"I don't believe you. You were gone for hours."

Irritation vibrated through him. "It's irrelevant, in any case. If you don't like how things are playing out, you're free to leave. You don't have to stay for the funeral; I'm sure you have more pressing things you need to do at home."

Macy was taken aback and for a split second felt like he'd just slapped her, but getting upset wouldn't move her agenda forward and she recovered quickly.

"Of course, I want to be here. I thought you'd need me, Caleb." Her face fell and she swallowed. "I thought... we had a relationship."

Great! Caleb's mind screamed. He felt like shit. Ten days ago, a week ago, so did he, but not in the same way Macy thought. And after seeing Wren, everything changed. It wasn't fair to Macy, but it was reality that he couldn't deny.

"We'll talk about everything when I get back to San Francisco; after this is all over." Getting back there meant to pack his stuff and figure out if he needed to sublet his apartment, but he didn't want to divulge that now. "Are you ready to go? Wren was just going to change, and then we can leave."

It wasn't long until Wren appeared, and after a short and very awkward silence, they were inside his father's BMW 640i and on their way. Macy made sure she was next to Caleb in the front seat, though he kept checking on Wren; his eyes flashing up into the rear view mirror. She was sitting quietly in the rich leather seats, and looking out of the window with a sad, contemplative expression on her beautiful face.

"Let's go to Hermès!" Macy gushed. "I was so happy to see they had one here! Is it far?"

The store was known for high-end leather goods, fragrances, and their expensive ready-to-wear clothing.

"Do you have the address?" It had been a few years since Caleb had been in Denver and while he knew the general vicinity, he wasn't sure exactly where it was.

After Macy rattled it off, Caleb asked Wren if she'd be able to find what she needed there.

"Hmm?" Wren looked up.

"Hermès," Macy said, a bit impatiently. "Can you find a dress there?"

"Oh," Wren was hesitant. "That's kind of expensive. Can't we go to a regular mall?"

"For heaven's sake, Wren," Macy scoffed. "You're a ballerina with the New York ballet."

Wren rolled her eyes before she could stop herself. "Actually, it's just a touring company, so that pretty much rules out that store."

"Really? I thought you'd be rolling in money."

Wren shook her head, her eyes widened, and her mouth flattened wryly. "No. Only a few of the top dancers in the world make huge money, and most of those aren't company dancers. I've been lucky, moving out of the Corps de Ballet sooner than most, especially since I didn't train in Russia or France. The men make more because they're in higher demand."

"Macy, let her be," Caleb admonished, feeling Wren's

distress. He wanted to quell Macy's inquisition of her. "We'll go to Pavilions. There are a lot of different stores there. I'm sure you can find something nice."

Macy opened her mouth, and then snapped it shut without saying a word. Caleb could tell she was seething, but he couldn't care less.

"If you'd like, you can drop me off back at the house and I'll ask Jared to take me around," Wren interjected from the backseat.

Caleb had already changed direction back toward the mall and he shook his head. "Not a chance." He glanced at Macy, silently interrupting her retort. The protectiveness he always felt for Wren was rearing its head and he wouldn't let Macy's selfishness dictate his actions. He was seeing a new side to her that he didn't like. He could see she was feeling threatened by Wren and it wasn't going to get any better when she discovered he'd be moving back to Denver and shelving the plans to start the engineering firm.

Caleb parked in front of the Nordstrom's store, one of the higher-end department stores at the mall, hoping that it would satisfy both women. The morning had started off clear, but clouds were rolling in and blocking out the sun as they all got out of the car and headed into the store. Macy reached for Caleb's hand and Wren, who was walking behind saw the gesture. Her heart fell. She would have preferred to shop alone to watching their PDA's all day.

"Look, I'm going to the dress department. I'll just call you when I'm finished and we can meet up," she said as Caleb pulled his hand from Macy's grasp and opened the glass door and waited for both women to precede him inside.

"No, Wren. I'll come with you," Macy stated quickly. "I shouldn't have been so selfish. I know this isn't a happy occasion." She smiled at Wren, who nodded sadly.

"I don't want to intrude," Wren said.

Caleb's hand lifted to Wren's shoulder and he squeezed it gently. "Wren, come on. Let's get you a dress, sweetheart." He could sense she was pensive, and her sadness was palpable.

Caleb wished the morbid business of the funeral was behind them, and the will had already been read. At least then, he'd know if he'd made the right choice. Judging from Wren's comments about a ballerina's salary, he felt confident that he'd done his best for her. The only thing uncertain was whether she'd want to move home to Denver, too. He hoped so, but if she wanted to keep touring, then he'd just handle Lux for the both of them.

They walked through the store to the escalators and followed the signs up to the Women's dress department. Wren immediately went through the available dresses to find all of the black options and was soon ensconced in the dressing room with her few selections. She closed the curtain behind her and started to try them on.

After the morning with Caleb, she hated seeing him with Macy. It was reality and she had to face it. Her eyes filled with tears as she took off her clothes and slipped into the first dress. It was simple with short sleeves, a scooped neckline, and was pretty fitted through the body. The hem stopped about two inches above her knee. The classic style was elegant and modest.

She swallowed at the thickness in her throat and wiped at the tear about to fall from her eye as she stared at herself in the mirror. She didn't really care about what she wore to the funeral as long as it was appropriate and respectful, and this would do fine. Her budget demanded she pick something she'd be able to wear again, and this dress could be used for various occasions, depending on how she accessorized.

She physically jumped when the curtain was yanked open suddenly. Wren's hand went to her chest and she gasped; startled. Macy was standing there with an armful of dresses. She barged in, and started hanging them up on the hooks situated on all sides of the small space.

"Oh, Macy, you scared me." This was the second time that Macy had invaded her privacy and Wren was annoyed.

"I brought you more choices. Look at this one?" Macy smiled brightly, the bright magenta lipstick a perfect compliment to her skin and dark hair. The dress she held up was made of chiffon and the skirt loose and flowing in a soft mauve but was inappropriate for the occasion. It would be pretty for a summer party, but this was a funeral. Some of the others Macy chose would be appropriate, but they were the best designers that Wren wouldn't be able to afford, and the one's she could afford were hideous; the style all wrong or designed for a woman two or three time's Wren's age.

Macy was so glamorous and Wren felt dowdy next to her. Caleb's girlfriend was always dressed to kill, and Wren was at a disadvantage because she barely had anything with her; let alone weather appropriate.

"I'll try it, but I think this one will be fine." Wren looked at the price tag and balked. As simple as it was, it was still more than three hundred dollars.

"You need two, right?" Macy asked holding up another dress.

Wren shook her head. "Maybe if I get a scarf or a sweater, I can wear the same one for both the visitation and the funeral," she said quietly. She didn't feel like shopping, and not with Macy's overbearing presence bombarding her. "Plus, I still need shoes, hose, and stuff."

"Caleb's loaded now. He can pay for it. I'm sure he'll want to, anyway." Macy shrugged off Wren's monetary concerns.

"That's okay. He doesn't need to. I travel a lot and so I don't like to have a lot of clothes. I'd rather have one dress that's versatile."

After more prodding from Macy and her refusal to leave the small dressing room, Wren acquiesced and tried on three more dresses. Caleb was waiting outside the small suite of rooms used for fitting rooms and she didn't want to take so much time. She decided that if she didn't argue with Macy, it would all be over more quickly. In the end, she still chose the first dress she'd tried on.

Macy got a better look at the locket Wren always wore under her clothes, which had been her main objective of joining her in the fitting room. The façade of helping Wren pick out a dress was the perfect excuse.

The pendant was much more beautiful than it was in the portrait, or the brief glimpse she'd had the previous evening in Wren's room.

"Wow. That's gorgeous. It was Celine's, wasn't it? I saw it

in the portrait."

Wren bent to pull on her jeans and quickly pulled her V-neck T-shirt over her head. For some reason she was irritated that Macy had been in Celine's room to see the portrait, and hurt that Caleb was obviously close enough to her to take her into his mother's room. "It was."

"What is it?

"A locket. It has Caleb's baby picture in it."

"It's beautiful." Macy reached out to touch it, intent on looking at it closer and seeing the picture. It could be partially seen through the filigree gate of the top section, but the picture that Wren had added of him when he was older in the third gate was hidden behind the first picture. The gates were layered and could only be viewed when the others in front were slid aside. It was like a secret between the person who owned the locket and the person who had gifted it.

Wren backed up a step and quickly returned the pendant beneath her shirt. Only the chain showed until it disappeared beneath the neckline. "It is."

"Then why don't you show it? Why hide it away in your shirt?"

Wren closed her eyes for a split second as she shoved her feet into the pair of old vans she found in her closet that morning. "I just don't. I don't know." She shrugged.

"Do you need anything, honey? Are the sizes alright?" An elderly sales clerk asked, thankfully interrupting Macy's inquiry.

Wren opened the curtain but bent to pick up a hanger from the floor, hung up the dress, and looked apologetically at the clerk. Macy turned and left the room without offering to help Wren remove the dozen dresses she'd brought into the room.

"I'm sorry, I'm just going to get this one dress." She handed the one she'd chosen over to the woman. "Can I bring some of these out and help put them away?"

"Oh, no dear. I can do it."

"I feel bad leaving this mess for you. I'd be happy to help," Wren said, and offering a soft smile as she picked up her purse and slung it over her shoulder; she grabbed several dresses from where they were hanging on the walls. There was a rack outside the dressing room suite that she hung them on.

Wren glanced out to see Caleb engaged in an animated discussion with Macy; his brow furrowed. It seemed intense and Wren looked away when Macy put her hand on his chest in a familiar way. "Would you be able to help me find a scarf and jacket to go with this dress? I don't have a lot of money, though, so something simple," she asked the woman.

"Oh, of course, dear. Do you have an idea of style?"

"Basic black. I'm hoping it will rely on cut for style, and a simple scarf with muted colors. Maybe grey and white, or grey paired with a soft pastel? It's for a funeral and wake. I'd like to be able to wear this dress to both. I'll need sheer black stockings and some basic black pumps."

"I can help you with the jacket and scarf, but the shoe department is downstairs."

"Would you mind just picking out the blazer and scarf? Whatever you add will be fine. I just really want to get this over with."

The woman nodded in understanding and went off to

collect Wren's requests. "Of course. I understand, dear."

When Caleb caught sight of Wren with the sales woman, he touched Macy on the elbow with his index finger. "Just a minute." He walked toward Wren when the older woman walked away. She looked stressed and frazzled. "Are you okay? Did you get everything you need?"

"I did find a dress and the clerk is going to find a couple of matching pieces. I still have to get shoes." She pressed the back of her hand to her forehead. "This sucks, Caleb." She looked up into his concerned face and shook her head. "I'm sorry."

He pulled her into his arms and against his chest in a tight hug. "For what?" He loved the way she smelled. Everything about her was softer than Macy, even her scent.

He could feel her shoulders rise in a shrug against him, still unwilling to let her out of his embrace.

"Everything?" her voice broke slightly.

Caleb bent to kiss the top of her blonde head, his lips moving against it as he spoke. "It's going to be okay, Wren."

"Is it?" Her arms were around his waist now and her fingers curled into his shirt.

"I promise."

"Are we buying the dress, or what?" Macy's impatient voice intruded. "I'm starving."

Wren pulled out of Caleb's arms, guilt flooding over her. Macy shouldn't have to witness her falling apart like a baby in Caleb's arms. She sniffed and smiled at her. "Yes. I'm just waiting for the clerk to come back with a scarf and jacket. I'll pay the bill here and go find some shoes. Why don't you two go to the food court while I finish up?"

"An excellent idea," Macy began, sliding a hand through Caleb's elbow to start pulling him away.

Caleb had other ideas and was already handing Macy money. "You go. We'll meet you there."

"I came to shop, not eat alone."

Caleb turned to Macy and put his hands on her shoulders. "Then shop. But if you're hungry, get something to eat and we'll follow in a few minutes."

Macy glanced in Wren's direction. The sales clerk had returned and was helping her try on the jacket by the cash register, and viewing her reflection in the long mirror outside the dressing rooms.

"Look, Caleb. I'm not going to let you brush me off while you hold Wren's hand. She's buying shoes, not getting open heart surgery, for God's sake. She's not that fragile. I'm getting sick of this pathetic big brother routine. I barely knew she existed before this trip. You can't be *that* concerned about her."

Anger exploded in Caleb's chest. "I don't give a fuck what you're tired of right now, Macy! Jesus Christ! Get over yourself for ten minutes!" His voice was low, but intense.

He left her standing there, mouth agape and went to pay for the dress against Wren's objections. When he was finished, Macy was gone and he didn't even care. If she wasn't in the food court when they were finished, he'd text her. He was beyond putting up with her unreasonable behavior.

He put his hand over Wren's as she started to pull her credit card out of her wallet and handed the woman his. "I've got this."

Wren shook her head adamantly. "No Caleb."

"I've got this, Wren." He put an arm lightly around her waist and nodded at the clerk to run his card. He bent down so he could speak in Wren's ear. "Rumor has it, I'm about to be loaded."

"Maybe it's all going to charity," she teased. "You might be dead broke."

He laughed. For the first time feeling light hearted since Macy confronted him in the great room earlier in the afternoon. "Even so, I'm still buying your dress."

Wren gasped at the total the nice old woman gave after ringing up the purchases. "Maybe just the dress and the scarf," she began.

"We're good." He shook his head at the sales lady. "Ignore her. We're good with this. Thank you." Caleb smiled and took hold of the two hangers protruding from the plastic bag and hauled it over the counter. "Have a great day." He winked at the woman.

"You two are so cute together. Have a nice day."

He smirked. "Thanks."

"Caleb, that's too much."

"Hear that? We're cute."

She punched him hard in the arm, but his muscle was hard and she was sure her hand was the more damaged of the two. "Ow! You don't need to—"

"Hush." He took Wren's hand and threaded her fingers through his, then headed her toward the escalator. "Now we need shoes, right?" He grinned down at her with one raised eyebrow.

"I only have flip flops and Vans. So, yes I do, but I'm buying them."

"Whatever," he said, amusement lacing his voice. There was no way in hell he was letting her pay for them.

The shoe department was to the right at the bottom of the escalator and Wren let go of his hand as she started to browse the tables laden with different types of shoes, organized by type. There were fancy heels and pumps, open toed boots, stilettos, and others with chunky or stacked heels. The dress had a simple elegance, and she wanted a shoe that would be as versatile.

Soon, a salesman was bringing out five different styles in her size. Caleb planted himself in one of the chairs in the middle of the department, the dress bag draped across his lap. As Wren sat next to him, she couldn't help notice the way many of the women and teenage girls perusing the shoes sending glance after glance in his direction. He seemed oblivious to their interest as he checked his phone.

The two years they spent at the same high school was laden with girls trying to get with him. If she hadn't known better, it could have been it's own varsity sport. Once she stopped cutting herself and dressing in disguise, and they were seen coming and going together, she was inundated with questions and pleas for introductions.

Caleb kept to himself. He was never involved in sports or after school activities; his fight club had been his sport; the one that kept his body honed. He never went to the school dances, and neither had she.

"Are you still fighting, Caleb?" Wren asked as they waited.

"Not as much. I did find one club in San Francisco and I fight occasionally, though not with the same frequency as in high school."

He wasn't fiddling with his phone anymore and she reached out to put her hand over his. "Caleb. This probably isn't the place, but I don't think I ever thanked you."

He looked at her, his eyes inquisitive. "For what? "

She shook her head softly. "Everything. Without the fighting, I wouldn't be a dancer now. Without you... I might have killed myself. You saved me from my mother, helped me have a life, and made me realize I was worth something."

He placed his free hand over hers, so one of her hands was between both of his. "Wren... you're worth *everything*." Emotions swelled and he swallowed at the tightness starting in his throat. His eyes started to sting. "Look at your life. You bring pleasure and beauty to the world. When you dance, it's like magic."

"I felt guilty every time you came home with a bruised face."

"You know my life was shit before you showed up. If not for you, I would have thought my mother died for nothing." He cleared his throat, knowing he was exposing much more than he intended to do in the shoe department at Nordstrom's. "Anyway, I would've been fighting regardless. I was already doing it, remember?"

"I know. But, you started doing it more often. Ballet lessons are expensive."

He laughed, his cobalt eyes locking with hers. "Don't I

know it! I wouldn't change it, though. Look at you now. You're like a butterfly, finally out of your cocoon." Caleb stopped. His words made him second-guess his decision. Half the estate might just be the shackle she didn't want. "I'm so proud of you."

"Okay," the salesman said, as he put a stack of boxes on the carpet in front of Wren. "I didn't have this one in a six, but I have a six and a half."

He began opening boxes and pulled individual shoes out of each one. Caleb watched in silence as she tried on each style, offering his opinion with a nod or shake of his head when she looked at him. He felt sorry that the close moment they had just shared had ended.

***

After the shopping trip, Caleb had showered and changed into a navy blue suit, a crisp white dress shirt, and silver and navy patterned tie. He'd already told Wren that he had a meeting with Jonathan before the visitation, and spoken to Jonesy about all the women going together with the driver to meet him there. Macy on the other hand was another story. She'd been silent and stoic on the ride home after they'd found her at the Michael Kors store buying a new spring bag. Clearly she was upset, and in all honesty, he couldn't really blame her.

He reluctantly made the trek from his room to hers to let her know what his plan was. Despite how he was feeling about the coming end of their relationship, he wasn't a big enough prick to blow her off completely.

Macy opened the door after a brief knock. She was dressed in a dark grey pencil skirt and pale pink blouse; and her hair was slicked back in the usual chignon she wore for work. The suit flattered her curvy figure and could be considered sexy, but not overtly so. She looked beautiful, and her makeup was perfect. Her level of sophistication was so different from Wren's, who was naturally beautiful and uncomplicated.

"Hey," he said quietly, waiting to be asked inside.

She turned away, leaving the door open to retrieve the jacket to her suit from the hanger in the closet. "Hi."

He walked in, closing the door behind him. "I have a meeting with my father's lawyer before the wake. Jonesy said she'd have something for you and Wren to eat in the kitchen and then the driver will bring you all over." His suit jacket was open and he shoved both of his hands into his pants pockets. "You look nice."

She let out a small sound of disgust, ignoring Caleb's compliment. "I'd prefer to come with you, now, Caleb. I've had enough of little Wren for one day."

Caleb stopped, and huffed with a short shake of his head. His eyes were incredulous as he looked at her. It was getting to the point that he couldn't stand having her around. "What is your problem, Macy? If you don't like what's happening, you don't have to come along. Wren has a right to be there."

Her face fell. "I'm sorry. Can't I just come with you?"

"It's a confidential meeting. I'll meet you at the funeral home in a couple of hours. If you don't want to have dinner in the kitchen, then you have the rental car... grab something on the way." Macy's back visibly stiffened and she took a slight pause slightly before donning the jacket and closing the one button in front.

"Is it about your father's will?"

"Among other things."

"So, why can't I come? It's no secret what's in your father's will. You're his only child."

"Jonathan asked I come alone." Caleb looked at his watch, impatiently. It was close to 4:30 PM and the service started at 6. "I don't have time to argue. I just wanted to let you know what I'm doing."

He began leaving the room, but Macy followed him through the house.

"I'll wait in the car or outside the room, but I'm not staying here in this mausoleum without you."

Caleb regarded her with calm indifference as she caught up to him. He was more than annoyed that she speculated on the content of his father's will, but he'd be damned if he'd show it. If she wanted to wait in the car, that was fine with him.

"Fine. I'll let Jonesy know you're coming with me." He walked into the kitchen calling the old woman's name, but she was nowhere to be found. "Jonesy?"

There was a small white board that she kept on the side of the large stainless steel refrigerator. She'd kept there for him since he was a small child, and he used to write down a list of food or other things he needed her to buy on her shopping trips. He quickly scrawled out a note.

Jonesy,
I have a meeting with Jonathan and I have Macy
with me. See you and Wren there.

Caleb

"COME ON." CALEB WALKED to the doorway that led from the kitchen into the garage, then stood back and waved her through in front of him. He had the key fob in his hand and unlocked the door as they approached the same grey luxury car they'd taken earlier in the day. After he held open her door and she was securely inside, Caleb walked around and slid into the driver's side.

Macy watched his every move with guarded eyes as she set her small bag on the light grey leather seat next to her.

"What's the story with you and Wren anyway?"

Caleb started the engine and was soon navigating his way out of the garage.

"Our story?" The corners of his well-defined lips lifted in a wry half smile. "Her bitch mother moved in on my dad not long after my mother died. I already had a deep hatred for my dad. I mean; I fucking wished I could kill him. I wished he'd died instead of my mom. She was the best person I think I've ever known. There was a bevy of the best doctors, but no one could save her, and at the end, my dad disappeared." The memory was still painful; Caleb's expression was stoic as he kept his focus on the road ahead.

As they pulled out of the gated community and Caleb merged into traffic, Macy continued. "That doesn't tell me anything about Wren."

"My mom was the face of Lux, and after she died, Veronica was hired to replace here."

"Right. She was that blonde model, right?"

"Yes. She became the new spokesperson, face, whatever. One day, my dad showed up with her and her kid, told me he'd remarried and the two of them were moving into our house. I wanted nothing to do with either of them."

"Wow. I'm sorry, Caleb. That must have been hard on you. How old were you?"

There was genuine sympathy in her voice that made it easier for Caleb to continue. Jonathan's office was about twenty-five minutes from the house and he decided that maybe she'd be more understanding about Wren if he told her a few of the facts. "Sixteen. I remember being so pissed I wanted to break something. Veronica was a plastic bitch, and I could see it from day one. Wren was barely visible, but I thought she was strange."

His eyes narrowed with the memory and his hands deftly maneuvered the car onto Interstate 25. "She looked different then. Her clothes were black, she used to wear this short black wig and a lot of dark eye shadow." He was introspective, like he was speaking to himself. "She acted like a scared mouse that barely spoke and didn't eat. She was skin and bones, and really screwed up. Even at school, she kept to herself and kids made fun of her. It was brutal."

Caleb cleared his throat and glanced at Macy who was listening with rapt attention. He decided to leave out the part about Wren cutting.

"Why would she disguise herself? I know that the Goth thing is big with some kids, but even at home?"

"Her mom was a mean, cold bitch, who couldn't stand it if anyone was prettier than her. Wren was much more beautiful. As she grew up, Veronica got meaner. I remember the first time I saw her as she really was. I thought I was dreaming. I'd just been in a particularly bad fight and I was in pretty bad shape... I didn't think she was real. All that golden hair, and her eyes without all that shit on them were... amazing. I'll never forget that moment."

Macy bristled in her seat. Clearly, there was much more to Caleb's relationship with Wren than she thought. She folded her hands in her lap and glanced out the window, letting him continue.

"When she told me the truth, I wanted to kill that bitch. I already hated Veronica, but after that, it was worse. I decided that Wren would never suffer under her hands or anyone else's again, and I wouldn't let her disguise herself anymore." He laughed bitterly. "I used my fight winnings to buy her clothes and enroll her into dance lessons. Dancing was the only thing she wanted, and with all this money," he waved around at the rich interior of the very expensive car, " Veronica wouldn't allow her to take classes."

Macy sighed. "That's too bad." Even she had to admit the situation sounded overly harsh.

Caleb's mind flashed back to a painful memory. "Yeah. I almost got arrested for assault once. Veronica went into Wren's room and hacked a big chunk of her hair off. Can you believe that shit?" The fingers of his left hand grazed his strong chin as he rested his elbow against the door. "It was gorgeous and she fucking cut it off."

"What did you do?" Macy asked softly, watching the emotion cross his features as he drove.

"I fucked her up. When I heard Wren crying and I went up there and saw what had happened; I lost it." He could remember it as clearly as if it were yesterday.

"Wren!" Caleb ran into her room at the sound of her sobbing. It was those harsh, wracking sobs that you feel in your chest, even if they aren't your own. "What the hell?" he asked in shock as he looked down upon her.

She was on the floor, leaning on her bed. On one side of her head, her hair was wacked off at the shoulder and he saw it, even though she had buried her face in her bent arms. Next to her on the carpet was a big chunk of her hair and a pair of scissors lying side-by-side. Seeing it, Caleb didn't need to ask what happened.

"That cunt!" he had bellowed. "I'm going to fucking kill her, Wren!"

He fell to his knees and gathered her close; her small form melting into him as she cried. His hand cupped her head and his other arm pulled her into the cradle of his arms. "I'll take care of this, Bird. I swear to God, she'll never touch you again."

After a couple of minutes, Caleb cupped her cheek with his palm. "Stay here, and lock the door when I leave."

"Caleb, don't get in trouble," Wren pleaded in a sad voice, her hand feeling at her head to assess the damage. Her chin started to tremble again. She'd have to get it all cut off if it

was going to look like anything.

"Just stay here."

He grabbed the scissors by the blades and shot out of the room like a rocket, slamming the door behind him.

"I had the scissors in my hand when I went to find my stepmother."

"Oh dear God! Did you stab her?"

Caleb grunted, and shook his head with the start of a devious grin. "No. I got my dad's electric beard trimmer out of his bathroom, then found Veronica, backhanded her, and sent her flying to the floor. It's the only time I've ever hit a woman, but it was so I could pin her down and mow a strip down the center of her head."

Macy couldn't decide if she was horrified or if it was funny in some twisted way. "What happened?"

"She screamed like a banshee and I went back upstairs with Wren and waited for the cops to show up. Veronica called them, and they hauled me to jail, but my dad posted bail a couple of hours later and Jonathan got the charges dropped."

They arrived at the law offices and Caleb pulled into a parking spot near the door. It was Sunday and the lot was completely empty except for Jonathan's BMW. When Caleb put the car in park, he glanced at Macy. "After that, my dad and I had an understanding that he'd keep Veronica away from me and Wren, or I was going to beat the shit out of her, and fuck the consequences."

"So, your dad was better after that?"

"He was less in my face, but he got back at me when he shipped me off to MIT."

"Why, if you didn't want to go?"

"That's another story. I have to go inside." He shut the car off, but left the fob in the middle console for her. "It's nice, so you might enjoy having the windows down, and of course the stereo. This shouldn't take long."

Caleb left Macy in the front seat of the car and walked into the elegant building that housed Jonathan's law firm. It was in an older part of Denver, and his offices were in an old Victorian house that had been renovated. The interior was indicative of Jonathan: elegant and majestic, with rich furnishings, fine wood and leather, with bookcases lining several of the walls.

Caleb knew the old house well, and had spent a lot of time in Jonathan's office when he was younger. He made his way through the halls to the back, past several other offices, to the largest one at the end.

Jonathan was in a dark suit sitting at his desk, with two sets of papers sitting in front of him. He looked up when he heard Caleb approach.

"Hello, son." His voice was warm and welcoming as he indicated a one of the two chairs in front of his desk he wanted Caleb to sit in. "Take a seat."

Caleb sat down, only nodding to the older man.

"There are a couple of things to go over, Caleb. Normally, the will would be sealed until the reading, but this isn't a typical situation and your father asked me to go over it with you to make sure you are fully aware of the choice."

Caleb's elbows were resting on the arms of the leather occasional chair he was sitting in and he opened his hands, palms up. "You don't need to. I get everything, or we split it.

What's to go over?"

"He just wanted to make sure you understood the five-year provision, and that I explained a couple of other things."

Caleb felt impatient. It was warm in the office and he had the urge to loosen his tie and unbutton the top button of his shirt. "You told me the other day. We can't sell for five years. If we walk, we can't give it to charity because of the implications to the stockholders. Both of us have to commit to the five years or we lose everything. Am I missing anything?"

"Not much. If you want to sell your shares after five years and donate the cash to charity, that's the only way it can happen. The shares remain with the company, and it remains a viable entity."

"Can I run it without Wren? I mean, if she doesn't want to stop dancing right away?"

"That's an option. What you work out between the two of you is up to you." Jonathan shook his head in silent contemplation. He'd known Caleb would be willing to sacrifice his own plans for his design firm, take on all the work, and still give up half of the estate for Wren.

"That's it, then." Caleb's clear blue eyes locked with Jonathan's. "Do I have to sign anything?"

"Not until the reading. All of the beneficiaries have to sign."

"Beneficiaries? You mean us, and Jonesy?"

"Your father left Jonesy a small sum of cash for her retirement, and he gave me one thousand shares in Lux."

Caleb felt Jonathan and Jonesy deserved anything they received and more. "Good."

"There's one more thing, Caleb," Jonathan said as he put one copy of the will back into an official looking envelope and sealed it. "Veronica does receive a small bequest."

Caleb was in the process of standing and buttoning the front of his blazer. "What?" His tone had lowered and took on a slight seethe at the mere mention of Veronica's name. "Why would Dad do that? Can we fight it?"

Jonathan shrugged. "It's not worth it. I've seen cases where the ex-spouse will go to court and try to contest a will, citing that they were in the process of reconciling. This would have been difficult to disprove because your father was an extremely private man and he wasn't seeing anyone else at the time of his death. Your absence also made that possibility likely. Veronica could rely on your estrangement with your father to keep any validity of your rebuttal in question."

Anger was starting to boil inside Caleb. He could feel the heat creep under his skin, his pulse quicken and his muscles coil as adrenalin started to course through his veins. He'd have to get a workout in later that night if he wanted to keep his cool. "So he caved and gave her a piece of it all, is that what you're telling me?"

Jonathan was smiling, which seemed to piss Caleb off even more.

"No. He gave her one hundred dollars."

Caleb paused, intrigued and beginning to understand the other man's amusement and his anger cooled instantly. "That's uh... funny." He smiled; then chuckled softly.

"If Veronica gets anything at all, she can't contest. If he stiffs her completely she may argue he was ill and overlooked her. If she's given a specified amount, especially one this laughable, his intentions are crystal clear. We wrote this in with a no-contest clause. It's for your protection, and Wren's."

"Will that hag be here for this? I'll throw in another hundred if she'll make herself scarce."

The two men laughed out loud. "No, she's not a principal beneficiary so she doesn't have to be in attendance at the reading. I'll notify her via registered mail next week."

"Well that bitch can smell money from thousands of miles away. I just hope she doesn't show up and harass us all. Especially Wren."

chapter
ELEVEN

THE PARKING LOT WAS ALMOST FULL to capacity when Caleb and Macy arrived at the funeral home.

Local and national news media vans were lined up outside, and reporters and camera people were filming live reports. He held up his hand when one of them asked him for a statement, and kept on walking without a word.

"The national news media is covering my dad kicking off. Awesome," Caleb muttered as they proceeded past them toward the doors.

"Lux Cosmetics is a global brand, Caleb. You had to expect press coverage of your father's death," Macy said simply.

She was right. Caleb was thankful that the actual funeral the following day would be closed to the public, with only a few very close friends and family in attendance.

When Caleb opened one of the double wooden doors

so Macy could enter in front of him, the odor of the place smacked him square in the face. He remembered that same scent from the three other funerals he'd attended in his life. If the way Macy wrinkled her nose was any indication of her distaste, she found it equally offensive. She was clinging to his arm and had made two attempts to hold his hand, but he was feeling emotionally closed off.

His defensive demeanor might be due to the wake, but he gave more weight to the combination of events that happened over the past couple of days. Macy's selfishness and her lack of compassion, the way his heart had literally leapt at the sight of Wren and having her close, and wanting her to remain that way, all added to his father's death. Caleb felt disengaged with Macy in every way, and it was just another unpleasant situation he needed to deal with.

The sickening scent of the mortuary was lessened by the bevy of flowers in the entryway and the many wreaths and large arrangements strewn around the room; on the floor, and on stands of varying heights. They were obviously sent by business associates, board members, and vendors who his father dealt with at Lux.

The funeral director had called him the day before and asked him if he wanted a private viewing, and he'd declined. He found the whole business of dying sickening and humiliating. When he thought about what actually happened to his father's body before it was laid out for people to leer at, he cringed. And really, what was the point to any of it?

Ugh.

The wake would require hours of time; going through

the motions of shaking hands and making inane small talk with people he didn't know or didn't remember, along with meeting people he didn't give a shit about.

The sympathetic glances in his direction said most were aware he was Edison Luxon's son. As he made his way through the room with Macy at his side, he wished he could skip the whole goddamned thing. Several people stopped him, patted him on the back, or shook his hand; many murmuring those meaningless comments people make after someone close to you dies.

"I'm so sorry for your loss, Caleb. Who's this pretty girl?"

"I loved working for Mr. Luxon. He was a great boss and will be missed."

"If there's anything I can do for you, let me know."

They were stopped multiple times by people anxious to offer their condolences, and he could sense Macy getting more and more pissed each time he introduced her as his friend. To give her credit, she pasted a stiff smile on her face and did her best to hide her ire.

His father's casket was partially hidden from Caleb's view by the line of people filing past it. It was located at the front of the room, with more and more flowers strewn around it, on the floor in front, and a large spray of white roses covering the lower half of the polished wood surface. The quilted white fabric on the inside of the lid was visible, but he only caught glimpse of his father's body as people filed by. His stomach lurched at the thought his father was actually inside. This was going to suck. He tugged uncomfortably at the collar of his shirt under the silk tie, wishing he could just take the damn thing off.

The sedan that had brought Wren and Jonesy had been parked out front, indicating they were already inside. Jonathan had followed Caleb and Macy from his office in his own car. Caleb's eyes scanned the room for Wren, looking for long blonde curls, still distracted when the funeral director approached.

"Hello, Mr. Luxon. I'm Alfred Baines." A hand was offered and Caleb shook it without thinking.

"Nice to meet you."

"You'll find a small room off to the side at the front for you and your family. It offers more privacy and you should be more comfortable in there." He handed them each a piece of folded white stationery with his father's picture and obituary on it. Caleb shoved it into the breast pocket of his suit without reading it.

"Thank you, Mr. Baines."

Caleb put a hand on Macy's arm to stop her briefly. "I'm going to go up and pay my respects. Why don't you go into the room Mr. Baines mentioned?"

Macy studied him for a brief moment. "Are you okay? I can come with you."

He shook his head in denial. He wasn't sure how he was going to feel and the last thing that Caleb wanted was to be seen showing any weakness. "No. I want to do this alone. I'll see you in a minute." Without waiting for her response, he turned and bypassed the line.

Those in front of him made way for him to take a moment alone beside the casket. Caleb stood and gazed down at his father for an obligatory moment. He felt sick, seeing his father cold and lifeless inside the expensive cherry wood casket. Edison's hair was still the same impeccable style he'd always worn, though with more grey than the last time Caleb had seen him, but he looked more peaceful than ever before.

Feeling morose, Caleb sighed; his lungs protesting at the tightness in his chest as he contemplated on the man he'd barely spent a week with since he'd graduated from MIT four years before. Guilt over his contribution to the estrangement of their relationship nagged at him. Maybe if he'd opened a few of those goddamned letters things could have been different, but a mountain of regret was useless now. It changed nothing.

He felt a warm presence beside him and Caleb knew without looking that it was Wren. The familiar scent of her perfume lingered softly in the air around him. Unlike Macy, he welcomed her nearness. She slid an arm through his, her fingers curling around his bicep, as she rested her forehead on his arm just below his shoulder.

Despite wearing the new high heels Caleb had purchased for her earlier at the mall, he still towered over her. His uneasiness settled in the same way it always did when she was near. His hand lifted to cover hers in silent connection.

"Are you okay?" she asked softly.

He nodded, still gazing down at his dad. "Yeah. You know, this is the first time I've been in the same room with him when he wasn't riding my ass for one reason or another," he said with a wry quirk of his lips. "I wish—" He stopped abruptly.

"I know, Cale." She squeezed his arm where she still held it. "Edison wouldn't want you to beat yourself up." Her tone was soft and pained. She desperately wanted to take away the ache she heard in his voice. Caleb was strong, and most people wouldn't pick up on it, but Wren did. "He knew he was the one at fault."

"It was easier when I hated the son-of-a-bitch." Caleb blinked at the sting in his eyes.

"Maybe, but that's not the life you deserve; to hate him or punish yourself forever. He wouldn't want that. "

Caleb slid an arm around the back of Wren's waist and moved to turn her away from the casket. "Come on. I don't want to talk about it now."

More people were coming in; the line was forming up the center aisle now, ushered by the funeral home staff. The chairs sitting in multiple rows were filling fast.

Caleb caught site of Dex and his parents about halfway back and he nodded at his friend. The two had kept in contact over the years, but Caleb hadn't been back to Denver to see him even once since the night they fought. It hadn't been easy for Caleb to move beyond the night when Dex put the moves on Wren, but eventually they had talked it out over the phone. Dex would have been insane not to want her; she was so beautiful, and it was Caleb's fault he'd never confessed his feelings concerning Wren to his best friend. He'd always held his emotions for her so close to himself out of guilt. How do you confess to being in love with a girl who you are supposed to protect and everyone else sees as your sister?

Dex looked quite a bit different; his hair was less edgy and he was wearing dress slacks and a button down. Growing up, Caleb had never seen Dex in anything other than jeans,

T-shirts and leather jackets. His old friend rose and walked up, offering his hand to Caleb and then going in for a brotherly hug. "It's good to see you, man. Sorry about your dad." He looked at Wren, and bent to kiss her on the cheek. "How are you, Wren?"

She smiled softly and Caleb could see the admiration in Dex's eyes. Some things never changed, and he didn't expect them to.

"You look good, Dex. Different."

Dex smiled. He was handsome in a rugged sort of way.

"Well, I couldn't be a thug my whole life. My dad has me managing the shop and we've expanded. We have three locations, now. Have you started your design firm in San Francisco?"

Dex was a first class mechanic. They'd both learned a lot from Darren growing up, but Dex had gone to trade school and learned how to run his father's business, while Caleb attended a top engineering university. It would have been the perfect combination for the two of them to go into business together, which had been their plan for years.

"Not yet. Might go on the back burner for awhile, now. I have to deal with Lux."

"Are you still fighting?" Dex asked.

"On occasion. I beat the shit out of the bag at the gym on a more regular basis." The two men laughed softly. Wren watched the interaction between the two of them, admiring them both. Both men were tall and fit, Caleb a bit taller with more of a classic beauty to his face. He had his mother's model features, though he was casually unaware of how people stared at him. Wren had always been acutely aware of him.

Dex put his hand lightly on the small of Wren's back. "Are you still with the touring company or back in New York for good?" he asked.

"Still touring, but we're on a break for a few weeks."

"I'd love to see you dance sometime."

"She's amazing. Stick around afterward and we'll get a beer at the house. Jonesy's been cooking for days. Bring your folks."

"Sounds good. I remember Jonesy's cooking."

Caleb hit Dex's bicep with his open palm. "It's good to see you."

It didn't escape Caleb's radar that Dex knew about Wren's schedule, which meant they'd been in touch. After he'd beat the shit out of him all those years ago, he was a bit surprised Dex still kept track of her, and that he neglected to mention it on any of their phone calls. It was probably nothing, but he couldn't deny that it still bothered him.

After Dex returned to his seat, Caleb and Wren found Macy, Jonathan, and Jonesy already waiting in the small room off to the side. The room was furnished with upholstered couches and chairs and was set up more like a living room. A few others, including his father's personal assistant and some of the board members, were also there.

Jonathan made the necessary introductions to some of the senior members of Lux's board of directors, and then they all took their seats.

Jonesy approached Caleb and put her arms around him. She hugged him, and he bent down to kiss her weathered cheek. "We're here for you," she said solemnly as she patted his cheek and pressed his mother's bible and her pearl and gold rosary in his hand. He was touched that she'd remembered to bring them with her. The dark brown leather and white beads blurred as he looked down at them in his hand. He swallowed at the tightness of his throat.

"I know. Thank you, Jonesy. This was nice of you to remember."

"Of course, honey. Celine would want you to have them with you today."

Given the turn his life had taken after his mother's death, Caleb wasn't all that religious, but she had been and the sentimental gesture touched him deeply. He held her rosary and her bible on his left knee after he sat down.

Caleb's right hand reached for Wren's as she sat beside him. He was unaware that he'd barely let go of her once since she'd joined him beside his father's casket. However, Macy was extremely aware, and sat in stiff silence to his left.

The reciting of the rosary seemed long; the same few prayers being recited over and over again felt monotonous and unnecessary to Caleb. The words to all but a couple of the prayers escaped him, even though he'd had them all memorized as a young child.

Sitting there, his mind was preoccupied. His father was the type to get down to business and dispense with anything frivolous, and he would consider this bevy of crying and praying unnecessary. Edison wouldn't have wanted a full-blown funeral. Caleb realized the formality was mostly for the press and the board of directors, who were no doubt taking advantage of any free publicity for the advancement of the company.

Caleb glanced past Wren at Jonesy who was sitting on the other side of her. She was staring straight ahead, and was struggling to hold it together as she dabbed at her eyes with a fine linen handkerchief. Caleb's chest expanded as he pulled in a breath. Obviously, Jonesy cared more about Edison than she let on. Caleb was thankful she'd been the one to arrange the funeral. The style of the service was likely what his mother would have also wanted, had she been alive to arrange it.

The scripture readings were delivered, and the hymns sung by people he was unfamiliar with. Jonathan would say the eulogy the following day at the funeral, then his father would be buried, the will would be read, and life would resume.

His father was dead and he couldn't change it no matter how badly he wanted to. He'd been robbed of his mother by cancer, and only now, after his father was gone, did he have any indication that Edison had actually cared about him. It was ironic how fucking cruel life could be, but there was something about the finality of death that demanded acceptance.

Wren's fingers squeezed around his; as if she could sense what he was thinking. He turned his head to glance down at her, to find her light blue eyes swimming in tears. Resentment and anger rose up and he felt ready to scream; his heart started pounding uncomfortably inside his chest. This was the real injustice; the time lost and the unknown of what his relationship should have been with Wren. He'd loved her for almost half of his life and nothing would ever change it. Not time, other women, distance, or letting each other down...

nothing.

Her brow furrowed as she recognized the frustration on his handsome face. "Cale, what is it?" she whispered.

He shook his head and squeezed her hand back, rubbing his thumb over the top of her fingers. "I'll tell you after the will is read. Let's just get through the next couple of days."

Macy couldn't hear the exchange between Caleb and Wren, given their whispers and the way Caleb leaned over so he could speak into Wren's ear. Anger boiled just beneath the surface and she shifted uncomfortably in her seat. She knew she had to tread carefully or risk losing him, but she could barely contain herself from an outburst; even as the wake continued around them.

After it was over and people were filing out, she bit her tongue yet again. Caleb was still hovering over Wren and Macy felt completely left out. He was polite to her, opening the doors for them both, but it was obvious in his actions and in conversations with others, where his focus was. Maybe she'd have some time alone with him in the car on the way back, given that Wren had arrived with Jonesy. Macy felt sure Wren wouldn't allow the housekeeper to ride back to the house alone. It played out exactly like she anticipated.

Jonathan hugged Wren goodbye as the five of them parted ways in the parking lot. Wren and Jonesy climbed into the back of the black sedan, Jonathan left in his own car, and she and Caleb were soon securely inside his father's car. They traveled caravan style back toward the estate.

It was dark and the lights of the city raced by the outside of the car, their reflections cast on the windows. Caleb's face bore the glow of the blue dashboard light. It was obvious he was deep in thought, but Macy didn't care. She was almost bursting with the words that she needed to say.

"What will happen tomorrow?" she asked.

One shoulder lifted in a slight shrug as he rested one hand casually on the wheel as he drove. "There will be a short service, then a few people at the house for lunch followed by the reading of the will in early evening. You don't have to stay for that if you want to catch a flight after lunch." His tone was casual and flat.

"You don't need to keep saying that." Macy was hurt and angry, but she tried to bite back a nasty retort. "So the will gets read, then you come home to San Francisco on Tuesday?"

He shook his head absently. "I'm not sure. With an estate this size, who knows when it will all be sorted?"

Macy turned to look at him more directly, her mouth tight. "What's to figure out? It all goes into escrow, Jonathan handles everything, and we get back to our life, right?"

The muscle in Caleb's jaw started to twitch and he shot her an irritated glance. "You shouldn't be so presumptive." He shook his head. He was tired of the cat and mouse game with Macy and he needed to lay it all out for her. "I may go back to San Francisco for a couple of weeks, but ultimately, I'll be coming back to Denver to head up Lux."

Macy's mouth opened and then she shut it again. She'd knew she'd better consider her words carefully because he hadn't exactly been loving or open to her since they'd arrived at this Godforsaken place. "I see. Well," she started slowly. "I'll have to resign and sublet my apartment, as will you, but—"

"No. I will, but you won't. I'm doing this alone, Macy."

"What?" She was stunned. "But, Caleb—."

He shook his head again. "Shit happens. The estate is massive. I can't just dump it on Jonathan, even if I wanted to. He's an old man."

"Then hire someone else!" she spat angrily. "You don't fuck your whole life just because your dad dies."

He huffed shortly. "It's not just my father dying, but thanks for your compassion."

Macy's eyes narrowed and fury made her skin flush with heat. She wished to hell she'd followed her instincts and snuck into Jonathan's office to eavesdrop on their conversation. At least, she wouldn't be blindsided but Caleb's change in plans. Her lips pressed into an irritated line and the hair on the back of her neck stood up. This had to be about the sister.

"I saw the way Wren was clinging to you like white on rice at the funeral. This wouldn't have anything to do with her, would it?"

"She inherits half of everything."

Macy's mouth pinched with resentment. It was just as she thought. "So! Sell the company, get your money, and get the hell back to your own plans. What about your design firm?"

Caleb was becoming impatient. "Isn't that obvious? Someone as smart as you should realize that it's on hold for now. There's a provision in the will that our shares can't be liquidated for five years."

"So she gets to pirouette off into the sunset and you're stuck here? And you *still* have to split it?"

Now, Caleb was pissed. Even he didn't know how it would

play out and he'd be damned if he was explaining himself to Macy. "I could have sworn you were all for my inheriting Lux." His eyes narrowed and his expression was hateful. "Oh, but that was as long as it was just me."

"Because the money would help with your own plans!"

"Yeah, right."

"Why would he saddle you with your little sister for five more years? She has her own career. What was he thinking?"

The gates of the estate opened and Caleb drove through them, up the lane, and around the back to the garage. The electronic door was already opening.

When the car was parked, Caleb turned toward Macy. "How many damn times do I have to tell you that Wren is *not my sister*?" he yelled. The elevated tenor in his voice took Macy aback and her eyes were wide as she looked at him. His words were hard and begged her to defy his control. "I can't speak to my father's intentions other than he was making sure that we didn't bail on the business he built with my mother before giving it a fair shot. I guess he figures five years is what is needed to give us enough time to see if we enjoy running it."

"Bullshit!" Macy's eyes flashed. The lights in the garage were on, but dimly lit. Caleb could see her dark eyes burning in rage. "Five years is long enough for Wren to get her hooks into you!"

Caleb's own fuse was short and getting shorter and the volume in his voice louder. "You know Macy, this has nothing to do with you! You have no right to be indignant about what I have to do, or that Wren is involved. I saw the way a fire lit under your ass when you realized Lux was short for Luxon. I'm not an idiot." Sarcasm dripped from his words. "Personally, I could have lived without the money, but it's not just about me."

He turned, and got out of the car. Slamming the door, he stood and waited for her to follow his lead.

"No," she seethed, stomping her way around the car. "It's about her."

Calm settled over Caleb. He nodded unapologetically. "Partly, yes. My decision to take on Lux is about Wren, but also Jonesy, Jonathan, the board of directors, the thousands of people Lux employs, and the stockholders! It's bigger than me, and my own selfish plans. Look beyond your goddamned nose for a minute. Jesus Christ!"

Fucking hell, he thought with a huff. *Macy was exactly like Veronica. Why didn't I see it sooner?*

"Let the board run Lux! All of our plans are ruined."

"*We* don't have any plans. The design firm was *my* plan. You were just helping me arrange the funding, remember?"

"Yes, and fucking you, in case you forgot," she said. The words were laced with venom.

"That's over."

"What?"

"You heard me. Even if I were fully invested in a relationship with you, which I wasn't, your true colors have surfaced on this trip and effectively killed it for me. I watched my stepmother use my father for years."

Macy sucked in her breath as if someone had knocked her in the gut. "Then at least be honest!" She steeled herself for Caleb's reaction to her next words, but at this point had little to lose. "What's the truth about you two, Caleb? Wren has your mother's locket."

Recognition of the implications registered on his face but he simply stared her down. "Yes, she does, and I already told you about Wren and me."

"I know there's more to it! The necklace is a family heirloom and should go to the woman you marry, so you might want to ask for it back."

"I gave it to her, and it stays where it is. You and I have only known each other a few months, so you can stop trying to make plans for me. It's been fun, but this is my life, not yours. If you'll excuse me, it's been a long fucking day and I'm done with this conversation."

"Are you fucking Wren, Caleb?"

He turned and glared at her, shoving both hands into his pant's pockets. "I'm not dignifying that with an answer."

"You must be, or you wouldn't have given her your mother's jewelry and be treating her like she's made of glass."

"Look, my reasons for giving it to her are between me and Wren! You don't know shit about what she has gone through or why we are the way we are, so back the hell off!"

"But, Caleb ..." She said in a softer tone. "I'm just trying to—"

"Enough!" He held up his hand to stop her from continuing her objection, his eyes burning into her as if he willed her to burst into flames.

He turned and started walking toward the kitchen entrance and Macy followed reluctantly. The physical distance between them screamed that they'd just had a major fight, but Caleb wasn't concerned about the conclusion that would be drawn by others in the house.

Inside, Jonesy was scurrying around the kitchen putting out the food she'd prepared over the last two days, buffet style in the kitchen, and Wren was helping her finish up.

Macy passed through and scurried down the hall to her room without a word and Caleb was thankful. The situation still wasn't resolved but he'd take the short reprieve.

Jonesy had hired a few people to help with service and tending the bar in his father's study, which was already filled with guests. The house was open and there were more people coming in the front doors. He found himself wishing he could just get a plate and a drink then head downstairs with Wren as they did when they were kids and were avoiding both of their parents.

"Caleb, what's up with Macy?"

"She isn't feeling well."

"Should I bring her something?" Wren asked innocently. "Some ginger ale?"

Caleb shook his head. "She'll be fine. Looks like you're busy enough."

"Go on into the other room," Jonesy instructed. She had several sheet pans and was cutting up various dessert bars into pieces and piling them on plates. "There are people you need to talk to and you'll need to eat, Caleb. We'll have this ready in a few minutes," Jonesy instructed in a motherly tone.

"Ugh." He groaned. "Okay."

Wren was filling two big glass bowls with fresh baked rolls to go with an array of meats, cheeses, salads and the desserts

Jonesy was plating. She glanced up and met his eyes. "Are you doing okay?"

Caleb nodded then turned away, pulled at his tie to loosen it, yanked it free from his collar, and then unbuttoned the top two buttons. He might have to socialize with these people, but he was going to be comfortable. "I'll just be glad when this bullshit is over."

Caleb made his way into his father's study and asked the bartender for a scotch and water. He leaned his right elbow on the fine wooden surface of the bar and glanced around. There were probably a hundred and fifty people in the house and he didn't know any of them. Looking at the animated way they were talking and the many smiles and laughs, you'd think it was an after hours gathering at the local country club.

He lifted the glass that the bartender had placed in front of him to his lips, glancing over the rim as he took a swallow. The amber liquid burned down his esophagus and settled warmly in his stomach.

His breath rushed out as he caught sight of a tall blonde woman blatantly flirting with an older man in a dark suit, who was clearly engaged in her exposed cleavage. Her posture was as elegant he remembered, but she was trash; pure and simple.

What the fuck was Veronica doing here?

Caleb straightened and set his glass down before he made a beeline for her. She was dressed in black, but her lips were covered in bright lipstick that was way to obnoxious for the occasion. He reached out and took her by the arm, turning her around, uncaring of the man she was speaking with or anyone else who would hear. Veronica was clearly shocked at the manhandling.

"Excuse me, I'm Caleb Luxon," Caleb interrupted the man speaking to his stepmother. "As a public service, I must remove this woman while you still have your dick and your wallet." His tone was flat, and his expression wry. The older man stood stunned, and cleared his throat as Veronica's mouth fell open as Caleb's sudden appearance took her by surprise. Her well made-up face stiffened. "Please excuse us." He took her arm and moved her a few feet away.

"What the hell are you doing here, Veronica?" The hatred he felt for the woman could be heard in every syllable. "Get the fuck out of my house."

Veronica quickly gathered her composure, pasting a plastic smile on her face as she looked up into Caleb's stern expression.

He hadn't seen her in four years, though he had to admit she was still well preserved. She was several years younger than his father, though the fine lines around her eyes and mouth were carved a bit deeper. "Did you miss your Botox appointment this month?" he asked scathingly. "You might want to schedule one."

"Uh hmm." She cleared her throat and smiled slyly. "Caleb, darling. Is that any way to treat your stepmother?"

"Cut the crap." Caleb grabbed her upper arm again and started pulling her with him to the front of the house. He didn't want Wren to have to deal with this bitch and wanted her out, now. "I should have expected you to show up. It's common knowledge that vultures buzz around carcasses."

"What a horrible thing to say!" she said shakily.

"You bring out the best in me, I guess," he said dryly.

"Caleb, stop! I want to see my daughter."

"Your daughter?" he shot in disgust. He continued to haul her through the entryway and out the front door as people gawked at the scene they were making. "Wren's not likely to fall for your bullshit lies anymore than I am."

He let go of her once outside, and the momentum carried her forward and she stumbled on the laid cobblestone of the driveway. "Why do you have to be so hateful? People can change."

"Not you." He lifted his arm, signaling Jared to pull the black sedan he'd hired for Wren forward. "Anyone with two brain cells to rub together knows that the only thing that changes about you is which poor bastard you're fucking for his bank account." He laughed harshly. "You must be getting better at it. That poor old man was what, ninety? Maybe he'll die before he can divorce you, but I guess that's the plan, huh?"

When the car pulled forward, Caleb didn't wait for Jared to get out and open the backdoor, instead doing it himself. He nodded to the car, silently demanding that Veronica get inside.

"I'm not leaving without seeing Wren," she insisted.

"She doesn't want to see you. Get out of here!" Caleb was furious, realizing that he had no clue whether Veronica still lived in Denver or if she'd moved. He didn't care.

"I have a right to see her."

"She's an adult. The only right you have is to get the fuck off my property before I call the police." Caleb took her arm and moved her toward the open door; the speed at which he moved had Veronica's high-heel clad feet shuffling and sliding underneath her. "Wren would be the first to say you're just here sniffing around for what you can get, but trust me; you're shit out of luck this time." He forced her inside the backseat, using his free hand to shield her head from the doorframe as momentum carried her backward inside the car. "Jared, get her out of here," he commanded.

"You can't stop me from being at the reading of the will, Caleb." Her voice had risen almost to a screech. "I called Jonathan an hour ago and he admitted Edison included me and Wren."

Caleb huffed out a laugh. "I'm aware." She was in for a big surprise. "Wren will be there tomorrow, and if she wants to speak to you, fine, but I swear to God if you so much as say one wrong word to her, I won't be liable for my actions."

Veronica gasped and Jared let out a laugh. "What are you laughing at?" she yelled at him. "You have no right!"

"Where should I take her, sir?" Jared ignored her, glancing over his shoulder at Caleb. He was still smirking, clearly unaffected by Veronica's rant.

"To the nearest street corner, I imagine. Don't let her berate you or give some sob story about how destitute she is. You work for me, so I expect you to be deaf to her lies. If she lives in town take her there, if not, dump her at the nearest Motel 6." He took a roll of bills out of his right front pants pocket, unrolled a fifty and flung it into the backseat of the car. "That should cover it."

"You've turned into a major bastard, Caleb," Veronica spat

at him. "I guess the fruit doesn't fall far from the tree."

"You're wrong, Veronica. I've *always* been a major bastard. Remember what I said. I can't stop you from showing up, but you will not do one damn thing to hurt Wren tomorrow." He used his hand to make a snip, snip scissors motion right in front of her face. "Don't fuck with either one of us, or you'll be very, very sorry. Hurt her and I'll do a lot more than shave your goddamned head."

He closed the car door in her face before she could say another word and then used the flat of his hand to pound on the roof of the car, signaling Jared to go.

Caleb shoved both hands into the pockets of his slacks as he watched the car pull out of the driveway. He inhaled as deeply as he could, trying to release some of the deep-seated anger boiling inside him. He hated Veronica as much as he ever did. His father's one hundred dollar bequest would stop any monetary claims on the estate, but that didn't mean Wren wouldn't suffer from a lifetime of wheedling from that bitch. He felt sure this was only the beginning.

His mind was working at the speed of light, and Caleb knew exactly what he had to do.

chapter
TWELVE

WREN RETREATED TO HER ROOMS after she was sure Jonesy didn't need any more help cleaning up.

Most of the mourners were gone, with only a few left in the den still talking with Caleb and Jonathan. She could only assume it had to do with the company. It was a massive undertaking and she was curious what Caleb was going to do. Would he move to Denver to assume control, or be silent partner, letting the suits handle the day-to-day operations?

She wanted to spend some time with Caleb so she could be sure of his plans. He'd been monopolized for the two hours since they'd returned from the wake, and given Macy's disappearance this evening, she was certain she would demand the small amount of free time Caleb would have the following day.

She hoped the other girl was feeling better, but Wren

didn't feel like going to her room to check on her. Macy had been standoffish at the wake, and Wren could only assume it was because she was still upset that Caleb helped her pick out her shoes rather than the sightseeing expedition that the other woman wanted. One thing was certain; the two would never be good friends.

She sighed as she took off the scarf and kicked off her shoes, leaving them lay where they landed on the area rug near her bed. She didn't have the energy to be tidy; her eyes were tired from crying and her heart was heavy. She was sad that Edison was gone, but sadder because after the funeral was over, there would be no more reason to stay. Her time with Caleb would be over soon and she wanted every precious second she could manage with him.

She wanted a bath; hoping the hot water would soothe away the tension in her back and shoulders. The sadness she was feeling was only getting worse and nothing would ease it. Distance and time would make it less intrusive, but there would always be that subdued sorrow that never went away. The hole that Caleb's absence left in her life created emptiness inside her chest that would always stay with her. She'd given up hope that it would ease long ago. It was part of her.

She struggled to unzip the dress by herself, bending her arms unnaturally behind her back to get it done. Finally, it was hanging up in the closet next to the new jacket she would wear with it, and she sat on the edge of the porcelain tub adjusting the water temperature. She plugged the tub and then added some softly scented bath salts that were part of the exclusive Lux line.

She stared at herself critically in the mirror as she removed the black lace lingerie. When she was completely naked, she couldn't help but compare herself to Macy whose curves were much more voluptuous and womanly. She ran her hands down her slender body. Her waist and breasts were small, and her pelvic bones were visible due to the concave curve of her stomach. She was muscular and had soft curves, but nothing like Macy, and Macy was the type Caleb liked, she thought dejectedly. In high school, the prettiest and sexiest girls were always around him. Some of her old insecurities crept in and she worked to push them away.

Her gaze moved upward over her perky breasts, collar bones and neck toward her face as steam started to fog over the mirror. That face. It had been the bane of her existence growing up. She slid her fingers over her cheek and jaw.

She swallowed at the pain building in her throat. Her face and the thick, long blonde curls were beautiful. Çaleb said so. Despite the many times her mother had told her she was ugly, stupid or untalented, Caleb belied it and with his help she came to believe it. Her eyes were clear and blue; glistening with unshed tears, and mirrored the deep sorrow she felt. Wren tried to ignore the pain rising up in her throat.

Her mother was a model and so naturally, her daughter shared her beauty. She'd hated the way she looked because her mother hated it. There wasn't a day she could remember after the age of eleven that Veronica didn't berate her with words so harsh no child should hear from anyone, let alone her mother.

The emotional pain had been unbearable. Wren could

pinpoint her mother's pivot to horrible to a day when one of Veronica's string of many boyfriends told Wren she was beautiful and that she'd grow up to be even prettier than her mother.

Something had snapped inside Veronica and in that moment, Wren's life changed for the worse. Her ballet classes were suddenly discontinued, she wasn't allowed to see friends, and her mother stopped being her mother. Everything she ate or said was ridiculed, the way she walked or wore her hair; criticized. Veronica did everything she could to make Wren feel ugly, worthless and miserable.

Her mind flashed to the many times when the emotional pain became more than she could handle, she'd resorted to cutting herself with razor blades or kitchen knives. Physical pain was easier to bear.

Until she learned to layer her face in pale foundation and darken her eyes with too much dark eye shadow, and added the awful black wig until she was basically unrecognizable. Her mother hadn't commented on the change but a miracle happened; the abuse reduced and Veronica basically forgot she was alive. It was lonely, but it was a better existence. It didn't matter that the kids at school were cruel about the way she looked; the trade off at home was worth it.

Wren sucked in a deep breath at the memories. She hid who she really was from everyone, including herself, until the night Caleb needed her to take care of him. His reaction had been powerful and he'd insisted she lose the disguise. She'd been scared, but she trusted him, and though Veronica's hateful behavior resumed, Caleb always stood between them, but he'd helped her much more than that.

She turned her wrist over and gazed down at the tattoo and tears filled her eyes. *Caleb, Caleb, Caleb...* his name resonated in her head. He'd stood between her and anything that could hurt her. She closed her eyes tightly, willing herself not to cry. She'd hoped they would reconcile to the point they could be in contact again, but now with Macy in his life, it might not be possible. Her heart was breaking and against her will, one fat tear squeezed from each eye. She shook her head, angry at her weakness, using both hands to wipe them away.

"Stop it," she commanded herself. Caleb might be a knight in shining armor but he wasn't hers anymore, and it was time she face it. Wren quickly pulled her hair up into a loose bun on top of her head, and stepped into the hot bath. The water was steaming and she had to sink in slowly. The tub was deep and comfortably sloped, and outfitted with twelve Jacuzzi jets that she decided to turn them on when the tub was full. She leaned back, closed her eyes and willed herself to relax.

The water was silky soft and felt amazing. Music was playing in her bedroom but was muffled by the closed door. Wren could hear the soft notes and she started to hum softly with the muted song. It was late and the bath would relax her so she could sleep.

The door to the bathroom burst open and the volume of the song suddenly increased. Wren's eyes flew open and she gasped as she quickly sat up. "What the hell?"

Macy was leaning casually against the marble vanity glaring down at Wren's naked body.

"Humph!" she snorted. "Looking at you, I can't imagine

why I'm even worried. Don't even think about wheedling your way in between Caleb and me. He's mine now, so don't be getting any ideas." She wagged a finger at Wren.

Wren instinctively covered her nakedness with her hands. "Why do you think you can just waltz in here whenever you want?" she said indignantly. "Get out! And take your threats with you. How dare you invade my private room?"

Macy was dressed in an expensive silk negligée in fuchsia silk. Wren's eyes widened at its gaudiness. The towel she wanted was sitting on the upholstered bench on wall beneath the window.

Seeing the direction of Wren's gaze, Macy raced to pick it up. She held it in her hands as her gaze narrowed on Wren. "Where Caleb is concerned, I dare any damn thing I want! Why are you mooning over him like a twelve-year old schoolgirl? It's gross anyway! He's your brother," she said in avid disgust.

Wren's skin flushed as she sat in the tub, her knees drawn up and her arms covering her breasts. "Get out!" she demanded again. "Or, give me a damn towel!"

Macy's face split into a nasty grin. "Not a chance. You're gonna listen to what I have to say. If you think you can come in here, bat your baby blues and have him on his hands and knees, think again!" Her tone was menacing and her nostrils flared.

Wren didn't think she'd ever hate another woman more than she did her mother, but Macy was running a close second. However, if Caleb really did love her, Wren didn't want to cause him problems, no matter her own feelings.

"I'm not mooning over him. It's really not like that," Wren

said evenly, shaking her head. It wasn't easy; Macy's words cut her to the bone, but she'd be damned if she'd give her the satisfaction of seeing her crumble. "I want him to be happy."

"How cute," Macy leered.

Wren realized that if she just let Macy say what she came to say, maybe the other woman would leave her in peace. "Can you let me get dressed and then we can talk? I'm getting cold."

Macy regarded Wren with guarded eyes, and Wren, now without the complete coverage of the water started to shiver.

"Boohoo." Macy folded her arms around the towel, completely ignoring Wren's request. "I see the way you look at him. He feels sorry for you, so don't mistake the obligation he feels toward you for more."

Wren bristled. "I don't. Give me the towel!" she commanded.

Macy looked at Wren with pure, unadulterated hatred. "I'll leave, but just one more thing... give his mother's locket back! He's too much of a gentleman to ask for it, but he wants me to have it. He told me some sob story about why he gave it to you, but it wasn't supposed to be forever."

Wren's jaw jutted out indignantly as Macy's vapid demand landed. Direct hit. Her eyes started to sting and she began to tremble, as the air in her lungs left in a whoosh. Caleb hadn't asked her for it in all the years since he'd given it to her, and it never occurred to her to give it back. She couldn't believe he would be so heartless in telling Macy the circumstances around it; not after their morning together. Her heart started to pound in her chest and she could feel the heat of embarrassment begin to creep into her cheeks.

Macy made no move to leave, and Wren had had enough. She no longer gave a damn about modesty. She stood up abruptly in the tub and the now tepid water rushed down her bare skin; some of it splashing onto the marble floor and the plush throw rug that lay by the tub. Lunging at Macy, Wren's hands fisted around the towel as she yanked with all her strength. A corner of it dropped into the water, but she didn't care.

She managed to pry it loose, but the momentum and the slippery floor sent her sprawling. She landed with a hard thud on her left hip and elbow. She'd be bruised for sure. "Uhhhh," she moaned in pain.

"If this is how graceful you are on stage, it's my advice to get a new job," Macy said sarcastically. "Cale doesn't like mewling little girls, so don't go running to him. He wants a real woman."

Wren's heart seized in pain; the fact that Macy was calling him Cale only made her burn with jealousy. She managed to rise to her feet and face Macy. She was hurt and furious, her body was throbbing from her fall and the insults left her emotions raw. She held the half-dripping towel in front of her with her left hand, but it didn't cover much. She pulled her right arm back and landed a full palm slap to Macy's face with all her might. The contact of skin on skin made a loud pop in the confines of the bathroom that echoed off the marble walls.

Macy's hand flew to her cheek as she stepped back in surprise. "How dare you!"

"You didn't expect that, did you? Get the hell out of here, right now!" Wren was seething, and frustrated tears filled her eyes as she railed at Macy. "Cale has enough to deal with, so don't you dare mention this to him, because if he asks me about it, I'll tell him the truth! He's had my back since I was fourteen, and he knows me better than he'll ever know you. I've never lied to him and he won't doubt me. Now get out!"

Wren whisked past the stunned woman into the attached bedroom, throwing down the towel and quickly pulling on some old grey sweatpants and a long sleeve T-shirt. She whirled on Macy, her chest heaving. "I might be smaller than you, but I promise I'm stronger! I said get out of here! Now!" she almost screamed.

Macy was still stunned by Wren's unexpected bravado, and walked quickly from the room; still holding her face.

When Wren was alone, she bounded forward, slammed the door, and then fell to her knees as furious sobs overtook her. She couldn't breathe and she couldn't see beyond the tears raining from her eyes.

She was heartbroken.

Macy would make it impossible for her to have any kind of relationship with Caleb in the future. It would be more than distance that would separate them and that filled her with unspeakable remorse.

Could he really have said those awful things about her? Did he really want to give the locket to Macy? She was going to lose it; her chest and emotions were about to explode. She got up and ran from her room, down the stairs, and out the back door. The night was breezy as she ran to the pool house; praying it had been left unlocked. She needed to be alone so she could come to terms with the future, cry her heart out, and

Caleb wouldn't be the wiser.

The pool house was the place Caleb said goodbye to her when he left for MIT years ago, and she gravitated toward it without even thinking. She couldn't bear the thought of life without him in it. It was one thing to live without him on a day-to-day basis... but how would she cope without the possibility of knowing him at all?

***

CALEB COULDN'T SLEEP. He'd given up after nearly an hour of trying.

Whapp! Whapp! Whapp! The sounds of his gloved fists hitting the cylindrical bag in the workout room was punctuated by his guttural grunts as he put all of his frustration and strength into it. He couldn't beat the shit out of Veronica, so the bag would have to do.

He tried to process the many emotions running through him. He was livid that Veronica had dared to show up at the house, and was worried sick that Wren would somehow fall apart when faced with that hag. The reading of the will and the logistics of moving to Denver, all had his guts tied up in knots.

He couldn't know how Wren would react to the inheritance being split, then being tied to him for at least five years. Part of him felt guilty about his decision. He knew that she had her own life to live, and he was honest enough with himself to admit that this was a selfish decision. He wanted a chance with Wren. The chance he'd foolishly thrown away nearly four years earlier when he'd slunk away like a coward after he'd made love to her. He hit the bag harder and harder, willing the conflict to leave his mind and heart.

"Ugh! Ugh! Ugh!" The sound of his exertion and aggression against the leather bag filled the glass-enclosed room. Perspiration was beading on his body and face due to his exertion.

He stopped and bent at the waist, breathing hard. He straightened and used one of the short sleeves of his T-shirt to wipe the sweat from his brow as it threatened to drip into his eyes. His teeth pulled at the Velcro closing of his boxing gloves one after the other, so he could remove them. He'd had enough for the night.

The muscles in his arms and shoulders were swollen and bulging from the workout, and his legs felt like jelly. He didn't know how long he'd been at it, but it had to be more than an hour. He hung up the gloves, kicked off his shoes, and then grabbed one of the small towels. He began to wipe down the back of his neck, face and arms. He planned on hopping in the shower, but was badly in need of a drink of water first.

The wet bar in the basement had an assortment of drinks, beer, soda and Perrier in the refrigerator, but no plain water, which was what he craved. His head fell back as he made the choice to go the kitchen. "Hell," he murmured softly, resigned to making the trek upstairs.

The towel now hung loosely around his neck, and he pulled one end of it up to dab at his forehead and eyes. His hair was plastered to his skin and he pushed it out of his eyes in irritation. The lights in the rest of the basement were off, but those illuminating the weight room were enough to see the furniture and the staircase.

Once in the kitchen, he glanced at the clock on the microwave on his way to the refrigerator. It was well after 1 AM. He opened the big stainless steel door, and leaned in to search the contents on the shelves. There were several containers of leftovers from earlier and half a dozen glass bottles of Voss water lined up on the top shelf. Caleb reached for one and was unscrewing the lid and chugging it down before the door to the refrigerator closed. *God bless, Jonesy*, he thought. It was his favorite brand. His head was back as he gulped it down; the cool, refreshing liquid was running down his throat when he heard the sound of the back door to the deck slide open and the low tones of a woman softly crying.

His head snapped up; his hand still closed around the almost empty bottle. He wiped at his mouth with the back of his wrist.

"Wren?" he called softly. "Wren?" Caleb's brow furrowed in concern.

The door shut with a quiet slide and soft click, and panic struck him. It had to be her. The crying belied that it was an intruder. The community was gated and guarded, and the property had it's own security, but he was still freaking out with worry. He set the bottle down, and moved toward the door. His protective instincts insisted he had to find out if she was okay and the reason she was in tears. The day had been long and it could be expected that she was feeling overwhelmed.

His bare feet registered the warmth of the cedar wood beneath his feet as he made his way down the two flights of stairs that separated the levels of the deck, and then onto the smooth concrete that surrounded the pool. June wasn't overly hot, nor was Colorado humid, but the early summer air was warm.

The pool house stood on the west side of the pool, which was landscaped with natural stone, waterfalls and foliage. There were motion lights attached to the deck that turned on automatically when he passed, and small recessed lights under the surface of the water that kept the large pool softly illuminated; the clear aquamarine blue surface pristine.

The structure in front of him had multiple paned windows practically from ground to roof, and contained two dressing rooms, two bathrooms complete with double showers each, and a main room outfitted with a pool table, a wet bar, several tables with chairs, and three plush couches. It reminded him of the clubhouse at his apartment complex in San Francisco, only nicer. The entire property was lined with an eight-foot privacy fence and Caleb had to hand it to his dad; nothing Luxon was ever half-assed.

There were three stone fire pits around the pool, and several luxurious upholstered chaise lounges and umbrella covered tables. Caleb hesitated just briefly before his hand closed around the brass handle of the one of the French doors that led to the entrance. They were also paned glass, and he tried to peer through for Wren. He didn't want to frighten her.

He didn't see her inside but decided to check anyway. He turned the handle, and gently pulled open the right door. The cool central air conditioning contrasted sharply with the night air as it hit his skin; the soft sheen of perspiration still lingering on his skin made it more pronounced. When Caleb stepped inside, the last time they were there together struck him. It had been the night before he left for college. His heart constricted at the painful memory.

He saw her then; her lithe silhouette stood by the far window. Wren's back was to him as she peered outside. The baggy pajama pants she was wearing didn't hide how small she was because of her close-fitting top. One arm hung at her side, and the other was bent up to her chest. The long blonde curls he was so fond of were twisted up into a knot on top of her head. The contrast between the bottoms and shirt made the pants look like they could literally fall off of her.

"Are you okay, honey?" Caleb called softly, moving slowly toward her. "What are you doing out here so late?"

Wren glanced over her shoulder, half turning toward him. Caleb could now see that her arm was bent because her right hand was fiddling with the locket that nestled on her chest. His heart stilled for a second and swelled to bursting. *She still wore it.*

She sniffed and then turned back to the window. "I'm fine." Her voice sounded thick, like she'd been crying. She didn't turn around, which was another tell tale sign that she didn't want him to see her face. "I'm just thinking about a few things."

He walked the rest of the way toward her and then put his hands on her shoulders, sliding them down her upper arms and then back up again. Wren's head cocked to one side, but she didn't protest. Caleb wished he could bend and run his nose along the graceful chord of her neck to get even closer. She smelled freshly sweet, like spring flowers and something distinctly feminine. He knew that scent and he savored it. His body remembered it as much as his mind, and his heart started to pound and blood started to flow like raging rapids through his veins. His head fell forward in surrender, as he silently acknowledged the hold she still had over him. His heart and body remembered her only too well. There wasn't a day he didn't think about her or remember how she came to life in his arms. It was bittersweet torture.

The estate was in the foothills, elevated above downtown Denver and there was a nice view of the city from the windows. Wren continued to gaze out at it, her fingers lovingly protective of the delicate gold and diamond pendant hanging on the fine, sparkling chain around her neck. The goosebumps breaking out on her skin were the only indication that he was affecting her in any way.

"Remember the last time we were in here? I don't think I've ever cried so much or as hard as I did that night."

Caleb closed his eyes for a beat, but then he continued his soft caresses of her arms and shoulders. "Yeah. It was a bitch."

"I felt like my whole world was ending. The only person I loved was leaving me." Wren's voice was soft and introspective, and he could hear a slight catch on the last word. His heart squeezed inside his chest. She loved him, then. He loved her, still. "I never really understood why you had to go."

His left hand continued down her arm until his fingers closed around hers.

Caleb knew Wren remembered it with as much pain as he did, but without the answer about why it happened. The memory was sharp.

That whole summer he'd let her think he was going to School of Mines, mostly because he'd been wracking his brain on a way to change his father's mind. Edison had put his blackmail plan in motion months before, but Caleb didn't want the cloud of sadness hanging over them for months before it actually happened. Wren had a recital in June, and then he and Dex had a road trip to Seattle planned for July. So when mid-August came, Caleb had no choice but to tell her he was leaving. Not just leaving; going halfway across the country.

He'd spent the day packing up the few clothes he planned on taking with him, and when he was done, he went to find Wren. She'd gone to the pool for a late evening swim after Jonesy had made dinner for them both. Veronica had been away on a photoshoot for Lux in New York, which allowed Wren to feel at ease hanging out by the pool, or making herself at home around the house. Even though Caleb's presence had stopped Veronica's blatant abuse, she was still mean and insulting enough to prevent Wren doing anything daring unless Caleb was with her.

Caleb had been a bit short with Wren when she'd asked him if he wanted to join her for a swim earlier in the evening. The hurt in her eyes was a foreshadowing for what was coming, and his pissy attitude was his own anger regarding what he knew he had to do, and the reaction that he was sure was coming.

He didn't want to tell her he was leaving. He knew she'd be afraid of Veronica if he weren't around to protect her, and all he had was his father's word that he'd keep Veronica in check. *Shit, he couldn't expect Wren to be brave when he was terrified himself.*

When he couldn't put it off any longer, he'd wandered down to the pool house with his mother's locket in the front pocket of his shorts. It was a beautiful night; the sun had already set behind the mountains, though it's rays left the sky many hues of blue, gold and purple. Wren was inside and had fallen asleep on one of the sofas.

Caleb could remember how small and innocent she'd looked lying there curled onto her side, hugging a towel to her chest as she slept. Her long blonde curls were still slightly damp from swimming, and there was a pink blush to her cheeks. Her lashes were long and dark on her high cheekbones. He'd managed to enter without waking her and he must have stood there staring down on her for five minutes or more, fighting his own emotions before he'd swallowed hard and sat down on the edge of the cushion next to her.

His fingers curled and he ran the back of his knuckles down the silky skin on the outside of her upper arm, hoping it would wake her. He could still remember how the warmth of her sun kissed skin had felt under his hand.

There were no lights on inside the pool house as twilight fell outside, but he could still clearly see her sparkling blue eyes as her lashes fluttered open and it registered in her mind that he was there.

"Hey," he said softly.

She blinked and sat up halfway, propping herself up on one of her elbows. The towel she'd been holding fell to the floor in front of the sofa as she scooted into an upright position. A frown settled on her face as she looked at him.

"I thought you didn't want to swim. Did you come out here to be a jerk to me again?"

He shook his head. "No. I'm sorry about earlier, Bird. I didn't have a great day. I was wrong to take it out on you."

Her chin jutted out as she stood up, walked a few steps away and then turned to look at him. Clearly, she hadn't forgiven him. "Is that why you're out here?"

The moment weighed heavy on Caleb. She was so innocent and trusting and he was about to hurt her. He hated his father more in that moment than he ever had. "I wanted to talk to you." He got up and walked toward her but stopped short. "I'm—" he hesitated. "Shit! I don't know how to tell you this, Wren." His voice was tortured.

Her eyes widened and fear settled on her face. "What is it? You're scaring me, Cale."

She was only sixteen, but she was so beautiful to Caleb. Her body was changing and her face was maturing. The gauzy dress she wore over her bikini left the outline of her body visible, but he hardly noticed. His heart was hurting too much.

"My dad says I have to go to MIT instead of School of Mines. In fact, I leave for Boston tomorrow." Once he started, he let the words rush from his lips.

"Where?" she asked in disbelief. "That soon?"

"MIT. The Massachusetts Institute of Technology. Classes start in a week and a half."

She started to shake her head as his words sank in and then she started to pace around the room. "But, you have a scholarship here, right? You can still be here with me if you go to—"

Dread settled over Caleb as he interrupted her. "I did. But that bastard arranged it so my scholarship was rescinded. He knows someone who knows someone, or some shit like that. Bottom line is that he gets what he wants, no matter who he has to destroy in the process."

Wren's face crumpled as her big eyes welled with sadness. She shook her head in disbelief. "Why would he do this?"

Caleb didn't want to tell her the real reason because he didn't want her to feel like it was her fault. "Because he's a prick, Wren! He wants to control everything and when he can screw with me; that's a bonus. You know how much I hate that mother fucker!"

Tears began rolling down her cheeks and she covered her face with her hands and her shoulders began to shake. "What about me? I don't want you to leave, Cale! I don't want you to guh—go."

He went to her and gathered her as close to his body as he could after she started to sob. "I know. I don't want to, either. But don't worry. I made him promise to keep Veronica away from you. He said he'd take care of you, and Dex will still be here. He'll look out for you, too." Caleb's voice was getting thick as it got harder and harder for him to talk. Holding the crying girl in his arms, he was on the verge of breaking himself, but he had to be the strong one. "Dex'll take you to the studio, and I'll send the money to cover your lessons as soon as I find a fight club out there."

"Dex isn't you." Her face was buried in his shirt and he

could feel the hot wetness of her tears soaking through as the fingers of both of her hands clutched and fisted desperately in his shirt. "What'll I do without you? What if you don't come back?"

His arms tightened around her and he hugged her harder, his chin resting on the top of her head. "Oh, Wren." He stepped back and put his hands on both of her shoulders. The pain in her face exploded inside his chest and he wanted to comfort her. His finger brushed her jaw and then he nudged it up with his thumb, silently demanding she meet his eyes. "Bird, look at me."

Wren sniffed and lifted her tear filled eyes to his. Caleb used one thumb to wipe one of her tears across her cheek.

"I'll always come back for you. Nothing will hurt you while I'm still breathing, do you hear me?" His voice broke and tears burned at the back of his eyes. He blinked to get rid of them as he cleared his throat. "Look," he reached into his pocket and brought out the necklace. He held it up, so she could see the pendant, dangling on the sparkling chain. "My dad gave it to my mom right after I was born. She wore it all the time. It was her very favorite thing. Check out that ugly picture inside." He tried to laugh as the index finger on his right hand moved aside the front part of the pendant. A picture of him as a baby appeared when the yellow gold and diamond gate moved aside. "It has my initials on the back, too." He turned it over to show her the engraving. "Will you keep it safe for me until I come back? Will you wear it?"

The sorrow on Wren's features didn't go away, but she did as he asked. She nodded. "Okay. If you want me to."

Caleb nodded. "I do. Everyday." He lifted the necklace and put it around her neck. The chain was long enough to go over her head without unfastening the clasp. It fell into the hollow between her small breasts and her hand instinctively went up to cover it.

"I will. Thank you," she said sadly, tears still raining down her face. Her chin was trembling and her face fell. "I still don't want you to go," she said, starting to cry as if the world was ending.

Caleb inhaled as his mind replayed the precious memory as if it just happened.

"Maybe we should talk about that." It was reckoning day.

Wren glanced over her shoulder and up into Caleb's face. Their eyes met and locked and then she nodded slightly. "I think we should."

Caleb pulled her with him and sat on the sofa, tugging her down on the soft cushion next to him. He didn't let go of her hand, and his thumb continued to stroke over the top of her fingers.

Wren curled one leg beneath her and faced him, leaning one shoulder on the back of the couch. The only light was that from the moon and the light reflecting out of the pool and through the windows. He was so beautiful and she wanted nothing more than to reach out and touch his face. She'd never forget that face as long as she lived.

Caleb's head dropped as he remembered her little body wracked with sobs as he said goodbye the day he left. She'd come down to his room as his dad waited for him in the car that would take them to the airport. She was even more upset than she had been the night before when he told her. Tears had rolled down her beautiful face in torrents as she begged him not to go, and it ripped his fucking heart out.

"Please, Cale. Don't go!" Her hands had clutched at his shoulders as her legs gave way beneath her. He'd caught her and pulled her into his arms, holding her tight against him, cradling her head with one hand while he whispered it would be okay over and over again into her temple.

She'd only been sixteen, and he would in Boston for four years. His father had said he'd do what was needed to ensure she would get an audition to Juilliard, and then make sure she attended if she was accepted... Caleb knew if that happened, she'd already be in New York when he came home to Denver. He'd been gutted at the prospect of never having time with her like that again. But it was the reality he faced as he left her behind... to save her.

Now, she sat gazing calmly up at him in the low light, her classic features so perfect; her skin creamy and translucent in the moonlight filtering in through the many windows.

He swallowed hard. He didn't know what was going to be more difficult; spilling his guts or not giving in to the urge to kiss her luscious mouth. He inhaled deeply, and then reached out to run a thumb down her cheekbone and then up her jaw. Wren's head cocked toward his touch as if she had no choice, and her beautiful eyes bore into his as if she were in a trance.

"My dad blackmailed me." Wren's mouth fell open in silent surprise. "He forced me to go to Boston. I never wanted to leave you. I was scared Veronica would revert to her old ways without me here to protect you."

Her blue eyes widened. "Blackmailed you, how?"

Caleb cleared his throat. "He was planning on filing for divorce and I knew what that would mean for you. You weren't eighteen yet, so she'd take you away with her." Caleb stopped as his eyes implored Wren to understand. His stomach hurt, and his throat ached. "If that happened, I wouldn't be able to protect you anymore. Who knew where that whore would have taken you, who she would have exposed you to, or if I'd be able to find you?"

Her expression registered her internal conflict. Pain, confusion, and sorrow filled her. Knowing the reason behind it didn't make it easier to remember. "So, he forced a commitment to MIT in exchange for waiting to file for divorce?"

"Basically." Caleb nodded and lifted her small hand to sandwich it between both of his larger ones. His hands were surprisingly soft, but his knuckles were scarred. "It didn't matter that I'd already been accepted to COSM and had a full ride. I argued with him like my life depended on it, but he said he'd already had my scholarship revoked by his golfing buddy so either way, I wouldn't be able to attend.

"Wow," she said seriously. "I guess that explains why things changed so much after you left. He must have felt guilty because he was really nice to me."

"He didn't trust me to make something of myself on my own, but he never talked to me, so how could he? He disapproved of the time I spent with Dex and Darren. He said he expected more out of me than being a grease monkey in someone else's garage. The whole thing infuriated me, and I hated him even more after that. I never wanted to lay eyes on him again."

Caleb tried to clear the regret out of his voice, but the memory was strong and made it difficult. "But then, I was so proud when you got into Juilliard." He grabbed her free hand, so now he held them both in his. "At least he kept up his end of the bargain about that."

As Wren watched the emotion play across his handsome face, she couldn't hold her own inside. First one, then another tear, tumbled from her large blue eyes and she reached out to lay the hand he wasn't holding on his chest. "Oh, Cale. I'm sorry you had to do that because of me."

He somberly cocked his head to one side. "Don't be. I'd do anything for you." He let go of her hand to reach up and wipe away an errant tear with the pad of his thumb. "Anything," he said in a throbbing whisper.

They sat there, face-to-face on the couch and all she wanted was to be in his arms, Macy or no Macy. This might be the last chance she'd ever have to be this close to him. Caleb bent his head and rested his forehead on hers; his salty and musky scent enveloped her. "Cale," she said, the ache in her heart, resonating in her voice.

He cleared his throat. "Don't forget that. No matter what happens."

Wren wanted to cry and scream. She felt cheated. If only they'd had a moment or two like this in the past; things would have been different. If only she'd gone to see him in San Francisco, or followed him back to Boston and confronted him about their one night together. The possibilities made her want to die. Now Macy was in between them and they might never have that chance. Her voice shook when she finally spoke. "I wish I'd have known. I wish so many things. For us."

"Me, too."

"Do you want the locket back?" It hurt to say the words, but she had to know.

His head snapped up and a hurt look crossed his features. "God, no. Why would you ask me that?"

"I don't know. I just... it was your mother's, that's all."

He let out a sigh of relief. "It's where I want it to be."

She closed her eyes, and Caleb's hand came up to cup her face. His fingers tangled in the silken strands at the back of her head at the same time as his thumb brushed along her jaw and tilted her chin up. "Wren." The one word pulled from him like a prayer that would save the world if it were ending.

Her hand closed around his wrist and she lifted her mouth, silently begging for him to kiss her. She was still crying, her heart cracked open as she waited. She had no right to want him given the other woman sleeping in the house, but she did. God, did she want him. He was hers first. He'd always be hers.

Caleb's breath rushed out over her lips and she sucked it into her lungs. She wanted every nuance, every touch; every second with him she could get. This might be the last time he'd ever touch her like this.

He froze. He didn't want to scare her and he didn't want to hurt her. It felt like she wanted what he wanted, and even though every cell in his body screamed for her, he didn't want to do the wrong thing. He could almost taste her, just by being this close; their lips hovering over one another.

She lifted her lips closer still and she brushed her lower lip against his upper one. Caleb groaned. "Jesus. Wren—" His thumb brushed her jaw over and over as his muscles coiled. His heart was pounding hard and blood was rushing like liquid fire in his veins. "You're playing with fire. Don't do this unless you're one hundred percent sure you want this to happen. There's no going back."

Wren didn't know what tomorrow would mean for them or what the consequences of this would be, but she knew for sure she would literally die if she didn't let this happen. Her fingers fisted into his shirt and she unconsciously pulled it forward, tugging him even closer, and then slid her hand up and over his broad shoulder. "I do, Cale. I'm sure."

She should consider Macy. She knew she should ask him about the other woman, but she didn't want the answer. She only wanted to feel him on her, over her, inside her like she'd fantasized and relived so many times.

"Oh, God." Caleb didn't need further encouragement as his left arm snaked out around the back of her waist and he pulled her roughly into his arms at the same time as his mouth took hers hungrily. His innate visceral response dictated his every move as he kissed her deeply. Wren's mouth opened to him as his tongue laved and made love to hers like it was the sweetest thing he'd ever tasted. It was ravenous and desperate heaven.

Caleb turned and pulled her onto his lap facing him, never breaking the kiss for a second. Her legs parted and her thighs settled on the outside of his. Both of Wren's hands slid into his hair and she pulled his mouth closer. They were feasting on each other, their mouths moving as if they were starving, but so perfectly in sync it was as if they'd kissed a million times.

His arm around her hips moved her closer and he could feel the heat seeping through both of their pants. His dick was huge, more engorged than it had ever been and it throbbed painfully. Her pelvis arched into his and his breath rushed out. He'd never wanted anyone more than he wanted her and every woman he'd ever touched was a sad substitute.

They were both panting heavily from their passionate play when he finally pulled his mouth from hers and buried his mouth in her neck to place slow, wet kisses so soft she began to tremble in his arms. "Uhhhh..." His hands explored her body, cupping her breasts through her shirt, his thumbs teasing her already erect nipples into a tighter pucker. "Wren." He said her name and his voice sounded pained. "I've wanted this forever... fucking dreamed about it."

His admission made her heart sing and having him this close, pressing his hardness into her softness was euphoric. He was all that existed for her and if the building were coming down around them, she wouldn't want to move. Her back arched and she could feel the outline of his erection pressing against her. Nothing had ever felt so good.

Her fingers were greedy as they roamed his body, detailing every curve of every muscle, committing every second of it to memory. Her lower body ached and opened, the emptiness becoming maddening. She rocked and rubbed against him seeking some small shred of satisfaction.

Caleb could sense the depth of her longing and it turned him on more than he could wrap his head around. It was yearning like he'd never experienced and he wanted to savor each touch and every incredible movement. He slowed his kisses and his touches became gentler.

When his fingers deliberately pushed up the hem of her shirt, the contact of her warm, smooth skin by his fingers he almost moaned in ecstasy. This was Wren; his little bird. His protective instincts overtook him. She deserved better than screwing frantically on a couch as if they were kids. He loved her, and he needed her to feel it in every breath between them.

"Cale," Wren whispered against his lips. "Don't stop." Her hand dipped between them and her fingers closed around his dick through the material of his sweats and his forehead fell onto her shoulder.

"Christ. I didn't plan for this."

"It's okay."

Caleb paused. "Are you protected? I won't put you at risk."

She nodded, a bit embarrassed to be confessing such a thing to Caleb. Periods and performing didn't go well together, so she took a version of the pill that kept her from having a period for a full three months. "It's safe."

"Wren." His tone was full of desire; his eyes hooded as he lifted them to meet hers intently. His hands came up to her head, to stroke through her blonde tresses, his index fingers tracing both cheekbones. "I want this." His finger traced her lower lip and pulled it down. "God." The word came out in a groan. "Do I want it."

Wren bent her head, intent on initiating another round of the passionate kisses. "Good," she whispered. Her lips ghosted over his and she slid her tongue out to hotly lick at his in a sultry assault. He gave in and soon their lips were giving and taking, tongues mating in glorious abandon, her hand working up and down on him, pulling out the reaction she wanted.

"Let's go to your room." Caleb felt like he was begging and he was barely able to stop exploring the secrets of her body or kissing her luscious mouth. He inhaled the scent of her skin. "You smell so good."

"We're alone here. Now. Let's stay here." After Macy making her room such a revolving door, Wren didn't want to risk it.

Caleb didn't argue and he gave in to her demands and the gravity of his own need. His hands made short work of her shirt, exposing the white lace bra as he pushed it up and off. Wren lifted her arms to complete the job at the same time as Caleb buried his mouth between her breasts, sliding his cheek over the gentle swells.

"You're so beautiful," he admitted. Wren was pulling at his clothes and soon his shirt and her pants had joined her discarded top on the floor.

Caleb took her weight easily as he stood up and turned them both around so he could lay her down beneath him. She was still wrapped around him, her heels hooked around his calves as he settled in between her spread thighs.

His dark blue eyes glowed almost black in the night as he bent to kiss her once on the mouth, then dragged his lips down her neck and over her collarbones. He made love to her with his mouth as he undressed her with slow measured precision. He pulled aside the lace cups of her bra, and Wren gasped as his hot mouth closed over one of her nipples as his fingers pushed down her pants and slid into her panties to touch where she'd been craving.

She gasped out his name as he worked her into a slow frenzy, teasing her clitoris, and then pushing into her heated body. He repeated it until she couldn't stand it, all the while going back for kiss after lascivious kiss. Wren didn't want it to end and she fought the orgasm, wanting to hold him and kiss him for hours, but eventually she couldn't stop it. Her body tightened, her back arched and she breathed out his name in a soft cry. "Uhhhhh, Caleb."

Caleb remained on top of her, his own body screaming for release, but he loved the erotic picture she made as she came in his arms. His gaze was intent on her face, though his whole body vibrated with desire. He could feel the throb of his heartbeat pound in his chest and his cock at the same time. He wanted to say the words, but wasn't sure if she was ready to hear them. This was a huge step, and one very late in coming.

When she stopped shaking and her eyes fluttered open, her eyes locked with his. The want in his expression made him even more beautiful. "Will you remember this in the morning?" Wren asked, almost so quietly that he wouldn't have heard if he still weren't so close to her.

"I remembered the last time. I have every second of it memorized. I've relived it a million times." His nose nuzzled the side of her head and he pressed his lips to her temple and then her cheek and jaw in a series of feather soft kisses that sent electricity through her entire body.

A soft intake of breath signaled her shock. "Then, why?"

"I was supposed to be protecting you, and I failed. I didn't protect you from myself. I was ashamed that I lost control."

"Oh, Cale." Wren reached for him, pulling his head down to softly kiss him on the lips. "I wanted you then, like I want you now." Love for him threatened to choke off her breath. "But what about Macy—?" Her mind flashed to the night in her room when Macy had insinuated she and Caleb had talked about marriage. Surely his presence here belied any of that.

"Hush," he shook his head. "We'll talk about it tomorrow. Tonight, it's about you and me."

After that there was no more talking. Heavy breathing and soft moans filled the silence as Caleb rekindled the ache deep inside Wren again until she was writhing beneath him. When he finally let himself take her and thrust deep into her body, he began moving inside her, filling her over and over again until he thought he'd die with pleasure. It was as eloquent and real, as absolute and as amazing as he remembered. Even more. This time, he vowed it would be forever.

They made tender and mad love all night, as Caleb poured all of the love and desire he'd been holding on to for years, into Wren. As the purple night turned into a pink and red dawn, Wren owned more than just his body. Being with Wren was much more than physical bliss and they worshiped each other over and over again. No one could ever know him or be as close to him as she was. They belonged together and deep down, he'd always known it.

They had a lot to talk about, the will to be dealt with, plans to be made, and lives to be changed, but Caleb's world was finally right.

Caleb knew he'd exhausted her, and yet he still wanted more. He smiled to himself as he quickly threw on his clothes. Wren had fallen asleep, but he could see that she was cold; especially now that he wasn't lying next to her to keep her warm.

Caleb covered her in a big towel, then gently lifted Wren's sleeping form into his arms before he carried her inside and up to her room. She sighed in contentment as he brought the thick comforter around her. He couldn't bear to leave her and decided to crawl in bed beside her.

After the evening they'd shared, there would be no harm in staying with her. Instinctively, Wren snuggled close into his side and he enfolded her in his strong arms. A happy smile slid across his mouth. Life couldn't get any better than this, he decided as he started to fall into a blissful sleep.

No matter what happened; Caleb swore he'd never let anyone or anything come between he and Wren again. Not ever again.

chapter
THIRTEEN

Rap! Rap! Rap! Rap!

Wren was startled out of a sound sleep by the sound of someone knocking on her door. She lifted a hand to her forehead and struggled to open her eyes. Blinking, her room came into focus, disorientation making her pause.

Caleb must have carried her into the house in the early morning. Love welled up inside her when she thought of the night before. She felt giddy and wanted to pinch herself. A small, satisfied smile curved her lips.

When the hard knocking interrupted her thoughts, Wren scrambled from the bed. The soreness in her muscles was a sweet testament to the full evening of love play with Caleb. When she jumped from the bed, she stopped and looked down at her body. She was completely naked and she almost laughed out loud because she was about to expose herself to whoever was waiting in the hall. She grabbed a large white towel from her bathroom and wrapped it around herself.

"Wren, dear! Are you awake? It's after nine and the funeral is at eleven," Jonesy's voice came through the closed door.

"Oh, Crap," Wren muttered as she hurried to the door to open it.

Jonesy was already dressed in a simple black dress that fell well below her knees and had three quarter length sleeves. She was carrying a wooden breakfast tray with a glass of orange juice, a cup of steaming coffee and a small plate of buttered toast. Wren motioned her to come in.

"I overslept," she stated the obvious and picked up the orange juice. She was thirsty and drank the whole thing down before setting it back on the tray that Jonesy had placed on the end of her bed. "Thank you, Jonesy. That was sweet of you."

"I guess so." Jonesy's eyebrow shot up, taking in Wren's sweat pants and shirt.

Wren nodded and went into the bathroom to turn on the shower. She glanced in the mirror wondering if Jonesy would be able to read what had happened the night before by just looking at her. Her lips were fuller; swollen from the hours upon hours of kissing. Her skin flushed at the memory and she wiped at the lower one with her fingers. Her hair was a mess, but her skin was clear. She was afraid that the stubble on Caleb's chin may have marred it, but she could find no ill effect. The only outward sign was waking up without any clothes on. It was a good thing Jonesy knocked and didn't just barge in. *Like Macy made a habit of*, she thought with disdain. Macy.

Shit. Wren cringed.

As the water temperature warmed, she ran a quick brush through her tangled hair then dropped the towel. When she stepped into the shower she immediately soaked her hair and reached for her shampoo. She wanted to hurry and get to the church early enough to speak to Caleb.

"Has Caleb already left?" Wren elevated her voice just enough so her words carried into the other room. The bathroom door was open and Jonesy was still waiting in the bedroom. Despite the water running, Wren knew they'd be able to talk if they both spoke loudly.

"Yes. He was up early. Obviously he has a lot on his mind, because he was in the kitchen dressed and making coffee by the time I got up. I wanted to fix him a nice breakfast, but he said he wasn't hungry. He seemed very preoccupied."

"He has a lot on his mind." Wren knew Caleb wasn't looking forward to this day, plus she wanted to know if Macy had gone with him, but she didn't want to ask. Did last night change anything between Macy and Caleb? She had a slight twinge of guilt but quickly pushed it down. Caleb was hers, first, and last night was magical. She wouldn't feel guilty about it.

Maybe Jonesy's lack of mention of Macy meant he'd left without her. The downside was that if he didn't, it would mean that she would most likely ride with her and Jonesy to the church for the funeral.

"After today, things should be better. That's if that woman doesn't get her hooks into him; I don't like her at all."

Wren had quickly rinsed the conditioner from her long hair and was soaping down her body. She paused for a beat at the coincidence that Jonesy was also thinking about the repercussions Macy brought to the table. She couldn't have said it better herself.

"Do you think Cale is influenced by her?" she asked.

"Hummph!" Jonesy snorted. Her disgust was clear, even from the other room. "I hope not, but I've seen the way she drapes all over him. When she can't find him she berates me about where he is."

Wren shut off the water and wrapped one towel around her hair and then one around her body before she stepped from the large, glass-enclosed shower.

"Caleb isn't the type to be controlled or to give a play-by-play of his schedule." She knew that he had always been independent and doubted he'd be pussy whipped by any woman. "He won't let her control him."

"She's going to try, I'm afraid. She was oozing all over him this morning. It was so distasteful, I was surprised he didn't go into insulin shock."

By now Wren had dried off and was starting to run a comb through her damp hair. "Maybe she was just concerned," Wren said, unconvinced. Macy had an agenda all right.

"She's a snake. I can see it from a mile away; I just hope Caleb isn't fooled by her polished, supportive act. Now that she knows his background about the company, she has dollar signs in her eyes. Women like that don't do anything without a motive."

Wren knew too well that Jonesy was on the right track, but she couldn't be sure money was Macy's only motivation. "Caleb is a catch even without the money," she said simply, realizing she might have slipped and given too much of her real feelings away.

The kind old woman appeared in the bathroom doorway and the expression on her face was sad. "Of course he is. I always thought you and Caleb might end up together. If something is happening between you two, don't you let that little conniving bitch keep you apart."

Wren's eyes widened as she looked at Jonesy's reflection in the mirror. Wren couldn't remember the housekeeper ever swearing in all the ten years she'd known her. It was clear evidence of how strongly she disliked Macy.

"I had the same dream. I've always loved him, Jonesy."

"I know, dear. It's as plain as the nose on your face."

Wren flushed in embarrassment. If it were this clear to Jonesy, did everyone else know? Macy's behavior clearly showed her suspicion. But, what about Caleb? Did last night mean as much to him as it did to her, or was it just one of those times you hear about; that everybody has sex around funerals as verification of life? She inwardly groaned and hoped her feelings weren't pouring out in her expression. "Even Lois Lane fell in love with Superman. Caleb is my Superman."

"I know. I love the two of you like my own family." Jonesy's weathered face was full of sadness, her eyes glassed over, and she swallowed hard. Her voice thickened with emotion. "You're like my own children or grandchildren and I hate to see you go your separate ways. I'm not sure what will become of me if that happens; you're the only family I have."

Wren was still wrapped in a towel but she walked over and put her arms around the older woman. "Oh Jonesy."

Wren hugged her tightly, trying to reassure her. "Nothing will change. Cale will take care of you. We both adore you."

Jonesy patted Wren's back. "Not if Macy has anything to say about it. "

Wren wasn't sure what Caleb planned to do with the estate or the company, but she was certain he wouldn't leave Jonesy out in the cold. "I don't know exactly what Caleb's relationship is with her, or what he'll do with the assets, Jonesy, but what I do know is that he won't turn his back on you. Macy, or no Macy." Wren had seen Macy trying to be close to Caleb, and while he was considerate of her, Wren hadn't seen him return her affection and it gave her a small ray of hope. She went to her dresser and gathered clean lingerie, taking them back to the bathroom to put on in privacy.

"Well, I can't stand her," Jonesy retorted. "Men think with the wrong head, if you ask me!"

Wren went into her closet to retrieve her dress followed by the difficult realization that Caleb had spent time in bed with Macy, too. Until she was able to see and talk to him she could only guess at his real feelings. "Truthfully? Me either. Did she go with Caleb to the church?" She finally asked the question that had been eating away at her.

Wren wished she could confide in Jonesy about her confrontation with Macy the day before and her night in Caleb's arms to get her advice, but they were running late. It might not be a good idea anyway. Wren stepped into her dress and turned, silently asking Jonesy to zip it up.

"Fortunately for us, yes." Jonesy slid the zipper into place and patted Wren's back lightly with one hand.

"I just hope she's thinking of him more than of herself. It's gonna be a rough day for him. He seems so strong, but I know he's more vulnerable than he lets on. Despite his estrangement from Edison, I know he's hurting." Wren was thinking of the way he'd melted into her arms in grief. "The first night I was home; the first time Caleb saw me, he lost it. We both did."

Jonesy nodded knowingly. "I don't know how he could avoid having unresolved issues. He doesn't need that gold digger muddying the waters. He has enough to deal with."

"I know. I can't lie; I've questioned Macy's motives, myself."

"That girl is out for number one, so thank God he has you."

"He also has you and Jonathan, Jonesy."

Jonesy stood up and started to leave. "Yes, he does. You'd better get dressed honey. Jared is waiting for us out front. I'll see you downstairs."

***

THE FUNERAL WENT BY in a blur.

Dex and his dad were there. Caleb saw them sitting in the pews when, Wren, Jonesy, Macy, and Jonathan took their seats in the front pew. Veronica was also in attendance, Caleb noted with disdain. He'd expected her to be there but even so, it grated on his nerves.

He'd kept Wren up all night, making love and talking, so he decided to let her sleep in. He had barely slept and he was tired, he wanted the day to be over with so he could talk to Wren and they could get on with their lives. He knew she'd still want to dance, and they'd have to work out the logistics. He was anxious to tell her how he felt; how he'd always felt and that he wanted to be with her. He was ready to do whatever it took to work it out.

Despite his exhaustion and the impending funeral, he felt happy. The night with Wren had radically changed the future. He was confident in his decision to give her half of the estate. She hadn't said she loved him, but he could feel it in every touch. Sex without love wasn't what he and Wren had shared.

Macy had been waiting to pounce the minute he was dressed and came upstairs for breakfast. Jonesy had his ready, but wasn't expecting Macy and the older woman had to scurry to make a plate for her as well.

He'd wanted to have some time to speak to the elderly woman alone and make clear that her place in the family wasn't going to change and he'd hoped to use the early morning to do so, but Macy had effectively ruined his plans with her presence. He couldn't remember a time when Jonesy hadn't been in the Luxon house and he didn't want that to change. When Macy indignantly demanded Jonesy make her breakfast, it made Caleb decidedly pissed off. Jonesy was the closest thing to a grandmother he had, and he'd be damned if he'd let anyone treat her like a servant.

In the car ride to the church, he'd debated whether to have it out with Macy over her treatment of Jonesy, but then decided it would be a waste of time. He'd already told her he'd be staying in Denver, but he wanted to make it clear that their relationship was over. In fact, he couldn't wait until she left to return to San Francisco. He wanted time with Wren before she had to go back to New York, but he needed to have that conversation with Macy first.

Caleb was preoccupied with all that needed to be done. He needed to go back to San Francisco for a few weeks to resign his position with his firm, sublet his apartment, and to pack up his things. Wren had another week or so of her break before she'd go into rehearsal for her next production, and Caleb hoped he could convince her to spend it with him while he packed up. She could fly back to New York directly from the west coast.

Caleb wasn't prepared for the sadness that overcame him during the service, especially at the cemetery. He stood between Macy and Wren during the short interment service and all he could do was stare at the large dark grey marble headstone with his mother and father's names on it. The date of death for his dad would need to be added, but his mother's was there and it choked him up. He was once again a twelve-year-old kid, who'd just lost his mother. His eyes filled with tears and he used one thumb to quickly brush one away.

Macy was clinging to him almost the point of annoyance as they left the church, during the ride in the back of the limo to the gravesite and on the walk to it. His eyes met with Wren's more than once and he could tell she was hurting when she'd quickly look away. He was certain she was feeling confused by Macy's behavior and his allowing it, after their night together.

Truthfully, he felt like hell over it. He wanted to be near Wren but he didn't want a scene. He needed to get the funeral and the entire day behind him before he told Macy he was ending things between them. They hadn't been physical in any intimate way since he'd set eyes on Wren the night she arrived in Denver.

A small rush of guilt overtook him. It hadn't been that long since he'd taken Macy to bed, but he never said he loved her. At the time, he hadn't thought he'd even see Wren, let alone that they'd share such an incredible night together. He didn't know how he bottled up his feelings for so long. After a night in her arms, he was ready to explode with love for her, and he didn't like hiding it from anyone... Mostly, he hated that Wren didn't know for certain that he loved her.

Wren stood quietly next to him; his instincts screamed to reach out, slide his arm around her, and pull her close to his side. Sensing his emotion, her small hand slipped into his and their fingers threaded together.

Caleb inhaled deeply as she squeezed his hand as the priest spoke a few words and said a prayer. There were only about thirty people in attendance and they drifted off, leaving Caleb, Wren and Macy at the graveside.

"Would you mind giving me a minute?" he asked of Macy. "I'll meet you at the car."

She glanced up into his face and Caleb could see the conflict in her expression. "Sure," she answered quietly and started to walk way, sending Wren a glance to see if she would follow.

Wren started to do follow Macy, but Caleb's hand tightened around hers. "No, stay." He shook his head, looking down at her. It was a sunny day and they both had on sunglasses so she couldn't see his eyes.

Macy's lips pressed together and she resumed her solo

trek to the waiting limo.

Wren's free hand moved up to close around the outside of Caleb's elbow. "Are you doing okay?"

He knew the day had been hard on her, too. "I'm okay, but I wanted to talk to you. It's over with Macy. I haven't touched her since I laid eyes on you again, and I need you to know that. I told you; there's no going back."

Wren had spent the last couple of hours wiping at tears, but her eyes started to burn again. She rested her head against his arm and shoulder, as they stood side-by-side facing the casket. She squeezed his hand again. He was still thinking of her. Her throat ached as she tried not to cry out loud. She nodded without looking at him. "Okay." It came out as a thick whisper.

"Okay," Caleb affirmed. "Did you see Veronica? Has she tried to talk to you at all?"

"I did see her, but Jonesy and I were running late because I overslept, so there wasn't time for her to corner me."

"Good. Just stay close so I can intervene if needed."

Wren's heart was so full of him she could hardly get the words out.

"I've missed you, Superman."

Caleb's handsome face split into a big smile and his heart suddenly felt lighter. He wanted to laugh out loud. This woman's respect and love was all he wanted in the world. The future looked bright.

"Are you ready to go?" he asked quietly, finally moving to wrap an arm around her shoulders.

"Yes."

Caleb and Wren walked to the waiting limo and the driver opened the door for them. Caleb waited as Wren slid into the seat across from Macy, and when he entered, it was Wren he chose to sit next to. It would have been disrespectful to hold Wren's hand or touch her until Macy knew where he stood. He couldn't touch Wren, but he'd be damned if she wouldn't be beside him.

***

"Wren!"

Wren turned around to see who was calling her name, though she already knew. She'd managed to avoid speaking to her mother for the entire wake and funeral, but now, waiting for Jonathan to read Edison's will, Veronica was here and quickly moving toward her.

Ugh! she thought.

Seeing Veronica was inevitable given there was cash on the table, but something Wren was not looking forward to. Her mother was a harsh and intimidating reminder of all she'd suffered at her hands.

Wren cringed and put up her hand to stop her mother's approach. The one thing she'd learned from Caleb was that words could only hurt you if you allowed them to.

"I don't have time talk to you now, mother," Wren said when Veronica stopped directly in front of her. Veronica was still beautiful, but in a stiffer, more plastic, sort of way. Her eyebrows were unnaturally frozen and her top lip barely moved when she spoke. Clearly, she's had some work done.

Veronica tried to hug her daughter, but Wren stood stiffly and didn't return the embrace. She searched for Caleb, who was deep in conversation with Jonathan and wasn't looking her way.

"Nonsense," Veronica brushed off Wren's dismissal. "They're talking and if I know lawyers, they never start on time."

Wren rolled her eyes. "I'm sure you'd know."

Veronica pulled at the lapel of her new black jacket, ignoring her daughter's jab to deliver one of her own. "This is nice fabric, but the outfit is boring, Wren. Surely you could have done better?"

Wren's eyes narrowed in hatred. One sentence in and her mother was finding fault. "This is a funeral, not a rave," she said wryly, registering the very low cut neckline of her mother's tight, body conscious dress. "But then, everything's a party to you."

Veronica smiled tightly. "There's no need to be nasty, Wren. Let's play nice, shall we?"

"What are you even doing here? I thought you moved to San Diego with your your latest victim?" She was unable to hide her disdain for the woman who had destroyed her childhood, and could have destroyed her entire life.

Veronica smiled and raised her shoulders. She neither confirmed nor denied whether she had a new man in her life. "I've been asked to be here! Eddy must have included me. Caleb probably thought he'd get it all." She sniffed haughtily.

Wren wanted to vomit at her salacious tone. "I can't imagine why." Wren waved her mother in the direction of the large conference table. "It's going to start soon, so let's take our seats."

They were in the conference room at Jonathan's firm; Westwood Barker. The room was modern with glass walls separating it from the rest of the office, a long dark wood table and sixteen plush leather chairs around it.

She gestured toward the table, but Veronica wasn't about to let her conversation end. Macy was sitting in a seat that Caleb had held out for her about halfway down the table and Jonesy was seated across from her. The room was large for the few people in attendance.

"Who is that attractive young woman?" Veronica pointed to Macy.

"A friend of Caleb's," Wren answered quietly. She was silently praying her mother would stop asking questions. "Sit down, mother."

"Friend or lover?"

"How would I know?"

Veronica's thin eyebrows shot up. "I thought you and he were as thick as thieves."

"Yeah, well don't think too hard, I wouldn't want you to hurt yourself," Caleb said sarcastically, breaking into the conversation. He hurled a dirty look in Veronica's direction and rested a hand on the back of Wren's back. "Let's get started," he said, nodding toward the other end of the table.

Veronica was happy to take a seat to Macy's left, and Caleb and Wren were seated on her right. Jonesy, seated across from them got up and moved, closer to the end next to Jonathan.

"Jonesy," Veronica nodded in her direction. "How are

you?"

Jonesy's obvious dislike of the woman was obvious. She huffed and didn't respond. Veronica's fake smile faded and was obviously embarrassed by the snub. She quickly turned her attention to Macy, introducing herself.

"That's a horrible idea; sitting the hag next to Macy," Caleb murmured in Wren's ear.

Birds of a feather, Wren thought. She simply nodded and took the seat Caleb had pulled out for her.

Jonathan joined them, holding a manila envelope. "Have a seat, Caleb."

When they were all seated, Jonathan placed the sealed envelope in front of him.

"Let's just get to it, shall we?" He didn't wait for an answer. "As you all know, Edison was not just a client, he was a good friend of mine for more than thirty years. I'm honored to be trusted with this task." He turned the envelope over and opened it, sliding the contents out on a table. There were several sealed letter envelopes, and the flat pages of the will. He cleared his throat and started reading in a clear voice.

"I, Edison Allan Luxon, residing at 530 South University, Denver, Colorado, declare this to be my last Will and Testament, and revoke any and all wills and codicils dated previously."

Wren could sense Caleb's uneasiness as he shifted in his chair. Could he really be worried that Veronica would get the bulk of the estate? Wren had no doubt that Edison had nothing but dislike for her mother. It was evident over the past few years when he'd shipped her off on work assignments or vacations without him much of the time. After speaking to Caleb, she realized now, that was part of the MIT deal to keep her away from her.

Jonathan continued: "ARTICLE I: Funeral expenses and payment of debt. I direct my executor to pay my enforceable unsecured personal debts and funeral expenses of my last illness, and the expenses of administering my estate from the funds in my main checking account at the Bank of Denver. ARTICLE II: Money & Personal Property."

Wren was grateful for her position between Jonathan and Caleb. She didn't think she could stand being next to either Macy or her mother, no matter what the circumstances. She'd seen the way Macy glared at her in the limo and several times since they arrived at the firm. Caleb's hand rested on the table next to her and she found herself wishing for him to steady her by holding her hand. She glanced at him out of the corner of her eye. He was sitting back in his chair, plucking at his lips; his eyes trained on Jonathan, who continued to read.

"To my housekeeper and longtime friend, Alice Jones, I leave the sum of one million dollars USD."

Jonesy gasped. "Oh my goodness!"

Caleb and Wren both smiled at her as she grabbed a tissue from her purse and dabbed at her eyes. "You deserve it Jonesy," Caleb said quietly, nodding his affirmation of his father's decision.

Veronica's lips pressed together in agitation. "Oh well, Eddie was richer than God. That's just a drop in the bucket." She was whispering to Macy, but everyone heard her. Caleb rolled his eyes and shook his head, and Jonathan stopped and shot her a disgusted look before he continued.

"To my loyal friend and attorney, Jonathan Westwood, I leave the sum of one million dollars, USD and one thousand shares of preferred stock in my company Luxon Pharmaceuticals, Incorporated. "

Jonathan paused briefly when Veronica made an annoyed grunt. He looked up at Caleb, who nodded again, reaffirming his approval of his father's decision.

"Uggmmmm." He cleared his throat. "Also, he and his firm will remain the attorney of record for Luxon Pharmaceuticals under their current and binding contracts & retainers going forward until expiration, at which time it may be renegotiated by the parties."

Caleb couldn't resist leaning forward on the table so he could make eye contact with Veronica. "Don't worry. I'm sure my father set you up with what you deserve." He pressed his lips together to hide a smile, but not before Wren saw the dimples appear in both of his cheeks. One eyebrow shot up for a brief second and she understood he was well aware of what was coming. Her head cocked when he met her gaze.

"To my ex-wife, Veronica Brashill-Luxon, I leave the sum of one hundred dollars USD."

She sat up in her chair as if there were a steel rod up her back. "Wait. What was that?"

Jonathan grinned. "If I may continue?" He glanced back down at the document. "No, this is not an error. One hundred dollars and not a penny more."

Jonesy, Jonathan, and Caleb were all watching Veronica intently for her reaction. Jonesy was the only one with any shock on her face, but was soon smiling with the rest of them. Wren's hand came up to her forehead as one elbow leaned on the arm of her chair as she braced herself for the outburst she knew would follow.

Veronica shot indignantly to her feet. "This is an outrage!" she spat. "Did you do this?" She pointed a red-tipped finger at Wren. "I bet you're inwardly rejoicing!" Her face was turning a mottled red as she stood there, fists clenching in protest at her complete helplessness.

"Go ahead, Veronica," Caleb said, casually amused. "Kick and scream. Have a fit. Hold your breath until you pass out."

Everyone in the room burst out laughing at his arrogant jibe, except him. His narrowed eyes met hers, daring her to challenge him.

"You think this is funny?"

He nodded, unaffected, then grinned. "I sure as hell do! Goddamn hilarious."

"With all due respect, Mrs. Luxon, you are divorced. You have to accept Edison's wishes," Jonathan added.

"No, I don't! I'll contest this in court! I gave him the best years of my life!" She literally stomped her foot. "The lousy housekeeper gets a million, and I get nothing? I don't think so!"

"Oh, God," Wren said quietly, wanting to sink down in her chair. Caleb's hand came down on her shoulder and gave it a quick squeeze as he stood up.

"No. You mean you sucked his dick, uh, I mean; *sucked him dry* for as long as he'd allow. But now that's over." Caleb shrugged wryly; his eyes snapping up to meet Veronica's unflinchingly. "Sucks for you." Jonesy started to blush, clearly in shock at Caleb's analogy. "Oh, sorry, Jonesy."

Veronica gathered up her clutch purse and shoved it under her arm, angrily. Her intention to leave was clear.

"You should wait." Jonathan put up his hand to halt her from leaving. "There is more at the end you should hear."

"Really, Jonathan?" Caleb asked incredulously. "Let her leave!"

"Caleb," Jonathan admonished with a shake of his head. "She should stay."

Caleb threw up his hands and took his seat again. "Fine."

Without a word, his stepmother sat back down in her leather chair, but she was seething and everyone knew it.

"I leave the remainder of all monies & tangible property (excluding the home furnishings- which are to remain with the respective estates), and all policies and proceeds of insurance covering such property, and all life insurance to be shared equally between my son, Caleb Allan Luxon and stepdaughter, Wren Elizabeth Brashill."

Veronica's eyes widened in shocked disbelief; so mad Caleb was sure her head was going to explode.

Wren's mouth fell open and formed the word "Oh." She turned her head to look at Caleb who was leaning back in his chair, waiting for her reaction. "But, I don't deserve—"

"Yeah. This is exactly what you deserve," he said. "It's real."

Wren's heart started pounding until it felt like it would fly from her chest, not sure how she felt about the inheritance. Money didn't mean she'd be in touch with Caleb. "Really?

You're okay with it?" she asked. "This is crazy."

His hand reached out to cover hers. "It is." His tone was reassuring, his expression softened and he smiled at her. "Go on, Jonathan."

Caleb heard Macy huff on the other side of him despite that he'd already told her Wren would receive half of everything. He wished to God that he still didn't have that confrontation ahead of him.

"This includes the art collection, cars, stock portfolio, and investments to be divided equitably among them by my executor's discretion after consultation with my children. My late wife, Celine Luxon's entire jewelry collection will go to my son, Caleb Luxon. My executor may pay out of my estate the expenses of delivering any of the tangible properties to the beneficiaries."

The will continued with the Denver house going to Caleb, the one in boulder to Wren and the vacation house would be put into both of their names. Wren was stunned and as Jonathan went through the document point by point, Caleb kept his eyes trained on her.

His chest swelled with pride that he could do something so significant for her, now happy that his father had given him this very important choice. He felt satisfaction that he could take care of Wren, but more, it was sheer joy that she'd be a real part of his life.

The stipulations about division of the Lux stock came next. Wren couldn't believe her ears at Jonathan's next words.

"As stated in Article II of this document, my LUX stock options are part of my portfolio and will be shared equally between Caleb and Wren. This represents the majority and controlling interest in the company. Any dividends will be shared equally or used to purchase more shares. The shares shall remain in your possession for a minimum of five consecutive years during which time you may not sell or gift them to anyone else. It is my wish that one, or both, of you assume control of Lux and the other to sit on the board of directors. At the end of the stipulated time period, you will decide the fate of Lux, by choosing one of the following options: 1. One of you may buy the other out, at or above fair market value of the stock at that time. 2. Continue to run the company together going forward. 3. You may give the shares to charity, with the stipulation that the shares remain together, the charity benefits by the dividends and the board of directors will hire a CEO to continue operations."

"You had me stay to hear this?" Veronica spat. Macy sat in silence, clearly uncomfortable as she listened to it. Caleb told her Wren got half, but not about the stipulation that tied him to Wren for five years. She was upset and angry, her mind working overtime to figure out a way to manipulate the outcome.

"We've got our work cut out for us," Veronica said. Jonathan was still reading and she was whispering to the other woman. She opened her purse and pulled out a Lux business card that had her cell number written on the back. "Call me tomorrow."

Macy took the card and nodded. Caleb was next to her, so she couldn't openly answer, for fear he might hear.

Jonathan finished reading. "It is my desire to provide for

you both, and that the company that I worked so hard to build with Celine will remain viable and any action the two of you take will consider the best interest of the stockholders and employees."

Edison named Jonathan executor and Caleb was thankful he wouldn't have to bear that burden. It was enough to quit his job and move.

"Lastly, there is a provision for relinquishment of bequeath. You'll all get copies of the document so you can read it for yourself, but it basically states that if you challenge the will you lose your bequeath."

Veronica glared at Jonathan, but it didn't phase him in the slightest.

"If litigation is initiated in objection to this will, the person bringing the suit will assume all legal fees for themselves and this estate regardless of outcome. Signed; Edison A. Luxon, dated and notarized."

He passed out a copy to everyone, and then handed one of the white, sealed envelopes to Jonesy, Veronica, and Wren. "Edison left personal letters to each of you."

"You already had yours," she said simply, and Caleb nodded.

"I let you read it, remember?"

Wren nodded.

Macy and Veronica rose from the table together and Caleb couldn't help but notice. His eyes narrowed. The last thing he needed were the two of them scheming to fuck everything up. He was confident that his father made sure the will could not be contested, but he still felt uneasy over it. He had to get Macy away from the older woman before she had an opportunity to work her over.

He touched the sleeve of Wren's jacket with an open hand. "I'll be right back."

Jonesy was talking to Jonathan and Wren went toward them. She hated that Macy's actions dictated Caleb's actions. Maybe she has some sort of hold over him and Wren didn't want to think about it. It hurt; making her insides burn.

Her eyes were drawn to them against her will. Veronica had left, and he was speaking to Macy alone in one corner of the room. They were touching; Caleb 's hand on Macy's arm, and her hand on his chest. It made Wren feel sick inside.

She put a smile on her face and went to thank Jonathan, then turned her attention to Jonesy. "Are you ready to go? I'm sure Jared is waiting."

Jonesy could tell Wren was off. Considering she'd just inherited millions, maybe she was in shock or processing. "Are you okay, honey?"

"Yes. I'm just tired. I'd like to go home and make it an early night."

"You don't want to wait for Caleb and Macy?"

Wren shook her head, sadly. "Not really. I just want to read my letter, take a bath and climb into bed."

"Okay, honey. I'll fix you something nice to eat and bring it to your room."

"I'm not that hungry. Besides, you've done enough for everyone this week. "

Jonesy didn't ask anything else and they started to walk out, but unfortunately, Caleb and Macy were standing on the end of the conference room by the door. Caleb looked slightly annoyed and Macy looked like she was pleading.

As Wren and Jonesy approached the couple, they stopped talking.

"Hey, are you leaving?" Caleb was disappointed. He wanted to ask Wren to come with him in his father's sedan, but he still had to take Macy home and she'd just asked him to take her out to dinner. Maybe he could use the time to speak to her like he needed to. At least in a public restaurant, she wouldn't be able to make a scene. Either way, he wouldn't be leaving with Wren.

"Yes. We'll see you at home?" Jonesy asked.

Caleb's dark blue eyes met Wren's lighter ones. "I'm—" He was worried Wren would get the wrong idea, but this was the fastest way to accomplish what he needed with Macy; and that was to end things. "Macy asked that we get some dinner, out."

Wren looked away uncomfortably. "Okay. Jonesy, I'll just wait outside."

"Is she alright?" he asked Jonesy, when Wren walked out.

"She's exhausted. See you at home."

Fuuuucccckk, Caleb thought. The last thing he needed was Wren thinking last night meant nothing.

Her eyes said it all. *How could you take Macy out alone after our night together?*

Caleb resolved to get dinner and his conversation with Macy over with as quickly as he possibly could.

chapter
FOURTEEN

C ALEB FELT BAD ABOUT WHAT he was about to do, despite Macy's cold demeanor since they left the will reading.

Macy had Googled and picked out a quiet Italian restaurant about half-way between the law firm and the Denver estate. It was an intimate, romantic atmosphere, with low light, hundreds of votive candles flickering around the room, soft music and white linen everywhere. It was the last type of place he wanted to be with Macy given the conversation he was about to have with her.

He couldn't help thinking how different it would have been if Wren were the one he was having dinner with, but nevertheless, he asked for a booth in the corner for privacy.

They were seated and the waiter had just left to retrieve a bottle of expensive Cabernet Macy had chosen from the wine menu.

Caleb's mind was occupied with about a hundred different things, and he was just going through the motions, but he couldn't help but be irritated by her presumptive behavior. He wasn't sure if it was the three hundred dollar bottle of wine, the fact that he didn't want to be out long enough to drink it, or if he was just so done, that everything she did irritated the shit out of him. If it were the latter, it wasn't fair, and he knew it.

"I hope you're thirsty. I'd rather have something stronger." His tone was wry.

Macy was put off by Caleb's demeanor. He was clearly agitated. He'd just inherited millions so why did he seem upset? She tried to lighten the mood by smiling beguilingly from across the table. "We're celebrating!" she said happily. "At least, we should be.'

He huffed, pushing the air out of his lungs with force as his brow furrowed. "Yeah, I just buried my dad today. Yay."

Macy's expression sobered. "Caleb, I know that's the unfortunate part, but it can't be changed. Why can't you be grateful for the possibilities? You can start your firm without assuming any debt."

He shook his head. "I told you that's on hold. Don't you listen?" If Macy noticed the muscle working overtime in his prominent jaw, she ignored it.

She laid one of the white linen napkins in her lap. "Why are you so angry? Are you upset that Wren gets half of everything? Is it that you'll be saddled with her for the next five years? I'll admit, it's not ideal—"

"Yeah. It is." Caleb was interrupted when the waiter came

to take their order. He didn't register what she ordered and he'd barely looked at the menu. "Just give me spaghetti," he barked shortly.

"With or without meatballs, sir?" The young waiter looked like he was afraid to speak.

"With. Please bring me a glass of MaCallan before the meal."

"Yes, sir."

"Caleb, you're going to have whiskey before the wine?" she admonished.

Caleb leaned back in the booth. "Who said I was having wine at all?"

He could see her physically deflate at his hard tone. "I just thought..." her words dropped off and he felt like an asshole.

"I'm sorry, Macy. Today's been a tough day and I'm exhausted."

"Well, why don't we have a nice dinner and then I can stay with you tonight?"

Caleb had wanted the distraction of the meal before he began the conversation, but he wasn't going to let her have any delusions and sugarcoating things never worked to his advantage.

"Look, Macy. I think we both know things have changed. You have your life in San Francisco, and now I have to take over Lux."

"We can work things out. I don't have to be in California. There are venture capitalists in Denver, too, or, I don't have to worry about that. I just want to be where you are."

He sighed heavily and ran a hand through his thick hair.

She wasn't going to make it easy on him. "That's crazy. We haven't known each other that long and even if I wanted to continue things, I wouldn't ask you to drastically change your life for a relationship that may or may not work out."

"At least be honest. That's not the reason, Caleb." Her eyes were hard and she picked up her wine glass and drank down half of it.

"No, it's not. I've seen a side of you this week that I don't like."

Macy audibly sucked in her breath.

"I'm sorry if that's harsh, but just because my bank account is larger, it doesn't change who I am. I don't give a shit about the money or even the business; other than there are people who depend on it, as I've already said. It's like you're deaf if I don't say what you want me to say."

She shook her head adamantly. "That's not true! I just want you to have your design firm, not give up your life for someone else's! Lux was your dad's dream, not yours."

"No, it was my mother's, and he worked his ass off to make it happen for her! Until she got sick, and he lost his mind. Then it was about survival and not letting the one thing he had of her die with her. I understand his motivation now."

Macy's brow wrinkled as she frowned at him from across the table. "Did you forget about how he treated you? You don't owe him anything. The company will survive! I was there! I heard your choices, Caleb. Let Wren step up, or let the board do it and be a silent partner."

"I didn't forget a damn thing!" Anger was building up inside him and the compassion he felt for ending things was quickly evaporating. "I'm not going to take the chance something happens to Lux, and I will never ask Wren to quit the ballet!"

Macy's eyes glassed over as she stared at Caleb. "No, you'll never ask little Wren to give up anything. Just give me up, give up the life we could have! I won't let you make me the sacrifice, Caleb!"

A couple at the next table glanced at them due to the raise in their voices.

"Keep your voice down," he commanded. His tone was firm, but he turned his volume down.

Caleb was ready to throw his napkin on the table and stalk out when the waiter brought his drink and sat it down in front of him, then picked up the open wine bottle setting on the table and refilled Macy's glass. "Your dinner will be out very soon."

Macy swallowed and pursed her lips, before picking up her wine glass again. She was livid, and Caleb could see anger simmering in her eyes.

"Calm down," he coaxed. "This isn't the place to fight."

"I don't want to fight. I want you to wake up. What do you expect to happen? Wren got what she wanted. Do you think she'll be running to you now? She doesn't need you anymore."

Caleb's teeth clenched, then he grabbed his glass and slammed his drink. "You know nothing about her. She never asked for anything."

Macy laughed bitterly. "She doesn't have to! You're so blind. I never took you for a fool. Maybe she was doing your dad to steal everything from you. Ever think of that?"

"Enough!" he seethed. Macy was grasping at straws and he wasn't about to fall for it. She would never make him doubt Wren, no matter what she said. "You won't change my mind by being a bitch about Wren. The opposite is true. It was *my decision* that she inherits half of everything, not my father's. He gave me the choice. What the hell do you think I've been agonizing over since we got here?"

"What?" she asked, her words halting in surprise. "Why? Out of some idiotic sense of duty?"

"No. To keep her in my life!" he burst out and Macy looked as if he'd slapped her. "I don't have to explain anything to you, and I wouldn't expect you to understand even if I tried."

Macy paused for a few seconds as she processed his words, and more, his conviction. She could see him soften whenever he spoke about Wren, but she didn't understand. "Cale…" she began, but he put up his hand to stop her.

"Don't call me Cale, Macy."

She poured herself another glass of wine, her feelings clearly hurt.

"I'm sorry. No one ever calls me Cale, except Wren."

"So, you're just going to give up everything for her?"

"I don't look at it like that. She's been a huge part of my life for ten years. It's just the way it is."

"Then why didn't I know anything about her?"

"Because I keep my relationship with her close to the cuff. Growing up, even Dex didn't know the truth. Don't take it personally." Even as he said the words, he knew it sounded absurd. Their relationship was casual, but they'd been intimate and now it was over. How could she not take it personally?

"What happens now? You're giving up your job?"

"Yes," he answered shortly.

"I can help you pack your things, if you want." She appeared resigned to the inevitability of the situation and the finality of his decision, but helping him would keep the connection open.

The waiter showed up at the side of their table with their meal and sat a plate down in front of Macy first, then Caleb.

"Sir, would you care for another drink?"

"I would, thank you." His appetite was dwindling after the conversation and he just wanted to get through the meal and check on Wren. "I think you should fly out in the morning and then in a few days, I'll go back, give notice at the firm, and put my apartment on the market."

"I see. Just like flipping a switch, everything is all fucked up?"

"Macy, I'm truly sorry. This wasn't planned, you know that." Caleb watched her face and he honestly felt bad for her. In the short time he'd known her, he would have sworn she wasn't the type to get overly emotional and could have sworn they'd been on the same page.

"I thought we had a good thing."

He had the grace to feel guilty. Truthfully, he didn't love her, and he never said he did, and they did have fun together, but the events of the past few days had changed the course of his life forever. "We had fun, but we both know it wasn't serious." He felt like he was trying to close a deal, but there was no way to make it a win, win.

"You don't have to be a prick about it, Caleb." Her mouth pursed and the look she shot him was filled with hatred.

"I didn't think I was."

She picked up her fork, looked at her plate for a few seconds, and then sat it down beside it. "Can we just go?"

"Yes." Caleb could barely hold in a sigh of relief.

When the waiter brought his new drink, he requested the bill.

***

ON THE WAY BACK TO the house, Wren sat in quiet contemplation for most of the drive home.

It was too dark to see the outline of the mountains from the right side of the car as she looked out the window, but the city lights raced by as Jared drove on the highway. Jonesy reached out and placed an old hand over Wren's young one when they only had a few blocks to go.

"Quite a day, wasn't it?" she asked. "A penny for your thoughts."

Wren turned her head to look at Jonesy whose features were shadowed due to the night and the dark windows of the limousine, which kept most of the passing lights from reaching the inside of the vehicle. Wren smiled sadly.

"My mind should be racing, I guess. I should be worried that this inheritance means I'll have to give up the ballet or that my mother will try to pressure me to support her, but all I can think about is Caleb and Macy."

Jonesy understood. Macy was like a clinging vine on the young man all day and she could sense Wren's trepidation. "I understand, dear, but don't worry about anything. You'll talk to Caleb and he'll take care of everything."

Wren was filled with frustration at the uncertainty of the future. "But that's not fair, Jonesy. He doesn't deserve to babysit me my entire life. He doesn't deserve to be responsible for me. I don't want him to be tied to me because of the estate and Lux."

Jonesy smiled knowingly. "Wren," she said simply. "I understand. You want him to be tied emotionally."

Wren's head bowed and she fiddled with the strap on her purse. It made her vulnerable to admit it, so she only nodded.

"You don't think he does what he does out of responsibility, do you?" Jonesy asked incredulously.

Wren shrugged slightly. "Cale always made me his responsibility. Maybe that's why his dad did this."

Jonesy shook her grey haired head. "I don't think so, honey. You'll see."

Jared had pulled up in front of the house and walked around to open the back passenger door. Both women slid out and made their way inside after thanking him.

"Do you want anything to eat?"

"Don't bother with me, Jonesy." Wren hugged her and kissed her cheek. "I'm just going to take a bath, read the letter Edison left for me, and then go to bed."

"If Caleb comes back and asks for you, should I tell him you're asleep?"

"If he asks. Goodnight. I love you."

"I love you, too, darling. Don't worry about anything. Just get a good night's sleep."

"I will." She started up the stairs, anxious to close her eyes, but curious about the contents of the letter. The envelope was pulled from her purse and she was ripping it open before she even made it to her room.

Wren let her purse drop and kicked her shoes off right inside as the door closed behind her before unfolding the sheet of paper with a short, handwritten note on it.

My Dearest Wren,

I wanted to tell you it was a pleasure to have you as my daughter for the few years I had you. I'm very proud of you for going after your dream and making the life you wanted for yourself.

If you're reading this, it means you've been bequeathed half of the estate and my equity in Lux. I hope that it will bring only good things to your life, including bringing you and Caleb back together.

It's only fair to tell you that there were two versions of the will and I required Caleb to choose between them. It was my fault that he left to go to Boston and away from you, and he was devastated. I wanted to right the wrong, so I put control over his relationship with you back into his own hands.

I'm certain he has not taken the decision lightly and has done what he believes puts you first. That's what he has always done. I've seen it a hundred times.

Have a happy life.
With love,
Edison

Wren was softly crying when she finished reading Edison's letter. So, it was Caleb that gave her half of everything, not his father. She wasn't sure if her heart was shattering, or if it was so full of the love she felt for him making her heart about to burst. She needed answers, but she was physically and emotionally exhausted. Two fat tears tumbled from her eyes and rolled down over her high cheekbones.

Laying the letter down on the end table to the right of her bed, she began to peel off her clothes, letting the new jacket and dress fall to the floor without a thought.

Soon the steaming water and soft lilac aroma of her bath water was soothing her nerves. The combination of the candles and soft scent made her close her eyes and relax in the luxurious gently sloped tub. Even with her eyes closed, the heat seeping into her muscles, and a conscious effort to clear her mind, it wasn't possible. She was sleepy, no question, but her mind tortured her with doubts about Caleb and Macy, when he'd be home, and his motivation for giving her half of his money.

When it came down to it, that was the bottom line and she had to face it. She inhaled deeply. The flickering of the candles glowed orange and black behind her closed lids as she lifted a hand and leaned her forehead against it.

Last night had been magical; so euphoric it was like a drug, so why did she doubt a single second of it now? The money would make life easier in some respects and harder in others. Without it, she could be sure what was between them was based on emotion. Part of her wished he hadn't given her half of the estate, then, if they ended up in each other's life, it would be because they chose it, and nothing else.

He hadn't said he loved her, but she felt so close to him; they were so connected, it was if they breathed for each other. That raw emotion was more important to her than any amount of money, more important than her career, or where they lived. If she could only have one thing from Caleb for the rest of her life, the only thing she wanted was his love. She wouldn't have any doubts if Caleb were with her, here, instead of being out to dinner with Macy. However, he was with Macy, so what if she'd misinterpreted the previous evening? What if it were only another weak moment? How could she be around him, if he was still involved with Macy?

A small sob broke from her chest as she let herself cry. It hurt too much to bottle it up inside and she wouldn't have been able to, even if she'd wanted to. How could she tell Cale that she didn't want the money without sounding ungrateful? The last thing she wanted was to hurt him or make him think she didn't appreciate the gesture, but could she tell him the truth? How much she loved him was the only secret she'd ever kept from him. Wren had overcome the things that used to intimidate or scare her, and she had Caleb to thank for it. By leaning on his strength, she'd been able to find her own confidence; yet, he was the one who held power over her and kept her in a place she was still very vulnerable.

When the temperature got tepid, she turned on the hot water faucet to add more, but when that cooled, too, she reluctantly climbed out of the tub, dried off and then pulled on a pair of old shorts and t-shirt to sleep in. Her lonely bed held no allure.

Wren didn't want to know what time it was as she brushed her hair and cleaned her teeth, then shut off the lights and climbed beneath the plush comforter of her bed. She was thankful for the comfort of the mattress and pillows that seemed to swallow her up and hug her body. Her eyes were tired from all of the tears, and she looked forward to the blissful blankness of sleep that would give her mind and heart a much-needed break.

She shivered for a moment, until her body heat began to warm the sheets and blankets. She rolled over and grabbed the opposite pillow, pulling it close to her chest to hug it. The faint scent of Caleb lingered, evidence that he had spent at least a couple of hours with her when he'd put her to bed last night and she found herself wishing it were twenty-four hours earlier.

There was a faint knock on her door and she immediately sat up, leaning her weight on one arm. The room was almost dark because the blinds were down.

"Yes?" she called. She hadn't locked the door, despite Macy's previous intrusions. "Who's there?"

The door opened a crack and a beam of light fell into the room and across the bed, causing her to squint in protest and she lifted a hand to ward it off.

"It's me," Caleb said softly. "Did I wake you?"

Wren's heart leapt at the sound of his voice. "I just got into bed a few minutes ago." There were no other occupied rooms on the second floor, but both of them spoke in low tones.

"I can let you sleep, but I thought you might want to talk about today."

She nodded. "I do. Come in."

He came in and shut the door quietly behind him. Caleb didn't turn on the light, and he didn't ask permission before he began to undress. The darkness hid most of his movements, but she could see the outlines of his white shirt after he removed his blazer and laid it on the upholstered chair by the window. Systematically, he kicked off his shoes, unbuttoned his shirt, and pulled off his undershirt, layering it all on the chair. When she heard the clank of his belt buckle, she scooted from the middle of the bed to one side, automatically making room.

Her heart started beating at the familiarity of his actions and she smiled to herself. He wouldn't see her blush in the darkness, as she bit her lip, but she felt the warmth spread into her cheeks.

"I love that your room smells just like you."

Pleasure rushed through her at his words. It was a simple statement, but the implications were huge.

When Caleb had disrobed down to his boxer briefs, he pulled back the covers and climbed in beside Wren. "You haven't told me to get the hell out, so I guess this is okay?" He settled back on the pillows and reached for her, and she easily settled into his arms, sliding one of hers across his hard abs and her head came to rest on his chest. She felt like warm silk against him, and the only thing that could have made it better were if they were both completely naked.

"Yes."

His arms tightened, and he bent his head to place a kiss on her forehead. "Are you okay with everything?" He hesitated for a beat, but continued when she didn't answer right away. "I'll make sure you don't have to give up ballet. I'll run the company for both of us."

"Cale." She tightened her arm around him and turned her face into the crook of his neck. He smelled of cologne and whiskey. "You didn't have to do that for me."

His fingers began threading the hair down her back in a rhythmic motion designed to soothe and relax. Mostly, it was because he couldn't stop himself from touching her. "Do what?"

"Split your inheritance."

He stilled immediately. "Damn it! How did you find out? Did Jonathan tell you?" His tone took on a bit of an angry edge.

"He didn't. It was in the letter your dad left for me. It explained about the two versions of the will."

Caleb's chest rose beneath her head as he inhaled a deep, regretful sigh. "I didn't want you to know it was my decision."

"Why not?"

He rolled to his side, shifting so they were facing each other in the darkness. He reached out and brushed the knuckles of his right hand along her left cheekbone. "Because, you might interpret the decision as selfish." He shrugged slightly. "It was."

Wren laid a hand on his bare chest. There was a light smattering of velvet soft hair and she pulled and played with it gently. "How could giving half of your inheritance away be selfish? I don't interpret it that way at all."

He shook his head. He could smell her sweet breath, feel the heat radiating between them. He wanted nothing more than to kiss her and roll her beneath him but this conversation was important. "Because, I want you in my life and the company ties will assure that. At least, for the next five years."

"Oh, Cale." Her voice wavered with the ache she felt in her throat. He was in her bed, so clearly the relationship he was after wasn't platonic. "That means a lot to me, but you didn't have to buy that. All you had to do was talk to me."

"I wasn't sure what was going on in your life."

"You mean beyond the times you checked up on me?"

Caleb couldn't help but smile. She knew him so well. "Yeah. I had to make sure you were okay, especially after that night downstairs."

She nodded against him. The way he left afterward still stung. "Why did you leave like that?"

"I was freaking out. It didn't matter how I felt about you, in the eyes of the world, we were—," He paused to gather what he wanted to say, lifting his arm up off of her and then letting it drop again.

"I get it," Wren said.

"At first, I was just relieved to put distance between us. I was ashamed of what happened, ashamed of the way I left it, and worried sick that you might get pregnant. We didn't use protection and I blamed myself. I felt like hell when I got back to Boston because I worried I'd ruined your life."

Her heart dropped. She'd never considered that he might feel anything other than regret and embarrassment. "I thought you only did it because you'd been drinking, and then afterward, were embarrassed you'd ever touched me. I didn't even consider I might get pregnant."

Caleb sucked in enough air to fill his lungs to capacity and then let it out in a deep sigh. "I did. I used to call home and check in with Jonesy a lot more often. I asked her to send me a bunch of shit I didn't need, because I knew she'd tell me if you needed me. And I hoped you'd call me, if it happened, but when I heard you were auditioning for Juilliard, I knew you were in the clear." The strain in his voice told Wren that those months had been as much a struggle for him as they had been for her, but for very different reasons.

"Juilliard was a good distraction, but I was heartbroken. That night meant so much to me, and it ruined us. I missed you every day."

"I was afraid you hated me, and I couldn't face it." Relief at finally being able to talk to her about it surged through him. "I was so mad at myself. You were my little bird and I took advantage of you."

Wren lifted her head to look into his face, and then shook her head slightly. "No, you didn't. I was of age and I wanted to be with you."

His eyes met hers unflinchingly, and his hand stroked the back of her head again. It was so soft, like a feather touch and it was all she could do not to melt into him. "But, I knew you looked to me to protect you, and I couldn't even protect you from myself."

"I'm glad it happened, Cale."

His arms tightened and she laid her head back down on his shoulder. The arm she laid across his midsection reached for his hand and they threaded their fingers together. Caleb felt the last piece of deceit between them vanish. "God, it feels good to finally tell you the truth. We belong together, bird."

Despite his actions of the night before and now, Wren needed clarification about the status of his relationship with Macy. She wanted to tell him she was in love with him, but not until she knew for sure it was over between them.

"What about Macy?"

He shook his head again, his brow furrowing seriously. It wouldn't be easy to tell her that his relationship with Macy was fairly new, and still convince Wren that he was in love with her. "At the risk of sounding like a dick, Macy and I were casual. We met at a time when I needed money to start my design firm and she had connections. One thing led to another and we dated; it was fun for a while, but it wasn't serious."

"Does Macy feel that way?" Wren was well aware the other woman felt threatened, otherwise, she wouldn't have done and said the things she had. She desperately wanted to tell Caleb, but decided not to add insult to injury. Macy was about to lose any chance with Caleb and that was punishment enough. "Intimacy changes things for a woman." Wren hoped he understood her double entendre. "She traveled across half of the country to be here for you."

"I didn't ask her to. When I was leaving, it was more of an annoyance than emotionally painful. Honestly, I just wanted to get it over with."

"She just showed up, then?"

"No, I knew she was coming, but I didn't initiate it. Wren, I told her that she and I don't have a future together. I'm moving here and she has a life on the west coast. That's that."

Her fingers stilled on his chest when he didn't say what she wanted to hear. "I'm sure she'd move if you asked her to."

Impatience erupted inside Caleb. The last thing he wanted to do was discuss Macy. "Probably, but obviously, I have other plans."

"Does she suspect it has anything to do with me?"

"Macy is a lot of things, Wren, but stupid isn't one of them."

Wren pulled out of his arms and sat up in the bed next to him. Calm settled over Caleb and he reached out to take her hand in his.

"I don't want to feel like you're sacrificing everything for me. You deserve to have your design firm, Cale. Maybe Jonathan still has the other version of the will. If it all comes to you, will you be able to sell everything, now? Then you can stop worrying about me."

Her heart was breaking but she owed it to him to think of him first.

"What makes you think I can stop worrying about you?"

"You can try."

His face twisted in frustration. Why was she doing this? "No, I can't, and we burned the other version so the will stays as it is."

"Why, Cale?"

"Your reptilian mother is just looking for anything she can use as a way to contest the will. But mostly, because I need to make sure you're taken care of, with or without me. Which you should already know!"

Wren smiled into the darkness, and Caleb saw the flash of

her white teeth. "Okay, don't get upset. What happens now?"

"I have to go to San Francisco for a few weeks, and Jonathan will step in until I can come back."

"When are you leaving?"

"That depends on you. When do you have to be back in New York?"

"We have rehearsals for the next show that start in a week. I have a contract until the end of the year, but then I can leave the company."

"As much as I'd love having you close to home, I can't let you give up dancing, Bird. That's not what this is about."

"Why should you be the one to always make the sacrifice? Besides, who says I have to give it up? I can dance here." Her career meant a lot to her, but what mattered most was being with Caleb. "Denver has a company, right?"

Caleb reached up and ran his index finger down her cheek in a loving caress. Her skin was like velvet beneath his touch, and his heart was full of love and anticipation for the future; a future he never let himself imagine was possible.

"We don't have to decide everything tonight." He lifted her hand and kissed the inside of her wrist, where the white horse tattoo covered her scars. "You stop arguing and kiss me." He brushed his lips softly back and forth over her tender skin.

Tingles ran over her skin starting from where he was kissing the inside of her wrist and then goose bumps spread out in delicious waves over her whole body.

Wren sidled up closer, and then bent forward at her waist and placed a soft, slow kiss on his mouth. Caleb's mouth came alive the second her lips touched his and he sat up, both hands coming to cup her head as he took charge. His open mouth slanted across hers and soon their tongues were waging a passionate war with each other as the kiss became deeper.

"I've been dying to do that all day," he ground out as his mouth teased hers, unwilling to break contact completely. "Mmmmm. You taste so good."

Wren's fingers brushed the soft stubble on his jaw just before Caleb leaned back and pulled her on top of him. He wanted her, there was no question she was aware of it. It was clear that Wren shared his feelings. His hardness was full and pressing into the softness of her stomach, as his hips pushed into hers and their legs tangled together under the covers.

"I want you," he said in an almost whisper, going in for another kiss, though he kept this one more reserved. He was conscious that they still had a lot of things to iron out.

Wren wanted to lose herself in him, anxious to have his mouth on hers, his hard body pressing and owning hers, but she hesitated. "Me, too, but Macy is downstairs, Caleb."

Caleb's arms tightened around her as she sprawled over him and he willed his body to stop its quest for hers. "I know." He kissed her temple. "I promise, sex wasn't my intention when I came up here. I just wanted to check on you and maybe sleep with you."

Wren let out a soft laugh. "Sleep, huh? That must explain why you're almost completely naked in my bed."

"Can't blame a guy for trying. I can be fully naked if you want me to be." He smiled and kissed the side of her neck in a series of delicious and very delicate kisses designed to seduce her despite his words or good intentions.

"I'm helpless with you, but aren't you tired? Plus, Macy—"

Wren snuggled into him, and Caleb's hands slid down her back and came to rest on top of her butt. He could see her logic, but he was reluctant to go to his own room. "Quiet. She knows I want to be with you. That was the whole point behind dinner with her."

Relief flooded through Wren. She could tell him about the way Macy had invaded her rooms and harassed her, but what was the point? Caleb had just said he wanted to be with her and they were some of the most beautiful words she'd ever heard. "How'd she take it?"

"She did fine," he dismissed. He didn't want to talk about Macy, Veronica, the funeral, Lux, or anything else. It helped that he wasn't convinced Macy was motivated purely by emotion. "I made my point. That's what matters."

Wren kissed the underside of Caleb's jaw and he started kneading her back. She wanted to tell him she loved him, but it was enough to be wrapped up safe and tight in his arms, warm in her bed and secure in the knowledge that they were choosing each other.

"Wren?" Caleb paused. His instincts picked up on her sudden sadness. "Aren't you happy? I don't care about any of it... all I want is you, and to know that you're happy."

She dropped her head to his shoulder and closed her eyes. He was so perfect. "I am. I'll just miss you, Cale."

"I've missed you for ten years." He rolled her over roughly, finally giving up his intention to stop himself from making love to her. "Let's not miss each other tonight," he said seriously as he started to make love to her. He touched her with reverence and awe, took his time kissing every inch as he slowly undressed her, and reveled in the soft sounds she made as he pleasured her with his mouth and hands.

There was nothing between them now; not time, distance, half-truths, pain or misunderstandings and he wanted to keep it that way. Caleb found himself grateful to his father for the first time in his life. The choice Edison had forced on him had conjured up everything he could ever want. This amazing, beautiful woman he'd always loved still trusted him unconditionally. She made him feel prouder, and stronger than he'd ever been. With her by his side, he was invincible.

All conversation stopped as he pushed into her willing body. Her flesh was hot and tight as she stretched to accommodate his size. He couldn't tell if the ecstasy came from her body or the way he loved her and it didn't matter. Their hands and mouths were desperate and clinging as they explored and devoured each other in insatiable desire, the longing almost unbearable. He moved on her and inside her, played her body like an instrument, and the closer he got, he still wanted more. The room fell silent except for panting breaths, sighs, and soft moans as love and pleasure started the slow build that Caleb controlled.

"I love you, Wren." He'd wanted to admit that to her for years and now there was no holding back. His body dug deeper into hers in long slow thrusts that drew out answering surges from her hips. It was like the most perfect dance Wren could ever imagine was playing out between them.

"Jesus, I love you so much. Promise you'll never leave me," he breathed against her mouth between kisses.

Emotion overtook her as his words registered a split second before he swooped and took her mouth in another hungry kiss. He tasted so good, and she was starving for him.

Her fingers curled into the flesh of his back, her arms and legs wound around him as tears filled her eyes. Her hips surged against his, her insides clamping down to hold him tighter. She wanted to get closer to his body, to let him feel what he meant to her; to melt right into him as love made her fall apart in his arms. "Oh, Cale. Oh, my God." Her voice cracked and she couldn't breathe. "I love you so much, it almost hurts."

Caleb was overwhelmed, even as his orgasm started to overtake him, his eyes started to burn and his chest felt like it would explode. It took a lot for Caleb to let down his guard, but he trusted Wren and with her, he could crack open. With her, vulnerability wasn't wrapped in risk; it brought the biggest gift of his life.

He turned and kissed her temple, as his eyes closed and he poured into her. "I know, Wren. Uhggggg," he groaned deeply. His body jerked and heaved against hers as he came hard. "It's painful as hell, but it's so amazing."

His arms were tight around her and he rolled on to his back, taking her with him as she fell apart around him; her flesh convulsing and quivering, pulling on his. His chest was heaving with the intensity of their lovemaking and the love that threatened to suffocate him. He could feel her hot tears fall onto the skin of his shoulder and neck, mixed with the warm rush of her breath as she struggled for control. They had just laid beautiful and passionate claim on each other and now, still wrapped tightly in each other's arms, his body still buried in hers, they stilled. Only their breathing came down slowly, and the thin sheen of perspiration covering their skin started to evaporate, making Wren shiver. She was on top and half of her body was bare to the air, so he bent slightly to grab the edge of the comforter to pull it up over her.

The fingers of one of his hands threaded through hers and his other soothed in long strokes down her back as she remained where she was on top of him. He knew she was crying and he blinked quickly to keep his own eyes from tearing up. Caleb wished he never had to move from her bed for the rest of his life.

"There's no going back for us. Promise me, Wren. He said it again, his voice growing thick. "I could lose everything and anyone and live through it, but I can't lose you."

She closed her eyes as her heart squeezed hard inside her chest. She never thought she'd hear more beautiful words. "I promise, Cale."

He relaxed against her, though his arms still held her close. Wren's head rested on his chest below his chin, and she could feel him breathe and hear his heart thunder under her ear, proof that he was alive and that he loved her.

"You won't lose me. Ever."

chapter
FIFTEEN

WHEN WREN WOKE AND MADE her way down to the kitchen, she found Jonesy had already started her day. A big bowl of fresh bread dough was covered with a linen towel and left to rise on the counter while the old woman puttered around cleaning up after herself. She was softly humming as she wiped down the cabinets and countertops. She offered Wren a glorious smile when the young woman walked into the kitchen.

"You look happy today, Jonesy!"

"I am!"

It took about a minute and a half for Jonesy to elaborate. "Caleb is out for an early run and then going out to lunch with Dex. And, hallelujah; I think we've seen the last of Macy!" Wren took a seat on one of the stools near where Jonesy was working, not bothering to get any coffee or orange juice. "She didn't look very happy when Caleb put her in that Toyota, I can tell you."

Wren nodded without thinking. Jonesy had no way of knowing Wren was privy to the other young woman's plans. She couldn't help a small sigh of relief. "That is a plus. How'd he take it?"

"Hummph!" Jonesy wrinkled her nose and rolled her eyes.

It was such so unusual to see Jonesy mocking anyone, it almost made Wren laugh out loud. "That good, huh?" She smiled.

"I don't know what he saw in her in the first place. She was about as nice as a wildcat in a fight with a rattle snake."

"I thought she was pushy, that's for sure."

Wren wished she could confide in Jonesy about Caleb, but didn't feel right about doing it before they both agreed.

"Pushy!" Jonesy scoffed. She took out a pan and put a few eggs on to boil, adding the cold eggs, some salt and white vinegar to the water. "She's a bulldozer!" She huffed wryly as she set a glass of orange juice and a warm mug of coffee in front of Wren.

"She's so sophisticated. I can see why Caleb would have been attracted to her."

"Until she opens her mouth, maybe. Don't you worry your little heart." She turned to Wren, reached out and patted her hand. "We all know who Caleb loves."

The corner of Wren's mouth lifted in a half smile and she lifted her eyes lazily. Jonesy had spot-on intuition. "Do we?"

"If you don't know, then you need your head examined."

"I wish it were that easy, but I have to go back to New York soon. At least for a while, anyway, and Caleb will be in San Francisco. "

"Ahh. You're worried that Macy will be there, too."

Wren bit her lip and nodded, picking up her coffee cup. "Yes. She will be. She lives there."

"I don't know exactly what's been brewing between you two, but it's been in the works long before that girl showed up." She went to turn the burner down to a simmer.

"But she's so..." Wren searched for the right word. "Determined."

"I see." Jonesy leaned back against the counter and crossed her arms across her chest. "What did she do? You can tell old Jonesy."

"She just," she shrugged. "Barged into my room a few times. At first, she pretended to be nice, but the last time, it was a full frontal assault."

"Does Caleb know?"

"I didn't see any reason to tell him; he's had so much going on."

"Don't start things off by keeping things from Caleb, Wren."

"I'm not trying to keep it a secret, but I don't need to run to him like I'm five."

Wren's phone was in the back pocket of her jeans and it started to ring. When she pulled it out and saw that it was from her mother she cringed. Veronica hardly ever called, and she'd only been to New York to see her once in all of the time she went to Juilliard or the years she'd lived there, since.

"Oh boy," she said in a deflated voice. "Just what I need."

Jonesy's eyebrows shot up as Wren answered. "Hello, mother."

"Wren, doll! How are you?"

"I'm good." Her tone was bland. No doubt Caleb would lose his shit if he even knew Veronica was calling.

"Can you meet Mummy for lunch before I leave town?"

Wren shifted in her chair and raised her free hand and started fiddling with her earring. "Um, well..." Her mother had the gift of selective retention and seemed to forget all of the mean ways she treated Wren when she was young.

"Oh, well, nothing! There's a nice restaurant in the hotel and then maybe you and that driver of yours can drop me at the airport. My plane leaves at 3 o'clock."

Wren couldn't find any logical reason to say no other than she just didn't want to, but the thought of several hours with her mother filled her with dread.

Jonesy looked at her pointedly, obviously interested in what Veronica wanted. Her disapproval was obvious by her expression.

"I'm not sure I can spare that much time, Mother."

"What do you mean, you aren't sure? For heaven's sake! How often do we see each other?"

Wren rubbed the back of her neck under the curtain of her hair. She was uneasy and it showed in her body language. Jonesy was making a slicing motion across her throat and Wren's mouth twisted wryly, her eyes widened and she nodded in agreement.

"That's true, but Caleb and I have some things to talk about before I go back to New York."

"Oh, pish! You can talk to him about all that business

nonsense later. This is more important, and I won't take 'no' for an answer. You're lucky I don't make you take me shopping."

"I hate shopping."

"So, be glad there's no time, then. I'll see you downtown at the Ritz Carlton in about two hours. I've got something important to tell you; something that can't be said over the phone."

Veronica's sugary sweet voice was a good indication that she was up to no good. Wren didn't want to see her mother because she figured she would try to strong-arm some way to get her to hand over at least a portion of her inheritance. On the other hand, she had to put on her big girl panties and face her demons. She was sure being clear that she had no intentions of giving Veronica an "in" or handing over any money would go a long way to a more peaceful future. The last thing she wanted was weekly phone calls or drop-ins from that hag.

"Okay."

"Wonderful, darling.

When the call ended, Jonesy gave Wren a stern look. Obviously, she expected Wren to share the details of Veronica's call. "You aren't considering meeting that woman, are you?"

Wren's head cocked to one side guiltily. "I'm not looking forward to it, but I know she will never leave me alone until she says her piece."

"Oh, she wants a piece, alright. Your bank account, and a pound of flesh." Jonesy was taking her aggression out on the bread dough she was punching down in the bowl before she turned and started pinching off a chunk to form it into a loaf, then put it in the greased pan she had waiting on the counter.

Wren slid off of the stool, walked around the island to Jonesy and put her arm around her shoulders to give them a squeeze. "I love you, Jonesy."

"I love you too, dear." Her hands were still in dough so she couldn't return Wren's embrace. "Just don't let that pariah intimidate you."

"I won't." She took one last swallow of the fresh squeezed orange juice that Jonesy had given her, and then started to walk from the kitchen. "That was delicious."

"Caleb isn't going to like you going alone," Jonesy called after her retreating form.

Wren stopped and turned back around so she could answer the housekeeper from the foyer that stood between the massive kitchen and the staircase. "I know, but I'm not thirteen anymore, and Caleb gave me a solid education on sticks and stones. My mother doesn't have the same power over me; I'm not a scared kid anymore."

Jonesy hacked off another chunk of dough. "Okay, but he isn't gonna like it."

As if he had psychic ability, her phone pinged and a text came in as she climbed the stairs and went into her room. It was from Caleb.

Thank you for last night. I'm meeting Dex for lunch. I didn't want to wake you. Jonathan wants me to meet him at Lux later. You can come along, but if you'd rather not, I can fill you in later.

You go ahead. Will I see you for dinner?

Yes. Why don't you give Jonesy the night off and we'll go out.

Wren smiled as warmth filled her like flowing honey, and she started to blush.

You mean, like a date?

Much more than a date.

***

WREN WALKED INTO THE beautiful hotel right on time. She just wanted to get this meeting with Veronica behind her. Her conscious nagged a bit. She should have told Caleb her plans, but he would have insisted he accompany her and his day would have been ruined. No; it was time she learned how to handle her mother.

Wren had on the best dress she'd taken with her to Bali. It was an aquamarine, cobalt blue, and white sundress with a flowing skirt that dropped to mid-calf and the bodice was fitted with spaghetti straps. She bought it because the darker color reminded her of Caleb's eyes, but walking into the elaborate lobby, she couldn't help feeling out of place.

She found the bell stand and asked directions to the restaurant, but the hotel had two. Leave it to Veronica to make it as difficult as she possibly could.

"Which one is the most expensive?" Wren asked the uniformed man who was clearly the bell captain.

"There is a coffee and breakfast bar, and the Elway's is right down that long hallway and to the left, ma'am," he said pleasantly, and pointed the way.

He smiled at her admiringly, and Wren answered with a small one of her own. "Thank you."

It wasn't quite 11:30 am, and the restaurant was filling up for lunch. Dark wood and various shades of orange upholstery oozed elegance in the understated way that said a cup of coffee was going to cost ten dollars. Wren rolled her eyes because she couldn't help herself.

She approached the hostess stand where a very tall and thin brunette welcomed her. "Good afternoon. Would you like the dining room or the patio?"

It was a beautiful June day, but Wren was sure her mother would not choose the breeze ruffling her hair, no matter how nice it was outside. "I'm meeting my mother, Veronica Luxon?" It came out sounding like a question.

"Oh, my gosh, yes!" she gushed. Clearly, the young woman had seen Veronica's face in some of the Lux advertisements. "Right this way, please." She motioned Wren to follow her through the restaurant to one of the curved booths against a far wall.

The booth looked out into the restaurant so Veronica saw her coming and waved her over. Wren was annoyed that her mother always had to take some sort of action to draw attention. She was elegantly dressed in a white suit, her hair freshly coiffed in an updo from a salon. Her fingers were dripping in diamonds, including the large rock Edison had given her for an engagement ring.

Veronica's face turned sour as the hostess waited for Wren to slide in before she placed a leather-bound menu in front of her on the bone china bread plate. "What are you wearing, Wren? This is the Ritz for goodness sake."

Wren slid into the booth, grateful for the size of it so she could keep a good amount of distance between herself and her mother. "Nice to see you, too, Mother."

Veronica was sufficiently sidetracked, like a dog that drops his ball when presented with a steak. Her bright red lips curved into a broad smile, showing her perfect teeth. She reached out a hand, hoping to take Wren's in hers but her daughter didn't comply, instead folding both of her hands in her lap after setting her purse on the seat next to her.

Veronica looked taken aback for a split second. "Wren, dear, is that any way to greet your mummy?"

Wren cringed. Why did she insist on that insipid label? It sounded off to Wren because it was completely fake, like everything else about her mother.

"I don't remember we ever lived in England, Mother, and I can remember years when you wanted me to call you Veronica. Nothing remotely related to *mummy*." Wren kept her voice dry and her guard up. "What's this about? Oh, besides a ride to the airport."

Veronica sat back and glared at Wren. "No need to get nasty. That stepbrother of yours is rubbing off on you. It's not attractive at all, Wren," she said indignantly.

Wren's mind screamed with hatred and a multitude of insults she wanted to hurl at her mother. "Haven't you heard? You're divorced. Caleb isn't my stepbrother, anymore."

"I'm still your mother and I won't have you speaking to me like that."

Wren shifted in her seat. The waiter came and asked Wren if she wanted a beverage. "Just water with lemon, please."

"Sparkling or still?"

"Still will be fine, but I'd love a lemon wedge with it."

"I'll have another vodka tonic," Veronica said before the girl could walk away.

"Yes, ma'am."

"It's a little early for the hard stuff, isn't it, Mother?"

"Look, I wanted to have a nice lunch, but since you're being so unpleasant, I'll get right to it." The bright red and overly long acrylic nails clacked on the surface of the crystal glass as she picked it up. "I know you're going to be touring, and Caleb has to get his house in order in California, so I'm very willing to step in and offer my help. I can move into the Bould—""

Wren's hair was tied up in a messy bun on the top of her head, but the hair on the back of her neck bristled, and Wren's eyes locked with Veronica's. "Wait, what? What do you know of Cale's plans?" she interrupted.

"Cale. That's so cute."

Wren's brow furrowed and she put up a hand to halt Veronica. She was about to ask a question, but she already knew the answer. "No, how do you know what his plans are?"

Veronica looked uncomfortable, cornered as she was by Wren's intuition. She reached up and patted the back of her hair nervously.

"Well, Macy mentioned it at the reading, and then I spoke to her on the phone last evening. She seems very nice and she loves Caleb. She just wants the best for him."

Wren huffed and shook her head, ready to bolt out of the restaurant without hearing another lying word. "First; no you won't be moving into the Boulder house. I'm not an idiot. I know exactly what you're trying to pull."

"I'm just trying to help you. Macy will be moving into the Denver house with Caleb, and they'll want their privacy, Wren. Be reasonable."

Wren felt like her mother was trying to herd her in a direction she didn't believe or want to go in, but despite telling herself to remain calm, she was affected. Her pulse increased, and she could physically feel heat seeping up her neck and into her face. "Caleb has no intentions of being with Macy. Stop lying. You won't intimidate, hurt, or cajole me into giving you what you want. Edison gave you more than you deserved in his will. That God-awful ring on your hand is worth a few million, so sell it if you need money."

They hadn't ordered, but the waiter made no move to approach the table during the heated exchange.

"How dare you say that to me? You have no idea what I put up with when I was married to him. I did it for you, you ungrateful brat!"

"Yeah. The best of everything, trips, having your face on the Lux brand, dripping diamonds, " Wren spat, venom dripping from every word. "You had it so hard."

It was as if the dam had broken and everything she'd ever wanted to say to her mother was gushing forth. "You poor thing. Anyone who ever met you knows you never do anything for anyone but yourself. I watched it through four husbands. I'm sort of surprised you haven't found another one. Caleb had you pegged from day one, and he was only fourteen!"

"Should have known you'd latch on to that little prick. He made my life hell!"

A smug smile settled on Wren's face as she began to scoot from the booth and throw her unused linen napkin on top of the table. "We're done, Mother. I don't ever want to lay eyes on you again. You won't get a dime from me, so stop trying. I despise you."

"You would have nothing if it weren't for me marrying that cold bastard, Wren. You should thank me!" Veronica derided.

If looks could kill, Wren would have dropped dead on the spot, but she smiled sweetly at her mother. "You know? You're right. Thank you, Mother."

"That's better. Now, it will end up costing too much money to contest the will, and that would be foolish. So, as soon as everything comes out of escrow, I'll take residence in the Boulder house and you can set me up with a modest bank account. I don't need much, Wren. Just a comfortable life."

Wren couldn't believe her ears and she almost laughed out loud. "You're deranged. You should seek professional help."

"Well, I won't be taking sharp objects to my skin, that's for sure."

Loathing reminiscent of what she experienced in her youth exploded inside Wren, and angry tears stung her eyes. The last thing she wanted was to start crying in front of the very woman who caused her enough misery to hurt herself. Her instincts were to flee and she found herself longing for Caleb's presence next to her. He wouldn't allow Veronica to treat her this way and she chastised herself for agreeing to see her at all.

"This is over. I'm leaving." Wren began to scoot the last couple of feet out of the big booth, but couldn't because Macy had appeared out of nowhere.

"Not so fast, Sunshine." Her lips slid into a salacious grin.

Wren's heart plummeted and she was stunned into silence. Veronica's intention was to tag team her with Macy. Both of them seemed desperate enough to do anything to get what they wanted. Veronica wanted her money, and Macy wanted Caleb and everything that came with him.

"Let me out of the booth, Macy."

"Calm down. You don't want to make a scene in a place like this. You and your mother are both sort of famous, and you won't do Caleb any good by making a fool of yourself. It will end up all over social media." Macy's tone was low and sounded soothing to anyone else listening, but Wren knew she was malicious in her intent. "We both know you won't embarrass him, so, sit there and listen up."

Veronica chuckled and waved the waiter over, who had her new drink. She picked it up and sipped it calmly while Macy did the dirty work.

Wren's heart was pounding so hard she could hear the beat in her ears. She was flushed and felt like she was going to vomit.

"I'm not about to let some little charity case ruin the life Caleb and I have planned. Especially, now." She opened her purse and held it open so Wren could see inside. Lying just inside the opening was a long white plastic tube with a pink lid on one end. Macy reached in and turned it over so the window with two pink lines showed. Her expression was egotistical and Wren wanted to die.

Oh, God, her mind screamed. She tried to suck in a deep breath but her heart felt as if it would fly from her body and she couldn't breathe. "It duh—does—doesn't prove anything," she gasped out.

Macy shrugged nonchalantly and Veronica squeezed the lime wedge perched on the edge of her glass into her fresh drink, completely unmoved by the events around her.

"Do you think Caleb and I have been playing Tiddlywinks, Wren?" She shook her head. "Oh, that man is virile, here's the proof." She held the pregnancy test up, uncaring who saw it or that it was completely unsanitary to bring it into a restaurant. "Even if he has you convinced he doesn't love me, he is an honorable man. We both know what comes next."

"I don't believe you, Macy. You're just like her," she said, pointing to Veronica. "You'll do or say anything to get what you want."

Macy's eyes bored into Wren. "When it comes to Caleb, you bet your ass I will. Do you really think I walked up to some random pregnant woman and ask her to pee on this thing? You're pathetic. Get real, Wren."

Wren felt hot, her chest tight, and she was about to throw up. Her eyelids drooped lazily and she tried to swallow down the bile. "Let me out." Her voice was soft and wavering. Macy was pleased with herself and neither of the two women cared that Wren was physically in distress. "I'm gonna be sick."

The manager came over to the table a concerned look on her face, just as Wren started to pant and push at Macy to move. She was having a panic attack and needed to get out of there or she would vomit what little she had in her stomach right there.

The manager was standing next to the table and recognized the urgency. "Should I call anyone, miss?"

"I jus—just ne—need to go!"

"Should I call an ambulance? Let her out, please, ma'am!" the manager insisted.

Macy finally complied, moving to let Wren out of the booth, but not quickly enough. Wren shoved her hard, sending her tumbling out of the booth and onto the carpeted floor. Macy's goal of avoiding a scene was moot when the restaurant fell silent as all of the staff members and patrons stopped what they were doing to turn their attention to Wren and Macy.

Tears were streaming down Wren's face as she scrambled over Macy and ran as fast as she could to the bathroom. The hand she had over her mouth was Wren's last effort not to puke where she was. She barely made it and had no choice but to vomit in the sink. She felt humiliated, heartbroken and furious. It only took a couple of heaves to completely empty her stomach of the orange juice she'd had that morning.

She was breathing heavily and her whole body was shaking. She turned on the water and cleaned out the sink, lifting her head to stare at her reflection. She used a paper towel to wipe at her mouth. Wren felt weak and wanted to fall to her knees and scream, but she couldn't do that in the bathroom of the Ritz Carlton. She sniffed loudly, trying to calm her breathing.

The woman who had helped her at the table followed her. "Are you alright? Do you need anything?"

Wren looked at the woman through blurry eyes. "I'd like

some water, please."

"Of course. Is anything else I can do?"

Wren shook her head, putting her full weight on her arms. "Nothing except I left my purse in the booth. Can you please get it for me? My phone's inside and I need to call my ride."

Oh, my God. What if Macy stole her phone and started texting Caleb with it?

The manager came forward and placed a hand lightly on her shoulder. "Okay. Just one moment."

The woman left and returned about a minute later and handed it to Wren who immediately opened it to check to make sure the phone was there. She breathed a sigh of relief.

"Have they left?"

"The woman nodded. "They have. Will you be okay, now? I can walk you out."

Wren nodded and pulled out her phone and dialed Jared's number. All she wanted was distance from Colorado and everything in it. She knew she should speak to Caleb but it would hurt like hell, and it wouldn't change anything. If Macy was pregnant, she'd still be pregnant in a few weeks when Wren had had some time to process. The last thing she wanted or needed was to be an emotional basket case when she spoke to Caleb. If Macy was pregnant with his child, she didn't want her break down to keep him from doing the thing his integrity demanded.

Sitting in the back of the car as Jared drove her home, she cried softly behind her sunglasses. She found herself wishing she had someone to confide in, and pour out her heartbreak to, but then, the only person she'd ever felt safe doing that with was Caleb, and she'd already come to terms with the reason why she couldn't talk to him. On the other hand, there was no way she'd be able to be near him and hide how broken she was. He'd see right through her, and Jonesy would tell Caleb the minute her back was turned.

Wren's head pounded and her stomach lurched again.

She could only come up with one alternative that would work for her right in this moment; she had to leave, and she had to leave before he got back from his meetings.

Could anything be worse? Just when she'd found Cale again, and now... she could lose him.

chapter
SIXTEEN

"W REN!" CALEB BURST THROUGH the front door to the house and bound up the stairs two at time.

After his meetings at Lux, Caleb was anxious to get home and talk to Wren. Jonathan was going to step in and run the company as he had been for the last few weeks, which would give Caleb time to get his affairs in order in San Francisco.

Hours had passed and he'd texted Wren twice. She hadn't responded and Caleb was getting worried. She hadn't said what her plans were so he was curious as to why she hadn't been answering her phone.

"Wren!" He knocked loudly on her door. He wanted to spend every second with Wren before she had to go back to New York at the end of the week. "Wren! Open up. I have some things to tell you!"

He leaned on the door, the palm of his hand flat on the fine wood. "Wren, come on. Don't play with me." He smiled gently as he said it. "I miss you."

When there was still no answer, he stepped back and took hold of the doorknob and turned it. Caleb was surprised when the door opened. The room was in shadows as the sunset dipped beyond the trees outside the windows, and the lack of light was a sure sign she wasn't in her room. The bed was made and the room was neat.

"Hmmm," he murmured before heading out of her room and back into the hall. Maybe she and Jonesy were already going through his father's things and packing them up for charity.

The house was massive and he walked to the other end of the second level to glance into his father's suite. "Jonesy? Wren?" Again, the rooms were silent and empty of life. He walked past the room his mother had occupied at the end of her life without checking to see if either woman was inside. It had been untouched so long, he didn't even consider it a possibility.

The house was quiet and as he walked through the main level he tried to remember if Jared's limo was outside. Today was the last day he'd hired him. There were plenty of cars in the garage that he, Wren, and Jonesy could use when needed. Maybe he'd already left.

The smell of freshly baked bread permeated the house, and four fresh loaves sat cooling on a rack on the marble counter, but the kitchen was conspicuously quiet. He moved from room to room, looking for life. Jonesy was getting older and so he considered she could be napping. But then remembered he'd told Wren to give her the night off.

He pulled out his phone, but still she hadn't answered any of his messages.

What the fuck? He was starting to panic. Wren was a grown woman, and she was capable of taking care of herself. It was obvious from her years in New York, but while she was in Denver and especially after what had happened between them, he was positive she'd keep him in the loop of her plans.

Caleb dialed her number but it went straight to voicemail, so either her phone was off or the battery was dead. His hand lifted to take a swipe through his dark hair.

This is Wren Brashill. Leave your name and a short message and I'll get right back to you.

After the beep that followed, Caleb spoke as he paced around the kitchen.

"Hey, where are you?" He realized how futile it was to leave a message on a phone that wasn't on or dead. "I thought you'd be here getting ready to go out. Call me. I'm starting to worry."

Jonesy's room was behind the kitchen near the spare one that Macy had stayed in, and he walked quickly down the back hall to check and see if she was home. Her door was shut and he felt guilty waking her if she was sleeping, but damn it, he had to know what was going on.

He tapped lightly with the knuckle of his index finger. "Jonesy?"

"Come in, Caleb," she answered through the door.

Relief flooded through him as he opened the door and peered in. Jonesy was sitting on an upholstered chaise lounge in one corner opposite her bed, with a book in her hand. There was a lamp on beside her to light the pages.

"Hey, I'm sorry to bother you, but I can't find Wren. We had dinner plans."

"Come in Caleb." She moved her legs to the side and patted the lower part of the chaise. "Sit down."

Caleb's guard went up; preparing himself to hear something he didn't want to hear. His brow furrowed and he shook his head, refusing to sit down. "Okay, this isn't good."

"She said she got a call from New York that they were having early auditions for *Giselle*. She has a chance to perform with the New York Ballet if she is chosen."

He threaded the fingers of both hands together on the top of his head as he peered down at Jonesy. Already, his heart was starting to pound and he struggled to swallow. He wasn't buying it.

"No. She would have told me. I've been texting and calling her for the past three hours. What else happened?"

Jonesy's expression was sympathetic and she looked pained. "That's all she told me, but..."

"But what, Jonesy?" Caleb bellowed, making the old woman jump, and he regretted yelling at her. His gut instinct told him this was bad. He stepped forward and sat down beside her. "Look, I'm sorry, but I'm freaking out. What happened?"

"Veronica called her this morning."

Caleb stood up immediately. "Jesus Christ. That woman is such a cunt!"

Jonesy's eyes widened in shock. "Caleb!" she admonished.

"I'm sorry! But, she disgusts me!" He began to pace, but

threw a glance at her. "What else?"

"I don't know all of the details; just that she asked to meet her downtown at her hotel. Wren went, then came home two hours later, packed her bags, and had Jared take her to the airport. She said her flight was at 5:30 and that she'd call you to let you know her plans."

"Well, she hasn't." Caleb's head fell back and he closed his eyes, placing both hands on his hips.

"Maybe she's telling the truth about the audition. The timing could just be coincidental."

"I'd agree, if she would've let me know about it." He glanced at his watch. It was after five so there was no way in hell he'd be able to catch her flight.

"What do you think Veronica could have said?" Jonesy got up and walked to Caleb, putting a calming hand on his shoulder. His face was pinched and

"You mean what could she have made up? She's a liar, but I thought Wren was immune to her tricks after all this time." He pulled his phone out of the pocket of his jeans and clicked Wren's number; which he had on speed dial. Again, it went straight to voicemail. She was on the plane so Caleb hoped that was the explanation on why he couldn't get through.

"It's me again. You left without telling me? Why didn't you call me, Wren? Please call me when you land in New York."

He hung up the phone in defeat. "This is just what I need. I have to go back to San Francisco and quit my job."

Jonesy patted his shoulder again. "You go do that. Take a little time. Both you and Wren have some big changes ahead, but you do what you need to do, and she'll get this audition out of the way. That ballet is one she's aspired to be part of, Caleb."

"As I said, I'd get it if she'd told me. There is more to it. What hotel is that bitch in?"

"Wren didn't say, but I'm fairly sure she's already left the city."

He nodded in disgust then turned and left the room.

Jonesy called after him. "Do you need me to fix you something to eat?"

"I'm not hungry, but thanks."

Caleb walked through the kitchen and down the back stairs. He was frustrated and pissed off. His first instinct was to beat the shit out of something but the prospect of hitting the bag wasn't as attractive as an actual fight. He had dialed Dex's phone number before he'd reached the bottom of the stairs.

"What's up?" Dex answered. "Miss me already?" He laughed into the phone.

Caleb huffed. "Listen, is there a fight we can get into tonight?"

"Is something up? I hear that old tone in your voice."

"Wren split without talking to me. Supposedly she has an audition, but the viper is involved."

"Oh, shit."

"Yeah. Wren's on a plane and I won't be able to talk to her for at least three hours and I can't just sit here."

"I'll check around, but it's Monday night, there won't be much. If I can't, we can get a burger and beer; maybe play some pool."

Caleb sighed. He'd missed having his best friend to hang out with. "Sounds good."

By now, Caleb was inside his bedroom and moved to flip the light on in the adjoining bathroom. He ended the call and set his phone down on the top of his dresser, intent on getting into a hot shower. Even if Dex did find a fight, the hot water might relax him in the meantime. He'd changed before lunch with his friend and he was dressed in black pants and a cream colored button down. He kicked off his shoes and quickly unbuttoned his shirt when out of the corner of his eye, he saw a white envelope setting on top of one of his pillows; the white paper contrasting sharply with the navy blue cotton pillow case.

Caleb started to unbuckle his belt and undo his pants, his shirt hanging completely open. He stopped dead as his heart dropped to his stomach. Whatever was inside had to be from Wren, and if so, it wasn't a good sign. He leaned over and picked it up, hesitant to open it.

"Fucking hell," he said, sinking down to sit on the edge of his bed. He ran a hand slowly through his hair and leaned back against his pillows leaving one foot on the floor. He stared at the one word written on the outside in Wren's perfect handwriting.

Cale

He might as well rip off the Bandaid. Waiting was a pussy thing to do, and he was no pussy. His lean fingers ripped off the end of the envelope and he pulled out the note. Something else heavier was inside and dropped onto his chest. It was cold and glancing down, he instantly recognized it.

His mother's locket.

He gave a slow, disbelieving shake of his head. She didn't just give something that meant so much back. Not after what had happened between them. He'd finally admitted he was in love with her; he'd bared his soul, and now this?

Caleb's vision blurred in the dimly lit room and his eyes started to burn. He wasn't even sure he cared what was in the fucking letter after that. It was the ultimate betrayal. What the hell did she think? That he'd make love to her, spill his guts and then she'd leave him? Was this payback for how he left after their first night together?

Pain shot through him, and his chest refused to expand. He felt like there were steel bands around his chest preventing him from breathing, his heart was racing uncomfortably.

He couldn't believe Wren would be so malicious. Veronica, yes; even Macy, but not Wren. He unfolded her note and squinted to read it under the low light, praying he'd find some sort of reasonable explanation.

Dear Cale,

I'm sorry I left without talking to you, but I knew I wouldn't be able to leave if I saw you. So much has happened in the past few days and I need to make sure that if we end up together, it's for the right reasons.

I love you for always taking care of me, but I don't want the money. My life would be nothing if it weren't for you, but this is about you and me. Not the money.

I'm not my mother. I know you'll say that you already know that, but I just need to prove it.

It's ironic that you gave me half of the estate to make sure I would be part of your life, and I'm giving it back for the very same reason. I need to make sure you know that I would choose you if you didn't have a penny to your name; if you had nothing to give me but your heart.

You can run Lux and I'll do another tour just like we planned. Then, if we don't end up together, I'll talk to Jonathan and figure out a way to give back the assets. It's your birthright, not mine. It's hard to hate my mother, when she is the reason I have you. I'd go through the bad stuff all over again, if I knew you'd be at the end of it.

I know everything inside of you is screaming at me right now, but please do this for me. Let's just take a break for a few months to make sure of each other. If you give me that locket again, I swear, I'll never take it off.

No matter what, you'll always be my Superman.

Love forever,

Wren

Caleb swallowed hard at the pain welling up that caused his throat to ache. His chest heaved with emotion as he bent his arm to rest over his eyes; his hand still holding on to the letter. His heart was breaking, but how could he be mad at her for this? If anything, he loved her even more.

"God, Wren," he said as if she could hear him. "You are so fucking perfect." The pain in his voice was tangible and two tears welled in his blue eyes, spilling out from his closed lids and running down the side of his face.

He bolted upright and grabbed his phone off of his dresser, instantly dialing her number. He knew she'd still be in the air and wouldn't answer. Maybe she wouldn't answer anyway, but he had something to say.

Caleb wished the sweet voice on the other end wasn't just a message.

"It's me, Bird. I got your letter and I'll do what you ask, but I don't like it. I love you, and nothing will change in whatever time you think needs to pass. I'll keep my distance, but talk to me. Please call me. I just got you back. I already miss you."

He struggled for a moment, the recording continuing through his silence. He didn't want to break the connection if this was this last connection he'd have with her. "I love you, Wren. Call me back."

After he ended the call, he called Dex.

"You didn't give me much time to look, man. I haven't even started."

"No, that's why I'm calling. I want to get a tattoo, then let's get burgers and beer."

"Okay. I'll call Scanlan's and see if he is open around 7:30. He's usually booked, but maybe since it's Monday he'll have an opening."

"I wondered if he was still in the city." It was the same establishment where he and Dex had gotten matching tribal tattoos done around their left biceps when they were kids. Darren had consented, but Caleb had forged a consent letter and then flaunted it in front of his father. Edison had been furious. "Just a simple one. Script."

"Cool. If I don't call back, it's a go; just meet me there."

"Right. Thanks, Dex."

"It's good to have you back."

"I was just thinking the same thing."

chapter
SEVENTEEN

IT HAD BEEN FIVE DAYS AND WREN still hadn't returned his calls. Caleb still called her everyday, hoping she'd eventually answer. Her letter said she loved him, and he understood her need for clarity and distance, at least for the time being. However, he didn't understand why she wouldn't talk to him. It was making him nuts but he was trying to occupy himself with packing.

He'd been back in San Francisco since Thursday morning, and he'd already started packing up his apartment. His kitchen was finished except for the drawers. One of them was full of his father's numerous unopened letters. His plan was to just throw them all in a box and go through them once he moved back to Denver.

The managing partner of his firm was not happy about his resignation, but he understood Caleb's new commitments.

Caleb had full AutoCAD software loaded onto his laptop, so he was able to soften the blow by committing to completing all of his current projects; even if it meant doing so from Colorado. He also agreed to take an occasional freelance job as needed. The two things together, meant he could leave as soon as his apartment was sublet. He had the money to buy out his lease, but it went against his convictions to throw thousands of dollars in cash to the wind.

Macy had been relentless in her calls and texts, before Caleb left Denver and once she knew he was in back town and it had gotten ten times worse.

Caleb had listed all of his furniture online and he had already sold his living room set, so the front room of his apartment was empty except for the stack of boxes starting to accumulate along one wall. Most of the boxes were marked for Goodwill or the food pantry.

Caleb grabbed a beer out of the now almost barren refrigerator. He'd been able to run, but no boxing workouts and he didn't feel like himself. Even though missing a few workouts wouldn't have an adverse effect on his body, he felt lethargic and he didn't like it. His stomach grumbled. He didn't have a lot of food left. He had a takeout menu from Chopstix hanging on his refrigerator by a magnet with an old 49ers schedule printed on it. He grimaced, looking through it. What could he order that wasn't completely bad for him? He needed protein, but he hated all the gloppy sauce that typically coated Chinese takeout.

He took a long pull on his beer trying to decide, when there was a short knock on his door. Taking his Dos Equis with him, he went to open it and was unprepared for who stood there. Macy stood in front of him dressed in black jeans, a bright orange tank top, and high-heeled sandals.

She came forward and wrapped her arms around him in a tight hug, and pressed her lips to his, though he was unresponsive. "I've missed you," she said against his mouth.

Caleb quickly pulled back, and moved away from her a displeased scowl on his handsome face. Macy's gaze took in Caleb's faded jeans, and old grey T-shirt with an open light blue plaid button down layered over top of it.

"What are you doing here?" he asked abruptly, continuing to stand in the doorway without asking her in.

"I thought you'd be glad to see me." Macy walked passed him without waiting for an invitation.

Caleb shook his head at her presumptive behavior. *By all means, barge in,* he thought. "It's only been a few days since you left Denver; nothing's changed since then. As you can see," he indicated around the apartment. "I'm getting ready to move."

"Yes." Macy had been at his apartment a few times and knew her way around. She went into the kitchen and opened the refrigerator, leaving Caleb no choice but to follow her. "Hmmm, nothing in there for me. You're out of bottled water."

"Thanks for the live action grocery list." He didn't feel like fighting with her, but neither did he stop what he was doing to focus on her. He grabbed one of the empty boxes sitting on the floor and opened the one of the four drawers he needed to empty, hoping his lack of attention would make her leave.

"Look, I was hoping we could make up, and play nice."

Caleb picked up the tray full of silverware and loaded the whole thing into the bottom of the box, and opened the next drawer. "Why are you here, Macy? I'm leaving. I've made it clear this isn't going any further. I'm not trying to hurt you, or be a dick, but as I said, nothing's changed," he said flatly.

"I'm pregnant. That's what's changed, asshole."

Caleb stood up holding a stack of dishtowels he'd just removed from the open drawer. He dumped them unceremoniously into the box on top of the silverware without caring how they landed. His blue eyes met her brown ones unflinchingly as he straightened. She was tall, but he still towered over her, and his face registered his revulsion. "Bullshit."

She pulled the used pregnancy test out of her purse and held it out for him. "Really?"

"It won't work, Macy." Caleb pulled out the next drawer, barely looking at the object in her hand. He had a brief moment's dread, but he couldn't allow her see to it. "You know I'll insist on a doctor's appointment, where I'm present, and there is a blood drawn pregnancy test. Now, *if* it's positive, which, I don't think it will be, I will insist on a DNA test as soon as it's medically possible."

"It is true, Caleb," Macy's tone turned pleading.

"Stop. Why are you doing this? I don't believe you, but even in the remote chance of it being true, it won't change a damn thing between us."

"Your child doesn't change anything?" she asked incredulously. "Are you crazy?"

Caleb refused to believe this was even a possibility. It

would ruin everything he hoped to have with Wren, and he wouldn't allow that. He leaned up against the counter across the kitchen from her and took another swallow of his beer. His casual and uncaring demeanor was not what she expected and he could see the anger building up and ready to blow inside her.

"You'll do the right thing by me, Caleb Luxon, or I swear, I'll—"

He wanted to come off as an uncaring asshole. If she was bluffing, this was the way to force it from her.

"You'll what? You can't blackmail me by holding my integrity against me. I have plans for my life, and if this turns out to be true I'll deal with it, but you and I are still done. Either way, we will not have a relationship, Macy." He shrugged and lifted the beer to his lips. He kept his eyes trained on her as he drank. He could almost see her squirm, her mind searching to find the right thing to say to convince him, which gave away her lie. Her mouth pursed and her eyes narrowed. Her rage was almost palpable. "What, no crying act?"

His words and how he was acting went completely against who he was, but he had years of watching a vindictive, manipulative woman in action, and his skill was honed to the point of artistry. When he compared and contrasted Macy and Wren, the truth was crystal clear.

"When did you turn into such a prick, Caleb?" she spat.

"When you tried to fuck with my life, I guess," he said flatly, completely devoid of emotion. "My future is with Wren."

"Don't be too sure of that!"

Caleb was about to open a third drawer when he stopped

and turned back to her. She was still seething, but her chin rose and jutted out.

"What did you do?"

Macy laughed bitterly, the sound filling the small space. Maybe it was because Caleb's own temper flared that made it seem so obnoxious.

"I said, what. Did. You. Do?" he yelled again, even more loudly. Macy didn't expect it from him and she physically jumped. "Tell me!" he railed, getting in her face as she cowered in front of him.

"I showed her the test and she believes me, even if you don't! I wish you could have seen her fall apart," she touted, smugly regaining some of her superiority.

"You are one ruthless bitch!" Caleb was beside himself. He felt that if he didn't punch something, his whole body would literally blow apart. He lunged toward Macy, but then turned away abruptly, fisting both of his hands in his hair. "Goddamn you!"

When he turned back to her fifteen seconds later, he was in control, but his mind was racing to figure a way out of the situation.

No wonder Wren had fled Colorado without talking to him. It didn't take a genius to figure out what happened; Veronica set up a meeting with Wren, then Macy ambushed her with a fake pregnancy test. He hoped it was fake or his whole world was about to come crashing down. His heart ached for Wren thinking how she must have felt when Macy launched on her. Especially, after the night they'd just spent together.

Caleb took a deep breath and smoothed back his hair

with both hands. "Let's go." He motioned toward the door. His keys and wallet were resting on the counter and he went in to retrieve them before heading toward the door of the apartment. He opened it and waited for Macy to precede him through the doorway. "Come on!" he blasted, when she didn't move.

Macy hesitantly walked through the doorway, glancing over her shoulder at him. "Where are we going?"

"Pacific Med ER. If you're telling the truth, you have nothing to lose."

The door closed behind him and Caleb pressed the button for the elevator that would take them to the underground parking garage and his Infiniti QX30.

Macy reluctantly followed. "Caleb..." she began.

He shook his head and hatred overtook him as he looked at her. He would not let her ruin his life and hurt Wren unspeakably with a lie. "Uh uh. I want to know, so whether you're pregnant or not, we're going to get a real test."

"I'll schedule an appointment with my OBGYN next week."

"No. We're doing this, right now."

"You can't force me to take a test, Caleb, and it won't prove paternity."

The elevator opened and they walked the twenty-five steps to where the dark silver car was waiting.

"You're right, but if you aren't pregnant, you won't be able to put me, or Wren, through months of agony.

"I won't take a test."

"Get in the goddamn car, Macy," Caleb commanded, pushing the button on his fob that unlocked the doors. "Now."

They locked eyes over the roof of the car but she made no move to open the passenger door and get in. Caleb's door was open and waiting.

"Why don't you believe me? We had sex, and we didn't use condoms the last few times."

"Yeah, because you said you were on the pill! I trusted you and you're fucking me over, so guess what? Now I don't trust you! Get in the fucking car!"

Slowly, she opened her door and slid inside. Caleb had the car started and in reverse before her door even clicked closed. "The truth is, I know in my gut there is no baby, Macy. You're far too narcissistic to be saddled with a kid. This is just a ploy to manipulate me, after I ended things."

Macy's stoic silence as she sat in the passenger seat was telling.

He pulled the car smoothly out of the garage and the apartment complex to merge onto Highway 101. "The worst part is that Wren is innocent. Nothing is her fault; she has done nothing to deserve this kind of vindictive bullshit game you're playing. I'll never forgive you for putting her through this."

"It's not what you think, Caleb. Just listen." Macy pleaded, turning toward him in her seat.

"Nothing you can say will change how I feel. I love Wren." Caleb glanced at Macy as he drove, and she was turned away to look out the window. He was angry enough to hope the words sliced her to the bone. "Do you get that? *I love Wren.* Right or wrong, kid or no kid; after this, I'm done with you, and you will stay. The fuck away from her."

Finally, his harsh words and stone cold demeanor got to Macy. She started to cry uncontrollably. Still, Caleb was unmoved.

"This is over."

chapter
EIGHTEEN

WREN WAS PHYSICALLY EXHAUSTED and emotionally drained. She'd just finished a grueling eight-hour rehearsal in New York City and had taken the train from midtown Manhattan to Jersey City where she had a small, studio that she shared with another dancer named Molly, whom she barely knew. New Jersey rent was much less expensive than that in Manhattan, and the apartment had been more like a storage unit to keep her things in while she was touring. Now that she'd landed a role in a New York City production, something had to change.

The commute on the train was over an hour, and she didn't have a car because parking in New York cost almost as much as her rent.

The strap of the bag she carried on her shoulder, dug into her flesh and her legs and feet ached with every step she took between the station and the brownstone that housed her apartment. The art of ballet was to make it look effortless and elegant; so graceful you almost appeared to be floating, but in reality, it was difficult and hard on her joints.

She'd wanted this role since before she'd graduated from Juilliard. Every ballerina wanted to play Giselle. The audition process had lasted two days and she only found out she was chosen earlier that morning, but her joy was overshadowed by thoughts of Macy and Caleb. She didn't mind the long days, but she despised the train rides, walks and long hours trying to sleep where her excruciating thoughts hammered through her heart and mind.

Each step she had to fight breaking out into tears, thinking that less than a week ago, she'd spent two amazing nights in Caleb's arms and she believed they had a future together. Finally. Her eyes were focused on the sidewalk in front of her, though she wasn't really aware of it because Caleb consumed her mind. She had listened to his messages over and over absorbing every nuance of love in his tone.

After the day she'd flown to New York and he'd read the note she left on his bed, he hadn't called again. Part of her was hoping he would, but she realized he had to be back in San Francisco and Macy would have surely told him about her supposed pregnancy.

Pain exploded inside her and ricocheted through her chest, causing a tightening of her lungs and heart whenever she thought about it. She guessed Caleb was reeling and trying to figure things out, or felt abandoned by her request of time. She tried hard to come up with an excuse that would explain why he'd stopped calling. It didn't really matter why, though; the result was the same. She missed him so much it hurt. She felt it in in every breath she took.

She couldn't help it when slow tears began to drip from her eyes, but she was thankful she was nearly home and she hadn't lost control on the train. Her face crumpled, and she used the back of her hand to wipe at her tears, holding back a sob. She swallowed hard at the lump in her throat. Everything hurt.

There was nothing she could do but wait the months needed to see if Macy was lying, and it would only be worse if she and Cale kept in touch; pretending and hoping it wasn't true, then being blindsided. The possibility was already crippling, and that would be so much worse. Wren hoped she'd be strong enough to handle it if it happened.

She rounded the last corner onto her street, and walked the last block and a half. She just wanted to get behind closed doors so she could let the pain pour out unabashed.

Even though it was getting dark, Caleb saw Wren coming as he waited on the front steps of the building where she lived. She was wearing frayed cutoff jean shorts, a faded burgundy T-shirt and sneakers. Her head was down as she walked carrying a sort of large duffle bag over her shoulder. Her face was flushed and her hair was in a tight ballerina bun at the back of her head. She looked exhausted and sad, but that didn't stop his eyes from devouring her.

When she was only a few feet away her head lifted and she saw him; their eyes locked and Wren's gate faltered.

"Cale." His name fell from her soft pink mouth. "What are

you doing here? I told you I needed time."

He stood up and stepped onto the sidewalk in front of her, just as she reached her building. His heart broke at the dark circles under her eyes and the tear tracks that were still fresh on her cheeks.

"Yeah, you did. You also said you'd never leave me."

Wren had the grace to pause. She had said that, but it was in the heat of passion and before she'd been clobbered by Macy's surprise.

"That's not fair." She shook her head incredulously as took a few steps back. "I'm not ready. Please, Cale."

"Oh, Wren," he said, pulling her roughly into his arms and tight against his chest. One hand cupped the back of her head, and he pressed his lips to her temple. She was so slight in his arms as her bag fell to the pavement and her arms slid around his waist, her fingers clawing at his shirt and flesh. She started to shake and he knew she was crying desperately. "You know why I'm here." Caleb's own eyes filled with tears. "I'm so sorry."

They stood there, uncaring of people walking or anyone spying from windows, as they remained locked together in a fierce embrace. Wren wasn't sure if he'd come to break the news about Macy in person, but even then, she was happy to see him. It felt good to have his arms around her, even if it couldn't be forever.

He kissed her on the temple again and his embrace tightened around her waist so he could lift her completely off the ground and into a full on hug. Wren's arms slid up and around his broad shoulders and she buried her face in the curve of his neck.

"It's going to be okay, Bird," he said softly, his lips moving against her skin. Something went right in Caleb's world, surrounded by her scent and holding her close. "Do you hear me?" Emotion made Caleb's voice crack on the last word.

Wren didn't want to let go of him, but she nodded, reluctant for the embrace to end. The past few days without him had felt like years. He smelled amazing and familiar.

Nothing in the world made her feel safer or as good as having Caleb's arms around her. She couldn't stop crying, uncertain if she was happy to see him, or if everything she'd been bottling up was just gushing out of her. "It hurts so much."

"I know. But I'm here, now." He finally set her down and bent to pick up her bag, but then slid his larger hand into hers, threading their fingers together. His thumb slid over the top of her hand again and again, as if he couldn't get enough of touching her. "Can we talk inside?" His deep blue eyes were sparkling with reflected light from the street lamps, his nose, forehead and prominent jaw casting shadows on one side of his face as he glanced around. "I don't like you walking the streets alone at night." It was a residential neighborhood, but it was still in the middle of the city. There were trees and cars parked on the side of the street where she lived, and his mind was analyzing all of the places someone could hide.

"Everybody walks in New York," Wren murmured as she slid the key into the lock with one hand and turned the doorknob with the other, pushing open the door to go inside.

"That doesn't make it smart."

"My roommate might be home."

"If she is, we'll go somewhere else, but this can't wait."

"Okay. Come up." Wren started up the short flight of concrete steps to the door of the large house that had been converted into six apartments, inwardly cringing; ashamed of her humble apartment. She had the key on a ribbon string that was looped around her neck. It was long enough that it allowed her to open the door without taking it off.

"That's smart not to carry the keys in your bag, but I still don't like you walking alone at night."

Caleb followed close on her heels making sure the door was secure behind them, and then followed her up the stairs to the second level. His eyes registered everything about the building, including the shadowed stairwell and the location of the mailboxes.

"Rehearsals go late sometimes, and I can't help it. I have mace." She bit her lip to hide a small smile. Caleb's protectiveness had always been a source of joy and made her love for him surge every time. That hadn't changed in all the years she'd known him. It still made her feel all warm and fuzzy inside.

"We have to get you a place in the city."

"The rent is outrageous in Manhattan. I'm hardly ever in New York, anyway. Traveling company, remember?"

Wren repeated the process with her key when they got to her apartment door. The studio was small and neat; old and sparsely furnished with an eclectic hodgepodge of things. One small lamp that had been left on illuminated the room with a soft glow.

"Molly?" Wren called inside as they walked through the door; then removed the ribbon key chain from her neck and dropped it on a small antique table in the entryway. "It doesn't look like she's here. I barely know her, honestly. Sorry about—" She paused and waved around the room. "All this."

"I came to see you, not your apartment."

Caleb sensed she was ashamed of her income situation, even though the inheritance would change that as soon as escrow cleared. This was a far cry from the mansion in Denver, or even his unkempt bachelor pad in San Francisco. It was literally just one room with a small kitchenette in one corner, two twin beds along one wall with a window in between them with mismatched bedding, a table with four chairs that looked like they were leftover from the early seventies, and a door that led to the barely there bathroom. There was one other door and Caleb could only assume it was a closet.

She shrugged and went to the small refrigerator and pulled out two bottles of water, and walked the few steps needed to hand one to Caleb.

"It's nothing to be ashamed of, Wren. Dancing is what you love."

"Macy didn't believe me when I said dancers don't have much money."

He had reluctantly let go of Wren's hand on the walk upstairs but he was anxious to kiss her, and had the urge to pull her into his arms and go for it, but he knew they had to talk first. He took her hand and tugged her gently with him to the sofa, and they both sat down. Caleb took a quick swallow of his water and then put the bottle on the coffee table.

"Speaking of Macy," Caleb began, taking her water and setting it next to his. "We need to talk."

Wren's eyes were wide and wary as she waited for him to continue. She was nervous; scared of what he was about to tell her. She sucked in a deep breath and braced herself for what was coming, when he took both of her hands in both of his as they sat facing each other on the sofa.

His deep blue eyes met hers unflinchingly. She had to see that every word he said was the absolute truth. "I know what she told you, but it was all a pack of lies. She and I are not having a baby together, Wren." His tone was filled with conviction, but Wren knew that it was too early for a paternity test.

Wren's eyes filled with tears and her lower lip trembled. "How can you be sure? It will be months before we can be sure it's not yours."

It suddenly dawned on Caleb that was the reason she asked that they take a few months apart. He could see the deep sorrow lingering in her eyes before she lowered them to look their entwined hands.

It had to be excruciatingly painful for her after the time they'd spent together. He'd lost his shit when Dex was only dancing with her, and again when he thought she was about to marry Sam. A child was the most permanent bond two people could have and he could only imagine how badly Wren must be suffering. If the situation were reversed he probably wouldn't be able to function.

"Wren." Caleb released her hands and then scooted closer so he could cup both sides of her face, using his thumbs to tilt her chin towards his. He rested his forehead on hers. "Do you think I'd let this go on for months without making sure? I couldn't do that to you. I'm sure, because I took her to the hospital and got a blood test twenty minutes after she tried to pull that shit with me. Not only is it not mine, there isn't a baby at all." His thumbs stroked her jaw and her fingers wrapped around both of his strong forearms. "But even if there were, it wouldn't change that you are the one I want to spend my life with," he said quietly.

"I was certain you'd marry her if it were true."

He shook his head; his eyes still intent on her beautiful face. The severe hairstyle made her fine cheekbones even more prominent. "No. I would have been a father, but that wouldn't make me let you go. Jesus Christ. All I've been able to think about was how you might believe her. I wanted to call, but didn't think you'd talk to me. I figured my only option was to give you space."

"It hurts that there was even a chance it could've been true. I hate thinking about you with her, like that."

He felt her pain as if it sliced right through him like a knife. He'd give anything if he could take it away. "I know, Bird. I can't change the past, but Macy has no doubt where things stand. She concocted this whole thing because she was desperate, because she was on her way out. She didn't care about me; it was all about the money. Wren, please."

Wren shook her head as a hurt expression settled on her face. "No, it is about you, Cale. How could she not love you?" Her voice was shaky, pain still present behind the words. "How could any woman not love you?"

His heart did a flip flop inside his chest. Every second that passed, she did or said something that only made her more precious.

"It doesn't matter how she felt, Wren. I know that sounds callous, but I never lied to her, and I never mislead her. I'm in love with *you*. You have to know that, because Macy did in the first seconds after you walked into my father's den the night we got to Denver. That's why she turned into a vindictive bitch."

"I can't seem to stop crying," she said as a small sob escaped. "Even now that you're here and saying all the right things."

Caleb chuckled softly, tilted her chin up further so he could kiss her mouth with gentle tenderness. His lips brushed and played with hers, his lower lip nudging her top one. "I know it's overwhelming. I'm sorry. I should have seen some sort of scheme coming. I should have protected you, but this; you and me, is what's real."

Caleb leaned back into a prone position, and pulled Wren across his body and she was lying on top of him, their legs tangling together. He nestled her into a full embrace, until her head rested on his chest. He lifted one of her hands to kiss the inside of her wrist, and then continued to hold it in his.

Wren enjoyed hearing his heart beating beneath her ear and the warmth of his body seeping into hers. "I hated leaving without seeing you."

"I wish you wouldn't have. I went bat-shit crazy when I couldn't find you. Jonesy told me that Veronica called you, and that you went to see her."

"Good old Jonesy. I knew she would. I hoped, anyway."

"What happened?"

"Mother and Macy ambushed me at the Ritz downtown. It was brutal. I think I had a panic attack. It was humiliating."

"I swear to God, I'm going to kill them both." Caleb closed his eyes, agonizing over what it must have been like. "You should have called me, Bird. Why would you fall for that? Veronica is like the anti-Christ. Anything she comes in contact with goes straight to hell."

"I went in knowing she wanted something, but I thought if I didn't go, she'd keep bugging me and months from now, I'd still be dealing with her. I didn't think it would turn out like that. I just wanted her to get out of my life."

"You're an adult. You don't have to see her. We'll change the phone numbers and have Jonathan get a restraining order if we need one."

"Macy is horrible."

"Yes, but she did well at hiding it until she met you."

"I bring out the best in people," Wren said with a sarcastic smirk, then closed her eyes. Crying made her sleepy, but she was conscious that Macy might walk through the door any minute.

Caleb was amused. "You do. Jonesy said you were auditioning for Giselle. How'd that go?"

"I was cast in the lead."

A slow smile spread over Caleb's face, pride filling him up. "I'm not surprised."

"There are two months of rehearsals and then it goes into production for the season."

"Will they take it out with a touring group next year?"

"Yes, but I don't have to do it, Cale. I'm not sure what I want to do, but I already miss you."

"We'll see each other. I can commute on the weekends sometimes."

Wren's head lifted and she met his eyes, a hopeful smile curving her lips. "Really?"

"We'll do whatever we need to do to make this work. I've missed your face. You're so beautiful, Wren." Caleb's index finger ran down her velvety cheek and he bent his head to kiss her.

Wren's mouth opened under his and his tongue slid inside. The kiss deepened when Wren's hands wound in his hair to cup the back of his head and instinctively, Caleb shifted her beneath him. Her legs parted to welcome him into the cradle of her body and he pressed his rapidly hardening erection into her soft heat. It wasn't long until they were making out like a couple of high school kids, kissing wildly and dry humping through their clothes.

Caleb pulled his mouth and collapsed on top of her with a groan. "Uhhhhh," he breathed. "I can't take this, Wren. Unless you want to give Molls an all-night show, we have to get out of here."

"Molls?" Wren's eyebrow lifted wryly, as Caleb climbed off of her to stand up, then turned his back and adjusted himself. Jeans and a hard dick did not work well together.

"Yup." His expression was coy when he turned back around. She was grinning so obviously she was aware of his uncomfortable predicament. "Come on. Get whatever you need for tomorrow and let's go into the city."

"I'm so tired, Cale. I don't want to run around Manhattan." Wren went limp, still lying where he left her, but her eyes dropped suggestively to the bulge still visible in his pants. She smiled suggestively. Wren was really tired, but she was enjoying the casual play with Caleb.

"Who said anything about running? We'll take a cab." He grinned, then bent and lifted her like she was a child before setting her on her feet.

"Hurry up. I'm about to take advantage of you, and we need a bigger bed, privacy, and room service."

"Pretty sure of me, I guess?" Wren went to the dresser that stood across the room and took a clean black leotard a pair of tights, and a short wrap skirt out of the top drawer. She went into the closet to get a light pink blouse and a pair of black jeans, and after swapping out her dirty clothes, she packed up the duffle bag Caleb had dropped just inside the door.

"Taking advantage of you is optional since you're wiped out, sweetheart. I'll run you a bath and order a nice dinner. We can just relax, and I'll rub your feet or something."

Wren giggled softly. "Or something," she repeated.

It wasn't ten minutes later, and Wren was falling asleep against Caleb in the back of a cab on their way into Manhattan. New York was a big difference from Downtown Denver or even San Francisco. Skyscrapers towered into the sky for miles and the city was bustling with people walking the streets in masses. The giant billboards, endless lights, honking horns and seas of yellow cabs and black sedans cutting each other off were unnerving to Caleb. Wren, however, was fast asleep with her head on his shoulder and clinging to his arm, oblivious to her surroundings. He had one arm draped over her legs; his hand wrapped possessively around her opposite thigh.

He couldn't believe how possessive he felt about her; how proud he was of all she'd accomplished, or how much contentment he had just knowing he had her heart. In a man and woman way, not because of how he'd always taken care of her.

Twenty-four hours earlier, his life could have come crashing down in an irreparable mess. He couldn't bear to think about it. Glancing down at Wren's sleeping from, cuddled so close against him, all of the bad thoughts fled his mind. They each had a horrible, dark past that brought them together, but the future looked incredibly bright.

chapter
NINETEEN

CALEB HAD CHECKED INTO THE Hilton Suites in Midtown Manhattan before he'd gone to find Wren's apartment. He dropped his bag off in the luxurious room. The suite was top of the line and he'd requested one with a big Jacuzzi bathtub. He'd been confident enough to hope Wren would spend the night with him, and if so, it would help soak away any aching muscles.

The second the door to their suite closed, Caleb dropped Wren's bag and took her in his arms. He'd been aching to go wild on her from the moment he saw her walking toward him on the sidewalk.

On the way to the hotel, he'd told himself that he wouldn't attempt to make love to her because she was physically spent. But once they were alone together, there was no holding back for either of them.

He quickly turned her around so her back was against the door. Instantly, he was pressing her into it with his own body. Desire drove them both, as they frantically grappled with each other's clothing during an assault of passionate kissing.

Caleb pulled at the hem of Wren's shirt, and she raised her arms so he could remove it more easily. "You don't need this," he breathed against her mouth, tossing it to the floor without taking his eyes off her. He was lifting her higher against the door at the same time his tongue slipped into her mouth.

Wren moaned softly as she felt the evidence of his desire pushing and pressing into her as he thrust slowly against her. Her fingers worked madly to free the buttons of his white dress shirt so they could hungrily explore his chest. It was delicious and frantic, yet it turned into slow, sweet torture.

Caleb pushed her arms up and threaded the fingers of both of his hands with hers, feeling the lace of her bra brush his bare chest. Her toned body was so small that the pressure of his hips between her thighs was enough to lift her and hold her firmly against the door. He could still feel the softness of her small breasts and the hardness of her nipples pressing against him and it was sexier than hell. The matching surge of her pelvis drove him insane with want. He'd been with more voluptuous women, but this was Wren, and no one was sexier to him. She excited him more than anyone ever had.

"I'm sorry, Bird," he panted against her mouth as blood surged in his veins, making his cock scream for release, and his heart tighten at the same time. "I know you're tired—" His words were more like a tortured groan. "—I had good intentions."

"Shhh... Just kiss me, Cale," She whispered in answer. "I want this."

Caleb freed her hands and Wren pushed his shirt off of his shoulders, exposing the hard ripples and planes of his body underneath. He reveled in the feel of her fingertips exploring his flesh. His elbows against the wall behind her prevented her from pulling the shirt free from his body, but her nails raked lightly over his shoulders and chest.

Wren felt ravenous and her greedy tongue ran along his lower lip.

Caleb's fingers curled against the wall. He responded by sucking her upper lip into his mouth, and flicking it with the tip of his tongue. When she sighed in pleasure, he kissed her deeply, invading her mouth and laving her tongue with his.

My God, it was amazing. He was so turned on and he craved release from the blissful agony that continued to build. Caleb repeated slow, hard thrusts as his hips pressed against her over and over; the thin fabric of her leggings did little to hide the radiating heat between her thighs.

Wren's body was already aching, but she was instantly on fire with her need for him. Her hips matched his with an answering rhythm that drove him crazy.

"Uhhhh, Wren. Jesus." Caleb's hand cupped her cheek and her hands wound tightly in his hair, both of them pulling each other deeper into another kiss. He couldn't help the way his hips rocked into hers and Wren responded with an answering ache.

He kissed her over and over, each one deeper than the last until finally he pulled back, his hot breath bathing her skin in heated pants. "Fuck, I want you," he ground out. "I love you, Wren."

Wren's eyes were closed; her breathing also labored. Though the passion sweeping over her was the most intense of her life, it was her love for Caleb that was her ruling force.

Caleb slowed down as his hands slid deftly down both sides of her body, his thumbs grazing the side slope of her breasts through her bra, and then pressing into her nipples. He tortured her with slow circles around the tender peaks.

Wren's head fell back in molten agony. "Caleb. Oh, God," she begged. "Please."

Her thighs flexed to hug his hips, and his hand continued down over her bottom to the back of her legs. He pulled her away from the wall and carried her toward the bed.

The room was luxurious, with the big king-sized bed near the picturesque window. The bright lights of the city shone in and it was enough for Caleb to see where he was going.

Caleb ran his mouth hotly down her neck and she arched it to give him more access until he could lie her down on the bed, he whipped his unbuttoned shirt off and let it fall to the floor.

Wren shivered at the loss of his body heat. It was June, but the air conditioning made the room overly cool. There was a gas fireplace in one corner and Caleb walked over to flip it on before unbuttoning his jeans and sliding the zipper down. His cock was swollen to the point of pain, but he was more concerned for Wren's comfort than his own release.

She was lying in the center of the big bed waiting for him and she looked so small. Her eyes intensely following every move he made and taking in every rippling muscle. She lost her breath at how strong he was; every move confident and lithe. And his face: God, he was beautiful. Wren sucked in her breath, willing herself to not lose control of her emotions. The last few days had been merciless and she was feeling fragile.

Caleb kicked off his shoes and then, with one knee on the bed, reached forward to pull first one, then the other of Wren's off, too. They landed on the carpeted floor with two soft thuds. Caleb's eyes met hers as he reached forward to the waist of her leggings and started to peel them down her legs, exposing firm thighs. Her dancer's body was athletic and toned. Caleb let his eyes slowly roam over every line of the soft swells of her hips and breasts, her flat stomach and defined abs. She shivered, this time not from the cold, but from the light brush of his fingertips against her skin as the dark knit fabric slid from her body. The intense look in his eyes as he stared down at her almost made her breath stop.

The barely there black lace panties and matching bra caused Caleb's mouth to go dry. "Christ," he said softly. "You're perfect." His fingers itched to touch her more intimately. The raw tone in his voice sent electricity through her as if he'd just licked every inch of her skin.

Wren began to pull the pins from her long hair, unwinding the coil that made up the tight chignon she wore whenever she danced. As he stood there watching, the firelight sent flickering cast of rays over his already golden skin turning it copper from the amazing play of light. He looked like a bronze statue, tall and strong perfection.

"Are you cold?" he asked softly.

Wren shook her head once as she shook her hair free. It fell in glorious blonde waves around her shoulders and down her back. Caleb wanted to run his fingers through the silken strands, kiss her senseless, and lose himself in her body. Forever.

"Come closer," she commanded, so softly he wasn't sure if he'd imagined it. She rose to kneel in front of him; perching her bottom on her feet, so she was eye level with his chest. She couldn't keep her eyes off of him. The light spattering of hair across chest lengthened and thickened as it trailed down his body and below the waistband of his boxer briefs. His open jeans hinted at the delights she knew were there and she wanted them off of him. She needed to touch every inch of his skin. His erection was obvious as it strained against the material at the top of his briefs.

Wren wasn't as experienced as Caleb and she should have been shy. She wanted to please him, to make him feel how much she loved him in every touch. She reached out and slid both hands lightly up his body, threading through the dark trail of hair and then smoothing their way up over his stomach and chest. She was teasing him; deliberately avoiding his cock.

Caleb's head fell back in pleasure and his breath left his body. His eyes closed as her name fell like an ache from his mouth. "Wren. That feels so good."

His reaction drove her on as she continued to caress his chest and shoulders, pushing his shirt off of them. Caleb let it fall to the floor and reached for her.

Wren leaned forward to trail kisses where her hands had been, then scratched her nails lightly down the outside of his arms, lifting his right hand to kiss the inside of his palm. She glimpsed some curved lines on the inside of his forearm and turned it over to get a better look.

"Did you get a new tattoo?" When she was able to get a closer look, her eyes shot up to meet his. "Oh, Cale." She bent her head to kiss the skin near it. She remembered how tender her tattoo was when it was new, and she was careful not to hurt him.

His hand threaded in her hair and pulled her forward and upward so she was on her knees on the bed while he stood next to it. His arm snaked out and wound around her waist and he hauled her hard against his body and lowered her beneath him onto the bed. His head bent and he started to kiss the side of her neck and shoulder as his body surged against hers. "Mmmm, hmm?"

Her words, in her own handwriting, were now permanently inked on his skin.

No matter what, you'll always be my Superman.
Love forever.
Wren

"When did you get that?" Emotion overwhelmed Wren at the same time he took control of her body, and tears flooded her eyes. His lips continued their hot, open mouth torture as he slowly placed a series of warm, wet kisses, and then sucked softly on her skin. It felt so good, her head lulled to one side as she gave him the access he needed. She could feel her body opening, craving the fullness he could give to her.

Caleb lifted his head so he could meet her eyes. The orange cast in the room made her eyes darker, but the love in them shone from them like a beacon. Her hands slid up his shoulders to hold both sides of his face as she waited for his answer. "The night you left me." His words were soft, but laden with meaning. "Right away. You have one that represents me, and I wanted a permanent reminder of you."

It was a dream she thought would never come true. Wren was content to just look at his face, so full of love. She could feel his desire pressing into the soft flesh of her tummy below her navel, but was also assaulted by the passion in his eyes and the way his fingers ghosted over the top swell of her breasts at the lacy edge of her bra. Finally, she pressed the flat of her hand firmly against the shaft of his cock as he'd been craving.

She pushed at the top of his jeans and boxers, moving them down over his ass and thighs, finally using one foot to hook into them and push them off. Caleb kicked them free and rose up on his knees and moved up the bed, leaning back on the pillows.

Wren's eyes widened at his cock as it bobbed proud and ready. It was full and thick and she wanted to wrap her fingers around it. Her breath left in a rush of air.

Caleb scooted up on the pillows and headboard. He wanted to make love to her, but he wanted to see her body and watch her face as he pleasured her.

"Come here, Bird," he commanded huskily, his tone soft. "Straddle my lap."

Holding her and having her hands on his body was almost enough for Caleb. She wasn't a girl anymore, she was a full-blown woman, and she wanted him. The love between them was tangible, permeating the air between them. Wren did as she asked and her eyes locked with his. Caleb 's gaze was intense, but never broke eye contact with her as he reached behind her with one hand and released the clasp to her bra. He slid the straps over her shoulders and down her arms until it drifted off. His hands raked down her back lightly, making her arch.

He huffed as the pressure caused the sheer black fabric to slide against his dick. He could feel the slippery heat through the material and he wanted the last barrier gone. His hands grabbed her hips and his thumbs rubbed over her hipbones. Wren was incapable of remaining still as her hips rocked into his to repeat the delicious sensation.

It was sweet agony. Caleb's head fell back and a guttural groan left on a sigh at the same time as he thrust upward. The head of his cock slid against her and they were both vibrating with need. "I love you and I want to make love to you."

Wren's eyes flooded with tears as a deluge of emotion left her helpless to his wishes. "Me, too."

"No more tears, Bird," his words were a mere whisper as he used his nose to nuzzle the side of her face. "I love you and I want to make love to you every day for the rest of my life." He let one hand trail down her body between her breasts, and over her stomach, until he reached the sheer lace. His fingers ran along the top of her panties.

Wren bit her lip, and reached down to wrap her hand around his erection. She loved seeing him writhe in pleasure and she wanted more.

Caleb couldn't take it. He sat up to slide an arm around her lower back and hips. He pulled her forward, and at the same time his other hand ripped the panties away and tossed them aside.

He didn't apologize for ruining the panties. Instead, he came alive beneath her, thrusting his hips so his cock could slide and push against her slick folds, as he pulled Wren closer and buried his face in the curve of her neck, leaving a trail of light sucking kisses with his open mouth. His free hand reached between them, and started rubbing small circles on her clit with his thumb.

Wren was bombarded with sensations more intense than she'd ever imagined possible. "Uhhhh, Cale," she breathed out his name. "God."

"Take me inside, Wren." His voice throbbed with desire.

Her eyelids were heavy, and she made a sensual picture as she complied. She lifted up and rocked forward to gain position and then slid down, fully sheathing him inside her body. The position made penetration deeper. Wren's knees were on the bed outside his hips and Caleb thrust up into her at the same time as her hips surged forward.

He groaned into her neck. She was the perfect combination of heat and slippery moisture, but also tight around him. Her muscles squeezed and pulled on his dick as he stretched her open, digging in deeper to her body with each thrust. It was hotter than hell.

"You feel amazing. We fit like a glove."

Caleb was overtaken with the need to have his mouth on hers, his tongue thrusting into her mouth in the same delicious rhythm as his hips against hers. Caleb's movements were slow and deliberate, already familiar with how to wring the most pleasure from her, and unable to help himself from wanting to draw it out. He kissed her deeply, again and again.

Breathing increased in tempo, words ceased, bodies pushed and pulled on one another, in an intimate dance that culminated in a shuddering and emotional climax.

Caleb gave in when Wren began to shudder in his arms, his mouth never leaving hers as he swallowed her soft moans and sighs of pleasure. The exquisite building of pleasure finally erupted in an explosion of bliss as a deep groan burst from him.

His arms wrapped around her tightly, as his body poured and continued to push into hers. Wren held him close, her arms around his shoulders and kissed the side of his face.

The room was warm from the fire and a light sheen of perspiration covered their bodies. Caleb still held Wren close as his breathing began to even out.

"I love you so much." He fell back on the pillows and rolled a little bit, so Wren could lie on the pillow next to him. His body was sated for the moment, but his heart was full and he wanted to look at her.

Her crystal blue eyes were soft, and the soft tendrils of hair at her temples were damp. He reached out and pushed one back behind her ear, then ran a thumb down the side of her face.

"I love you," his words were simple, but they touched Wren deep at her core.

She scooted closer and pulled one of his hands into hers

and then close to her chest. "I love you, too."

He continued to stroke her arm. "That was incredible," he said. His deep blue eyes were intense and his expression somber as he studied. "Are you hungry?"

Wren's pink lips curved up into a smile. That wasn't what she expected after the look on his face seconds before. "Translation: you are."

"Yes. Starving." Caleb kissed her briefly, and then bounded off the bed, uncaring of his nakedness. His hair was mussed from her fingers running through it. "I'll run you a bath and order room service. Figure out what you want." He tossed her the menu he found on the desk by the bed.

He went into the bathroom to clean himself off and start the water for a bath, being careful to adjust the temperature. Wren had followed him and was already climbing into the tub.

Caleb glanced at her reflection in the mirror, admiring the lines of her body. She was in perfect physical condition, but when she lowered her body down, he could see she was stiff and sore.

She met his eyes. "Why do you look upset?"

"I'm not. I just know how hard it will be to be apart from you."

Wren nodded and slid down further into the clear water wishing she had some bubble bath. "I know. We've done it for years, Cale. A few more months won't kill us."

He turned away from the mirror and grabbed a clean towel and wrapped it around his waist then leaned on the vanity, folding his arms across his chest. "Just because we've done it for years, doesn't mean it's okay. It's different now."

"I know that, but I'm not sure what to do. It's a lot to figure out when it's all so new."

"It's not new for me. I've always been in love with you. I think from the first time I saw the real you. You were so ethereally beautiful. Like an angel."

Wren's expression softened as her heart rocketed through her chest. "I wish I would have known you felt that way."

Caleb's brow furrowed. "Didn't you?"

"I hoped so."

"I'll be right back."

He left the room and returned within twenty seconds. He opened his hand and the locket fell from his fist, to dangle in front of her. "I gave you this when I left you before Boston. It's the only real thing I had left of my mom, and I gave it to you. You had to know what that meant."

Wren felt at a disadvantage lying in the tub, exposed. She looked up at him, her eyes imploring. "I know. It meant everything. I never took it off."

"Until *you* left *me*. It killed me, Wren."

"If you ended up with Macy, I thought you'd want to give it to her."

"Why would I give this to anyone else? Ever?"

Her shoulder lifted in a half shrug. "You said you wanted me to keep it until you got back from Boston."

"I know what I said, but it wasn't what I meant! You know me better than anyone. How could you not see what you meant to me?"

Wren's heart squeezed. She'd caused him pain at the same time he was causing it for her. "Because in all of the time we knew each other, you never— "

"Crossed the line. I know. Because you were younger than me, and because our parents were married!"

She rinsed off quickly and then began to stand up, reaching for the towel she'd left near the tub's edge. Her feet slipped on the porcelain and she wobbled. Caleb caught her, easily lifting her out of the deep tub and helping to wrap her up in the big, fluffy white towel. He reached for one of the velour robes that were provided by the hotel and pulled the towel free of her body before and helping her on with it.

"Is that the real reason you bolted after that night in the basement? Was it really because I was younger, or because you felt like you didn't protect me? I was eighteen by then."

"It was a big part of it, but seeing you with Dex, my whole world imploded." He lifted his head and looked into her face. Her hair was damp on the ends from the bath water. He took a lock of it in his hands. "I was afraid you'd hate me and I couldn't live with that. I guess it doesn't matter anymore."

She took his big hand in hers and pulled him into the other room. She pushed on his shoulders so he would sink down to sit on the bed's edge. She wanted his eyes the same level as hers.

Wren lifted a hand and cupped his jaw. "Of course it matters, Cale. I could never hate you." Her hands came to rest on the bare skin of his shoulders. He met her eyes reluctantly and she bent to place a soft kiss on his lips. "I've dreamed about you every second since we met. I wanted you to look at me like a woman, but as you said, I was younger and I was afraid to tell you how I felt."

His arms moved around her to pull her closer until she was standing between his knees. Caleb dropped his forehead to her stomach, rubbing it back and forth against her.

Wren's hands dropped onto his shoulders and his arms slid around her waist, the soft velour sliding against his skin. She hugged him tight and kissed his temple and the side of his face and his jaw. Her eyes were full of tears when she pulled back. "So may I have the locket back? I promise I'll keep it safe for you."

A slow smile spread across his lips. "I don't want it back. I'll give it to you if you marry me."

Wren's eyes widened in shock and she gasped softly. "Really?" she asked tremulously, afraid she'd heard him wrong.

He nodded and bent to kiss her softly on the mouth, tenderly teasing. Tears started to rain from her eyes and Caleb gently wiped them away with both of his thumbs.

"I didn't plan on asking you while you were wearing a bathrobe and me a towel, but I needed you to know, once and for all, who I want; the only woman I'll be making babies with, is you, got it?" he asked sincerely, nuzzling the side of her face with his nose. "I know I should be kneeling before you with the engagement ring that's in my bag, but then I'd be forced to let go of you to get it."

Wren's heart was hammering so hard she felt it would fly from her chest as Caleb watched the tears fall down her flushed cheeks. Her chin was trembling as she nodded, and then her voice broke on a sob. "I love you so much, Cale. A ring isn't important. You're what matters. "

"I love you, too, Wren," he said softly, bending his head to take her mouth with his. "You're a part of me. Forever."

epilogue

CALEB WAS LOOKING FORWARD to a busy weekend. Wren had a performance of Swan Lake, both evenings and a Sunday, at the Denver Performing Arts Center. The Colorado Ballet was more than willing to add her to their company when Caleb and Wren both decided the distance and time apart was too much. But that was four years ago, and life was good.

Caleb had acclimated to his role managing Lux and the company was flourishing. It was a huge conglomerate and he had the best in the business heading up research and development, quality control and marketing departments. Jonathan was still their corporate attorney and Wren sat on the board of directors with him and several of the major stockholders.

They were launching a new line of fragrances, but their

makeup line was solidly successful. They changed the color palettes each season and added a new skin care product occasionally. It was rewarding to know he was carrying on his mother and father's legacy.

His love of design hadn't diminished and he and Dex started their design firm. It was grueling at times to be involved with two companies, but design was what he loved, and Dex was a talented mechanic who understood how things worked. He did an amazing job selling their services for industrial design and custom automobiles. Dex ran the day-to-day operations, leaving Caleb to contribute designs and consult when necessary.

Caleb had invited Jonathan and his wife, and Dex and his family to Wren's matinee performance the coming Sunday. Jonesy would be there as well, and then they were all going to have a barbeque at Caleb and Wren's afterward.

Caleb and Wren.

Caleb smiled at the thought.

The Goddard preschool wasn't exactly the most convenient given the awful rush hour traffic. Interstate 25 always seemed to have construction and the backstreets were congested. It was the best preschool in the city, and though it would have been easier to have a live-in nanny, they considered interaction with children to be very important. "Grandma" Jonesy volunteered to babysit, but she still insisted on doing her household duties, even though Caleb and Wren treated her as one of the family.

Caleb got out of the car, and smoothed down his light grey silk tie, unbuttoned his cuffs and rolled the sleeves of his crisp white shirt up to his forearms. He'd removed the jacket to his Tom Ford suit and laid it across the passenger seat of the Infiniti SUV. It was great for family treks into the mountains for camping or skiing and Drake helped him pick it out. He was only three, but he and Caleb were inseparable whenever Caleb wasn't working, or Drake wasn't sleeping.

Many parents were picking up their kids and the parking lot was full. When Caleb walked through the door, he nodded to one of the caregivers who knew him. She pointed into one of the playrooms where Drake was playing with cars on a racetrack with two other little boys. He shoved both hands in his pockets in a casual stance as he watched the interaction.

Caleb felt the rush of love he always did when he looked at his little son. Drake's head covered in hair the same shade of dark brown as Caleb's, and his eyes were the same light blue of his mother's. He was busy talking to the other boys, pushing a little red racecar along the plastic track. Caleb watched him push it up a hill and then let it go. His expression was intent; taking the task so serious.

"See? My car is the fastest!" Drake smiled in glee and scrambled to retrieve the car at the bottom of the hill before another little boy got to it first.

"No, mine is!" A little redheaded boy answered.

"Uh uh," Drake shook his head adamantly and pointed to the other little boy's toy. "See, that's a truck. It's not aerdo-dynamic."

Caleb chuckled happily at his son's explanation and the pronunciation.

"He's very smart," the teacher said, with a smile. She was

an attractive young woman, and it was evident she thought he was attractive in the way she always looked at him. He made a fine specimen dressed for the office; his tailored shirt didn't hide his broad shoulders or the strength in his arms. His hair was combed and held in place with a light amount of hair gel. He was professional, powerful and confident, which most women found to be a lethal combination.

His smile broadened and his white teeth flashed as he sauntered past her toward his son. "He's the son of an engineer, and he's curious. He sits on my lap when I work sometimes and asks question after question." His fatherly pride emanated from every pore. "Was my wife here earlier?" Caleb already knew the answer but he wanted to remind the woman he was married, and happily so.

"Yes. Around 3:30."

Caleb nodded. "Good. Hey, buddy!"

Drake's little head turned and his face broke out in a grin. "Daddy!

Drake struggled to get to his feet and then took off in a run toward Caleb who bent to scoop him up in his arms. He'd just turned three, and was just past the toddler waddle stage, as Caleb liked to call it.

Chubby little arms hugged Caleb's neck hard, and Caleb rubbed his son's back as he held him with one arm. "Did you have a fun day?"

Drake nodded. "Yup! We played outside on the slide!"

"Did you see Mommy?"

"Yeah. Are we going home now? I'm hungry."

Caleb set his son back on his feet. "We're going to Mommy's

studio. Get your shoes on." The little boy ran to a cabinet that held row after row of cubbies and pulled one out. His shoes were inside and he came back holding them in his arms. Caleb crouched down on one knee, hoisted his son to sit on his leg and helped him on with his shoes, then scooted him off and took his hand.

"Where's Yark?" Drake asked on the way out the door, looking up at Caleb questioningly.

Caleb smiled at his pronunciation of his twin sister's name. She was the spitting image of Wren. Wren let Caleb name them both, and now he had three little birds. It warmed his heart thinking about them. Wren was a wonderful mother. He was so proud of her. She worked hard. She was the lead in almost every production, and no matter how tired she was, she still made time for her children and her husband. The dance class with Lark was a good example. She taught three classes a week in pre-ballet just to spend time with her daughter. They were like two peas in a pod.

"Lark is at the studio getting her dance lesson. Didn't you see her leave with Mommy?"

Caleb opened the back door of his SUV and lifted Drake into one of the car seats. Both of the vehicles they drove the most had two sets of car seats to avoid switching them back and forth. Drake shook his head then took the sippy cup of juice Caleb had brought for him. It would tide him over until dinner.

When he was behind the wheel and buckled in himself, he glanced at Drake in the rearview mirror. "You didn't?"

"Nope."

It was opening night for Wren and Jonesy was going to keep the kids and feed them dinner, but Caleb needed to pick up his daughter and take them both home before he could meet Wren at the theater.

Caleb never got tired of watching her dance and he never missed a performance. Lux supported the theater with large donations and they had one of the balcony boxes just off the right of the stage. While he invited employees and managers to join him on most evenings of the performances, he always went alone to all of Wren's opening night performances. It had become a ritual; he'd fill her dressing room with white roses and then they'd spend a romantic night with candles and champagne afterward. It was always something he looked forward to.

Drake's eyelids were drooping and his head lolling to one side by the time they arrived at the same dance studio that Wren took classes as a kid. Every time he pulled into the parking lot, he was hit with the sweet memory of the first time he'd surprised her and signed her up.

Caleb couldn't leave Drake in the car, so he found himself pulling the empty sippy cup from his little hands, unbuckling him and pulling his pint-sized body into his arms. Drake's head fell onto his father's shoulder, his eyes fluttering open, to quickly shut again.

Caleb was well known at the studio and so walked in and went into the studio he knew Wren was teaching the class. Lark was in the front row, dressed in pink leotards, tights and a matching tutu. The other little girls all had on similar getups. They loved dressing up and it helped keep their attention on the lesson.

Wren saw her husband walk in with her son sleeping on his shoulder. He flashed her a beautiful smile and she nearly lost her breath. He was so handsome and her heart still raced at the site of him. She made a kissing motion with her mouth and his smile broadened as he took a seat on the bench that ran along the back wall of the studio. Wren stood in front of the mirrored wall, facing the little ones, who all watched her every move, except for two who were distracted by each other.

"Okay, remember first position?" Wren asked them all. "Jessy, heels together, like this. Watch me."

Caleb watched Lark. She stood up straight with her little arms curved gracefully as she waited. He could see her face in the mirror and her little forehead was furrowed into a frown as she glanced at the little girl to her left who was bent over at the waist and touching her toes. "That's not first position," she said.

"Lark," Wren admonished gently, shaking her head.

"Well, it isn't," Lark returned matter-of-factly.

Wren had to bite her lip to keep from smiling, but Caleb chuckled softly. He loved it. Both of his children were quite precocious, but he told himself that intelligent children were bound to be. The room upstairs that used to be Wren's was now redone in pink, with teddy bears in tutus painted on the walls. The adjoining studio was unchanged and his little girl played in there quite often, and spent more time there having private times with her mother.

"Bend your knees; Plié, then up on your toes; relevé." The little girls watched Wren and themselves in the mirror, except for the one next to Lark who sat down on the wooden floor and held on to both of her feet. "Plié, relevé." Wren repeated the words slowly as she went through the movements. "Plié, relevé."

"Remember second position? Your feet stay the same, but you move them a little apart. Stand tall, and hold your arms out like this. Bend them a little at the elbows, and have ballet hands. Do you see how I'm holding my fingers?"

Despite having the twins, her body was unmarred. Caleb couldn't help take in her slender curves, unhidden by the leotard and chiffon wrap skirt she wore. He glanced at his watch. It was almost six, which would mean the lesson was over.

A few more instructions and Wren went to change the music. "Okay, these last few minutes are free style. You can do whatever you want!" Wren turned on a clean version of "Cake by the Ocean" that she knew her little girl particularly liked. As the little girls started jumping around and randomly twirling, Wren walked toward Caleb. Her hand reached out and slid down the back of his head, and then she sat down and leaned in to kiss Drake on the cheek. "Wake up sleepy head. Jonesy is making Pizza."

Caleb leaned toward her and she met him in the middle so he could place a soft kiss on her mouth in greeting. She closed her eyes and savored the way his lips lingered on hers. Caleb's hand reached for hers as their mouths separated. "Mmmm," he said so softly she barely heard it with the music playing.

Wren's heart and body quickened at the sound. "How was your day, babe?"

"Good. How did rehearsal go? Are you tired?"

"I had a class this morning, and then rehearsal afterward, so I'm a tad tired. Maybe the schedule is getting to me."

"But you're so beautiful doing it. And, I know you love it."

"I do." She cupped Drake's head, her fingers lingering in his silky hair. "I have to go straight to the theater after this, Cale. I have stage call at 6:30."

The song ended. Wren dismissed the group, and right away Lark bolted over to her father. "Hi, Daddy. Did you see me dance?" she asked excitedly. Her bright blue eyes sparkled.

He smiled and lifted her up so she could sit on his knee. "I did. You were incredible, sweetheart. Just like Mommy!" He kissed her temple. "Are you ready to go home?"

"Are we going to Mommy's show?"

"No, Grandma Jonesy is waiting for you and your brother. She said you guys are having a pizza and movie night. She made Rice Krispie Treats, too."

"Yay! I love Kispie Teats!"

Wren and Caleb both laughed. Drake stirred after his sister's presence and voice intruded on his nap, lifting his head as Caleb rose with both kids in his arms.

"Go ahead, I'll grab her stuff and put it in my car."

Wren loved seeing Caleb with the children. Their relationship was so beautiful and the way he was with them made her love him even more. They both had rotten parents, but the opposite was true for their babies. Drake idolized Caleb and Lark adored him. She knew how they both felt because love for him made her heart flop inside her chest every time she looked at him.

She leaned in to give him a kiss goodbye, just before he turned to leave the studio with both kids still in his arms. "See you later, Superman."

The End

Special Interest Stuff

There is a RELEASE WEEK GIVEAWAY
& a NEWSLETTER sign-up link,
so you receive ALERTS at the at the end of this section!

Remembrance Trilogy Readers

You will be happy to hear that I'll be offering the complete series in
a box set with extra content for a limited time, coming soon.
(The extra content will include the outtakes
I've written in the past, but something NEW, as well.)
This set will be at a special price for a couple of days only
so those of you who already have the series will have an
opportunity to get the extra content without breaking the bank.
KEEP WATCHING FOR IT.
(Because it depends on a few things when I can get it done.)

FAMOUS Readers

Many of you have asked for a follow-up to The Famous Novels and
I'll be writing a novella called After Famous, coming soon.
Keep your eyes peeled!

After Dark Readers

I've had many, many requests for a book for Aaron and Becca, and maybe one for Kyle. You'll find two titles on the UPCOMING Titles list that I think you'll like.

Again... Stay tuned!

If you haven't read all of these books; why the hell not? GO!

RELEASE WEEK GIVEAWAY

Go here!

http://www.kahlenaymes.com/release-week-giveaway

Newsletter Sign-up

Go here!

https://app.mailerlite.com/webforms/landing/v7t7ko

About the Author

Kahlen Aymes is a USA Today bestselling author who writes steamy romance novels that cross genre lines between New Adult, Adult Contemporary, and Erotica.

Kahlen has been on several bestseller lists including Barnes & Noble, Amazon, Smashwords, Publisher's Weekly, iBooks and USA Today! She began her writing career without ever planning on publishing a single word and won multiple awards in the world's second largest fan fiction community, including BEST Author, BEST RPF, Best All-Human that Knocks You Off Your Feet, and several others! Encouragement and support from her readers was what prompted her to publish.

Her interests include reading, as well as writing, theater arts, cooking, roller skating, and going for long walks. She is the proud mom to one teenage daughter and two golden retrievers, who basically rule her world.

Kahlen has a strong love of writing and romance, and you can count on her to deliver strong, relatable characters, deep and detailed plots, sexy love scenes, and emotion overflow!

Connect with Kahlen

Facebook: https://www.facebook.com/kahlen.aymes.
author?fref=ts
Goodreads: https://www.goodreads.com/author/
show/5768062.Kahlen_Aymes
Twitter: @Kahlen_Aymes
Instagram: Kahlen.Aymes
Pinterest: https://www.pinterest.com/kahlenaymes/

For merchandise, signed books, Julia's recipes, missing scenes,
events, my blog, and series playlists: **OFFICIAL WEBSITE**:
KahlenAymes.com

**For news, giveaways, appearances, and book discussion
sign-up for my newsletter here:** https://app.mailerlite.com/
webforms/landing/v7t7k0

**To hang out privately with me on Facebook, join our
READER GROUP:** Kahlen's Book Babes https://www.facebook.
com/groups/252301134873105/

Request an eBook autograph at: http://www.authorgraph.com/
authors/Kahlen_Aymes

If you have interest in joining Kahlen's STREET TEAM, please
contact us at
Info@KahlenAymes.com

Rights information: Info@KahlenAymes.com

Other Books By Kahlen Aymes

The Remembrance Trilogy & Prequel

Prequel: Before Ryan Was Mine
1. The Future of Our Past
2. Don't Forget to Remember Me
3. A Love Like This

The After Dark Series

1. Angel After Dark
2. Confessions After Dark
3. Promises After Dark

The FAMOUS Novels
1. FAMOUS
2. More Than FAMOUS
3. Beyond FAMOUS

Upcoming Titles

Soulmate
Daddy After Dark
Rock Me After Dark
After Famous
Trading Yesterday
Unfinished Business
Marriage Material
Covered in Rain
Love Notes
You, and You Alone

Made in the USA
Middletown, DE
26 October 2016